WHAT REVIEWERS ARE SAYING ABOUT
ENSNARED BY INNOCENCE...

"Witty, Enchanting and Roaring Hot!
I think I've found a new author to binge! I would
definitely recommend it as a good gateway book to
shape-shifters or to lovers of historical romance."
5-Star Goodreads Review

"I would give this a 10/10 rating. Beautifully written by
a very talented author... PLEASE read this brilliant
novel. I cannot wait for the next in series."
5-Star BookBub Review

"Oh. My. Goodness! This story caught my attention
from page one. It is a fresh take on the shifter
genre. This Regency novel had every element a girl
could want: several mysteries to solve, smokin' hot
heroes and sensible, funny and courageous
heroines."
5-star Goodreads review

"I thoroughly enjoyed this regency romance. It is the
full package of emotions with intrigue, angst, mirth,
fear and steamy sex scenes."
5-star Goodreads review

"New-to-me author **Larissa Lyons' writing style kept me glued to the story** with all the twists and turns. She took great pains to use authentic period language. It was easy to understand and helped the story come alive with authenticity. **Without a doubt, this author is going to the top of my favorite historical novel author list. I really loved this twist on the traditional historical romance novel.**"
5-star Goodreads review

"**This book has it all:**
-Regency Romance. With Regency England slang. I'm a sucker for it
-Cursed Shifters
-Sexy, dark, secretive, brooding hero
-Fiesty, intelligent, independent heroine...
So yes, brooding lord and innocent, young ladies. Ancient curses regarding shifters. And time travelers. And very hot. **Yep, this story had it all has it all.**"
5-star BookBub review

"**Fantastic Story!!** I really enjoyed this book!" 5-Star Reviewer Emily P.

"I love the fact this is **shifter and regency** all rolled into one...I was amazed by the storyline and couldn't help how addictive I found this text...**I loved the originality of this book** and thought it really stood out for many reasons... **A true talent for writing...**"
5-Star Review

ENSNARED BY INNOCENCE

STEAMY REGENCY SHAPESHIFTER

LARISSA LYONS

Ensnared by Innocence, 2nd Edition Copyright © 2021 by Larissa Lyons
Published by Literary Madness.

First Paperback Edition: August 2021
First Large Print Edition: August 2021
Second E-book Edition: August 2021

ISBN 978-1-949426-29-8 Paperback - Rev. 10.2021
ISBN 978-1-949426-34-2 Large Print
ISBN 978-1-949426-69-4 E-book

Proofread by Judy Zweifel at Judy's Proofreading; Edits by Elizabeth St. John; Cover by Literary Madness

At Literary Madness, our goal is to create a book free of typos. If you notice anything amiss, we're happy to fix it. litmadness@yahoo.com

CONTENTS

I thought thy heart had been wounded with the claws of a lion.

Wounded it is, but with the eyes of a lady.

— SHAKESPEARE, AS YOU LIKE IT

1

THE PREPOSTEROUS PROPOSITION

I LEAVE *this recordation for my beloved sons. Erasmus and Nash. My heirs. Who will one day, pray God, live to manhood and conduct themselves in a manner more gracious, more fitting to their station and responsibilities than I have managed.*

My dear offspring who I cannot believe I condemned to such a fate, however unknowingly.

A fate I share but one that was not known to me until after you were both conceived. (And which also no doubt explains the sparsity of children in our family, and siblings for you both.)

The urges for The Change first came upon me in the summer of the year I turned five and twenty. It was not yet the middle of July and yet I sensed the stirrings of what I would eventually learn was my animal blood. My feline side, if you boys will only set aside skepticism and believe. Please, sons, heed my warnings, for you do not want to be caught unaware as I—and irreparably harm the woman you love.

To see the fear in her eyes when she looks upon you and beholds a monster. A beast. Your inner beast. The lion, untamable. Unstoppable.

Deadly?

I pray not. 'Tis why I locked myself away, in this, my 28th year, the third of the curse. Why I place armed guards at the door for the entirety of the month.

As I battle the inner demon once again, my only consolation is knowing that you both are still too young to remark upon my absence.

Too young to question why Papa turns into an ogre toward the end of the hot, sultry summer months.

Too young to recall how severely I injured your mother...

⸻◦⸻

LONDON, ENGLAND
MAY 1812

"LORD BLAKELY, pardon the interruption. Might I beg a word with you?"

Erasmus Hammond, Marquis of Blakely, looked down his long patrician—scarred—nose at the intrepid female who dared interrupt the boisterous group of men he currently conversed with.

Delicate, feminine young ladies such as this one definitely did *not* mix with his oft-beastly ways. Not unless they wanted to be torn asunder.

He didn't recognize her, but judging from the looks

his companions aimed her direction, they did. The meaning behind the smirks and elbow jabs was unmistakable, confound it.

Just what he didn't need—another wedding-minded miss setting her cap for him. Every Season he remained unmarried, it seemed his value on the marriage market escalated. Despite the air of libidinous rake he cultivated in public—and indulged in private—his attraction as an eligible mate only increased with each year that passed, as though snaring his dissolute self would be something of a coup. Hardly.

Where was her chaperone?

"Gracious me," he drawled as sarcastically as he could manage, "a bold little muff, are you not?" He gestured to his chortling companions, hoping the crude comment would be enough to send her heels flying. "Approaching *me*? Here?"

Here, at Lady Longford's crush, celebrating the engagement of one of her many offspring, the place teeming with too many people and too much perspiration, offensive odors he chronicled as easily as breathing. Odors he tolerated, along with the boorish twaddle that surrounded him, because unlike some others he could name—ahem, his brother for one—Blakely bore his responsibilities, took them very seriously indeed.

Yet, no sweat-drenched, unpalatable odors emanated from the brash one before him, he couldn't help but note. So she wasn't here to dance and make merry?

Dance and make a marriage, more like. Is that not the ultimate aim of every young chit here?

Blakely grunted at the thought, taking her in.

The very definition of English miss—blonde, blue-eyed and insipid—stood before him. Granted, she was a trifle taller than perfection allowed these days, and her face looked decidedly powdered—smelled powdered too, the pale artifice likely hiding all manner of spots, blemishes and daunting imperfections.

But when she shifted, allowing the shawl curved within the crooks of both arms to slide, he noticed the two-inch expanse of skin between the short, puffy sleeves of her gown and her long gloves. Two inches of implausibly dark skin, which forced his attention back to her face. Caused him to study...to linger. Beneath the powder, 'twas smooth as silk. At least that's how it appeared, making his fingers twitch with the sudden urge to test the observation.

So she wasn't hiding spots? Perchance only an unfashionable liking of the sun? As one who spent more time than he'd like in the dark, that alone piqued his interest.

"Please, my lord?" She scooted further around the column separating his small group from the dance floor. "I promise not to take but a few moments of your time." So earnest. Her voice so very serene, even as he scented her... What was it? Fear? Frustration? Apprehension that her asinine errand—approaching him, of all people—would prove unsuccessful?

Of course it would. It has to.

Trying again to discourage her, he glanced around the ballroom, purposely avoiding her gaze and employed his loftiest voice. "I do not believe we have been introduced and therefore, most regretfully, I cannot begin any manner of discourse with—"

"But we have," she had the audacity to interject. "It was three years ago at the Seftons' ball. We danced, but I have no expectation that you recollect the encounter."

He didn't.

And he knew she was shamming him. If they'd met, if he'd been near her for a dance, he'd remember her scent.

A remarkably fresh yet earthy fragrance that appealed to him on so many levels 'twas dangerous. Dangerous for them both.

She stood her ground and spoke calmly, despite their eavesdropping, snickering audience. Taller than most women, she came nearly to his chin. Hers was tilted at such an angle he suspected she must practice the determined stance in front of a mirror.

More than that, most fresh-faced elegants weren't bold enough to approach him directly, and he couldn't help but admire this one in spite of himself. He almost hated to crush her spirit but dissuade her he must. Innocents were not for him. Especially now.

It was nearing the time of year he had two choices: Either secret himself away and privately battle his demons. Or find the wildest women he could to exorcise away his fiendish tendencies through exhaustive, nightly rounds of intense prigging. Smashing choice, that. No wonder he always chose the second, more sociable option. Something he seriously doubted would appeal to this one.

"By all means, do forgive me," he stated, matching her tranquil tone. "But, alas, you are correct. I do not remember you." There was more jostling from his cohorts. They knew the type of female he preferred—and the kind he avoided at all costs. Though several years beyond the schoolroom, the flaxen-haired miss in front of him definitely fell into the latter category.

Even so, he was surprised how her poise drew him. And if he tipped his head…just so…

Ah, yes, he *could* look straight down the front of her pale blue gown, to furtively gaze at the womanly endowments not quite hidden beneath. Of course, he had no business looking at her dugs, none whatsoever.

"A *word*?" she insisted, angling her chin a fraction higher. "Consider it imperative."

Imperative? Intrigued despite his better judgment, he inclined his head in a show of assent.

'Twas odd, how her voice drew him, all calm assurance instead of the more heated, sultry tones he was used to hearing from his experienced lovers. Would she maintain that cultured, confident manner in the throes of passion?

What of it, man? She's not for you.

True. So very true.

Especially now, with his latest suspicions? With even more danger surrounding London than before…

Had he missed one? Failed to pick up on a potential wrong-side-of-the-blanket Hammond offspring? Had all the sacrifices, the years spent miring himself in the dungeons of the *ton*, seeking out the most dissolute, reckless individuals, praying they were only human—and nothing more sinister—been all for naught?

Shaking off the dread that accompanied him these days like a persistent and bothersome fly, he followed her a short distance further, away from the periphery of the crowded dance floor.

When she reached a secluded corner and stopped, he did as well. And found himself curious, if only remotely so, why she had approached *him* directly—and without a formal introduction. Totally unheard of in the upper realms of the *ton* he inhabited.

"Lord Blakely, I have a proposition I would like to put forth to you." For all her height and assured poise, she seemed dainty, almost fragile, standing before him.

"By all means, please do." His curiosity grew by the second. And so did the reluctant attraction running rampant through his veins. Which would never do.

Never! Do you not have sufficient responsibilities, man? Ferreting out who's destroying—

Blakely shook off the annoying reminder, the one that settled fear and concern heavily on his shoulders; far more pleasant to ponder the diverting package before him. "State your case," he encouraged in as droll a voice as he could cultivate, "so I may rejoin my crew."

When she hesitated, glancing behind her, he took possession of the gloved hand nearest—which brought her attention swiftly back to him. He then lifted it to his lips and kissed the air over her fingers before releasing them. Instead of scaring her away as he'd intended, a blush flared up her chest and over her face, delighting him, which was patently ridiculous.

Blushes were for maidens; whores were for him.

So why was it that the tinge of pink flushing her cheeks fascinated? The slight color was difficult to discern beneath the powder and her unfashionably dark skin but he saw it clearly nevertheless. Unbidden, curiosity rose regarding the extent of her exposure to sunlight. Where might the golden hue leave off and pale porcelain begin?

And why do you care?

Aye, definitely time to curtail their conversation. "You were saying? A proposition, I believe. I weary of being here," he lied. "Speak in haste."

The pale blonde ringlets surrounding her face swayed as she took a fortifying breath, readying for battle. "I know I presume much, but I would be eternally grateful if you could see your way to posing as my betrothed until—"

He laughed outright at her outrageous request, drawing the attention of several guests. Sobering, Blakely stated, "Completely out of the question. But thank you for asking. I needed some amusement this evening."

When he turned to leave, her hand shot out, latching on to his arm with surprising strength. He halted and peered at her gloved fingers until she removed them. Damn if a bolt of *need* hadn't flashed through him at the contact. Astonishing, for he'd just dallied with the amorous and very accommodating Mistress Rose of the Crown & Cock not twenty-four hours before.

"Lord Blakely, please. Hear me out." She rushed on before he could say yea or nay. "It would be a pretend betrothal, a farce if you will, lasting only a few weeks. Surely you can find it in your heart to assist me for such a short time? I will pay you handsomely for your trouble and release you publicly from our agreed-upon understanding after you fulfill its terms."

"We have no understanding," he felt compelled to remind her. "But for the sake of argument, your reasoning is faulty. How would this assist you in any way? For upon becoming affianced to me, not to mention later breaking said betrothal, your reputation would be tantamount to ruined."

"That has no consequence," she said rather convincingly. "I only want the *appearance* of a betrothal for the remainder of the Season."

Which only intrigued him further. What manner of eligible miss cared naught for her reputation? 'Twas a young female's only currency, all her real blunt controlled first by her father and then by her spouse. "And why is that?"

"My reasons are my own."

Stubborn chit. He half wished he couldn't see her so clearly in the candlelit ballroom. What was it about her that drew him?

The unspoilt scent of heather and fresh air? The sunshine she exudes? The hint of freedom from the chains that bind you to London as surely as if you were locked in Newgate.

"If you will not explain yourself, why should I even consider your ridiculous proposal?"

That willful chin lifted again. "Because I will pay you."

"Not enough, not for what you ask." She had no *idea* what she was asking, what being near her the next few weeks might cost him. Or her.

She proceeded to name an amount that sent his head spinning.

Good God. He'd just been propositioned by a bloody heiress.

To fight the deceptive allure she represented—because it wasn't called a *leg shackle* for nothing—he shifted his weight, tightened the muscles in his legs. "You are a piece of intriguing baggage, I'll grant you that. Why approach me and not some other titled gent in need of the ready and likely to agree?"

"Your standing as one of the most sought-after libertines in the *ton*," she stated baldly, her face flushing even more. "It suits my purposes quite well. And your title, for another reason. Not every marquis has a character such as yours."

"I do not know whether to be insulted or flattered." The inexplicable urge to touch her cheek stormed through him. Since when did he care about cheeks? He fisted his hands and anchored them firmly at his sides.

"I mean no offense, I assure you, but it is not in me to cavil at the truth. You and I both know that you have no intention of marrying this year, and I need someone of your...*ilk* to best ensure the successful outcome of my plan."

He made a noise in his throat, one that could indicate he was considering her asinine idea, which was absurd—because he wasn't. Neither was he convinced he wanted his *ilk*—well-suited to her asinine plan or not—to be what he was known for. Sought after for.

"I only ask that you show me the same courtesy and give me your honest reply posthaste." Again, she looked over her shoulder, as if expecting a dragon to swoop in and steal her away.

Come to think on it, he was surprised they had

been left alone this long. "And what is your next course of action, should I turn down your oh-so-tempting offer?"

"Sarcasm does not become you, Lord Blakely," she admonished him.

"Do not talk down to me," he told her, instantly irritated with himself. With her. Why was he still wasting his breath conversing? Why not simply tell her nay and be done with it? Why did he long to touch so much more than her cheek? To see her hair down, her dress gone and her legs wrapped around his waist?

Damn it, where was his control? It seemed to have abandoned him the very moment *she* abandoned her good sense and approached him.

"Forgive me," she said contritely. "The stress of awaiting your reply has put me quite on edge."

"Which is understandable. Considering you have propositioned a man who has not the faintest clue who you are."

"Lady Francine Montfort, my lord." She sketched the briefest curtsy on record.

"Please continue, Lady Francine Montfort." He committed her name to memory; her scent he'd never forget—even if he tried. "When I refuse to be a part of your outlandish scheme, what will you do?"

"*When* you refuse?" She arched a single, chastising eyebrow.

How the hell an eyebrow lift could make him feel small only strengthened his resolve. *Say nay and be gone!*

"If you persist in claiming you have already decided"—she gave a prim little huff—"then there remains no further need to waste your time. Or mine. Good night."

This time it was his hand that halted her retreat.

She spun silently on slippered feet back to him. "Yes, my lord?" Her tone had turned icy.

Blakely released her at once, the tingles attacking his palm something of a surprise. "Humor me, then. *If.* If I decline. What is your plan?"

"Why, I will speak with the next person on my list. Perhaps *he* will be more agreeable."

Unaccountably, disappointment stirred in his chest. "Oh? So this is not an exclusive offer you make to me alone? I am only one in a long line?" *And no doubt farther down the list than your pride deems acceptable.* "Lady Francine Montfort," he continued, and it was an effort to maintain his droll façade, "I must confess I am crushed by the knowledge. Quite."

She looked over her shoulder again, distracted by whatever it was she sought. "If you must know..." Her gaze swung back to his. "You are my preferred choice and the first man I approached, but as you are determined to thwart my sincere overtures, I must move on. I beg of you, please do not speak of this to anyone. It—"

"I would not dream of it."

"Are you positive I cannot persuade you to at least consider my proposition? You have yet to hear my terms in their entirety and yet you are refusing me outright."

"There is more?" The entreaty in her sky-blue eyes was almost enough to convince him to reconsider. But then he saw past the appeal, to the innocence.

Pity. He didn't deal with innocents. Ever. Only those

women already hardened by life's experiences, women who liked having their precious egos petted as much as they liked having their slits stroked. Women whose purses he was not averse to lining and who were willing to overlook his behavior, if, in the midst of things, he got a little rough. Certainly, his carnal appetites were too wild for the virtuous dainty before him.

Somewhat regretfully, he opened his mouth to decline.

"Frannnny!"

The screech interrupted him.

"How *dare* you!" An older woman charged at them from the side, brandishing her fan like a bayonet and casting him a glare as if he were Lucifer come to life. Which perhaps he was—for even considering corrupting her charge.

"Franny! You *evil* child!" Sky-high plum-colored feathers stuck out of a forest-green turban, agitating the air above her mottled face. Ire definitely did not sit pretty on this particular matron. "What *are* you doing, talking to *him*?" the woman hissed. Her voice carried like that of a general commanding his troops. More than one curious head turned toward their secluded corner. "Come away this instant!"

"But, Aunt," Lady Francine protested, casting him a commiserating glance. "Lord Blakely and I are only conver—"

"The Lord Blakelys of this world are most certainly *not* for the likes of you, gel. Now come along." A full head shorter and three times as wide as her niece, the harridan grasped Lady Francine's slim arm and tugged.

Pale-blue eyes gazed at him as she silently succumbed to the forced retreat. Just before she disappeared from view, her mouth formed the words, *The garden?*

And he, purveyor of pleasure and avoider of innocents, found himself nodding in assent.

Damn his hide.

2

CONSIDERABLE CONSIDERATION

To my Cherished Sons ~

My dearest Erasmus, my darling Nash,

Your father intended to give all contained herein to you both, while he was alive, to allow you time to read and absorb, to laugh and deny, to answer any and all questions you might have (and he expected the number would be monstrous).

More than anything, he expected to be here to help you through the terrible ordeal he's convinced looms on the horizon for each of you.

Alas, Fate has intervened, separated him from me, from you both, so many times when he could have remained at home, instead of either off traveling, seeking a solution to what he always termed The Blighted Curse or locked away in hell. One of his own making, did he but know it.

When I think of all the time lost because—

Nay.

No more of that now. In the last weeks since he's been missing, I have cried too often and too much. I must be strong now. Strong for all of us. For the sake of my darling boys and just as much for myself.

For, if what your father feared most has come to pass, the difficulties plaguing our family may only now be beginning. My only solace is that he took some time off to be with friends, to relax and bond again, before—

Nay. I shall not anticipate wretched news. Not when I have hired someone to look into his last known whereabouts. Keeping the truth of things from you both, while I remain strong, waiting for answers, is taking a toll.

<u>When</u> do I share everything? I know not.

Only be assured, when I do finally reveal the accompanying pages, that the information within is no jest nor joke. 'Tis the heartfelt admissions and ponderings of a man walking an invisible line, a path he had no inkling how to traverse. A man navigating that impossible line, praying he would not fall to his death—nor cause that of any others.

A man trying to care for his family the only way he could.

I pray you will forgive him, and me, for keeping this from you. Had either of us any notion he would not be here for you now, the information contained in his letters and in his father's journal would have been shared so very long ago.

With equal parts love, for the men you are growing into, and anguish—for the trials I suspect await you...

Your loving Mother (Who also hopes you will now understand why I banished that wretched gold kitten to the stables. The one you brought me last Easter. So soon after your father's disappearance, I could not abide that vile creature under my roof.)

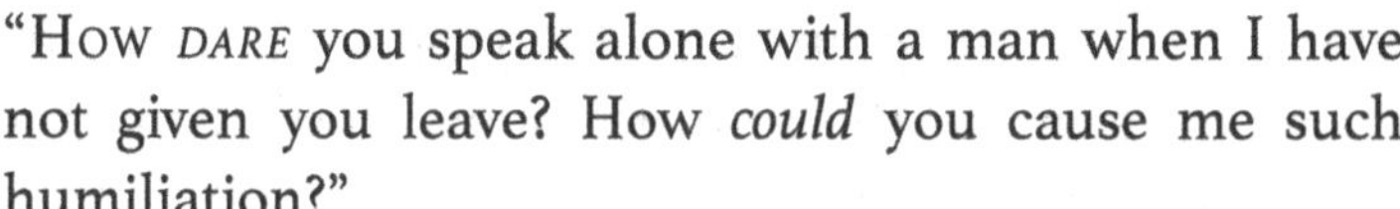

"HOW *DARE* you speak alone with a man when I have not given you leave? How *could* you cause me such humiliation?"

Lady Francine Montfort suffered through the scolding from her aunt. Over the years, Francine had perfected the art of appearing to listen while her mind raced over a hundred different topics. All of which were far, far away from her aunt's latest ramblings and —at this moment—centered instead directly upon Lord Blakely.

Oh, she'd known who he was even without a proper introduction. His rumored exploits were practically the stuff of legends, definitely tittered about—if not by first-year debutantes, then by their chaperones.

Lord Blakely had secrets. Ones that drew her as nothing else.

After all, did she not have her own secrets? One in particular she kept from the world.

Beyond that, Back when her parents were still alive and she their devoted only child, living life with no thought nor care beyond that of having fun and ensuring those around her did the same... Back when she and her childhood friend Katherina dreamt of naught else but finding beaus to kiss and dance with, once they made their come-outs...

Back then, before tragedy had affected them both, how was she to have ever suspected the men of her acquaintance--discounting the one she'd just approached--would leave her lukewarm at best, cold at worst?

Not a single one of her suitors over the past handful of years had incited the urge to kiss them or touch them, the impulse to press her body against theirs. Not once, not even on the rare occasions she'd danced a waltz with a gentleman of the *ton*.

Yet tonight, as she'd stood close to Lord Blakely?

Oh my fearsome frowns and deeply rasped growls! Just being so very near him made her insides spark as never before. Made her long to grasp the muscular arms beneath the expensively tailored tailcoat, to touch the seductive angle of his side whiskers, ease the strain furrowing his brow.

Silently, she laughed at herself, realizing how easily she could count another two hundred ways she wanted to touch him without taxing her brain in the least; the same most certainly could not be said for how taxing it was, enduring yet another of her aunt's lectures.

And that knowledge, regardless of whether he met her in the garden later or not, could set her mind at ease on one point: She *did* know how it felt to want a man. To crave his touch down to the depths of her soul.

"Why, to approach such a disgraceful rake! A libertine of the first order! Franny, I am nonplussed at your selfish lack of care..."

Her breath eased out on a peaceful sigh...

In public, he conducted himself with complete refinement—outwardly, at least. Inwardly? Why, the few times she'd been fortunate enough to glimpse a moment of weakness in his carefully cultivated, haughty exterior, she'd seen a peer carrying the weight of the world on his broad shoulders. One who drew her mightily.

A few nights ago when she'd first concocted her Plan of Genius—or so she hoped and prayed, as the alternative was Dire indeed—she could fathom approaching no other man to pose as her betrothed, no matter that she'd spun taradiddle about having an entire list of potential paramours.

Pretend engagement or not, one's betrothed was expected to take certain liberties, and after her single wretched experience, compounded by evading the revolting clutches of her latest suitor—a creeper if there ever was one—Francine knew full well she'd only put herself within touching distance of Lord Blakely, not some other unknown scapegrace. Only the man she dreamt about.

"What about your cousins? Did you even *think* to give their reputations a thought? *Any* consideration at all? And after I welcomed you into my home and raised you as one of my own..."

Francine nodded and attempted to assume a suitable expression of guilt—and after the barrage went on longer than usual, an appropriate amount of contriteness. While, in actuality, she was calculating the mathematical probability that the touch from any other man in the *ton* would have affected her in quite the same way as Lord Blakely's.

When she'd devised her plan and let her mind flit over possible candidates, his name had gravitated to the top. To maintain her freedom and safeguard her future, she needed the protection an alliance with him, or someone like him, would provide. And she needed it immediately.

In a number of weeks, she would have successfully avoided the marriage trap her aunt appeared intent on netting her into. At the moment, a false betrothal would shield her from Aunt Prudence's seemingly desperate efforts to secure her a husband and instead leave Francine in the position to concentrate on what she *did* want. Which certainly *wasn't* a husband—and all the control they wielded.

Not if her "condition" was turning out as her mother's had, which Francine suspected was the case. Though successfully concealed so far, she absolutely had to secure her inheritance to guarantee her future happiness and what she did want: The ability to maintain her independence. To live life on her own terms, to make her own choices, not be locked away. Hidden, neglected, or forgotten if some unknown, tight-fisted or heavy-handed husband had his way.

After all, not many women were as fortunate in their choice of spouse as her dear mama. Look at Aunt Prudence. Her first husband had been such a grumbler, he'd squeezed any semblance of friendliness and caring right out of her by the time he died.

Uncle Rowden, her second husband and Francine's uncle by marriage, was often away from home (not that Francine blamed him). He left the running of everything including his London household and the rearing of her children—and by extension her niece—to his critical crank of a wife.

But Lord Blakely, now? Why, if one needed a

pretend paramour for a short duration only, she could think of no one better.

He'd already rescued her once, if he but knew it. And rescue, drat it, was what she needed again.

No matter that she'd thought she could retain her single state easily enough until her majority, Aunt Prudence's resolve to see Francine wed and out of the house knew no bounds of late. Only days ago, she'd inadvertently left Francine alone with the most recent unsavory suitor—and directly in harm's way.

Aye, time for assistance.

Assistance from the man who'd fascinated her from the beginning. The moment that led to her developing a *tendre* for the often austere lord she'd studied from afar. The man with the commanding, captivating air that made everything in his vicinity burn brighter.

Late-summer, it'd been, after their first full Season (hers and Patience's, Temperance not yet out). A neighbor of Uncle Rowden's country estate held a ball, commemorating the end of a house party and invited everyone in the vicinity, giving Temperance a chance to attend her first grown-up event.

Returning from the ladies' retiring room, after helping Patience repair a ripped hem (albeit, with crooked stitches, but strong ones that kept her dress from tripping her further), her cousin had skipped ahead, not wanting to miss a second of dancing if she could help it. Leaving Francine and her more sedate pace alone in the long hallway.

But only for a few seconds, given the trio of boisterous bucks who burst from behind a closed door, crowding into the narrow hall right in front of her. Behind them, the room they'd left, dark with shadows, teeming with energy, voices. Giggles. A squeal or two. A couple of grunts.

Francine knew now what could go on behind closed doors, even at a respectable setting—hadn't she been caught behind one herself recently?

But that night, things were different. Confronted with three hulking male bodies, pressing in without permission, awareness sharpened her senses. Sexual awareness. But not the good sort she'd felt near Lord Blakely earlier; nay, this had been an edgy, intimidating sort, the kind smart girls and intelligent women ran from.

Only it was most difficult to run when strange men gripped your upper arm, loomed close behind you. In front of you. Gave your heart and stomach a dark thrill you didn't quite want but couldn't ignore either.

"Hansen! Get back in here." The order was barked from within the gloomy interior. "Crandall! By the devil, where did they get off to?"

Accompanied by shuffling noises, a whined, feminine "Do not leave me, Blake, we're not finished yet" coming from within, the stranger's voice she'd not heard before touched her every bit as fiercely as the fingernails that scraped up the side of her neck.

"Stop that," Francine told the man at her side, the one who hovered closer as if to inspect the scratches he'd left. "Let me go!" She jerked her shoulder free of the other's hold, but bumped into a solid wall behind her when she tried to skirt around the trio. A solid wall of the third man, who leaned forward, breathed hotly over her nape, and grunted of all things.

"Tyndale!" The intriguing voice again, this time closer and followed by a storm of fire and heat—and then blessed rescue.

Rescue when the tallest man of them all, the owner of The Voice, stormed into the hallway, firing off orders in a language she didn't recognize. As though realizing it, he quickly repeated himself in English, cursing the roysters who'd invaded her person and violated her space back from whence they came, evicting the three with authority and leaving the hallway bereft save for the two of them.

Leaving her overheating from the tips of her toes to her sizzling eyelashes as she beheld—for one brief second more—the man she'd soon learn had earned one of the worst reputations in London, yet somehow also commanded the respect of just about every other man in the *ton*.

'Twas Lord Blakely who had rescued her that day, sparing her a glance that lasted naught but a second, but inciting her interest, demanding her curiosity, and earning her devotion, however distant, upon his equally brief bow and murmured, "My apologies, miss. I do hope you are unharmed," before ducking back inside, slamming the door behind him, and roaring recriminations at the men he'd freed her from.

Francine blinked. Waved her hand in front of her face, trying to cool off temperatures that soared every time she thought of him. Of how he'd looked in that oh-so-brief moment—haggard. Tired. Suffering under the weight of responsibilities, yet assuming them all the same. Attractive. Powerful. Thoroughly compelling.

Though his timely rescue made her appreciate him,

it was the dark haunting she sensed in his soul that fixed her attention upon him.

Never one for fickleness, her idle interest had only deepened with time, something that was brought home with utter certainty in the last few minutes of mental wrangling:

For after being close enough mere moments ago to count the folds in his snowy-white cravat, see the tiny nick that scarred his nose right at the midpoint and recognize the haunted loneliness still smoldering in his russet eyes—despite his irreverent air—she'd just decided that what she wanted above all things was Lord Blakely. Any way she could get him.

She still felt the imprint of his hand where he'd gripped her arm. Her lady regions still twitched from his invigorating presence, directing her thoughts into entirely new realms. Her intention *had* been to pay Lord Blakely only for his time and the use of his disreputable reputation but now... Now? Francine was seriously considering adding an entirely new element to her offer. One that included *herself*.

His wavy black hair, attractively shaped side whiskers and penetrating eyes were the cornerstone of illicit fantasies. Hers, certainly. Who knew that up close he would look so dratted...scrumptious? His appearance put her in mind of a seductive demon. One sent to Earth with the sole purpose of tempting and tormenting young—and not so young—females. She could easily imagine herself ensnared in his fierce embrace and delighting in every aspect of it.

How soon could she escape Aunt Prudence and go

to the garden on the chance he'd decided to meet her? Not until after supper, surely.

She patted the sides of her dress, searching for her spectacles.

"Do you have *any* idea what kind of man Lord Blakely is? What type of scandals he and those awful *cubs* of his participate in? Such a carousing band of rabblers! How Lady Longford could even *consider* inviting them..."

Ah. Blakely's Cubs, Francine thought, abandoning her search when she remembered that Aunt Prudence had made her leave them at home.

Blakely's Cubs...

She'd heard whispers of the debauched revelries that took place at The Den, one of the more notorious London hells, but hadn't realized the connection.

Now that she thought back to the group of young men surrounding Lord Blakely, vying for position next to him and doing their best to command his attention—she'd watched their blurred forms for ages before working up the gumption to approach him—she realized he must be one of the patrons of the infamous club. A thrill of excitement flashed through her stomach. If anything, this only made him more appropriate in her eyes.

"He is *known* for affiliating with the lowest grade of society. Three-quarters of the *filth* he associates with do not come close to ranking invitations to the best events."

Barely restraining the smile that threatened, Francine commented, "But are we not all attending the same fête tonight?"

Aunt Prudence ignored her.

So she added, "And he was at the Seftons' ball three years ago. Or did you not know?"

But her aunt was adept at hearing only what she chose to. "Why, the very thought of one under *my* protection even being in the same room with that blackguard! It destroys my soul to see you behaving with *such* utter disgrace, Franny. If you persist in such outlandish behavior—"

"Persist?" Francine was finally compelled to defend herself. "When have I ever done anything to cause embarrassment to your family?" Had she not voluntarily delayed her own come-out a year or more beyond what was customary, waiting for Patience to reach an age where they could debut together, only out of consideration for her aunt?

An aunt who now sputtered before replying. "All those flowers you play with. It is not the least seemly."

"Aunt, they are herbs and vegetables, not flowers and they supply food to your table."

"*Well.*" Her aunt could harrumph with the best of them. "And your face is as brown as a chestnut, despite the powder." Aunt Pru poked a finger to her chin and turned her head hither and yon. "*Unseemly* is far too mild a term for what you have done to your skin. Makes you look like a veritable Gypsy."

"With this hair?" Francine was grateful she'd found at least one thing to laugh about during this conversation. "I seriously doubt anyone will be mistaking me for anything other than a bland English miss."

"*Miss* is right."

Aunt Prudence would latch on to that word. Drat!

"'Tis high time you started behaving as a *proper* English miss and let me procure a match for you. Both of your cousins have already done so, such *grand* alliances and without a word of protest from either of them. Why you will not just *follow* along and behave as they..."

It was to be expected when Patience went along with her mother's scheming and betrothal arranging, accepting the first man to offer. After all, Patience took after her father in looks (with thin, mud-brown hair and a nose several shades too large for her mouth, giving her a perpetually pinched look), and she followed her mother in temperament. Given that, she hadn't exactly been lauded a success in her early Seasons.

But Temperance, now? The cousin who had recently taken to asking everyone to call her Tempest... Her quiet acquiescence had surprised Francine.

When she'd first come to live with them, not long after her widowed aunt had remarried, Francine had thought she and Temperance, her younger cousin, might form a bond beyond family and become true friends.

Despite the five-year difference in their ages, they'd shared several meaningful conversations deep into the night when they should have been in the Land of Nod. Yet only a short while later, Temperance changed, becoming aloof and flitting about much like her older sister—the both of them behaving, more often than not, as though not a meaningful thought existed betwixt their ears.

At the time, Francine had not the fortitude to

pursue an unwanted friendship nor to discern the impetus behind the sudden shift, not when she still grieved the loss of her parents with nearly every waking breath.

And though she'd tried to reach out a few times since, her every overture was rebuffed, Temperance making it clear as sunshine she'd no need of Francine as anything more than her elder cousin, someone to be friendly toward, share the occasional smile or laugh with, but certainly not as a bosom companion to be confided in.

As to Patience? Only two years younger than Francine, peevish in the extreme, and evolving into the very epitome of her mother so thoroughly it erased any disappointment Francine might have felt over not pursuing a relationship with the cousin closest to her in age.

Contrary to her current preoccupation with unpleasantness, Aunt Prudence had been convivial once upon a time, according to Francine's papa. Even going so far as to follow her heart into an alliance firmly disapproved by their parents. When the man she'd eloped with fell victim to *his* parents' edicts and joined the church (else continue to be cut off from their deep pockets), it seemed he took to heart all the Thou Shall Nots and moral restrictives the Good Book espoused while not embracing any of the more loving examples and positive biblical teachings. Becoming harsh and critical, unforgiving and somewhat of a gaoler if the stories Temperance initially shared were to be believed.

At least Lord Rowden, her aunt's new husband,

cared not about restricting the interests and activities of the female members of his instant family. In truth, he seemed rather apathetic about the lot of them. That very afternoon, she'd overheard her aunt complaining to her spouse. "'Tis most unseemly, *still* unmarried at her advanced age. She continues to be a *horrid* example for the girls. Simply appalling."

"Leave the gel alone," her uncle had mumbled. Blood relative or not, she always had liked him better. 'Twas easier to be ignored than hounded.

Though Uncle went on to murmur something soothing about her own daughters and their recent engagements, Aunt Prudence had proceeded to list all of Francine's deplorable, headstrong ways, much as she was doing now. Bandying a harangue about *all* the suitors she had secured for Francine—and how their "ungrateful niece" better accept the latest one if she knew what was good for her.

Living in such an environment, where her aunt thought she had the right to manage Francine to her whims, rankled. After seven years of such treatment, not to mention witnessing her aunt and uncle's unenviable, lackluster marriage—combined with the tales she'd heard about her aunt's restrictive first—Francine vowed her last few months in their household would be on *her* terms.

As would the direction of her entire future, hence her proposition to the powerful Lord Blakely.

"The sooner you acquiesce and accept Lord Peterson's perfectly amiable offer, Franny, the sooner we can *all* move on..."

As Aunt Prudence's current tirade showed no signs

of slowing, Francine's determination grew. She refused to resign herself to suffering her relative's unjust complaints and machinations any longer. She refused to allow herself to be browbeaten into a *mésalliance*, when all she really wanted was freedom.

Freedom. Just the mere thought filled her lungs with ease, promised to lessen the constriction of tightly laced stays—and an ever tighter-wound aunt. Because the longer the unfounded ranting went on, the more restrictive her stays became. The more determined her resolve...

If Aunt Prudence insisted on constantly bombarding Francine with her lack of a suitable match, then Francine was convinced the next best thing was to secure for herself an *unsuitable* match. And who could be more unsuitable than the condescending, philandering, devilishly attractive Lord Blakely?

<hr>

CLAIMING A PREVIOUSLY SCHEDULED assignation and smiling gamely through the ribald comments thrown his way, Blakely decided to forgo the last several hands at the card tables and instead chose to explore the very depths of the Longfords' elaborate garden.

If their earlier encounter was anything to go by, he suspected Lady Francine would be waiting for him in the most secluded section of the extensive grounds—the darkest portion in the far corner, studded with more trees than the rest of the formal, planned-out gardens. Fortunately, he knew exactly where that was, after having met a rather immoral widow there at a previous ball.

His senses acutely attuned to the night, he easily made his way past seven-foot-high hedges, the occasional topiary and a number of benches, gazebos and arbors until arriving at the private setting.

Which was decidedly empty. *Damn.*

Ah. Just as well.

He was due at The Den. If he delayed significantly longer, Adam might question how the evening went. Come to think on it, with her shockingly bold approach in front of others, Adam was sure to hear of it regardless. But not from Blakely; for he, more than most, knew how to hold his tongue.

He'd put in his appearance as required tonight, so his duties, socially, were once again fulfilled. Now to focus on his unending responsibilities—

A giant sigh heaved from him as he scanned the area one last time. Hoping...

But nay, nothing.

Intent on banishing a specific exasperating female from his mind once and for all, he resolutely dismissed the lingering pang of disappointment. "Asides," he attempted to console himself, "the last thing I need right now is such an annoying distraction."

Don't you mean intriguing?

"Vexing baggage, too bold for—" He cut off the internal debate when he heard someone approaching. His heart gave a strange, unfamiliar lift.

"Too brave for your own good, are you not?" he whispered, a predatory smile curving his lips as he secreted himself away in the darkest shadows while he waited for Lady Francine to arrive.

Scant minutes later, she did, tiptoeing her way through the unlit paths. The shawl that had concealed her upper arms inside now trailed behind, gently flowing from the delicate hand that gripped it. She moved hesitantly, searching out each step before she took it as if in the dead of night she didn't quite trust her vision. But he could see her clearly.

Her elegantly simple features and the nondescript attire that failed to do her justice indoors transformed in the starlight. The celestial reflections caused her skin to gleam pearlescent, lightening her unfashionably tan exterior to one of cream.

Cream he wanted to sample. Especially after viewing the tempting expanse of her chest visible with her shawl discarded. The salacious swell of her bosom invited his attention more than any he'd seen in recent memory. But he had no business thinking of her diddeys again, even though he could easily see their outline above her stays and beneath the thin fabric of her gown.

She really was a fetching thing, if one could look past the unnecessary face powder, which was easy enough. *If* one could look past the unmistakable stamp of *virgin*. Which he couldn't, no matter how part of him longed to. Nay... He was here to decline her offer in person. Nothing more.

Her courage approaching him earlier deserved no less.

She'd almost reached his hiding spot. He was about to step forth when two whirlwinds came skipping noisily down the path, paying little heed to the dim light. Knowing he didn't want to involve the latest arrivals, he retreated behind the trunk of a tall tree, further concealing himself as they raced the rest of the way.

"Franny! There you are," a female with an unfortunately large nose huffed. "We have quite exhausted ourselves, looking *all* over for you."

At the peevish announcement, Lady Francine Montfort fisted her hands around the shawl and swung to face the young women. "*Francine*," she stressed in a low voice. "Please refrain from calling me Franny in public. You know how I detest it."

Montfort. Something about the name nudged at a memory, like one's tongue poking at a sore tooth. What was he not recalling?

"Mother is simply *livid* at your disappearance."

"She sent us out here," the other one said, a bit younger than the first and with a decidedly appropriately sized conk. "Looking for you, that is. Instructed we not return without you."

"There is no need to concern yourselves. I shall return inside before overly long." She spun in a slow circle, gesturing to the gardens around her. "Do the crickets not sound lovely? After all the people and hours inside, I just need a bit of fresh air. Alone."

She sounded admirably convincing. If she hadn't invited him to meet her, he'd feel he intruded on what was meant to be a private moment between Lady Francine—never Franny, he made a mental note—and nature.

Given what he already knew about her, he knew

she and Nature shared an attachment. One he was unaccountably envious of, so hardened by battling his own traitorous nature.

When was the last time he'd stopped to enjoy the breeze upon his cheek? The sound of a cricket or call of a bird? Sunshine and a rare, quiet moment for himself? Not since losing his parents. Not since becoming the Marquis.

"Mother will positively *rage*." The older one put that unfortunate nose to use and gave an audible sniff. "You know she *detests* it when you act the insociable bluestocking, Franny."

"Aunt Prudence chooses not to like anything that is not perfectly proper, boringly suitable or prepared by her new French chef." Lady Francine's shoulders rose and fell on a loud exhalation. "Can you not simply tell her I had the headache and am lying down?"

After sneaking a quick glance at who he assumed was her sister, no matter that the two didn't resemble each other in the slightest, the younger one shook her head. "That would be telling Mother an untruth."

From her low groan, he could just imagine Lady Francine's irritation. He smiled, watching with interest when she lifted a hand to her forehead and flicked herself with a light snap of her middle finger.

"Ow. Now my head does ache. You will not be telling a whisker."

Blakely fought back a laugh. So did the younger one.

"But, Franny..."

"Patience..." Lady Francine said at full volume, then

murmured low enough he was sure no one but him heard, "you are surely trying mine."

She peered through the gloom and spotted a nearby bench, then promptly reclined full-length on its hard surface. Her feet hung off the edge, exposing several inches of stocking-clad legs. His fingers suddenly itched with the need to slowly graze upward toward her thighs, to determine exactly where her stockings ended. By gads, he was half tempted to agree to her outrageous offer.

Don't be a fool!

In quick succession, she thumped her forehead thrice more. "There. I *do* have the headache and I *am* lying down. There is no need to mention that I remained outside—it's immaterial. Simply tell your mother I shall return when I feel rested."

"You are *so* clever!" the younger one applauded, literally clapping her hands together.

"Mother says you think you are too clever, Franny. But she still holds out hope that—"

"Please. No more." Lady Francine's deep sigh filled the air as she remained on the bench, her fingers drumming impatiently on her stomach. "Do you not want to return to the dancing and your admiring beaus? Your came-up-to-scratch suitors that so please your mother? Wait..." She paused and made a great show of turning her head while sniffing the night air. "Does it smell like rain to you?"

"*Rain?*" the elder exclaimed, causing Blakely to bite his tongue to keep from laughing outright. There wasn't a cloud in the sky. "We had best go inside immediately. Rain would absolutely *destroy* our hair."

"Oh, that would be *dreadful*," the other agreed in a mocking tone that had him now biting his lips to remain silent.

"Aye, dreadful," Francine added dryly.

"Rain!" the older one repeated, as though they discussed a veritable deluge of vipers thundering down upon them rather than the possibility of a few harmless water droplets. "You *know* what moisture does to *your* hair, Franny. Best mind you come with us now."

"As if I could forget," the reclining Lady Francine muttered to herself. Then louder and brighter, to her persistent companions, "The sooner I have a moment or several to myself, the sooner I am likely to join you inside. For the sake of my hair, if nothing else, will you please—"

"Going!" the younger one trilled, dragging off her sister despite the continued grumbling that they ought to be bringing "Franny" with them.

"Do come in soon, though. Else Mother may come looking herself," the younger one advised, sounding more mature than she had thus far, still tugging her sister back. "One of *your* recent suitors is here to renew his address."

"Aye, you *really* should consider accepting him, Franny. Mother says his rank and standing in the *ton* is comserate with yours and that he would make you a *very* suitable match."

"Commensurate," Francine corrected, even as both girls—finally—turned to speed from the garden. "And 'tis Franc*ine*," she called after their retreating figures. "Oh, why do I even bother?"

"Because you know they are nothing more than ill-educated, flighty females but they remain family, so you feel responsible for them all the same." Blakely stepped from the shadows, exposing himself on several levels, if truth be told. "And though part of me is loath to admit it, I have begun to feel a measure of responsibility toward you, at least in part. Come, make your full proposition. I promise to give it due consideration."

3

THE METTLESOME MISS AND HER BOLD BARGAIN

My senses are remarkably acute. I see better than my peers, hear better than them. My sense of smell? Oh gads, should there be a rotten rodent rotting below stairs? My blighted nose will not let me sleep until ferreting out the offender.

When I can lose myself in some relaxing endeavor for a few moments, I can almost forget the curse I bear. But then something as simple as playing a game of piquet with my peers brings it roaring back. Either when one of them taps the cards mindlessly on top of the green, or picks at a corner with the edge of a fingernail. Or, heaven forbid one raises the stakes higher than he's comfortable with and starts to sweat.

I become aware of it all. My nose flares, their perspiration turns pungent, and I feel as though I'm suddenly on the hunt. For what? I know not.

I only know my very cells respond with an acute awareness that leaves me both in awe and mentally rebelling—

hating with every cognizant thought in my brain what I have become. A beast. An uncontrollable monster.

A lonely man, who remains afraid to engage with his young sons or love his wife, uncertain when the demon side might take control and render those closest to me lifeless.

It is a wretched, desolate way to live...

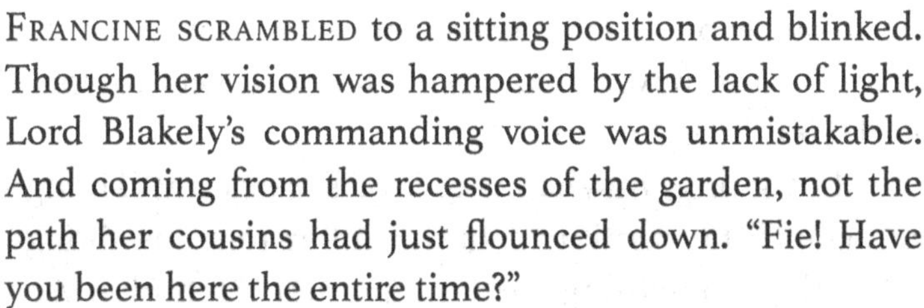

FRANCINE SCRAMBLED to a sitting position and blinked. Though her vision was hampered by the lack of light, Lord Blakely's commanding voice was unmistakable. And coming from the recesses of the garden, not the path her cousins had just flounced down. "Fie! Have you been here the entire time?"

"I have."

What a rotten thing for him to witness! And after he'd deigned to meet her too. She knew her chances with him were ruined now that he'd beheld her childish antics with her cousins. Oh, why couldn't she maintain "a more proper decorum", as Aunt Prudence pompously phrased it, for more than a minute?

She stood and faced him, shaking out her petticoats and skirt. "I am certain after observing that interaction, you are quite ready to turn tail and depart, are you not?"

"I make it a point never to turn on my tail."

The cryptic remark seemed to hold more meaning than she could infer. After a moment, she stopped trying. "Lord Blakely, I promise what you saw is not—"

"You lied earlier," he accused, "claiming that we have been introduced."

Caught, she confessed, "We did not exactly meet at the Seftons'"—or dance, much to my disappointment—"but I first saw you there."

And have fancied you ever since...

As though laughing at her, the cricket chirps became louder, almost drowning out the hard pounding of her heart.

"You are quite the sauce box, are you not?"

"You find me overly forward? Impetuous?" Better to be a sauce box than married to an unwanted suitor. "Were I not, how could I have found a way to speak with you?"

"Intriguing, mayhap. Bold, of a certainty. Though reluctant," he continued in a somber tone, as though admitting something he'd rather not, "I find myself considering your offer."

"You are? Why, that's smashing."

"As to that, there remains significant doubt." Three long strides and he was standing directly in front of her. "Tell me your terms, then I shall decide."

The allure of his body heat and untamed presence only firmed her earlier resolve. She squared her shoulders. "My terms have changed."

"They have?" His deep voice washed over her again. "To what? Upon further reflection, you have decided not to pursue your scheme?"

"Actually, I *have* changed my mind but...um..." Her voice wavered as she searched for the right words. Francine's confidence in the appreciable talents of her intellect was resolute, but making an offer based on her questionable physical attributes was harder than she'd expected.

He shifted, easing away from her and the damp night suddenly permeated her gown. "I should be relieved to hear that you no longer intend to go through with this farce," he said. "That you have no need of me now. Oddly though, I am crestfallen."

"There exists no need to mock me, my lord. You do not have to be a...a..."

"An arse?" he supplied, stealing the word right from her thoughts, the scoundrel. "Be assured that was not my intention, but I daresay you have made the right decision. I am convinced of it, though my regret at the news cannot be denied." He stepped back as if to leave.

"Wait." Francine lunged to grasp his arm. "You would have me believe that you are quite run aground at the thought I no longer need your help? We both know I'd have to be a complete nick-ninny to believe that."

Muscles flexed beneath her touch but she held firm. "What now, little miss?"

At the mocking tone, she released him. "You do not understand. I have not changed my mind about *you*, Lord Blakely, or the pretend engagement. 'Tis just that... Upon my word, this is difficult."

"You obviously have more to say. Come, let us sit and you can state your piece." He guided her to the bench she'd reclined on earlier and they both sat down, a respectable distance between their thighs—one she longed to close.

"What is it?" His wine-laced breath was warm as it wafted past her cheek, combating the slight chill in the air. "Am I now to conclude that no longer am I your first choice? That after making my acquaintance tonight, you have now decided I shall not suit?"

Lord Blakely turned away and faced the shadows.

In profile, the planes of his face outlined by the starlight, he seemed more vulnerable, more open to injury than Francine would have thought possible. She could just make out the casual fall of his overlong hair, the slash of black side whiskers against his well-defined jaw, the barely discernible curve of his lips, almost lost in the burgeoning folds of his neckcloth, now that he'd bowed his head. Lips she desperately wanted to touch with her own.

Or perhaps she only imagined the details, having committed them to memory earlier.

"Cannot say I'm surprised," he muttered, as if to himself. "Are you now moving on to candidate number two? Who is he, by the way?"

"Lord Crandall," she tossed off the first name she thought of, hoping he was still unmarried, "but that is of no consequence because—"

"Lord *Crandall*?" His head whipped around and he fairly glared at her, his eyes suddenly taking on a shimmering golden glow. "Have you truly lost your wits? He delights in being an unprincipled reprobate, one who will eat you up and spit you out, bones and all. Come to think on it, I might too, but at least *I* would regret it afterward."

Her fingers returned to his sleeve. "You do not understand."

.   .   .

"Damn right I do not. How you could even contemplate the *possibility* of propositioning that rakeshame is beyond me. Crandall is an unconscionable mundungus of a man, certainly *not* a knave someone like yourself should—"

She laughed. "Now you begin to sound like Aunt Prudence."

That comparison shut him up.

"I did not mean to imply that I have revised my assessment of your suitability for my proposition. Not at all."

Blakely knew that her words were meant to reassure him. How was it they did...and didn't?

"'Tis only that I have altered what I want from you and what I am offering in return."

"Go on."

"My circumstances still necessitate that you pose as my betrothed."

"How do I know you shall end the farce? Jilt me in truth? You could simply be angling for a prime title."

"Let me put your mind at ease. For one, if all I desired was a title, I would have accepted Farnsworth two Seasons ago."

A duke, no less.

So I'm not the only one who sees something in her. Blakely might not be bosom chums with the man, but knew him to be better than many. And she'd turned him down? "He proposed?"

"His Grace most certainly did—through my uncle, who brought his suit to me. I declined the same way."

He stifled a snort. "Farnswimpy becomes flustered,

somewhat tongue-tied around a prime article like yourself."

"That is of no matter." So quickly she discounted his impromptu compliment. "Secondly, I have no interest in marrying or considering anyone for a husband. Truly, I do not. I am much more concerned with my freedom. Too concerned, I assure you, to barter it stupidly away—to you or any man. And we both know..." Uncharacteristically, she hesitated. Then turned toward him until their knees barely nudged. "May I speak plainly, without fear of wounding your feelings?"

He'd have to have them first. "By all means."

"If my intention was to secure a husband in truth, would I not have, um, sought assistance elsewhere?"

And there he went, experiencing another strange clip to his pride. One that did not sit well in the least. "I am considered a magnificent catch, I'll have you know."

"Aye, you possess a title," she rushed to assure, a little too quickly to his mind. "A good one. And your pockets brim, your estates produce. But you also whore and gamble and have secrets that—"

He snaked an arm out to capture her wrist. "What makes you say that?"

"I see—sense them." And if that didn't turn him up mute. "Come now, let us, for a moment at least, have utter and complete candor between us. Would any sane, marriage-minded miss—one with an analyzing brain and a modicum of true wit—really choose you?"

He did not know whether to be rudely insulted or hugely impressed by her observations. Unsettling, though they were.

Unsettling in the extreme.

Before he could ascertain why, she rushed on. "Now that we have confirmed I shall jilt away, you need to hear the rest of my proposal. For, in addition to the playacting, the faked betrothal, Lord Blakely, I would like to request you to be my lover."

Shock held him immobile. Dirt from his last hunting excursion must be lodged in his ears. Blakely shook his head. "Repeat that."

"I want you to be my lover. If you would not mind overly much, that is. During the tenure of our agreement," she added, as if only doing it for a specified duration made her request any less surprising.

Did she have any idea what her words did to him? What the *idea* of prigging her was doing to his body? He stood abruptly, forced his fingers from her wrist and stalked away from the temptation she presented. A vision of mounting her filled his mind. Of riding her feminine, shapely arse until she moaned and wept around his cock as he pounded into her so hard, so deep, she screamed. And begged for more.

The thought fired his blood to the point of pain. *Insane.* He'd always been able to manage his desires. Always. His mind might not have dominion over The Change but through years of practice, he could remain sheathed inside a woman, experiencing her release—which somehow tamed the feline atoms of his being—until just before he erupted, always vacating her warm fancy in time and spilling his seed harmlessly.

Knowing full well the dangers of passing on the curse, he'd refrained from siring any bastards, but he couldn't say the same for the others who shared his burden.

He could control his lust, *his cells*, tonight. But for how much longer? He looked past the hedges, gauging the position of the stars beyond. By midnight, Hercules would be almost overhead. In less than three months, the sun would enter the constellation Leo and his control would be precarious at best. Deadly at worst.

Did that give him enough time to fulfill her request *and* satisfy his burgeoning lust? Still not looking at her, he swore. "You do not know the entirety of what you ask."

She stepped in front of him, caught his gaze and captured him as surely as if she'd snared a hapless hare. "Perhaps not, but I want you to show me."

"Why would a virgin want to align herself with someone like me? Your reputation will be destroyed." Why in the hell was he arguing with her? She'd just invited him to fuck her, for God's sake.

It seemed some shred of nobility remained in him after all.

"Do you not understand? At four and twenty—and nine months," said as though he should consider her ancient, indeed, "I should be considered on the shelf by now but my popularity has not waned, not among a certain caliber of men, ones I have absolutely no interest in." For the first time, her composure slipped, voice cracked as agitation lent a panicked edge to her tone. "Can you not see? I *want* to be publicly ruined— or, at the very least, publicly *claimed* by you. Then my aunt will have to abandon her ridiculous notions of managing me into an unwanted marriage." She dropped her gaze, lowered her voice to a whisper. "Aside from that, I... I am not a virgin."

Not a virgin? That was news. "You have been with a man before? Sexually?"

"Aye," she confessed in a small voice.

There was that at least.

"Only once. He was a boy, really, not a man." She tipped her head up, braving his gaze. "Not to refine overmuch, but I was numb with grief at the time. 'Twas directly after my parents died and before my aunt and uncle traveled to Papa's country estate—my home—to bring me to live with them. I did not object when he..."

"Who?" And why did he care?

"A shopkeeper's son I had known for years. Not well, mind." Her eyes flitted away before returning. "I just wanted to *feel* again. And I did. Only remorse after. Not any pleasure during. And, well..." Her face pinched as though she tasted something bitter indeed. How was it she managed to maintain her calm and serene tone —even while sharing something so very intimate? "Since I did not enjoy it in the least, I chose not to repeat the experience. Not that I have been the least tempted, because I have not."

"Then why bring it up now? Why ask me to bed you?"

Her eyes glistened, speaking to every part of him that wasn't a barbarian. "Because when I am close to you, my womanly urges make themselves known. And I want to experience it again, the physical knowing of a man. With you. In particular."

Bloody hell.

At four and thirty, he'd had almost a full decade to

familiarize himself with his body's altered abilities—
and limitations. His thoughts raced over what he and
the others who shared his burden had discovered since
The Change began...that the only way to mitigate the
animalistic tendencies was through sex.

Surrendering to the instinctual need to mate, which
heightened throughout the summer, channeled the
foreign energy that drove him into an outlet other than
altering his form. The singular act of swiving a wench
was the only thing that subdued the wildness, calmed
his blood and allowed him to function even remotely
like normal during the time his control was at its most
tenuous.

Which shouldn't be for weeks yet, so why was lust
stampeding his very being right this moment?

Because of the surprisingly appealing morsel
before him?

He stepped to the side, away from temptation.

Temptation followed—Lady Francine matched his
action. "Lest you forget, I shall compensate you handsomely once our time is finished—"

"What do you take me for?" he all but spat. When
had his pantaloons gotten so dreadfully tight? "I am
not a three-penny upright or licentious lord with
pockets so empty the Devil dances in them at his
leisure. I have absolutely no interest in your money."
Only your*self*.

"Please, my lord. I only need the protection of our
false betrothal until I reach my majority, which is not
terribly far off. Then you will be released from our
agreement and I promise not to make any further
claims on you."

A clue, finally. Something to take his mind off what his body craved. "Tell me what has happened, that you now require an official betrothal, especially one for such a brief commitment."

She hesitated. He could tell she was deciding what to reveal. Would it be the truth or an invented story just to garner his sympathy and agreement? Did he care? It wasn't as if he was ready to bare his soul, so who was he to judge? When she remained silent, he persisted, "Well? Have you need of me or not?"

"I do!" she sputtered, talking fast. "Aunt Prudence has been pushing suitors toward me for a while now, but this latest batch seems unaccountably determined, very unsavory, one in particular. He accosted me at the Farmingtons' rout last week. If not for my quick actions, I shudder to think what might have become of me."

Hmmm. Turning rather melodramatic, wasn't she? Just how much was she embellishing this need of hers, for the protection of a false betrothal? "And what actions were those?"

"After he ripped my dress—"

She paused when a growl emerged from his suddenly tight throat. "Go on," he gritted out past the restriction. If the blackguard had ripped her dress, by God, then nay, she wasn't embellishing a lick.

"Well, after that..." A small smile curved her lips. "I allowed a rather heavy piece of statuary to connect with his head."

"*Allowed?*"

"Heaved it with all my might, if truth be told." She lifted one shoulder in a light shrug, that belied the seriousness of the situation she'd found herself in. "Both he and the statue toppled to the ground, but only the expensive plaster shattered, not the cheap buffoon, I'm afraid."

"Good for you." He no longer even cared what they were discussing. She was captivating his mind as much as she'd seduced his body.

"Lord and Lady Farmington were adamant that I no longer attend anything hosted in their home, no matter that they were great friends of my father's."

He laughed. "'Tis their loss."

"And it will be mine, if you do not agree."

Like a dog with a bone, she returned to the motivation behind this impromptu meeting. "When would it end? Our performance?"

Lord Farmington... Great friends. *Montfort.*

Recognition snapped like a bolt of lightning slamming into his heart. "*You* are the Duke of Swanhart's only offspring?"

"Aye, the very one."

Every person who wasn't a complete chowder-head living in southern England knew of the Heartsick Duke, as he'd been dubbed, his first two wives dying in childbirth, his third suffering three miscarriages before birthing a healthy baby.

But not an heir, to the collective gasp of the *ton*, only a "mere" girl.

"I knew your father," he managed to impart without a fleck of emotion. "He called on me once." Upon news of his own father's demise, the duke had arrived in person to honor his long-time friend, to pay his respects. Swanhart had offered to lend his support any way he could, left written recommendations on Runners, if the new marquis—Erasmus—wanted the suspicious circumstances of his father's demise investigated, suggestions for solicitors, stewards, even a good vicar should his soul need nourished. He'd even come laden with foodstuffs and pantry supplies, offering a stunned, grieving man of nineteen all manner of support.

And *this* was his Infamous Miracle Child? A babe magical enough to be born healthy to an older duke yet defiant enough to be born *female*?

Gads. Even more reason to help her.

"Your mother?" he asked and his somber tone wasn't feigned in the least. He'd mourned privately upon news of the duke's death, listened with interest to the gossip over lack of obvious heir...just rumors of some distant relative off in the Americas. "What became of her?"

"They perished together, my lord. Carriage accident. A rainstorm...a ravine." He saw her lips tremble before she firmed them, heard the shaky inhalation she couldn't stem. "And to this day, speaking of it is difficult for I miss them both terribly."

"Then, pray, do not talk of it further."

She accepted the counsel with a gracious nod. "Once I turn five and twenty, my inheritance will be released into my control and I will no longer be under Aunt Prudence's thumb," she resumed her narrative, even as his mind swirled at the prickles of added responsibility. "The position is not a comfortable one, I assure you."

"I do not doubt it." His lips curved in a reluctant

smile as his admiration grew. *Your father would be pleased with how elegant and articulate you have become,* he thought but knew better than to say.

"I realize my situation may not sound severe, but I have been besieged by suitors in recent months and here I thought my advanced age would have put them off by now. A distasteful lot—men quite unfamiliar to me or those with unsavory reputations. Aye!" She hurried on before he could interrupt—wanting to scoff at the idea of anyone considering this young miss plagued by "advanced" age. "Before you argue, men with reputations as grieviously lamentable as your own, but ones without your trustworthy character."

And while that unexpected praise threatened to make him lose his head, she kept on, still speaking swiftly and yet with an edge her quiet words had lacked before. "Men I have no desire to become conversant with, much less legally bound to. Men overeager for my hand that I could not trust to enact the farce. Nor to end it. Several of them have become insistent of late, pressing their address regardless of my wishes and completely ignoring my staunch refusals."

"You ignored *my* refusal earlier tonight," he reminded her.

"Only because you had not yet heard me out."

"You have my full attention at present. Why me, specifically?"

"Your reputation, for one. It will quite unhinge my aunt." Her dimpled smile charmed him. "And yet, you are still welcomed throughout society. Add that to your title, and you should see why you alone are perfect for my needs."

He sensed there was more, something—or mayhap several somethings—she wasn't telling him, yet, truth be told, every minute spent in her presence mitigated his desire to protest, to turn her away and have nothing more to do with her. He was almost relieved when she continued her logical-sounding litany.

"As a duke's daughter, I dare not attempt the pretense with anyone holding a title lower than yours. My aunt would not possess the audacity to proclaim *you* an unfit suitor in public. I shall only have to endure her vocal protestations in private. I am counting on our courtship to shield me from her overzealous efforts and the unwanted beaus who hound me like the plague. I do not know where she dredges up these relentless rakes, but I am not interested in marrying. She pointedly refuses to accept that."

"Does it not occur to you that she covets your money?"

"It has, but Papa left her a considerable sum in his will, to compensate her for my care, as well as a portion just for her. He also provided generous dowries for both my cousins, to the chagrin of my uncle, if truth be told."

"Your aunt obviously thinks she is entitled to more."

"But I offered!" Lady Francine paced a few steps away, then returned, her growing agitation palatable. "Thinking that was why she seemed so determined to marry me off but only to men *she* approved of, I asked her if she needed additional funds but she declined, affronted by my even approaching her. With both my cousins recently becoming engaged, I thought her attention would turn to planning their weddings, but no, her efforts only seemed to have redoubled in my direction. I can only assume, then, that 'tis my presence she finds objectionable. She chastises her daughters if they emulate any part of my person or behavior. Heaven forfend they order a bonnet like mine or express an interest in learning anything beyond watercolors, embroidery or how to set a fine and boring table. Nay, it is *me* she objects to. I intend to move out and live on my own the moment I am in possession of my funds."

"And you believe masquerading with me would enable that to occur?"

"I do, while giving me a modicum of peace in the meantime. I confess, hearing my reasons out loud, even I begin to fear they sound paltry. I have lived under these circumstances for years, why can I not continue a few weeks longer?" Her chin firmed, tilted once more until she regained his gaze. "Because they do not *feel* the same, I tell you. She harbors such growing animosity toward me and I am clueless as to its source. Her determination has escalated to the point I confess to having lost far too much sleep over puzzling a solution. Will you help me, please?" She stared at him with an open, endearing expression, one that made him long to grant the peace she so craved. But that wasn't all he wanted to give her...

Her spirit, her intellect—even her determination— they drew him as much as the outward package.

How he wanted to bend her over, forge his way through her tight crevice and plow into her sweet depths, scrape his nails along the skin of her back and taste the delicate flavor of her nape. By the saints, he wanted, no *needed*, to corrupt this not quite pure innocent. What did that say about him? The irresponsible actions of his grandfather had done more than damn their family. It seemed, with his current inexplicable affection and predilection toward corrupting Lady Francine, they had damned his soul as well.

"Please." She interrupted his ruminating.

So he barked, "What?"

"Consider." A plea. Heartfelt.

"Considering."

"Hmm…"

He grunted, his mind racing. Running over reasons why not. Clinging to the reasons why.

"Still?" She actually let more than thirty seconds pass that time.

Had he ever before bantered wits with any female? Had he ever enjoyed an initial conversation with one as much? Nay, never. "Aye."

"*Still?*"

"Unrelentingly."

"*Harrumph.*"

At that, he couldn't quite stifle the foreign snicker that emerged, that turned into a full-out laugh. "Vexing baggage or not, you are quite unexpected."

"Exceptional."

All right. He'd play again. "Entertaining."

"Vastly."

"Moderately." Best not let her charms—nor how they affected him—go to her head.

"Enticing?"

"Enough."

"Engaging?" With just the right amount of emphasis to bring them back to why she'd approached him in the first place. *An engagement.* The protection he could offer. Or so she thought.

"Enough!" he all but roared, trying to maintain his outward expression of hauteur. It didn't alarm her one bit.

"Enjoying?" This asked quietly, that beautiful, soothing tone wrapping around him in such a way he wanted nothing more than to curl around her and purr.

"Exquisitely." Why had he not met her sooner? Sought her out before? Claimed a dance? A carriage ride? Her body?

Responsibilities.

An absent brother. A missing cousin.

And lest you forget, you could turn into a damn lion at any time and eat her for breakfast.

Eat her? For...breakfast?

Which would imply they'd spent the night together...

Which would become a reality, if he agreed to her terms.

And suddenly, he—the man who put responsibility toward others before himself since the moment his father died and he assumed the title—wanted nothing more than to selfishly consent.

Ensnared by an innocent. What was his world coming to?

"Very well. I agree." He was a weak, weak man.

"Only..." Of a sudden, she hesitated. What now? "I

do not want any unintentional consequences. Can you prevent conception?"

Of course he could. And that she'd asked it so plainly? At that, his respect notched higher. "I have never sired a babe and have no intention of starting now," he told her in all honesty. "Aye, I can prevent it. Ensure there is pleasure between us but naught else."

"Very well, then. We are of one accord? You will pose as my betrothed?"

"I will, and I shall also awaken your body to the pleasures to be explored between us. With one stipulation," he added when she started to look more joyful than he had a right to even behold. "I will squire you about town and effectively put my claim on you in order to protect you from any further offers or unwelcome suitors. However, regarding the physical aspects of our association…"

"Yes?"

How in the hell could he phrase this delicately, yet still convey the potential danger?

He couldn't and gave up trying. Better to scare her off now and forgo any momentary oblivion he might find in her arms than to suffer—or force her to suffer— anything like what his cousin once caused. Poor Phineas. Losing his wife like that.

Nay! I'll not have spirited Francine's demise on my conscience. Never that.

Blakely stepped forward and grabbed her hand. Roughly, he placed it on his cock, curving her fingers around the width of his mounting erection and holding them there when she instinctively attempted to pull away. "My sexual proclivities are renowned for a reason. I have extensive appetites. Ones I am not sure you can satisfy or will even want to."

Her fingers flexed, tightened on his shaft. Now that her initial reluctance had waned, curiosity seemingly took its place. "Oh but I do. I want to experience what all the fuss is about and, as I have no intention of marrying in truth, this is a prime opportunity."

"Your flattering words make me feel so very wanted," he said sarcastically, hating how he even cared that he was being used simply because she was curious. And hating how his body responded so furiously to her hesitant explorations. All thought and will centered in his groin— and both were disintegrating by the moment.

"I did tell you that I approached you before asking any others. That you were my first choice." Her fingers prodded and probed, causing him to swell under their regard—even *after* he lifted his away and off, clenching his fists at his side. "In truth, you are my *only* choice. The list, the others... Those were clankers. Forgive me?"

If she continued to explore him *just so*, he'd forgive her anything.

Since when are you so far gone for a female? One who's made it a habit to lie?

Biting the edges of his tongue to distract his mind from the journey her fingers took along his length, he gritted out, "No more bounders. Not a one. Lie to me again and our association is over."

He had to be able to trust her—if he had any hope of keeping her safe.

"Never again. I promise."

"In turn, I will tell you that I shall endeavor not to be seen with another woman during our farce, which would likely cause speculation. In exchange, I require that you make yourself available to me anytime I desire it and absent yourself when I require that as well." There. If he felt his control slipping, he'd simply order her from his presence. That should assuage his conscience.

"Done."

Her easy assent, after hounding him so very thoroughly until he capitulated and fell in with her plans, raised a red flag. "Do not think to gainsay me on this at a later date, Lady Francine. You *will* vacate yourself from my vicinity at once, if I so order it."

"Of course. No more clankers, remember? My word is good, my lord. You may depend upon me to honor my side of our bargain."

She had no idea what she'd just agreed to and he was too damn selfish to tell her.

4

THE NICK-NINNIES NATTER ON
(FORMERLY, THE INTERRUPTION)

Six years now I have struggled with the Beastly Change. With the threat of turning into a monster without fore-thought or intent. In an effort to learn more, to see whether there was any discernible pattern I might use to predict The Change, I began charting the urges the third year.

Through that, I discovered they intensify as the sun travels across the sky in its ecliptic, heading toward the summer constellation Leo. Even before it enters the area dominated by the confounded constellation, the battle begins in earnest.

Lion? Or man? It is a toss-up, minute by minute, hour by hour...

Yet once it's firmly there? Our daytime sun seated directly where the invisible-to-my-eye constellation resides? It happens: without diligent, exhaustive effort, I lose all control.

ELATED WITH HIS ACQUIESCENCE, with the present location of her hand, Francine rushed to assure him, "I promise you, Lord Blakely, you will not have cause to regret our agreement."

Did she convey her complete and utter sincerity?

Hard to concentrate when such different sensations assaulted her questing fingers. "Upon my word, you shall not regret our bargain."

"I already do." His actions belied the grumbled words as he ground himself into her palm, returning his hand to cover hers and hold her securely against his erection. His other hand curved over her cheek and ear, and he tilted her face up for his kiss.

She lifted onto her toes, melting with anticipation. Their lips a hairsbreadth from connecting, he stilled. Drat it. "Why did you stop?"

"Someone's coming."

"Are you certain?" She couldn't hear anything beyond the gentle rustle of leaves and her exhilarated breaths.

"Hush now." His urgency conveyed itself and she froze.

"Quickly. Over here." Keeping hold of her hand, he strode toward the shadows and trees where she suspected he'd hidden earlier. He pushed her back into the tall hedge and shielded her body with his own, standing so close her breasts were mashed against his chest. Utterly delightful.

"Lord Bl—"

"Shhh. Wait. Your shawl? Do you not have it? Stay here."

In seconds, he was back, shoving it between them, leaning into her just as close as before. "I still do not hear—"

"Quiet, please." He bent down and gathered the fabric of her evening gown and petticoats beneath, scrunching the layers toward the center and then trapping them between his legs. Legs that were pressed intimately against her own. "Your dress," he whispered on a dark husk that brushed her ear, "the color's light enough, they'll see it."

The sensation of being so close to him, his scent... his *hardness*, convinced her that she'd done the right thing, approaching him with a proposition that included her body, even if she hadn't been completely truthful about her reasons. She may have sworn not to lie further, but he hadn't inquired whether any other falsehoods remained between them.

So she'd no reason to feel guilty. Or so she kept telling herself. "What are—"

"Shhh." His mouth touched her neck, the soft admonition barely reaching her awareness. An involuntary shudder racked her frame. "Do you still not hear them?"

"Hear what?" she murmured as quietly as she could, nothing but normal, everyday nighttime sounds greeting her ears, plus the occasional distant laugh from inside the Longfords', the low thrum of party-goers too far away to concern herself with.

Just then, distant footsteps penetrated her eardrums but still so far off she wondered how he'd—

"*Them*," he whispered and his lips wrapped around her earlobe, obliterating thought. But not action—a squeak escaping her parted mouth.

"Mmm." His tongue joined in the play, the tip bathing the bottom of her ear, tracing the outer curve... diving inside and making her stomach feel like it received his erotic attentions, all swooping and boggled.

She leaned into him, loving the unfamiliar pressure of his large frame pressed to her tall one and how he made her feel decidedly diminutive for once, even as her head twitched from his tickly kisses.

Where else might he delve and lick? Take that talented tongue and draw forth such exquisite reactions from her? She couldn't wait to find out.

Eyes wide open, she stared over his shoulder, lower now that he'd leaned down to lasciviously attack her ear. Pray God, they weren't about to be discovered. The unexpected treat of having his mouth on her flesh was too wonderful, too necessary. She released her hold on the shawl and wrapped her arms around his waist, pulling him closer. His male length nudged her stomach and her fingers scrambled beneath his tailcoat and waistcoat, to sink into the muscles of his back through the fine lawn of his shirt.

His tongue was still doing devilish things. It skated from her ear to caress the sensitive skin just beneath, sending streaks sparking down her neck and shoulders. A shudder trembled through her.

"*Where* could she have gone off to, damn that gel!"

The shock of hearing Aunt Prudence's strident tone

speaking such coarse language had Francine stiffening, her enjoyment of touching Lord Blakely evaporating.

"Stay still," he released the skin of her neck long enough to rasp. "I do not believe they can see us." Then he promptly returned to silently sucking on her and rubbing his form against hers. Oh, glorious heavens. Her body responded, even as her mind grappled.

"I do not have the tolerance for this," an impatient male voice complained. "You bloody promised she would have acquiesced by now. To date, I have seen no sign of such submission. My patience grows thin."

Beyond Lord Blakely's shoulder, she glimpsed two shadowy figures entering the shrouded circle where only a few feet and trees—plus the bench—separated them from sure discovery.

"Be patient," Aunt Prudence hissed, sounding incensed. "I told you, *wed* her, then *bed* her. I guarantee, her fortune will be yours, and that is several times over what I—"

"Are you positive you cannot just take what—"

"I told you, *this* is the only way, but you have not much time. Her majority comes and then 'twill be too late..."

Francine gasped. She recognized Lord Peterson's peeved tones. The louse had been her most determined suitor to date *and* the man whose hard head had cracked the statuary. Dismayed by the interruption, irritated it was *them*, she tried to skirt past Lord Blakey, ready to charge after her treacherous aunt.

.   .   .

"STAY," Blakely breathed as he tightened his grip on Lady Francine's arms and straightened, holding her steadfast against the hedge when she would have confronted the interlopers. "Trust me."

"And I told *you*, Prunie," the petulant voice continued, "I at least need to have a go at her first. Got to sample what you would have me buy with my freedom and my cock, you see. Cannot consent to wedding the prissy little piece if I cannot find something worth fucking about her, now can I?"

Another strangled gasp worked its way from the lovely Lady Francine's throat. Acting on instinct, Blakely covered her lips with his, pressing hard against her closed mouth to keep her from giving away their location. This was one starlit encounter he wasn't yet ready to conclude.

Beyond that, his senses easily picked up on her surprise. Bugger that her annoying aunt was close by; he'd wager one of his carriages Francine would come out of this near encounter with more knowledge than she claimed before it began. And he wasn't thinking about the physical aspects of her education either.

But by damn—lusty lions and fornicating felines, the physical aspects! 'Twas enough to go to any man's head, and for one with a weakness for wenches this time of year?

Not a weakness, his saner self tried to assert. *A need of women. A use for females. 'Tis all.*

They don't make you weak. You use them to make you strong.

Certainly. That.

Whatever.

Shoving aside the voice so he could concentrate on keeping her hidden, he gave over his every thought to the unique individual in his grasp.

Already, the delicate flavor of her skin had enticed his lips to leisurely saunter from her adorably compressed mouth over her ear and neck, savoring and staying in the moment far longer than he was accustomed to. Typically, he'd have a wench's skirts over her head and his mouth sucking on her fancy by now.

But there was something about this one—something more than the innocence. He couldn't quite decipher what, but then she shifted, her lips seeking his, and he quit trying to ascertain what it was about the contradictory female in his arms that held him in her thrall. Instead, he kissed her back and felt as if he were basking in the sun when she responded and her mouth yielded—*opened*—beneath his...

The first foray of her tongue was heaven.

So pure, so goddamn lovely.

So *very* fuck-worthy in his opinion. Peterson was a fool. Blakely recognized the knave. A fortune hunter if there ever was one. A card cheat too, or so he'd heard, not bothering to sit across the tables from his sort.

He pulled her closer, blocking out the others. Unexpectedly, given her earlier reticence, she kissed him harder, spearing her tongue against his—all clumsy, innocent abandon and he growled. Lost.

"Did you hear that?" her damnable aunt asked. Blakely cursed his lack of restraint.

"Just some animal, I wager," Peterson replied in a petulant tone more suited to a bantling in full tantrum than a grown man. "I thought when you left her to me at last week's rout, I could finally nab a taste. Instead, the bitch left my head aching for two days. Two days, Prunie! She owes me for that." The grudged epithet made it patently clear the man planned to collect—and it wouldn't be pleasant. "You owe me far more than I think marriage to that resisting draggletail will be worth."

"She is an heiress, I tell you!" the girl's chattering bore of an aunt hissed.

Damn biddy. Didn't appreciate the jewel in her midst.

"An heiress of the *first* order. Plenty rich enough for you to deal with her eccentric ways for a bit. Or *not...*" He heard the old trot's bosom heave in an aggravated grunt. "After she is yours, I care not what becomes of her. Just move off, *away* from London, if you... Before you do anything *permanent*."

At that, Blakely saw red. Liquid red. The blood of these two scattered from here to Herefordshire if he let the beast have its way. If he lost control—and did what he damn well wanted—dispatching these two blights upon humanity to their own southerly afterlife. But the fresh sprig of innocence in his arms didn't need to see that, experience his unchecked wildness in the worst of ways.

As to that, if he uncaged the monster, who knew what might happen? He'd certainly never been willing to risk it before, and he wasn't now.

He kissed her harder, fiercer, trying to blot out the reality of the conversation taking place just a few feet beyond. Drank in her sweet essence and wished he could taste more—all of her. Imprint the unique flavor that slid so deliciously over his tongue.

It was a kiss of unmatched passion, aye—on his part at least; for Francine, he sensed it was rather a kiss of discovery, spared a thought to wonder at how majestically they would come together once she had experience and knew what she was about. But more than that, it was a kiss of soothing, of consolation. Of apology. Trying to erase the horrific words and sentiments she'd heard bandied about her beautiful self so carelessly.

Ah, Francine.

The little determined innocent most assuredly needed saving. How could he contemplate thus, when being with him—near him—was the complete opposite of salvation? When his very presence threatened to destroy her soul, mar her body, taint that innocence he found so beguiling?

And because worry was nothing new to him, but worry over a female, one he barely knew, was, he brought her closer to his body, pressed her along his entire length and kissed her with every ounce of authentic human male still residing in him.

"Are you sure we cannot come to an arrangement for your younger daughter instead?" Peterson piped up, sounding excited for the first time—rather than vengeful. "Now there is a prime piece I wouldn't mind prigging. No ugly spectacles distorting her face either. I would be willing to forgive your entire—"

"You forget yourself. *My* daughters are not for the likes of you."

"You dare be so derisive toward me, Prunie? You, who has amassed quite the—"

"Shht! Not *here*."

Not here? You won't discuss your debts, but you'll blithely banter about your niece's death?

Good God. The woman was unhinged.

And Lady Francine lived with that? Day in and day out?

His ardor knew no bounds. As he somehow aspired, with his fervent kiss, to block out the terrible reality surrounding her.

"Come now," her aunt said so brightly, Blakely wanted to rip her to shreds all over again. "We shall check the gazebos, then return inside. Franny may be back by the dance floor by now, either dancing or watching her cousins."

"What made you think she would be out here?" A slap sounded. "Stupid moth—blame thing flew into my eye."

"My girls confessed they saw her amid the hedges when I threatened to cut off their pin money, but I remain appalled at..." The harridan's voice faded as they walked from the garden. He could still hear every word but chose to concentrate instead on the woman shaking in his arms.

He withdrew his tongue, angled his mouth, gentling the pressure upon Lady Francine's soft lips, easing himself from the haze of desire that gripped him so fiercely.

So she hadn't been exaggerating. If anything, she'd understated her aunt's attempts to marry her off—and secure a bloody fortune. Grasping harpy.

"I knew..." Lady Francine said in a haggard whisper, and he watched the tip her tongue flit over her bottom lip. "I..." Her words faltered and she swallowed, seizing his upper arms. "I knew she had been excessively eager to see me wed, but I thought she only wanted me out of their home, had tired of me encroaching upon her hospitality. She always says I'm a bad influence...too independent..."

Blakely hated the way her confidence had been shattered.

"How could she? To *him*? She cares not at all about me. I knew that. Knew it, but *this*? Her evil machinations are so far beyond what I ever would have fathomed..."

He hated the way the determined, confident miss of earlier had been replaced with a subdued shell.

"I had no idea..." A tear slipped from one blinking eye. "*Prunie?* Just how well does she know Lord Peterson? Why would she contrive to give me over to him, knowing I find him unpalatable?"

He hated more how his only recourse, in helping her, would also put her at risk.

From *him*.

Another tear followed the first, a glistening trail of disappointment and betrayal. He watched them track down her face and bent to wipe the tiny droplets away with the touch of his lips. "'Twill be all right, for I shall help you."

She swallowed back the tears and smiled, a pathetic tilt of her lips that caught at his heart and made him want to pound her aunt and that filthy-minded cur she'd had with her into the ground. "You will?"

Even now, he heard the uncertainty in her tone, so at odds with how fearlessly she'd first approached him. Had that only been such a short time ago? It seemed like the minutes had slowed to seconds, time passing with infinitesimal care, excruciating slowness, as if the universe were giving him time to reconsider his rash offer of assistance. But he didn't want to reconsider, not when such a delightful armful was depending on him, had come to *him* for salvation.

"Does your aunt gamble much, at parties and the like?" He stroked his fingers along her neck, back to her nape and secured them there. "I suspect she is too far gone with the Devil's books and that Peterson's holding her vowels. A substantial sum. And you suffer because of it."

She bit her lips to still their trembling. "Aye. That makes sense. She often finds the card room when she escorts us to social events."

How could he erase what she'd discovered tonight? Return that exasperatingly bold confidence to her now crushed demeanor? "Here now, tell your sham of a suitor what to do," Blakely invited, expecting her to name a ball or event she wanted his escort to. "How may I best assist you?"

"Make me forget," she said swiftly, staring up at him from between damp eyelashes. "Show me the pleasure you alluded to, what we just started." The smile turned tremulous and she bravely wiped her eyes. He heard her heart pounding. "Now. Tonight. Then come to the house and offer for me tomorrow."

She gazed at him, waiting. Challenging. Expecting him to turn her down.

Blast his soul. Lady Francine had just presented him with the one thing he wanted more than any other —herself.

Now it was up to him to decide just what to do about it. His conscience or his cock? Which was stronger? Which would allow him a modicum of peaceful slumber when he retired that night and the nights that followed?

There was only one possible answer. He drew air into lungs gone tight and opened his mouth to deny her. To deny himself. To do the *right* thing.

She gave a little whimper and wilted before him. Blinked fast. Tried again to smile.

His conscience or his cock?

Consigning his conscience to the Devil, Blakely decided he'd deal with repercussions later. Didn't he *always* put others before himself, ever since his father asked it of him? Wasn't he always available, guarding, keeping tabs on those who might not know how dangerous they really were?

Hadn't he handled everything by himself, financed everything, year after year, once Phineas disappeared and Nash ran off? Wasn't it his turn to think of himself for once?

For once...

FRANCINE BIT her tongue to keep from pleading. Why was he taking so long to respond? Had her blatant request—or hearing her aunt and Lord Peterson discussing her in such terms—given Lord Blakely a disgust of her? But no...he'd kissed her like a man possessed. Like a man beyond interested in continuing what they'd begun.

Perhaps she was mistaken? It wasn't as though she had substantial experience, not beyond that one regretful time—or defending herself against more recent and unwelcome encounters.

She gazed up at him in the darkness and forced a casual shrug. "Disregard my hasty words. The evening grows late and I'm sure you would rather be elsewhere."

With an edge of wildness, he cupped her face, stunning her into silence. When his thumbs pressed into the corners of her lips, she had to subdue the sudden urge to lick them. "Lady Francine Montfort, the *only* place I would rather be is inside your body."

At his words, her abdomen tightened, thighs clenched and she gave a single nod.

Abruptly, his fingers left her face only to caress down her neck, over her collarbone, grazing across her breasts with the sheerest of touches, until they settled firmly at her sides. "Starting now."

Oh, how wondrous!

Hands around her waist, he picked her up and shoved her back against a tall tree. "*Oommph.*"

"Did not mean to be so rough."

"'Tis fine. Really." Was that breathy voice hers? "Please continue."

Laughing softly, Lord Blakely knelt before her and his warm hands curved around her ankles, tightened and rose, skimming the length of her legs until they reached the top of her stockings, where he paused and looked up at her.

Why had he stopped?

His features were a study of shadows. She sensed his countenance more than saw it—the intensity in his dark eyes, the concentration he focused upon her flesh. Her lower regions pulsed at his nearness, eager for his touch and the mastery she knew he'd command. Her fingers crushed her skirts and petticoats, lifted them, and his hands guided her legs apart.

"I smell your desire," he said thickly into the silence.

Someone opened the ballroom doors, allowing laughter and light to pierce the shadows, if only just. Enough that with the moon which had risen overhead she could finally, finally see enough to do more than imagine.

This taciturn, tall, powerful specimen kneeling between her legs? 'Twas truly the stuff of dreams. Of happiness found and joy remembered.

She bunched the material in her hands, holding on to it like an anchor when his fingers eased beneath the layers of fabric shielding her Venus mound from view. She hardly dared to move when his exploring touch brushed against her curls. The contact was insubstantial, practically nonexistent.

So how was it that she felt him everywhere? Invading every part of her as the effects from such a nebulous touch careened throughout her body, slamming against every nerve ending and creating a burn so combustible, so unforgiving, she felt like crying?

He rimmed the edges of her opening, the slick sound his fingers made against her wetness unmistakable.

Aye, she'd touched herself a time or thirty—what curious woman nearing twenty-five hadn't? But—

Her breath caught as he firmly stroked along one side again. But her fingers certainly never made her feel like *this*. She yearned, aching. "Please. Do not make me wait."

"Eager little innocent, are you not?" he murmured, and somehow it sounded like praise.

"I told you"—my, she sounded winded and her stomach kept twitching, every time he touched her a little differently—"I am not innocent."

"I know what you said. I have not forgotten." He leaned in and inhaled. "I happen to disagree. Heartily."

She couldn't remain still any longer and wiggled her hips, restless. He pushed one long, blunt finger inside her passage. It slid in easily, flowing into her body as if it belonged. Her muscles gripped him and held tight when he would have pulled away. Her hands fluttered, releasing her gown, and she grasped for purchase upon his shoulders.

"You are so swollen, *drenched*...ready for me." Now he sounded proud, and she couldn't stop a tremulous smile from curving her lips. *Thank you, body, for whatever instincts you're heeding.*

Who knew, that with the right person, this would feel so grand? Not hurt at all. Except for the gnawing ache growing in her abdomen and lower. A fierce pressure that wound tighter every second.

He added another finger, thrusting them both high. At the exquisite sensations, she almost lost her footing. Though he steadied her, he didn't halt his motions. Her body was rocking against his touch, taking his fingers farther inside. New vibrations bombarded her, growing outward from her slit, encompassing her trembling thighs, her stomach—which clenched with every forceful thrust of his hand—but still, she ached for more... Needed it all.

"I need." He echoed her desire as he growled the words, unfastening his pantaloons with his free hand. The stars shone down benevolently, the considerate moon beaming just enough as he released his shaft and fisted it. Her tongue slipped from her mouth to wet her lower lip. She wanted...

"*A taste,*" he said, reading her mind again. "I must taste you."

He rotated his fingers inside her, capturing the essence that flowed forth. Easing his hand free, he ran his fingers under his nose, staring at her, inhaling...the act so horridly decadent, so impossibly sensual, that it would have stolen her wits if she'd had any to spare.

Stars and seduction... Her senses spun faster than the overhead canopy. "My, you are debauched."

The whisper only sounded like a compliment.

"Aye, I am." And he took it as such, nostrils flaring, that haughty bearing of his only increasing.

Then he stood, still holding his erection and holding her gaze. How was it his eyes seemed to blaze? As if lit from within...a fire that raged in his soul. For *her*. Gracious, she was burning up.

He came close enough to kiss and placed his longest finger between their lips, proceeding to lick it clean with slow, thorough swipes of his tongue that touched her mouth as he washed the juices from her body off his.

Francine smelled herself, felt the pressure of his finger against her closed lips, felt his moist flesh traverse over his finger, caressing her mouth with each torturously slow glide of his wicked, delightful tongue. A mew of protest, of yearning, escaped her trembling lips. She longed to join in but inexperience held her back.

Her lower muscles spasmed, wrenching her hips forward.

"All done," he said, rubbing her lips with the pad of his finger before removing it.

Warm flesh nudged between her legs. Thicker than before...

Francine moaned, staring into his smoldering eyes and slanting her pelvis, desperate to impale herself.

"Share?" he invited, placing his second naughty, coated finger at her mouth.

He'd now proven her earlier assessment accurate—he was a tormenting demon and she was so very wicked. For even considering...

She unclenched her jaw and her tongue came out, just barely grazing his slick skin. Salty tang invaded her senses, made her head spin and her senses swim. For though she'd touched herself before, she'd certainly never *tasted*.

A second later, his tongue met hers and he slid his finger away, replacing it with his mouth. She mimicked his actions, licking his tongue with hers. At once he tensed and withdrew.

"Come back," she begged, her tongue bereft. "I was not finished—"

Then he was there, giving her what she needed,

licking her lips, plunging his tongue inside her mouth the same instant he drove into her body.

Yes.

Pure sweet sensation burst through her. Her cleft expanded, acclimating to him...his breadth, his length. He held himself motionless, breathing into her mouth.

She wound her fingers in his hair and guided him even closer. That released his restraint and he ground their lips together, thrusting his tongue deeper and gliding it sinuously over hers. She felt consumed. Alive. Gloriously alive.

No need to bemoan that it wasn't bright enough to see every single detail. She could remember how black his hair, how strong his jaw. She could remember the haughty way he'd first looked down his nose at her and the sardonic tilt of his lips when he'd instantly declined her proposition. She could smell his scent—*man.* Primal, spicy, sex-crazed man.

But most of all, she could feel him—feel his hands curved around the back of her head, feel his fingers burrowing past the dangling ringlets and through her upswept hair, feel the weight of his palms as he released her head to trail his hands over her shoulders and down her back...and lower. She could feel his staff lunging inside her, feel her inner muscles rippling along its length. Clasping tight, pulling him higher. All the way into the depths of her body. Oh my, oh-mazing.

Who needed to see when they had Lord Blakely making them *feel?*

A moan escaped her throat and she swirled her tongue against his. He dove deep in her mouth, exploring every hidden recess as his hands came to rest on the swells of her buttocks. She sucked harder on his tongue and he gripped her arse firmly, holding her snug against his length. Francine lifted her feet from the ground, allowing him to support her weight. The moment she wrapped her legs around his waist, her body convulsed around his shaft, pulling him in until she sank so far down, their pubic hair met, tangled. Tied her in knots. Thrilled her to her core.

This is what she'd been missing. And she hadn't even known it. Real feeling. Real emotion. *Desire*—wanting to be close to another human being. Wanting to be pummeled from the inside out. She forgot every concern that haunted her and gave herself up to the night, to this man. This experience. She tugged his hair, loving the unexpected wildness of their coupling.

His grip tightened on her bottom, lifting her until he almost slid free, then he brought her down, crashing into his abdomen. Ankles crossed for leverage, her thighs squeezed his body, telling him without words, *More. Harder!*

He listened.

The tips of his fingers delved inward toward her most private regions and he spread the cheeks of her arse. Cool night air assailed her anus. Francine hugged his shaft with her passage, amazed. This wasn't a dream. It was real.

Lord Blakely's strummer. Inside her. Pleasuring her in ways she hadn't thought to ever know.

He grunted and pulled away from her mouth to latch on to her collarbone. His hips pumped, driving his long rod in so deep it hurt. Wonderfully.

He braced her against the tree trunk and shifted his

arms, wedging his fingers between her thighs and his to caress her intimately. The top of her cleft was on fire. He touched and teased.

She squealed and screamed.

The bark of the tree scraped against her back, snagging the delicate fabric of her gown, but Francine didn't care. Again, he lunged, thrusting higher. His fingers pinched and rolled her flesh. His hands grabbed her arse and held tight. She pulled his hair harder, unable to temper the force of her actions.

She loved his raw power, the way he touched a part of her she'd held back for years, stifled first under the weight of grief, then under the strident propriety of her relatives, now freed thanks to his rugged stimulation. With no thought nor care to decorum, Lord Blakely physically adored her body in such a manner she felt truly cherished.

His teeth sank into her shoulder and she exploded, fire erupting along her channel, within her abdomen, encircling her heart.

Tears of joy, of release, flowed down her cheeks as he heaved and pounded into her. Then he wrenched himself free, climaxing to the side with a growl that echoed throughout the garden.

5

ANXIOUS ANTICIPATION

The armed guards deliver raw meat once a day through the iron grill I had installed. In my saner moments—before this yearly hell starts in earnest—I have convinced them I'm training a cross breed. A new type of hunting dog, one paired with a wolf. Or perhaps one of those thought-to-be-extinct cave critters...

Pah. Better to secure my place in Hell with a lie than a lion—dining on some unsuspecting human.

Just the thought sickens me. Anguish rolls through my veins in lieu of blood. What has befallen me? Could my days be any more wretched?

Could the day be any more glorious?

The light from the window shone brighter.

The bird calls sounded cheerier. The late-morning chatter from her cousins less insipid.

Even last week's embroidery efforts didn't appear quite so disastrous when she held the piece up for inspection.

What a truly spectacular day!

At least, that was how it'd seemed—two hours ago.

Francine sat in the drawing room peering through her spectacles at the embroidery floss mangled about her fingertips, above the cut-off gloves. Despite how many times her aunt complained and insisted she purchase a new pair, Francine had trimmed the finger fabric away so she could better attempt some modicum of decent stitchery—hopeless attempt, though it might be.

How she'd rather be outside, sans gloves altogether, with her hands palm-deep in the earth, vacating weeds from their expired reservation in the garden.

But remain indoors during calling hours she must, on the distinct possibility that Lord Blakely would pay a visit and ask for her hand.

If, that was, he hadn't changed his mind.

If last night hadn't been a trick, or a lark.

Spark with the naïve, bespectacled chit, take what she recklessly offers and depart.

Nay! He'll not treat you thus. He cannot, part of her insisted.

While the other, more cautious part demanded, *And just what makes him different from any other arrogant, indulged lord of the ton?*

His inner demons.

His what?!

And there it was—the truth laid bare. Some of it at least. For ever since that first, awed glimpse of him at the Seftons' ages ago, she'd sensed they both battled inner torment. Secrets that were theirs alone to bear, kept securely hidden from others—except in rare, brief unguarded moments.

Secrets. Such as the silly reason she kept attempting needlework even with her decided lack of talent. Especially despite how it actually pleased her aunt to see her engaged in such a domestic endeavor. Not that Francine ever went out of her way to thwart her aunt—well, not excessively so, if she were being completely honest. Neither did she relish making an effort to please her aunt, either. Certainly, not lately.

Nay, she stitched—or attempted to—because it made her feel close to her mother's memory. The quiet, repetitive task bringing recollections to the fore, ones that produced soft sighs and happy smiles. Ones she didn't want to let fade.

Her secrets? The cause was easy enough to identify. After Mama lost three young babes mere days from the womb, she and her fourth-born had become especially close. Much more than typical for a duchess and her young daughter.

Whether cavorting through the manor, playing hide-and-go-seek together or running free over the estate, swimming in the lake, even the Latin lessons Mama insisted would benefit their only living child as she matured, Francine and her mother were more than family. They were friends. Confidants, even.

Oh, they both had friends their own age as well, and each had their own individual interests too. Mama couldn't abide dirt anywhere—much less seek to invite it upon her person or beneath her nails, and Francine would rather walk behind the carriage and shovel up after Papa's matched bays than spend an afternoon plying a needle and thread as Mama had once been so very accomplished at...

And then later, when Mama's condition became worse, Francine would read to her, find other ways they could still ramble about the manner and estate grounds, even if slower.

Neither had Papa been excluded from their antics. One winter when storms stranded travelers nearby and Papa learned of their plight, he'd invited the family in out of the blizzard and played along with a twelve-year-old Francine who pretended to be a maid of all work instead of his daughter. He and Mama had laughed about it for days afterward.

She shut her eyes against the pang of memories.

Heartwarming though they might be, they also invited comparisons to the present. The present that, given her current environment, was decidedly lacking. Squeezed both eyes hard, needing to block out the memories that came after. Clenched the floss a bit tighter and breathed through the pain of loss. The loneliness.

Relocating from the boisterous, playful existence she'd known for most of her sixteen and a half years to the perfectly proper, exceedingly dull and critical abode of her aunt and uncle hadn't shocked the joy out of Francine, only sent it scurrying underground.

Is that why you like to dig in the dirt?

She relaxed her eyes and fist, allowed a small smile.

Nay. I like watching things grow. From an unremarkable seed to a magnificent bloom. To a flower or a fruit. Herbs or vegetables. It mattered not what the end result, only that seeing the change, the growth, and knowing she'd had a hand in it comforted her as little else.

Cut through the placid pall that hovered over and around her since moving to London and cleared the fog, made way for the sun.

Much like your Lord Blakely?

Only if starlight be sun. And his darkness something I can cut through…

Why she was so certain he had secrets, heavy ones, perched upon his broad shoulders, she couldn't quite explain. But just as she knew—sensed—right before a bud poked through the dirt that it was on its way, *she knew.*

The haughty, droll, seemingly self-sufficient man she harbored a secret *tendre* for needed her. And Francine was determined to find out exactly what she could do to help him.

If, that was, he actually deigned to appear today.

She'd like to repay him for the gifts he'd given her last night—not only of his promised assistance, but the gift of *feeling* again.

Multiply that by his unintended rescue several years ago, and why, 'twas no wonder she thought frequently of the man. All right, *constantly* of the man…

Now Lord Blakely's secrets?

The ones she instinctively knew existed and longed to know more about?

Instead of assuaging her curiosity or dampening

her interest, time spent in his presence only sent her need to know more about him soaring.

After the act of passion she'd experienced in his arms last night, he'd efficiently gone about setting their clothing to rights, retrieved her shawl from the ground and placed it about her shoulders. Then he took her by the arm and escorted her to their host's back patio, just steps away from where guests laughed and danced, having no thought nor clue to the monumental event that had just occurred in Francine's body. In her life.

With a bow and the gentle application of his lips upon the back of her gloved hand, Lord Blakely had stated, "I will call upon you tomorrow to pay my address. Be ready to receive me at three o'clock."

Then he was gone, leaving her to wonder if his slight emphasis on the word *receive* meant what she fancied it might.

But it was half past five already. Why give her a time if he didn't intend to honor it? He had raised her hopes, only to dash them with his tardiness, the scurrilous beast.

Determined to accomplish something this afternoon other than counting minutes that passed far too slowly, she once again smoothed the threads of floss. Her forehead pinched, a sharp tug that stole her attention. Ugh, she was straining again.

Breathe slowly. Ease the pressure away.

She consciously unknit her brow, blinking several times, then concentrated on seeing the far corner. Things were more blurred than usual and her eyes felt especially tired. *That's what you get for embroidering three hours straight.*

Burford, her aunt's butler and Francine's favorite servant in the townhouse, had checked on her twice in the last hour, no doubt wondering why she spent the long afternoon toiling at her least favorite task. Why had she not succumbed to the splendid weather beckoning her outside and into the garden?

Mayhap she should have forewarned Burford she might have a caller. But as it happened so rarely these days—without her aunt's scheming behind it—the notion might have given the elderly servant heart palpitations. *Mayhap you do not want to let anyone else know of your rash actions of last night in case they do not bear ripe fruit today?*

No matter how hard she tried to concentrate on her handwork, the doubts kept plaguing her. Had he entertained second thoughts after agreeing to pose as her betrothed, or was it her request they become lovers that caused his hesitation? Why had he been so intent on intimidating her? Requesting that she as much as vanish at his leisure, then expressing such surprise when she instantly agreed?

Of course she'd agreed. Having come so close to obtaining what she wanted, she wasn't about to quibble over anything that might interfere. She was determined to be *all* that was agreeable—in every matter—to ensure Lord Blakely had no cause to regret their bargain or to desire anyone other than *her* at his side for its duration. If she made it her goal to satisfy every one of his desires, then he would have no reason to wish her gone, and the time until her birthday would fly by without compare.

If he appeared today.

Her aunt and cousins had already retired to their rooms for their daily restorative, leaving Francine to wait alone—thank goodness—but what could be keeping Lord Blak—

Pain shot through her hand.

Drat!

The needle had gone straight into her finger. Clenching her back teeth, she yanked it free, popped the digit in her mouth and sucked.

Rattish rodents, but that hurt! Eyes watering, she willed the pain away and sucked harder on the stinging spot.

Burford knocked once and announced a guest.

Lord Blakely stepped into the room, his gaze immediately catching hers, then avidly going to her mouth.

How was it he always caught her at her worst?

She stood abruptly, pulling her finger free and curtsying—when she'd much rather be cursing. Her embroidery fell from her lap to the floor, but she at least salvaged her spectacles before they slid from her nose and disembarked as well.

Behind the visiting lord, the servant's grey eyebrows climbed skyward, toward his receding hairline, vast curiosity reflected in his expression, as he backed out, leaving the door wide open.

Gulping down the disquiet circling through her middle, she turned to face the man she most wanted to see. My, oh my. In daylight he proved every bit as intimidating, as intriguing, as he did in starlight.

He was here! He'd come as promised.

Come and made an already pleasant day—if one

discounted her recent bout of anxious worrying—that much more enthralling.

"Lady Francine. I trust you are having a pleasant afternoon?"

His voice was deeper than she recalled.

His height just as impressive.

Her reaction to both rolling through her as though she'd been knocked asunder by a boulder of lust.

"My lord. Welcome." She curtsied again, noticed her fingers still clenching the spectacles, so she quickly folded the earpieces and crammed them in her pocket.

It took everything in her to hold his gaze, to see the awareness in his he didn't try to disguise. Along with the amusement dancing in his eyes as he bent to rescue her mediocre efforts at needlework.

"I have come to speak with your guardian about your hand," he said very properly, then winked, spoiling the effect.

She reached for the knotted handiwork he held between them.

"You are decidedly late," she commented lightly, working to keep any accusation from her tone.

"Ah, but I am here."

Said as if his presence hadn't been a foregone conclusion.

Had he seriously considered changing his mind? Discomfited by the thought, she hastily dropped another curtsy. *A third? Just how nervous are you?* "For which I am most grateful, my lord."

When she again straightened, he raised one finger and tapped her cheek. "Leave off the powder from now on. I want to view your countenance in its natural state henceforth."

"Tell that to my aunt."

"I shall."

"Franny!" Her aunt's shrill preceded her presence. "What is this Burford tells me about a caller?" Aunt Prudence bustled in, instantly aghast at the identity of Francine's guest. "Blakely, you fiend! How *dare* you darken my door! You are most certainly *not* welcome in—"

"Madam," he began, and Francine rather liked the way he snubbed her aunt by forgoing any formal greeting or acknowledgement of her own courtesy title. "I would like a word with your husband."

"He is in the country. Departed this morning, so you will have to leave and—"

Francine heard his muttered, "Smart man," and stifled a laugh. Her finger felt better already. As did her confidence. *This* was the man she easily conversed with the night before, shared her secrets with and hoped he'd eventually confide his as well.

"Then I will speak with you, madam, though we both might wish otherwise."

Her aunt sputtered a protest but only minutes later —after unceremoniously overriding every one of her aunt's objections—Lord Blakely had officially proposed, Francine had accepted and he'd summarily dispatched her still-harping aunt so the two of them could have a few private moments.

"You were very masterful. I am in alt over how well you handle her," Francine told him once they were blessedly alone, and he'd dispensed with his gloves and swept her into his embrace. "Did you see how her eyes nearly quit their sockets when you told her you'd come to claim my hand and would brook nothing but her complete cooperation?"

"The privilege of being a marquis, my dear."

"I was half afraid you were not going to call," she confessed, though in truth, it had been more like seven-eights.

GET A HOLD OF YOURSELF, man! Frighten her off. Before you do something she'll not live to regret.

"I was unavoidably detained." Blakely wasn't about to tell her how he'd debated with himself, weighing the benefits to them both, versus the risks to Lady Francine should they pursue this charade.

In the end, his conscience had decided for him. He wouldn't have a moment's peace until he assured himself she wasn't in any lingering danger. He shifted, angling his hips toward the inviting warmth at the juncture of her thighs and lowered his head to take possession of her lips.

Then he caught sight of the reddened marks on her flushed skin. The marks his abrasive, day-old beard had left the prior evening.

He tilted her head to better see and almost came undone.

"Did I do this?" he demanded, tugging the collar away from her neck to expose the wicked bruise that marred her shoulder.

She shivered at the contact and he felt like a lout.

"I love how your touch burns across my skin."

God, she was innocent.

He'd injured her to that extent—and hadn't even known? He released the fabric and cursed. "I shall never touch you again," he said rashly. "I pledge it with—"

"You had better."

"Upon my word." They were halting the madness now. He'd already marked her? And with The Change weeks away yet. "I shall still enact the farce, but I vow, I will not—"

She took his hands in hers and captured his full attention with one glance from those shining blue eyes. "You had most certainly *better* touch me again."

"Beg pardon?" She wasn't issuing recriminations?

Why should she? You do it enough for the both of you.

"I am quite fine, I assure you." Her thumbs stroked over the back of his hands. "Did you not notice the color?" Her chin dipped toward her shoulder, inviting him to look again.

Fading green and yellow, not purple and fresh, you clodpate.

"'Tis already yellowing. It happened last week, not last night. Quit coddling, it's unnecessary. I would much prefer you tell me how you received the scar on your nose."

"Ahem. I think not." More disconcerted than he wanted to admit, he pulled away and walked to the window.

Amused laughter spilled from her. "Lord Blakely, I do declare that you are blushing. Have I not shown my integrity, my trustworthiness by all that I confessed to you last eve? Will you not grant me the same consideration?"

"In a fight. With my brother." And that was all he was saying on the matter.

"I did not realize you had a brother."

Which told him something else about her. She hadn't looked him up in *Debrett's*, chased down his family tree before chasing *him* down...

He wasn't quite sure why that should matter but it did. Made him seem less like a prize to her. More like a person.

He spun to face her. "We are no longer close. He is living abroad." Or on a ship. Or in a dungeon. He never knew anymore.

"And what might the two of you have fought over?" She looked at him thoughtfully. "A woman, perhaps?"

"It was several years ago," Blakely excused himself. He couldn't very well tell her it *was* over a woman. The female in question had already lost consciousness, from several rounds of ferocious fornicating, and they'd both wanted another go at her. "It was not one of my finer moments."

"I shall conclude by your evasive answer-non-answer that it *was* about a woman."

"I believe, Lady Francine"—he stalked toward her, intent on making her forget this unpalatable line of questioning—"that agreeing to participate in your outlandish scheme and coming up to snuff so quickly should give me a measure of anonymity upon certain select subjects."

"So it should."

He breathed a sigh of relief—

"But speaking of women…"

That caught in his throat.

"Did you find me satisfactory last evening?"

Any more and he'd actually consider proposing in truth. If not for the pesky, life-endangering concern that ruled his existence.

Refusing to dwell on his unwanted reality, he hauled her against his rigid flesh, his broad palms dwelling instead on the lush curve of her derrière. "What makes you ask?"

Her eyes flashed to his, then dropped away. "Your reputation along with your assurance not to publicly indulge with other women during our engagement." She ran her hands along the sleeves of his tailcoat until they rested on his shoulders. He felt her touch clear to his toes—and everywhere in between.

"What of it?" His words were strangled.

"I have another proposition for you, Lord Blakely."

"Call me Erasmus." 'Twas not an appellation many used. Reserved for his mother, mainly, most calling him Blakely the last fifteen years—or, in more intimate settings, the abbreviated Blake.

He wasn't sure if it was his slight history with her father, or his even slighter history with her, but for whatever reason, it seemed important.

Something to set her apart from the others. "After all, we are engaged, are we not?"

"Thank you for the honor." Her fingers worked their way to the front of his shirt, toying with his neckcloth, completely destroying the Maharatta that had taken his valet far too long to fashion. She could untie every one of his damn neckcloths, if he could just hold her like this, breathe in her fresh, clean, *vibrant* scent. Bask in her presence. Both calming and invigorating.

"Erasmus, I confess, last evening went far beyond my every expectation and I..." She gave a little wiggle and he allowed her to take a single step back. Her eyes went from studying what her fingers were doing to focus instead on his groin. Hard as stone already, his erection was easily visible beneath his buff pantaloons. If this kept up, he'd need to darken his wardrobe. "I want to meddle again. *With you.*" Keeping her head directed downward, she spoke those unexpected, hushed words to his eager anatomy. Then she angled her gaze back to his, her normally porcelain cheeks brimming with pink. "That is, during the term of our agreement, I would like to propose that you avoid *privately* indulging with other women and give me the opportunity to satisfy all of your carnal desires."

As if he even had to think about it.

But he did, Blakely *knew* he did.

He paused, gauging his own response.

Stirrings of arousal stampeded his blood but little else. His teeth, nails, his *control*...they all remained intact. He ran a hand over his jaw, testing the thickness of his whiskers. Normal. Good. He still had some time before the urges strengthened. Last night he'd been so far gone he hadn't paused to sufficiently consider how much mastery over his feline cells he commanded—not once her toad-eating aunt and scrub of a former suitor had appeared. He considered them now.

"Hmmm." He made a show of hesitancy. "And in exchange for satisfying my desires, what might be expected of me in return?"

"I shall allow you to fulfill all of mine."

Could there be another woman on the planet as perfect for his needs?

"So do you agree?" She gave a little jump, adorable in her enthusiasm. "To my latest proposition?"

"I will go one better. I shall claim you so thoroughly, in public *and* in private, that you will forever be safe from moneygrubbers like Peterson and your aunt."

"Splendid!"

But could he keep her safe from himself?

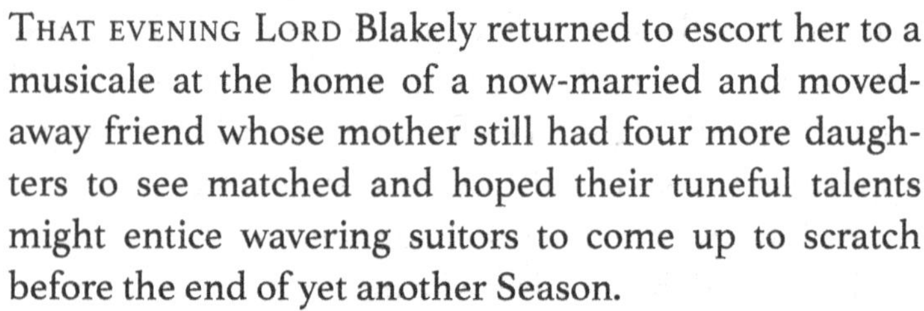

THAT EVENING LORD Blakely returned to escort her to a musicale at the home of a now-married and moved-away friend whose mother still had four more daughters to see matched and hoped their tuneful talents might entice wavering suitors to come up to scratch before the end of yet another Season.

Recalling her friend's decided *lack* of talent in the instrumental arena left Francine sincerely doubting this would be the case. But no matter, their home was grand—as was the company who'd just handed her up the steps to his conveyance with a light stroke upon the back of her glove before releasing her fingers.

Of course, Aunt Prudence and Francine's cousins had also been invited to share the ride in his majestic carriage —Aunt Prudence wouldn't have it any other way. Once they were all seated and en route, the barrage began.

"What *will* people think?" Aunt Prudence complained across the carriage, fixing Francine and

Lord Blakely with what could almost be termed an evil eye. "Your marriage announcement coming on the heels of one *singular* meeting? 'Tis preposterous! Void of *any* semblance of authenticity! And put those *horrid* spectacles away, Franny. They make you look like a bluestocking. 'Tis absolutely appalling."

Knowing better than to argue, Francine slipped them off and tucked them into her reticule. Next to her, Lord Blakely—Erasmus, she reminded herself—lifted her gloved hand and placed it near his knee, ignoring Aunt Prudence's gasps of protest. "Anyone who matters will mind their own business," he said, leaning over to douse the lantern, plunging them into darkness. "Everyone else will assume that your niece charmed me with just one glance. One dance."

He spoke with such conviction that even knowing it was a falsehood—they'd never danced and it'd taken substantially more than a *glance* to convince him—the words warmed Francine down to her slippers. Touching the fine silk of his breeches with her fingertips increased the heat flowing through her until she felt like fanning herself. Even through her gloves, his nearness made her burn.

"Add to that," he continued, "how could I be anything but honored to escort my betrothed and her delightful family about this fine evening?"

Did anyone else notice Erasmus hesitate over the word *delightful*?

"Well, I think it's quite gran-dose," exclaimed Patience. "Marrying a marquis! I am quite green over it. Mother found me but a mere viscount."

"Grand*iose*?" Francine prompted, but it flew over the girl's head and out the window.

"Just like a fairy tale," Temperance enthused on a sigh. "Lord Blakely has *swept* you off your feet. Papa will be so excited."

"Your papa will be nothing of the kind," muttered Aunt Prudence, berating her daughters for their show of support. "Having *such* an outlandish event occur with him from town? Why, I never..."

Francine took advantage of their preoccupation to tilt her head toward Lord Blakely. "Thank you again, my lord. For everything."

"'Tis my pleasure."

"Lord Blakely?" Temperance spoke into the void. "Do you mind if I inquire about your family coat of arms?"

"Not a bit."

"'Tis a particular fascination of mine, you see, and—"

"Hush, girl. You think he is in possession of time sufficient to entertain you and your nonsensical obsessions?"

"Madam, let the lady speak."

"Thank you, my lord. I could not help but notice yours has three lion charges, when the one included within my research volume on heraldic histories only shows two for the Hammond family name. Do you know, perchance, who changed it and why?"

Francine couldn't help but be gratified when her aunt huffed with irritation and blustered about. Good. She hadn't yet browbeaten the intellectual curiosity out of her youngest. Not for lack of trying, Francine knew.

While Erasmus answered, his hand tightened upon her own, crushing her palm into the muscled strength of his thigh. Banked nerves fluttered to life in her stomach. When might he touch her again? Without an audience?

While she mentally calculated the distance her fingers would need to travel to encounter illicit terrain and acknowledged how very much she wanted to touch him without the barrier of clothing, he proceeded to answer her cousin, correcting her where needed and informing everywhere else.

Even Patience joined in a time or two, not sounding the complete jolterhead, which in and of itself proved a minor miracle.

Fortunately their animated conversation left Francine free to indulge in all manner of lustful imaginings—and now that she knew exactly how wonderful knowing him in the intimate sense was, the daydreams she currently entertained brimmed with so much more detail than her vague imaginings of the past.

Every time he spoke with tolerance and ease in his fine voice, her appreciation grew and she slid her hand fractionally closer to his groin. By her figuring, at this rate she'd reach the summit of his thighs about the time Aunt Prudence lost complete and utter patience with her offspring. Francine couldn't stop the grin that lifted her cheeks.

Too soon, the carriage rolled to a creaking stop and swayed in place. It was several moments before she noticed the heavy silence permeating the interior. Francine shook off her own amusing, debauched thoughts. "Have we arrived?"

"I have just informed your aunt that she and her charges will be exiting my conveyance. We shall join them for the musicale in a few moments."

"*That* is not done. Franny cannot be left *alone* with you! In a closed carriage. Anywhere!"

Lord Blakely's coachman opened the door and lowered the steps, allowing light from the townhouse to spill gently into the carriage. "Lady Francine is my affianced, and unless you want your husband learning the sordid details about your association with Peter—"

"*Shhht!*" her aunt veritably shrieked, drawing curious looks from her daughters. "Very well." Aunt Prudence swept her girls out the door so fast Francine felt the breeze from their exit. "But if you *ever* mention—"

"Madam." Lord Blakely leaned forward and spoke directly into Aunt Prudence's face. "Do not presume to tell me what I may or may not do. Your gambling days, as they affect your niece or any part of your household, are at an end."

The pale glow spilling from the windows and open door of the home they'd reached, combined with the carriage's exterior lanterns, gave Francine enough light to see her aunt stumble.

"Girls! Go inside *this* instant." Her aunt turned back to Lord Blakely but Francine couldn't make out her expression. "G-gambling debts, my lord?" Aunt Prudence remarked in a docile, toadying voice totally foreign to her usual strident commands and caterwauling. "Why, whatever *could* you mean? I am *not* one to dabble at the green cloth—"

"Your vernacular alone belies your protest," he told

her coldly. "I have secured your vowels from Peterson. I know exactly how much you lost to him and that he was blackmailing you with your debt and on top of that working to extract exorbitant interest. Now, madam," he spoke with an unhurried cadence that only stressed the threatening undercurrent palpable in his tone, "you are in debt to me. Do not, I repeat, *do not* ever interfere with Lady Francine's actions again. I may have bought Peterson's silence but mine is not for sale. If you go against me on this, I will make your ill habits known— gambling with money you do not have to lose, trading the reputation, the very life of one in your care." He made an incensed, hissing noise, that even knowing wasn't directed at her, made Francine jump. "And if that were to come out? Then, madam, your precious daughters lose their reputations, quite likely their beaus, and your standing in the *ton* becomes tarnished beyond redemption. Have I made myself clear?"

"Pre-precisely, my lord." Aunt Prudence's entire demeanor had changed. "I trust I will see you inside?"

"You will. Later."

Aunt Prudence stepped back and Lord Blakely nodded to his servant to secure the door once again.

In the darkened interior, Francine stared at his shadow and felt her world tilt on its axis once again. "How—how did you confirm such a thing? Secure her vowels? And so quickly?"

"It seems your dear aunt has developed a penchant for gaming and deep play. I made some discreet inquiries and discovered she was in to Peterson for over fifteen thousand pounds. Not counting the insane interest that was accumulating."

Fifteen? *Thousand?* "But that is—"

"A bloody fortune. I know."

"I shall pay you back, my lord."

"Erasmus," he reminded her, his voice going all dark and smoky. "No you will not. What you will do is sit there silently while I sample your body's perfume again."

That brought an immediate blush to her cheeks, a tingling to her loins.

"I will?" she murmured, hardly daring to hope.

His warmth caressed her collarbone when he leaned forward, guiding one hand under her skirt. A whimper escaped her lips just as his mouth neared hers.

"Very good, Francine," he practically purred. His fingers delved beneath her petticoats and shift, then grazed up her stocking until he reached the bare skin of her inner thigh. She held her breath, afraid to move and break the spell. "Very good, indeed."

His lips and tongue danced lightly over her mouth while his touch edged nearer forbidden territory. He slid his tongue past her lips, his fingers past her feminine curls.

She moaned around his tongue, finding the unexpected texture to it arousing. Had it been this rough before? She couldn't remember, but thinking about last night took too much effort, especially when he was stroking her tongue with his, licking the roof of her mouth. Did all men kiss this way?

Restless, she shifted her hips. His fingers delved, parting her folds to circle her entrance and slide inside the wet welcome. "Ummm." She couldn't stop the welcoming, eager sound from escaping.

With a hiss he jerked back—distancing both his mouth and his hand—until he was gazing at her in the darkness and no longer touching her anywhere. His piercing eyes glowed as he stared at her lips.

Her heartbeat suddenly clamored between her thighs. "I ache for you. Please, Erasmus, touch me again."

She sensed his satisfied smile rather than saw it, and then from the soft noises, could tell he was licking his fingers clean, right in front of her. "Debauched, indeed."

He made a satisfying murmur at the husky accusation. How she wished she could see him.

The raspy sound of his tongue swiping over his skin caused Francine to go rigid. The flesh he'd left empty burned. "Touch me again."

He leaned forward and licked her lips. She tried to capture his tongue and pull it into her mouth, but he evaded her attempts. She gripped his forearm, ready to launch herself into his lap, but he broke free.

"Lady Francine, I do believe we have a musicale to endure." He chuckled, and it had a slight edge to it. *Good. The beast isn't unaffected—just pretending to be.* "I mean enjoy. During every note of every measure, I want you to anticipate the moment when I will take you tonight. Because I will."

6

THE WYLDE INTERLUDE

ERASMUS, you shall be a man soon. Your eighteenth year looms close—but so does The Change.

Do I tell my serious, overly responsible son of the fate that awaits him? Do I rob him of what should rightly be his last few years of unfettered freedom? More to the point, when do I tell you what I discovered last year? When your mother joined me at the hunting lodge while I was near insensible from waging the fight I do every summer? Brave lass holds my heart more every year we are together. (Have I mentioned she even convinced me to cast off that last mistress some years back—and it didn't take a significant amount of coaxing, either.)

I continue to appreciate and value her more with every day that passes.

Even when she defied my every order and defeated my guard (hard to obey the master when the master's wife holds a loaded dueling pistol up to your ear—or so I gathered once

I became myself again). I lose time during much of the battle. Lose my memory too, have I told you that? So much of the blame weeks I grapple, defending myself against The Change, is a bloody haze when it's over.

Regardless. Son, she seduced me. Aye, you read that right. That sweet-smelling sweetheart of a woman who has suffered so much at my hands, seduced me when I was nearly insensible, so damn fearful of harming her again.

And the gentle loving she blessed me with? Well, upon the completion of it, Erasmus, I swear I was blessed with hours of normalcy.

Or as near normal as a half-beast can experience when the Roho wa Simba is so strong.

Does the act of sex subdue the urges? Tame the beast?

I sit here and ponder, both that and exactly when to share all of this with you.

Is it just sex? Or perhaps love? Will this only hold true with a woman who owns your heart? Or would any woman do? Or was the calming of savage urges significant only because it was your mother—my love?

And do not think I jest in this, for 'tis not a laughing matter. However, I can promise you tossing one off by frigging your own pipe will not suffice, else I'd have become a tame pussycat by now.

AFTER SUFFERING through deplorable music and sitting next to the delectable Lady Francine, Blakely was aroused to the point of pain and enjoying every miserable, trying second.

He'd half expected that spending more time with

her—fully clothed—would dull her appeal. Never before had he committed himself to so many consecutive hours in the company of one such as her, but if anything, 'twas he who was duped. Anticipation? Bloody hell. If he didn't take her soon, he'd turn into a raving beast all by himself—by choice—and cart her off... Ravish her thoroughly against the nearest wall and roar at anyone who dared interrupt.

Are you listening to yourself? Have you gone mad? 'Tis not a matter for jests!

Confound it.

As if he could change at will. Risk the lives of those close to him? By the devil, he spent so much time fighting The Change each year, that even *contemplating* doing it by choice shocked him to the tips of his sometimes clawed toes.

Mayhap the strident tones assaulting his eardrums were scrabbling his common sense, scrambling his judgment?

Thank heavens they'd dallied in the carriage.

That spontaneous episode ensuring they arrived sufficiently late that all of the seats near the performance area were taken. He and Francine occupied a perch upon a settee in the last informal row that had been arranged to accommodate those invited, satisfyingly distant from her aunt and cousins.

Although, the younger one had proved surprisingly entertaining, with her exuberant questions about his coat of arms and heraldic symbols, showing a more intellectual bent than the other two gossipy harpies, retrieving a pencil and paper from her reticule, making notes by the meager light after she pulled the window curtain aside. Even going so far as to invite him to call her "Tempest, now that we're going to be family"—to the hissed disapproval of her mother—when she laughed about Miss Temperance Comberlander being such a veritable mouthful. Dismissing with a light shrug the rumbled criticisms from her mother and older sister the more she asked...

And Francine? Those subtly inquisitive fingers of hers only allowing a fraction of his mind to remain on the impromptu history lesson; the rest of his thoughts entrenched firmly in the vicinity of his groin.

Much as they were now.

Her alluring scent rising up to capture his riotous thoughts. Sunshine, heather and lust. Combined with the delicate fragrance of lilacs she wore tonight, a new scent to catalog. The combination persisted in going to his head, kept his mind firmly on her instead of circling elsewhere, seeking solutions to the growing concern surrounding his cubs.

He should be analyzing the list Adam had made, shared with him last night, the list comparing the known locations of certain men against dates of the horrid acts he now knew had been committed closer to The Den than comfort allowed. But nay, one more scent reined in his concentration, tethered it and him— right back to the woman at his side.

Where he so easily identified her own heady aroma —that which was wafting from between her thighs. Damn his overly astute nose. Damn him and his earlier teasing. His reckless actions had only served to whet both their carnal appetites and he paid the price for it now, his tongue pulsing with the need to taste her again. Everywhere.

Lady Stanton's well-hyped (erroneously, it seemed) musicale wasn't even halfway through the interminable first set. The way things were progressing, he'd never make it to the interval without bursting through his breeches and tossing up Francine's skirts to claim her right here in the back of the Stantons' ballroom, converted for the event.

That would certainly be living up to his reputation, now wouldn't it? Plunk her into his lap and bang away. 'Twould ruin them both. Completely and forever.

She was driving him to think like a dull swift.

Gads. Rather than howl his frustration, he sought distraction by means of her wit.

Below the piercing tones coming from the youngest Stanton on the pianoforte, he bent his head to whisper, "Since your aunt has been offering your hand to any marriage-minded man in the *ton*, and even those who are not so inclined, I am curious how you have managed to remain unclaimed thus far. Did you make it a practice to crack statuary over all their heads?"

A subtle smile curved her lips before she spoke. "Most subdued their suit when I expressed disinterest. For those who chose not to, I simply made myself unpalatable." She addressed him from behind her gently waving fan, her eyes riveted on the elevated plat-form at the front of the room. Was she refusing to look at him intentionally? Or did she truly enjoy this hash?

"Why is that, I wonder?" He no longer made any pretense of paying attention to the performance. "Is it not the ambition of every young lady to marry, manage her own home and have a family?"

"Not when stifling your true self is the price and freedom is the cost."

She spoke so quickly he almost missed it, but her words repeated themselves in his mind. Freedom...that mattered to her. She'd mentioned it more than once. Before he could ask what she meant by the rest, she added, "The only thing standing in my way is time. And my aunt."

"She will not be haranguing you further."

"What about our agreement?" At that, she glanced at him, then smartly snapped her fan shut and then open again, waving it furiously. A burst of air huffed past his jaw. "Now that you have taken care of Aunt Pru, there remains no need—"

In case she harbored any ridiculous notions of ending their betrothal early, he blurted, "There stands every reason to keep up our pretense."

Was that relief? A softening in her posture, surely.

"I concur," she said, relaxing the motions of her fan and gazing again at the stage as if enraptured. "We shall continue our association until the agreed upon time several weeks hence. Correct?"

He wanted her attention on him, not the butchered music blasting his sensitive ears. "Do you remember every facet of our bargain?"

Behind her fan, he saw one cheek dimple when she replied, still without looking at him, "Are you referring to the part where you satisfy my desires?"

"Minx." At least he knew he had her full attention.

"I refer to the aspect where you satisfy mine. Any time I ask."

Her hand stilled. "Are you asking now?"

Applause broke out, covering the stifled groan he couldn't contain. Lady Francine Montfort would be the death of him yet. "Nay, not quite. But I shall. Sometime tonight. Be ready."

"I am ready now, my lord." She turned to him and mouthed, *Erasmus.*

"I know," he said with a smugness he didn't try to dampen. "I smell you."

He knew she got his meaning when her eyes widened and that fan started flapping again like a bird in flight.

⸺⸻◦⸻⸺

ALMOST EVERYONE in attendance was there not for the audible abuse being heaped on their ears by Lady Stanton's unmarried daughters but in anticipation of the Grayson String Quartet, which was scheduled to perform selected movements from *Haydn's Opus* 76 directly after the interlude. Francine had been looking forward to hearing the compositions for an age.

Yet she couldn't deny how the anticipation for that singular experience paled in comparison to what she currently had waiting for her this evening—Lord Blakely and whatever intimate activities he thought to indulge in.

By the time the second youngest daughter screeched to a halt on her flute and Lady Stanton announced the interval intended for guests to stretch their legs, visit the "necessary"—if necessary—and mingle, Francine's wrist ached.

She'd never clutched a fan so tightly, nor wielded it with such vigor.

Neither had she ever been so nervous—or excited—in her life. Muscles discovered during her illicit garden encounter last night contracted quite without her permission, anxious to repeat the performance.

Amid the milling throng of stalwart listeners, Erasmus escorted her to the refreshment tables, his proprietary air unmistakable. Accomplishing his part of their agreement, he was making his claim on her known to one and all.

As they roamed through the large rooms, Francine marveled at the attention they garnered from those present.

To the eyebrow-raised expressions of incredulity several of his friends directed their way, Erasmus only nodded and smiled, dismissing them and conveying without words his wish to be left alone.

To the multitude of behind-the-fan whispers and hushed murmurings—accompanied by many a dark or jealous look—from a number of the various "ladies" present, he turned a blind eye, ignoring the edge of their surprise and disappointment with such aplomb that she could only marvel further.

How fortunate! That she'd amassed the courage to approach him so boldly—no easy feat—and that he'd acceded.

It might be considered unfashionable to be obviously devoted to one's intended, but given how he treated her, combined with his insistence that their farce continue, even with her aunt's immediate threat dispatched? Well, Francine was over the moon. To have such a man at her disposal—if only for a short time— why, 'twas the closest thing to a blissful marriage she could ever hope to attain. Add to that the amorous turn her plan had taken and she must be the luckiest woman alive.

As though he'd read the tumultuous thoughts tumbling through her mind, he gave her a pointed look. "You seem content. Shall I take that to mean you think you made the right choice, approaching me? I shall assume, then, that you are still willing to abide by my terms."

"Of course. I am all that is agreeable."

"Hmm. Debatable." One of the men that had surrounded him last evening before she'd first approached him, started in their direction. Erasmus noticed and, with a single glance, a tilt of his head, sent the fellow scurrying away. Then he again fixed his penetrating gaze on her. "Well, Lady Agreeable, are you prepared to service me now?"

She laughed off his naughty teasing. "You make me sound like a dumbwaiter, my lord."

"Ah, but dumbwaiters are particularly suited to *servicing* their masters, are they not?"

"For shame, my lord. I do not believe I have given you leave to claim *mastery* over me." At least not yet. "And you know how very much I look forward to the professional quartet secured for later."

"Mmm." The sound was noncommittal; the look in his eyes almost pleased that she hadn't jumped to do his alluded-to bidding without thought.

"Even so," she commented lightly, taking a sip of the ratafia he'd procured for her as they claimed an empty spot along one wall, overlooking the milling throng, "I do not believe I could have selected a better man to enact my sham of an engagement with if I had spent days compiling a list of suitable candidates instead of mere seconds."

His arm across her waist tightened, swinging her to his opposite side when a rather inebriated man, totally in his cups, staggered by. "Ah. There goes your Lord Crandall. Still happy that your first choice fell in with your scheme?" he countered just as casually.

"Must you remind me?" Francine took another sip, purposefully looking away.

"Mayhap I want to hear it again."

She swiveled her head to give him an arch look, but willing to flatter his ego nevertheless; he had been remarkably patient with her oft-vexatious relatives. "There never was a second choice—it was you or no one at all."

He made a low, pleased noise in his throat. The knave seemed to be fighting a smile as he indicated the unsteady man who'd just passed. "Not even that fine specimen?"

"Particularly not. He takes snuff," she confided. "Flakes of it are always hovering at the corners of his lips."

"Unsightly," Erasmus agreed.

"Untidy."

"Undignified."

"Intolerable." Francine shuddered in mock horror.

"Indubitably."

"Effectively."

"And with that, my dear, I do believe you have quite *effectively* put a halt to whatever topic we were conversing upon. Unless, might you permit me to inquire—just what is it we are now discussing?" He placed her empty glass on a tray and lifted her hand, bowing over it as if they were being introduced for the first time.

"You may inquire." Francine tried to muffle her laughter but failed miserably. "But I have not a clue."

"Pardon the interruption, my lord." A servant behind Lord Blakely stood, nervously shifting from one foot to the other, seeming somewhat out of breath. "You are Lord Blakely, correct?"

Erasmus inclined his head. "Aye. What is it?"

"Very well. I've found you." The servant released a loud sigh and held out a folded, waxed-sealed note. "I was instructed to put this into your hand directly." He followed through when Erasmus held out his palm. Then in a much quieter tone, looking furtively from side to side, the young man leaned in and said quietly, "I was told it's most urgent, my lord, that you read it with all due haste."

Behaving as though such an odd occurrence was nothing out of the everyday ordinary, Erasmus retrieved a coin from his pocket and held that out to the servant.

"You may consider your duty dispatched," he said with a surprisingly serene air.

"My lord. Thank you." The man bowed himself off, leaving Francine rather startled.

When Erasmus made no move, she pointed to the note. "Are you not going to read it?"

He hesitated, as though about to say something, then, a small muscle ticking in his jaw, he did so, quickly severing the page from the wax closure and opening it, turning toward the wall, as though retrieving another glass, not making it obvious to anyone but her what had his attention.

She heard the gasp, saw the slight paling of his features that he so quickly erased. When he turned back to her, in complete command of his expression once again, one would never guess that whatever he'd just read had prompted such a reaction.

"And now, my dear, I most heartily regret that I must step away for a moment. Do forgive me. I am needed elsewhere. I—"

Once again, he stopped himself from saying something. He took her gloved hand, gave it a soothingly tight squeeze, brushed his thumb over the back in an unmistakable caress and met her gaze, allowing his to show the molten heat he'd kept banked the last hour or more. "I shall return to escort you home before the night is through, have no fear. Sooner if I can manage it."

Then he was gone, striding off, leaving her staring at the immaculate, enthralling precision of six foot, three inches—or thereabouts—of strong, powerful, *tortured* man in one bang-up fine assortment of attire...

For he'd dressed quite formally for the evening, going so far as to wear black knee breeches for the occasion. Above which the fitted burgundy tailcoat displayed his broad shoulders to perfection; below which, white silk stockings graced his lower legs above the buckled shoes.

Despite her curiosity over the note that had troubled him so, she couldn't help the little heartsick sigh that escaped, watching the muscles in his lower legs flex and move as they made their way toward the door, taking her stalwart protector—and the devastatingly attractive view—away.

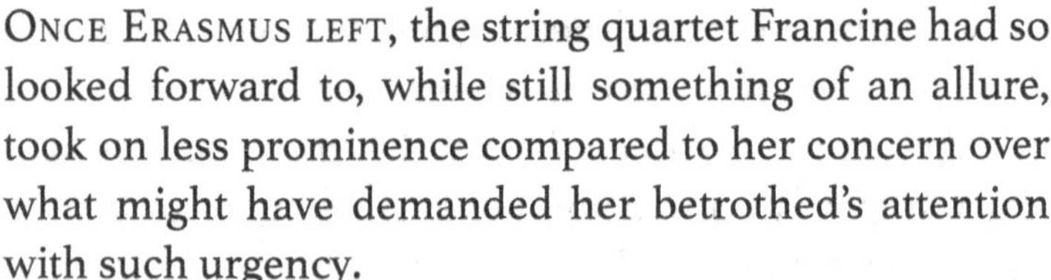

ONCE ERASMUS LEFT, the string quartet Francine had so looked forward to, while still something of an allure, took on less prominence compared to her concern over what might have demanded her betrothed's attention with such urgency.

Nevertheless, not one to wander aimlessly when there might be things to learn, she sought out the Stantons' middle daughter, knowing they shared an interest in mathematics and curious whether Louisa had made any strides in her efforts to learn the probabilities surrounding Vingt-un depending upon what was already visible on the table, as she'd expressed an interest in calculating the last time their paths crossed.

Instead, finding her friend surrounded by beaus despite the horrid harpsichord melodies, Francine decided to explore the open and candlelit areas of the large townhouse, inviting guests to enjoy. Quite massive, even by London standards, the prior Lord Stanton going so far as to purchase the one next door and combine the two, creating a lively space for gatherings, as well as other vast rooms not often found in town.

Two staircases, several turns and a long hallway later, she found herself perusing the majestic portraits in the upstairs gallery. Surprisingly, she was the only person taking pleasure in that particular pastime, now that the few others who'd been there when she arrived had left, murmuring about locating refreshments and retiring rooms before the music began anew.

Upon reaching the far end of the long gallery, she craned her neck to inspect a painted family from another century. "Hoops galore," she whispered, in awe of the exorbitantly wide panniers that supported the sumptuous dresses worn by the females depicted in the portrait. "How did they sit? Use a chamber pot?"

At that particular image in her head, a light snicker escaped. Before the sound died down, hushed voices beyond the arched doorway captured her attention.

Was that her youngest cousin? Whispering intently on the other side of the door? Despite her uncertainty, her feet refused to move, no matter that listening in showed every bit of ill breeding her aunt liked to unjustly accuse her of.

"...speak with you most candidly, my lord, if you would but allow it?" That *was* Temperance, most assuredly; Francine had heard the exact hushed, low whisper when they used to confide in each other and didn't want to wake any of the household.

She stepped closer to the hinges, even dared to glance through the small crevice before hesitation took her a single step away, allowing only her ears and not her eyes to be privy to what occurred on the other side.

"By all means, Miss Comberlander, I believe 'tis imperative, of the utmost importance in fact, that two people seeking to spend the rest of their time on this earth together can and do speak to each other with nothing but plain honesty between them."

'Twas Lord Wylde conversing quietly with Temperance, the man she'd recently become engaged to. Renowned for his fastidious appearance, he easily rivaled Beau Brummell as an arbiter of men's fashion, one others sought to emulate, his waistcoats always sporting the most detailed embroidery and vivid colors, his neckcloths the most intricate of arrangements. When he wasn't fluid perfection on the dance floor, Francine had noted, he had the most precise, regal manner, reminding her of those in the military, but without that experience himself—or so she thought.

"Without reservations muddying the waters," he continued. "So, aye, speak plainly if you would."

"I am relieved to hear you feel thus, however it pains me to say this..." Even Francine could hear the hesitation in Temperance's voice. "The unadorned truth is, my lord... Lord Wylde, I-simply-do-not-see-the-two-of-us-spending-our-remaining-days-together," she rushed out in one long word. "Indefinitely, that is. *Ad finitum.*"

The man gave a quiet grunt after the Latin addition. "You do not, do you?"

"Please know, 'tis nothing against you, specifically. Nothing at all. In actuality, I find you a very fine specimen indeed. Very cordial, extremely pleasant. You have been nothing but amiable in all your dealings with my mother as well—no mean feat, I admit. And I appreciate the conversations we have had to date, however brief, and find you a magnificent dancer, if I may be so bold."

Francine couldn't help but wonder, with all that her cousin found to admire in the attractive lord, why on earth wouldn't she want to marry him?

"Well, then?" the lord in question questioned, blatant curiosity in his tone, as though he wondered the same thing.

Another couple entered the gallery across the way and Francine had to restrain herself from shooing them back out. As long as they stayed on the opposite side, there'd be no chance of them eavesdropping as well. That thought should have made her feel guilty enough to move.

It didn't. If anything, she leaned closer to the crack along the door and tilted her head to better hear how Temperance responded. But Lord Wylde wasn't yet finished.

With a quiet dignity she could not help but applaud, he added, "Might you now enumerate the reasons *why* I shall not suit as a forever mate? If I am to be jilted for a second time in as many years, I believe 'tis fitting I understand the rationale, do you not agree?"

"Of a certainty," her cousin rushed to assure him. "And that is the truth—exactly *what* has given me the most pause."

Francine had all but forgotten the furor over the public jilt two years ago, his from-the-womb betrothed taking off mere hours before their scheduled nuptials —at St. George's, no less—eloping to Scotland with the fourth son of another family, one with a much less illustrious reputation than Lord Wylde himself had possessed (up to that point).

It wasn't so much that the woman had discarded their union for one not considered anywhere near as grand, but that she had done so with such a lack of consideration for his reputation—literally abandoning him in front of everyone already in attendance at the majestic church. With nothing more than a note, delivered by a hired messenger, not even a family servant, only minutes before the event was scheduled to begin.

"In truth, Lord Wylde," Temperance continued, sounding truly regretful, "it is because of how very comfortable I do feel with you, that we ought not marry. I believe we would be doing both ourselves an extreme disfavor."

"Disfavor?" he queried, making no effort to hide how flummoxed he was at her attempted explanation. "When we already get along tolerably well? When a budding friendship might become something more?"

"But that is my point exactly!" Temperance said with the most animation Francine had heard yet, starting to sound more like a *Tempest* indeed.

Her neck was starting to hurt, still staring at the antiquated painting, as she was. But at least her seeming fascination with the piece had induced the other couple to circle, before they'd reached the far end where she stood, and start making their way back toward the entrance, thus preserving the remainder of her cousin's privacy—that which Francine herself was still invading.

"I do not want to *tolerate* a life's mate, my lord, I

want to rejoice in him, and him me. And again, please forgive my blunt speaking..." Temperance was all quiet earnestness now. "But friendship is all it would ever be between us, of that I am quite confident."

"Are your affections fixed elsewhere?"

"As those of your prior betrothed were? Nay, they are not. I answer you with all honesty. There is no one else I have a *tendre* for, no inkling nor cravings in any direction, save those I harbor toward the future.

"Nonsensical in the extreme or not"—once again, Temperance's voice expressed both regret and enthusiasm—"I cannot help but wish for more, for myself and for you."

"Damn me, Miss Comberlander, I begin to regret not wooing you in truth. You are a fine young woman and I have no doubt will make some man a perfect match. Would that it could be me, but alas, I understand, more than I care to admit, what you share."

"I fear it sounds rather fickle of me, but I wish not to feel *quite* so very comfortable with a man I am to be sharing such intimate and enduring activities with. To put it bluntly, Lord Wylde, I could not think of you more as a brother had we grown up together since the time of leading strings. Please, be as forthright with me now. I meant it when I said I do not want to harm you, nor your reputation, further, and I regret, abominably so, that this most assuredly will.

"If, for whatever reason, you have your heart set on marrying me, I will go through with it, with as much equanimity as I can muster. And I vow to be faithful henceforth. Regardless—"

"Halt." It sounded as though he took a step forward,

possibly touched Temperance_to stem the heartfelt avowals. "Nay, I shall not require nor request such a sacrifice on your part, nor of mine. For if truth be known, I only offered for you out of a sense of protective pity." My, oh my, the things one learned listening at cracks. "Now I hesitate to share this with you, but believe it is information you deserve to know. I was casually gaming at a house party, hosted by the parents of a friend of mine, where your mother was in attendance.

"Though she was bosky at the time, I regret to inform you she made remarks about bartering you, your future, to more than one insalubrious type present. She had an amazing run, and continued to win each time such an outlandish thing was mentioned, but when it happened a third time, and the cards I was dealt gave me their blessing, I did all I could to secure you from her, unwilling to risk your hand being transferred elsewhere. And to someone who might be lacking in my, shall we say, sense of moral fortitude?"

Francine couldn't help but gasp and staggered into the corner, abandoning her desire to listen in upon the heels of that revelation.

Dastardly rakes and scurrilous scoundrels, but her aunt was truly, truly vile.

So, Francine had not been the only dependent Aunt Pru was willing to sacrifice over her unhealthy addiction to gaming?

Nor did *Tempest* sound anything like the mutton-headed flit-about she often did at home and in the presence of their other relatives, all of her words pronounced accurately, all of her reasoning quite sound. Leading Francine to conclude she herself had been outwitted by her quick-thinking cousin. Definitely time to find out why.

On silent, slippered feet, she retraced her steps to the other side of the gallery, where an elaborately wide settee resided under an equally wide family painting, this one showing their country estate, she assumed, the peaceful, rolling green hills, beautiful three-story manor house and picnicking throng helping settle the maelstrom of thoughts surging through her baffled brain.

7

A WILD INTERRUPTION

Meet me outside. At the mews.
Another has been found.
—A

TWO BRIEF LINES that struck sheer horror into his heart, sent terror slicing through him yet again. *Another?* God in heaven, when would this stop?

"WHAT THE DEVIL HAPPENED?"

Foregoing any manner of greeting, Blakely's demand blasted the pungent air of the Stanton stables the moment he ducked inside the long structure and found his quarry. Air redolent with leather, horseflesh *and* their leavings. His nose having delivered him to the corner Adam inhabited, the one furthest from the beehive of activity taking place closer to the main entrance.

Not unexpectedly, given the elegant throng attending the auditory festivities tonight, just a wall or several away, the space was crowded with enough carriages, horses, and their coachmen, tigers and grooms, that two more men, conversing in hushed whispers, shouldn't rouse significant interest. To make sure, Blakely stepped deeper into the shadows, his formal dress glaringly more out of place than the working-man's type attire Adam preferred.

"Who is manning the club if your arse is here?"

The same age as Blakely, give or take, Adam had his own secrets—staggering ones—Blakely had learned of quite by accident. The brawny, sandy-haired American from the Texas frontier had come to London on his own quest—and to Blakely's aide one evil, misbegotten night, assisting him with some wretched business, then staying on. From stranger to confidant in the span of a few short hours. Despite his peculiarities, a man Blakely trusted as no other—not even his erstwhile, missing family members, damn their hidden hides.

Where the bloody hell was Nash? He'd usually show his furry face by now. Damn buffoon grew out his own whiskery bristles into an unfashionable beard, thinking 'twould mask The Change. Not hardly, especially not given the careless way his brother insisted upon dressing, eschewing any manner of more formal garments befitting his station.

While Blakely had always used his birthright and his title—his arrogant bearing easily exaggerated given his naturally reserved inclinations—to keep most at a distance, Nash did the opposite: letting his long, untrimmed hair and untamed beard, and the casual dregs he dressed in, combined with an intentionally surly nature to keep others away and maintain his privacy.

Adam wasn't much better, foregoing any effort at the impeccable appearance Blakely depended upon so... Adam with his horridly plain bandanna tied around his neck in lieu of a neckcloth. His unusual pantaloons a stiff, thick texture, much looser around the legs and longer than typical. His upper lip taken over by a giant, furry caterpillar of a mustache—totally not in vogue. Totally "Texan", circa 1790s—according to his pseudo-assistant and true friend.

"Baywick stayed," Adam answered now, mentioning one of their doorkeepers. "Add to that, with what happened, I ushered out everyone who didn't belong, made sure those who did were tucked in tight, and locked the doors with Bay keeping watch."

Blakely nodded, already his body tensing for the news that was imminent. "What transpired?"

"A third body has turned up."

Damn it. "I suspected as much, from your note."

Knew with utter certainty, you mean.

But hearing it confirmed proved worse than suspicion. *Fact* gripped his innards in a vise and threatened to squeeze the humanity right out of him. *Fact* made him want to turn savage, to rail against a world where innocents could lose everything—and in the most vile ways imaginable. "Who? Where?"

When?

One of their regular "ladies"—a bird of the game, a

strumpet, a flash girl, a whore...a harlot (though he tried to dissuade use of these latter two)—"employed" by The Den had been missing for a handful of days. He cringed at the very thought of seeing the young mother as the other two had been. Shredded. Hardly recognizable.

But he had to ask. "Diane?"

"No, thank God. This one had hair much blonder than hers. Wavy too." When they both knew Diane bemoaned her straight-as-sin dark locks. "And that's about all I can tell you. I can't believe this has happened again." Adam swore, colorfully and loudly, drawing the attention of more than one busy groom.

"Mind your voice," Blakely said quietly.

"Forgive me." Adam pressed the base of both palms into his eye sockets and spoke through gritted teeth. "I just cannot rid myself of the sight. No matter that the streets here are dark as the inside of a wild boar's hairy arse, I still saw way more than I ever needed to. It's imprinted on my brain." For a second, it sounded as though his friend were gargling glass as a shudder trembled through his frame. "And, oh God, the smell..."

The flies were already bad enough this summer. After what they'd both helped clean up three weeks ago, Blakely knew whatever Adam experienced this night was more than many could handle.

Adam lowered his hands and gave his head a quick shake. "Never you mind. You don't need the details. I know you've already seen enough yourself."

And he had. For it had been Blakely who had stumbled across the second body to be found in the general vicinity of his club. Blakely who'd uncharacteristically struggled with a combination of panic and uncertainty upon discovering the gruesome sight without warning...

Thinking instead his nose was simply leading him to an abandoned sack of discarded kittens, a spilt butcher's cart or some lazy gadabout's weekly refuse. Not realizing until he turned that last corner, curious, wishing he was enough of a dandy to carry a handkerchief at all times so he could have attempted to blot the stench...

Wasn't until seeing another form—bent over the prone one on the ground, tucked away in a begrimed alley, doing unspeakable things—that he'd been faced with the true depths humanity could sink to. Not even the tragic circumstances surrounding the appalling, impossible death of his father had affected him so.

He turned to the wall now, braced his hand on the rough plank, and cough-retched, but nothing came up. Pure anger at the monster responsible and absolute conviction that he'd do all he could to stop the madness settled the nausea, thank goodness.

Business still needed tended to, sickening circumstances aside. "Unknown to us or not, she still needs—"

"Already done, E," Adam interrupted, using the casual abbreviation of his given name they'd finally agreed upon—after the chucklehead kept calling him *Fitzwilliam* for some asinine reason. "By the time I arrived, there was enough muscle to move her—what was left of her." Adam swore again. "I brought a blanket. Someone else had a cart. Just like last time, I paid a couple men to start digging. Woke your preacher man to say a few words over her once they were done."

After news of the first unclaimed, unrecognizable body had reached his awareness, before the attack and death that occurred not far from the club, Blakely had purchased a small plot of land near a parish cemetery, but not officially part of it. He'd then greased the open palm of the man of the cloth sufficiently to ensure a simple burial, doing what little he could and hoping it would be the last. Hoping in vain, as it appeared.

A couple stalls over, several stable boys started up some rollicking, ribald tune.

"Drunk off their arses," Blakely remarked, seeing the two bottles they'd passed around in the last few minutes, only fractionally envious.

When was the last time he drank to excess? Had he ever? Or even considered loosening the tight stranglehold he forced on himself long enough to sing like an idiot?

Adam slapped the wall with such force that it groaned. Then he did it again, twice, before halting and catching Blakely's gaze. "My apologies for interrupting your evening out. I—"

"Nay. No regrets." Blakely took hold of Adam's wrist and gave a squeeze. "You did exactly the right thing."

Blakely released him when the muscles relaxed, Adam fisting what must be a stinging palm, but not abusing the blameless wood further.

"The investigator?" he queried, seeking to distract his friend. The one they were looking to hire.

"I'll have a report on that and the other information we discussed tomorrow night."

"Very well. Give me but a moment. I shall make my excuses and accompany you—"

Nay! You escorted Francine and her chatty relatives—

Blakely swallowed his words and started over. "I will direct my coachman to wait for Lady Francine and family, and return with you."

"No." After outwardly expressing his grief, Adam had crumpled against the wall. It seemed to be the only thing holding his friend up at the moment, despite the steady conviction conveyed in his tone. "It's unnecessary, E. I rode. The moon's bright enough, and after what I saw, it helped clear... I couldn't stomach the thought of *walking*. Not through London. Not at night.

"Even if I do feel twice as big as most of these city pipsqueaks, I don't want a damn pickpocket plying his trade anywhere near my person. Nor anything more sinister."

Pipsqueak? Blakely allowed himself a small smile at Adam and his peculiar turns of phrases, ones he'd learned long ago to stop asking about.

"I need to ride," his friend was saying, "before I turn in for the night and don't mind being by myself for a while."

During the last couple of sentences, Adam's demeanor underwent a bit of a change, as he shifted, lounging a bit more comfortably—as much as one could against a splintering plank wall. He brightened. "*Lady Francine.* That reminds me—what's this I heard tonight at the club—you've *offered* for someone?"

The bawdy song to their right got louder. Lewder.

Blakely was tempted to join in—anything to avoid

discussing his arrangement with Lady Francine Montfort.

"When were you going to tell me of this, pray tell?" Adam clipped out the words, echoing the speech patterns of an upper-crust British gent in an accurate imitation of most of their patrons. "I am aghast with insatiable curiosity, my lord."

"And when you go all mocking and 'my lording', dear sir," Blakely said, his customary polish back in place, while employing every bit of sarcasm his friend had—if not more. "I am rather tempted to plant you a facer."

Adam guffawed. Straightened from his lounging position against the wall and tipped his—invisible—hat, a thoroughly mocking motion. "I daresay, milord, I should very well like to see you try."

Bugger the insolent man. They might be near the same height, with Blakely topping his friend by a scant inch or two but the sheer breadth of Adam's chest, the muscular arms that needed custom-tailored shirts along with extra fabric, meant that any true fight between them would come out a near tie. Had they not proved that the night they'd met?

Blakely was still smiling grimly as he made his way back inside, found the room reserved for tending to one's personal business of a private nature, and attempted to wash off the nauseating hum of the stables and sordid secrets. Of mews and murder.

Tried to shake off the dark horror of the night and replace it instead with the fresh innocence beckoning to him from a delicate conundrum of forthright honesty and perplexing stubbornness.

Needed to banish the images conjured in the last few minutes with the untainted passion and clean, sultry taste of his affianced.

The stark contrast of where his mind, and his nose, had just been and what—*whom*—he now focused on did not escape him. Light versus shadows. Sunshine versus stables. Sweetness versus stench.

Life.

Versus death.

The most basic of differences. Only Francine, each time she'd crossed his mind today, represented so much more than simple daylight or sunshine.

Hope circled round those spiral ringlets, errant thoughts of her ever since last eve prodding his spirits upward, lifting his heels... Somehow making the burdens he carried seem not quite so cumbersome. Made him start to dream.

And that would never do.

Not if he was going to keep the beast locked tightly away, shoved deep, wedged into a box in the far reaches of his being, with the lid bolted tight. "Damn distraction, is what she is."

And after what he'd just learned?

She was all he wanted to think of.

Rather than ask her aunt or the unpleasantly impatient Patience—both of whom he nodded to, then moved swiftly on, before they or anyone could waylay him—Blakely made his way back to the refreshment tables where he'd been handed the blighted note. Took a deliberate, hearty inhale all the way into his lungs... And let his nose lead him where he wanted to go.

You're going to defile her if you don't take care.

He ignored the scold.

The garden last night, her exuberant, uninhibited response—even when he was purposefully approaching his lascivious worst—had to have been an aberration. No prim little miss of the *ton*—a duke's daughter, no less—could be as innocently wanton as he recalled.

As untutored yet ardent.

Just how far are you intending to corrupt her?

However far she'd let him.

"FRANNY!"

Her name was a veritable shriek.

Francine looked up and blinked, having removed her spectacles to rest her eyes as well as her brain so the whirlwind that circled closer was nothing more than a whimsical blur.

"I mean, Fran*cine*!" This time, a happy shriek, as her cousin rushed forward and pulled her up for a tight hug. "Oh, dearest, you heard all of that, did you not?"

Temperance released her only to plop down on the settee and tug Francine down beside her. "Or at least enough to realize the truth?"

The spontaneous hug had quite taken her aback. For it felt lovely. "*Several* truths, if I am not mistaken."

"Oh, Francine—and forgive me, it may take a short while for me to stop with the detestable 'Franny'. I never, *never* wanted to hurt you. Have been counting the days until ghastly Patience's nuptials and going-away afterward will render her wretched self gone from the house so I may confide in you once again!"

"Temperance?" Francine retrieved her hands and fumbled with her spectacles, sliding them over her ears and up her nose to see the welcome sight of her dear cousin, all blonde, ethereal hair—with the slightest tinge of red—and pale green eyes exuberantly beaming at her, the tepid muslin gown of pastel pink not doing a thing to subdue the vivaciousness the younger woman exuded. "Tempest?"

"I know! I know. My sister has been *so* very jealous of you. Fiendishly obsessed with it, if truth be known. Threatened constantly to steal jewelry or some such nonsense from Mother and place it among your possessions, trying to see you ousted from our home. I could not bear to see that happen through nought more than her odious selfishness. Especially not when you were so distraught over your parents—and so very young."

Francine had to stifle the absurd laugh that threatened to bubble forth—she might have been a mere sixteen when she came to live with her aunt, but dear Temperance had not yet turned twelve.

Her cousin leaned in close as though offering the utmost of clandestine confidences. "Lest we forget, we both *know* what happens to young ladies cast out without any financial or familial wherewithal. I could *not* be the instrument of your ruin."

In her youth, Temperance must not have realized how they could have simply gone to her new stepfather —or mayhap, she didn't know him or his character sufficiently at that point. But so easily they could have sought his counsel and rendered Patience's outlandish threats ineffective. There was no conceivable way her aunt would have cast her out, not given Francine's standing as the daughter of a duke, nor given the funds ultimately involved, but perhaps neither did Tempest know where her dowry monies came from, that so much of what she and her family now enjoyed had been funded through Francine's inheritance, the portions her father's will had left to his sister, on behalf of her own children.

Now that the thought flitted across her mind... How was it Uncle Rowden hadn't maintained management over the money? Most likely, her aunt had not remarried when her father's will was drawn up. Certainly, her father had no notion that his sister, once married to a vicar, had since turned to gaming and the like.

None of those points mattered now, not when Temperance's animated, bright presence proved such an unexpected and joyous balm.

"As I matured and started to rebel against her, anytime I emulated you or even so much as mentioned you in conversation, she renewed her threats, adding to them in ways that do not bear repeating. I was always concerned that Mother was just self-centered enough to believe her claims. Can you ever find it in your heart to forgive me?"

"Of course." Francine swallowed the emotion knotting her throat. "Have you any idea the relief I now feel? At being able to converse with you as we did in the beginning? On equal footing once again." Which was the absolute truth. But neither was she about to reverse years of learned self-sufficiency upon the strength of one conversation or one night. Time—and her cousin's actions henceforth—would demonstrate the veracity of the claims.

Tempest squeezed her forearm. "I have missed you so. You have no inkling how very difficult it has been, to pattern myself off her, to call you Franny—a thousand apologies on that—so she would never suspect a thing."

Francine grinned. "I confess, if I never hear that name again, it will be too soon. Really, cousin, you belong on the stage. All this time—feigning?"

Temperance giggled, sounding for the first time tonight her younger age. "I know! Playing the pudding-head can be thumping fun, I admit. 'Twould serve Mother right if I did walk the stage. I vow, after her betrayal—did you hear that part? Trying to *gamble me*? As though I were nought more than one of her hand-written vowels?"

"I did. Forgive—"

"Nay! I am so thankful you know. Really, 'tis a monstrous weight lifted." Temperance circled her eyes skyward. "I cannot believe I was so naïve as to think things might improve once Patience became engaged, especially before you. She always considers everything such a competition."

"A competition? With me?"

"Constantly! You *do* know that was why she took such an instant dislike to you? She thinks she has been found wanting since the *moment* you moved in. 'Twas not long after you came to live with us, while you were still very much grieving...emotionally if not visually. We had gone out walking, shopping more likely, the four of us, and I overheard more than one of our acquaintances remark to Mother how very much *you and I* looked alike, as though we were the sisters, and Patience the extended relation. That put her nose out of joint unlike anything I have seen before or since."

Tempest chuckled. "Not that her nose has ever appeared as though it were quite *in joint*, as it were, but still, she took strong aversion to hearing compliments about you and I from that moment onward." She sobered and leaned in. "She is every bit as wretched as Mother, and I have felt so very alone, pretending for all these years to find you as unpalatable as they. I swear, that has never, *never* been the case. I have been vastly relieved—in alt!—over your own engagement. And to Lord Blakely, no less! Knowing that you have found someone for yourself has been utterly divine."

Not ready to discuss her Lord Blakely, not with everything still so very new between them, Francine instead proposed, "Let us make a fresh start, shall we? However you need to maintain peace between your sister and mother, please do so, and with my blessing. Inconsiderate family members or not, they are still yours, and I would never take them away from you. And what is all this—please forgive me, but aye, I confess to raptly listening once I recognized your voice —have you and Lord Wylde now broken things off?"

"We have." Temperance sighed, as though already regretting her decision, but when she spoke, her voice held conviction. "Lord Wylde is such a dear. He even agreed that we will wait and make the announcement *after* Patience's wedding. If I do anything to take the attention from her before the ceremony, we both know she would find something else to bemoan or become vindictive over—you should have heard her vicious complaining after Lord Blakely's visit this afternoon. 'How *Franny* rated a *marquis* when I am *younger* than she is! It's *not fair!*' I was quite tempted to thump her in the bone box, but refrained."

Of a sudden, she stopped speaking, aimed her eyes toward the ceiling, deep in thought. "Hmmm." Her gaze returned. "Could I be forgiven for wondering just what Mother lost—or perhaps *won*—in order to get Lord Hansen to take Patience off our hands?" They both shared a stifled giggle over that. "Amusement aside, I need time to consider what treachery I have learned about Mother tonight, and how best to go on."

"Speak to your stepfather, mayhap?"

"That is something to consider, certainly. But I do not want to rush anything. Ergo, Lord Wylde and I agreed to maintain the farce until after Patience's marriage is accomplished, and then I shall act the shrew in public, before soundly slapping his face or some such scandalous nonsense, and bidding him *adieu*. Hopefully, if I appear distasteful enough, that may help preserve whatever reputation he may still lay claim to. Restore or at least prevent further damage."

"That is remarkably magnanimous of him— permitting a second jilt when the first was so very public. He—"

"Ladies." Lord Blakely strode through the door and straight to them.

Francine's heart gave a decided lurch.

He greeted Temperance, and one would think that gave Francine a moment to gather her wits. But no...

For he leaned down, on the side opposite of where her cousin sat, and placed his lips at her ear.

"'Tis delightful to find you and your cousin in accord," he breathed hotly over her skin, before giving her neck the briefest of kisses. "Meet me near the back staircase. You have four minutes."

8

DARK DISCOVERIES ILLUMINATED

Erasmus William Charles Hammond, for you and you alone I leave these last words.

As my firstborn son, my heir, I owe you the greatest apology. For what I'm about to request—nay, to demand—places an even greater burden on you than I have set forth previously.

Son, as the future marquis, you have an underlying responsibility to the title, our lands and people, and to the Hammond fortune. A responsibility toward your brother. Your cousin. And any others there may be like you—bastards we know naught about.

My scapegrace brother has like as not sired by-blows, though one can hope not prolifically. And if the Saints be smiling on us for once, not <u>male</u>. Since, from what I have gleaned, only the males of our line are doomed to suffer the curse, not the ladies.

Pray God I am accurate on that assertion.

However, dear Erasmus, as the ~~owner~~ ~~possessor~~ <u>inheri-</u>
<u>tant</u> of the highest title in our lineage, it's your responsibility
to not only nurture the estates and tenants and ensure they
continue to thrive, but to see to the individuals of our line
prosper as well. To seek out any others, oversee their actions,
to find the strength within you to set forth boundaries,
restricting their wild behavior.

To prevent any more innocent lives from being ruined.

Aye, I am damning my soul all over again because I'm
tasking you with caring for them all: seeing that any of the
cursed Blakely line—whether recognized legally or not—is
kept within the bounds of propriety. Kept from committing
atrocious acts that might get themselves, and by association,
the rest of us ~~hanged~~. Hung? Hell, son, noosed around the
neck with silk over rope is still sufficient to have any one of
us crying cockles.

<u>You</u>, Erasmus, must save them all, and yourself as well,
uphold the family honor all while determining how you best
go on. Do you marry? Become priest-linked and continue the
line—<u>along with the curse</u>? Do you embrace celibacy and
remain unwed? Avoid tiffing, at all costs? (The life of a monk
is not one we're well suited to, son... I tried when the urges
first came upon me, how I tried.)

Or do you succumb to the lure of sexual revelry I now
suspect will—at least on some levels—allow you to remain
human? As human as the inner beast will permit...

<hr>

TWELVE MINUTES later Francine was still searching for
the dratted stairs. Had he meant the servants' stairs or
was there another set for family use? Was he expecting

her inside the narrow stairway, or simply on the landing? And had he meant on the same floor as the portrait gallery or the one below, where the ballroom had collected chairs and stage, for the performances?

The *Haydn* piece had long-since started, but the sound of her drumming heartbeat drowned out the hauntingly beautiful notes of the violin, viola and cello strings.

She could be forgiven then, for her inability to arrive on time, which was the direct result of taking her leave from Temperance—without alluding to the romantic nature of the assignation she was heading to —and being so eager and subsequently so flustered, that no matter how she tried, she could not locate the referred-to "back" stairs. It wasn't as if Lord and Lady Stanton provided diagrams to every guest, outlining the whereabouts of each feature in their monstrously large home.

Not to mention that she'd practically flown downstairs, to make a stop of a personal nature, before seeking his specified rendezvous.

Blakely found her wandering around upstairs, silently opening every door on the landing. He made his presence known by coming up directly behind her and pulling her to him. She barely muffled her squeak of surprise. "My lord! I did not hear you."

"Where have you been?" he snarled in a throaty whisper, his lips hovering near the juncture of her neck and shoulder.

"I—" Shivers fluttered downward and attacked her stomach. Not wanting to be caught so flagrantly flouting convention, she slipped from his grasp and spun to face him. She couldn't very well confess she was horridly lost, could she?

"I stopped off at the ladies' retiring room," she told him, which was the truth. And which also brought an entirely new, slightly disconcerting, topic to mind. "Two women were discussing how you would not remain satisfied for long with your new bride and would return to prowling—or did they say *plowing*?—before summer's end." Oh, why had she brought this up? She sounded the jealous fishwife. "Likely long before. Either way, I should not think it matters, since ours is not a real betrothal."

And why did that knowledge discomfit instead of comfort?

The candle in the nearest wall sconce flickered and then went out, leaving his face in shadow. "My dear, I am truly disappointed." He reached forward and adjusted the lace edging the neckline of her gown. "You did not strike me as one who listened to idle gossip."

"Strictly speaking, I don't, not usually, but..." His long finger worked its way beneath the lace shielding the upper swells of her breasts...wiggled inside the tighter fit of her stays... Her breath caught, just as he grazed the point of one nipple. "But I—I heard them speaking of your cubs."

"Oh? Merely speculating, I have no doubt..." He sounded quite bored. "Of things they know nothing about." With his other hand, he pulled the neckline of her gown and shift down, completely exposing the top of one breast.

Below stairs, the quality of the music changed, becoming more intense as though the beautiful sounds sought to express every nuance of feeling his attentions wrought.

Her body swayed toward his. "Tales of orgies and...*things*," she confessed in an airy voice. One she tried to firm before finishing, "How could I not listen, I ask you?"

"Orgies? You would have me tell you more of that? I think not. Contrary to what gossip would have you believe, I do have *some* scruples."

As though to contradict that claim, his scrupulous finger circled her flesh.

"Not... That." Well, not particularly that, but she was curious. And embarrassingly breathless.

What happened to decorum?

Decorum could hang—when his touch made her tremble so. Made her ache as though naught else mattered—save his next touch.

"So, you want to know all about Blakely's Cubs, do you?"

All she really wanted to know was his mouth upon her breast, but as experiencing that singular blessing was completely out of the realm of possibility, considering they were still standing in the hallway, she bit back a moan when his thumb twirled around her areola and somehow managed, "If you are willing to—ah—share that with me." He plucked her nipple between thumb and finger now, eliciting a moan. One she attempted to muffle. "I would, of course, see it —*mmm*—as a confidence and treat it as such."

"Very well. When you inquire so sweetly... Ah, but you are not trying to, say, distract me from doing this?" The plucking motion changed to a full-out palm caressing the mound of one breast. "When I want nothing more than to lick your nipples? Suck them into my mouth this very second and drown in your unique flavor?"

"Distractions, indeed," she practically panted.

Then, deciding 'twas only fair she gave him the same, she quickly tugged the glove off one restless hand and twined her fingers up the back of his neck and into his thick hair. Grabbing hold and tugging, tugging harder, the more his palm and fingers explored.

He gave a soft grunt, then eased the taunting, retrieved his hand from within her bodice and anchored it behind her back. "In actuality, I have made it a practice to take certain wayward males of the *ton* under my wing. You may consider it my noble attempt to keep them out of trouble. 'Tis all." As though to divert her from any further questioning, he slid his other hand round her back as well, lowered both along the fabric of her gown until he spread them over the halves of her bottom to cup her fully. Firmly.

"Mmm." Her back arched, pressing her flesh into his palms.

Are you a strumpet in truth, now? Anyone could happen by!

He'd hear them, I've no doubt.

Oh. Right you are. Carry on, then...

"So, umm..." She couldn't quite stop her hips from squirming closer to his groin. Or was that his hold— tugging her forward? "You are not fostering these young men to satisfy your urges for some tenebrous and drunken debauchery? Even more wicked than what you have already shown me?"

"HARDLY," Blakely confessed, wondering how their conversation had taken such a turn. "Though I cannot deny participating in such a time or two." *Or wanting to share with you so much more.*

"What exactly precipitates your association with these men? If they are not particular friends? And have proven prone to 'wayward' tendencies?"

How could she ask such a question, with his hands intimately molding the supple halves of her arse? With how she pressed against him with such abandon he could still recall the precise way her beaded nipple had forged its imprint into his skin? "My intent to keep those so-called cubs safe."

"From what?"

Her fingers grazing his scalp, pulling his hair robbed him of caution.

"Themselves. Their own baser natures, if you will. Young men, when left to their own devices without guidance or wisdom from their elders, often prove dangerous." Dangerous? Had he ever been in more danger than he was right now? "At least that has been the case in my experience."

Get a grip on yourself, man! Frighten her off. Before you do something she'll not live to regret.

Aye, he should. Before too much time passed, rendering him a full savage and it too late to show her any tenderness at all.

He already knew sex tamed the urges. Sex.

But rough, fast sex. Hard sex. Not the type of loving a lady such as her should ever be forced to endure.

What about *lovemaking*? Would that help at all when the time came?

Dare he chance it?

"Am I nothing but a charitable endeavor, then, much like your cubs?"

Leave it to Francine to cut straight through the flesh and bone and get to the heart of the matter. "You are the most vexing female I have ever had the fortune to meet." His staff thrust against his breeches so fiercely he almost didn't care whether someone chanced upon them. Then she'd have to marry him in truth—and if *that* wasn't the most asinine notion he'd had, he didn't know what was. "If you did start out as a 'charitable endeavor', you have quickly turned into something else entirely."

Blast! This is what he had to guard against. He couldn't develop bloody *tender feelings* for the chit. He damn well knew better.

"Your eyes are glowing again," she commented, staring at him with a rapt expression. "Like sunset upon the ocean. It is as if they change color when—"

"I am sure you are quite mistaken." *S-E-X*. It's about sex, he reminded himself, massaging the flesh of her arse so firmly she groaned. *Sex.*

Getting sex whenever he wanted it, certainly when he needed it, to enable him to fight off the feral urges that would soon be rising to the fore. If they weren't already. At that very moment, his blood sizzled, heating his veins and increasing the latent power that always hovered beneath the surface. Whether the cause was irritation with himself or desire for her—or the need to purge tonight's atrocious knowledge from his mind if only for a brief while—he wasn't sure and chose not to contemplate further.

He ran his tongue along the bottom edge of his teeth. Smooth. It wasn't *Felis leo* burning in him. It was *him* burning for *her*. Blast her not-so-innocent charms.

"Come." He jerked his head from her hold, released her from his, set her gown to rights and caught her ungloved hand. "I am taking you now."

"Where?"

"The first private place I can locate."

<hr>

WHICH HAPPENED to be a secluded alcove, hidden from view by nothing more than a long velvet drape. The olive curtain was the only thing that separated them from the mass downstairs listening to the professional musicians. Erasmus led her behind the drape and secured it, giving them a measure of privacy, however precarious.

In the instant before they were enshrouded in darkness, Francine glimpsed a ceiling-high window centered in the alcove; it, too, was draped. So no light from that quarter. Standing just inside the curtain, she huddled, waiting. *Needing.*

Pushing back anxiety that rose like a spectre, ready to snaffle her wits, send her huddling. Oh, not because of what she suspected they were about to do but because it was as black as pitch.

She hated total darkness. So very absolute when

one was indoors and not outside among nature's nurturing presence... Where the sounds of birds, bugs and breezes kept one company.

Listen. You're not remotely alone.

The soothing sounds from the quartet vied with the choppy cadence of her overly loud breathing as sexual awareness competed with inane fear.

Clothing rustled. Fabric whispered against skin. Something dropped. His cravat? Maybe his tailcoat? *What* was he removing?

So much easier to concentrate on that, on *him*, than the idea of being alone. In the dark.

"Francine." His low, soothing murmur threatened to quiet the fretful apprehension that endangered her peace when darkness hovered and obscurity loomed.

Again, he rasped her name, his warm hand cupping one side of her face, stilling the silly terrors further.

"You really cannot see in the dark at all, can you?" he asked in a low voice.

"Nay, I cannot," she whispered back. "Why?"

"Because I am standing in front of you, stripped nude. And you have not flinched."

"Noooo. Really?" Shock, dismay, the sharp bite of excitement, all rivaled for superiority. Excitement won heartily and she took a small step forward. "Naked— Completely? *Here?*"

"You look dumbfounded, my little dumbwaiter," he laughed softly. "And nay, not here. Not completely. I am not that far gone, not yet, however much I might wish it were so. But my waistcoat is undone, my breeches unfastened and yet you do not seem inclined to join me."

"One moment." No other prompting needed, she turned toward the remembered wall, carefully pulled the strings of her reticule off her arm, bent at the knees and flailed with her outstretched hand until she found the solid surface, placing her small bag upon the floor, along with the glove he'd stripped off.

Standing, she angled back toward his heat and lifted her still-gloved hand, encountering his hard chest, covered in nothing more than his thin shirt. "I am inclined. Very much so."

As though her touch lit the flame, embers in his unique eyes flared to life, set them afire. She imagined the radiance from his glowing eyes enabled her to see, him at least—if not their surroundings.

Which was patently ridiculous! Or was it?

Because as Erasmus began peeling the glove down her arm, it was as though she watched him watching her... She most assuredly felt her heart turn over in her chest at the sensual journey he made of removing a simple evening glove, journeying the fine linen from her elbow to her fingertips with exquisite attention to detail, allowing his touch to linger over every portion of skin he exposed. How was it his touch upon her mere arm caused the moisture in her mouth to evaporate? And to accumulate lower, directly between her thighs?

She licked lips gone dry and forced herself to remain still, no matter how part of her wanted to rip the curtain from its moorings and flood light into their tiny alcove so she could see every bit of this encounter, not just the fanciful visions she no doubt embellished in her mind.

"What about your spectacles?" he asked in a

hushed tone, stripping the glove off completely. "You're wearing them now. Do they not aid your vision?"

The tingle that had begun in her fingertips made its way down to her toes, which curled in her slippers. Had he said something? All she could think about was the nearness of his chest. The heat now assaulting her fingers. "Hmmm?"

"Your spectacles," he reminded with a light laugh, bending to kiss the newly exposed crease of her elbow.

Her entire arm caught fire. "They do not prove sufficiently helpful, not in dim light."

He lifted his shirt and placed both of her bare palms against the muscles cording his stomach. They twitched under her touch. Hard as iron, warm as a forge. Her fingers flexed, tracing the delineations.

"Touching is better than seeing," she whispered, closing her eyes to better envisage every heated second. The music and mood created by the beautiful strings wafted up and around them, creating a bewitching space. A place transported far away from the small nook in a large London home and into an enthralling escape, one inhabited by no one save the two of them.

Erasmus shifted, grasping her wrists. "A padded bench is two steps to your right."

He led her to it and sat down. When she moved to do the same, he stopped her with a gentle touch to her waist. "Not yet. Remove your gown."

She stood transfixed, unable to move, anticipation, longing—a level of boldness she'd never known—surging through her at his nearness, at the certainty of what they were about to do. Knowing their proximity to the other guests, how very forbidden their actions, only heightened her desire.

"Francine?" His voice firmed. "Your gown. I want it off tonight."

"You cannot expect me to do that here!" Though a wicked part of her wanted desperately to comply...

His hand settled heavily upon her hip. "You promised to obey me. In all things—"

"I never!" Her lady bits throbbed at his nearness. She wanted to jump naked into his arms and thwack him all at once.

"Shhh," he cautioned, nuzzling his face into the modest cleavage left exposed by her neckline. "In all things pertaining to the physical aspect of our agreement, I was about to add."

Had she promised that? His breath was hot. Whiskers abraded her chest. Her nipples ached. "Are you going to kiss my bosom?"

She felt him shake with laughter, the rapscallion. He held her still when she would have jerked away and thwacked him after all.

"You are so damn innocent," he said into the valley between her breasts, barely suppressing his mirth.

"I am not. I already told you." It was an effort to keep her tone low. She was starting to sweat, their innocuous little space quickly becoming hot and sultry. "Especially not after what we did last night—"

"What we will do again now if you will only acquiesce and obey." His hands slid to her back, over her gown, where he proceeded to trace a path down every vertebra of her spine, starting from her nape and stopping only when he reached the sensitive indentation leading to her bottom. He palmed the fleshy area, squeezed her backside, pressing the fabric inward with his lower fingers. "Unless you are overly chafed. *Here.*" His fingers snagged against the delicate fabric as he urged them deeper between her legs. "Are you?"

"How can you ask such a thing out loud?" she said by way of distraction. She wasn't about to confess how very tender she was nor let such a thing stop her, not when his touch only increased how aroused, how moist and *swollen* her netherlands felt. Staunchly refusing to acknowledge any of that or how trembly he made her, she stiffened her knees. "Nay, not sore at all."

"Liar," he laughed softly. "For shame, Francine. 'Tis totally against your word."

"All right. Yes, but not *too* sore."

He kissed each of her breasts through her gown. "My hearing's beyond excellent. No one will approach within thirty paces without my knowing. And aye, I am going to lick and suck on your *bosom.* Now take your blasted dress off before I rip—"

Francine leapt to obey. At the promise of his lips upon her flesh, her gown fairly flew off, landing somewhere in the dark magical space, leaving her in shift, stays, stockings and slippers. She balanced her hands upon his shoulders, feeling skin and cloth where his shirt had parted and she began to explore him, touching his collarbone, his neck...

The music grew louder, gaining in tempo, a swift barrage of melodious notes that filled the air, further insulating them from the realities of life occurring beyond their private haven.

· · ·

THAT WAS A SURPRISE. So, his brave, bold lass found utter darkness unsettling?

Yet another reason you ought not be dallying with her. Your cursed soul is nothing if not dark.

Yet dally he damn well would.

Did he not deserve the solace, the escape her presence afforded, if not forever, then for a few precious moments? For his sanity, if not his life.

Selfish, man.

Damn necessary.

He gripped her waist harder, held on tight to both his conviction and his woman, lest his conscience gain the upper hand.

After the mews, the sordid *news*, he needed oblivion as he'd never needed before.

And damn his rotten soul, for the next few minutes, he would *take*.

And if you scare her off for real this time?

Then so much the better.

Beyond determined, Blakely swung one leg over, sitting astride the bench, forcing his hold to gentle, calling on his human will to temper the maelstrom of agonizing desperation tied up with want and need.

Barely shielded by her shift, thrust upward by her stays, the tops of her breasts jiggled in front of him as her fingertips danced across his jaw, his cheeks, along his nose—

Putting his olfactory senses on alert. "I smell dirt on your person." Not the earthy, sunshine scent she always exuded. "Dirt."

Her touch stumbled to a halt above his eyebrows.

She jerked back, taking those tempting mounds

farther from his mouth. "Are you saying that I'm *dirty*? That I stink? I washed just before—"

"Nay, sweetheart. As always, I think you smell divine. I'm talk of literal earth. Soil." Clean and fresh, unspoilt by city refuse.

She drifted back, closer, as he spoke. "After you left, I did some weeding." Which explained much. "'Twas that or listen to Aunt Prudence complain about your spontaneous—"

"Hush now. When we are together, like so, I would rather that woman not cross either of our minds."

"Agreed." The word breezed from her lips as gently as a butterfly might land upon a petal. Her hands fluttered about his shoulders before going round his neck, her nails digging in—exquisitely so—above his nape. "Consider thoughts of anyone other than you banished henceforth."

He pulled her shift down and feasted on the glorious sight. "By God, Francine, you might not be able to see well at night but you, my dear, are a vision."

Her sigh of pleasure rewarded the compliment but he sought other bounty. He cupped both of her breasts, pushing them toward each other. A noticeable delineation crossed both creamy globes, the upper swells several shades darker than the flesh below. Just how much time did she spend outdoors? The milk-white skin led directly to her hard-tipped rosy nipples.

His thumbs circled the stiff points, fingernails edged over the nubby flesh. He meant to tell her what she was missing, describe how she looked to him. He intended to, if only he could find the words...

"Oh." She pushed herself into his hands and sank

her fingers deeper into his hair. He wanted to tell her how *her* nails digging into his scalp felt better than they should, how satisfaction roared through him when she shuffled ever closer, bringing her breasts to his lips—which he proceeded to take full advantage of, flicking his tongue over the invitation of one nipple.

He wanted to tell her how the curious juxtaposition of *innocent seductress* fired his blood in a way he'd never experienced. Most of all, he wanted to describe how her demure blonde ringlets had fallen free in her haste to remove her gown, how the loose curls cascaded down the sides of her neck and made her the most beautiful thing he'd ever seen.

He wanted to tell her all those things. But he couldn't.

His lips were occupied.

"Umm. I, um, like to garden," she puffed over his head, just the lightest of sounds. "And dirt...you—*ah*—know goes along with...umm..."

His tongue swirled around the puckered flesh, drawing more moans of appreciation from the delight who bewitched him so. Her beauty—her beauteous reactions to him—helping blot out the horror he'd discovered a few weeks ago and revisited tonight.

"Mmm. Herbs and such," she gasped. Her nails scraped along his scalp, raising his hair, his desire. "Plants and...um, *passion*."

Stifling a growl, he drew upon her breast, sucking the appetizing tip into his mouth and drawing hard. His nostrils flared. The womanly scent of her cream overrode the remnants of dandelion and fennel he'd just identified.

Heated petticoat or further discussion on garden plants?

Not much of a dilemma, was it? He released her breast and rolled the damp bead between his thumb and forefinger while his other hand went to his fall. He needed to climax, to discharge his seed before he bent her over and forgot himself. "Stand over my face."

Ignoring her startled gasp, he shuffled her back and scooted forward till he could recline upon the settee. He was still in control, by damn, and it was going to stay that way. "*Now*."

Using her hands to guide her, she sketched her way up his body with a tortuous precision that left him gritting his teeth and wishing to God he'd never freed his blasted erection. Too blame slow for him but so elegantly, he didn't have the heart to tell her to hasten.

When she reached his shoulders, she carefully arranged one leg over his chest, bracing her knee next to his head. "Do you mean like this?"

Her scent surrounded him. Near his face, her velvet slit pulsed, glistening with moisture. He could practically hear the heartbeat reverberating between her thighs. His pelvis contracted, instinctively rising up, his cock seeking her heat, but he tamped down the urge to plow into her. He wasn't an animal—not tonight anyway.

But his blood felt like liquid fire rushing through his veins, burning him from the inside out. And he needed her release to douse the flames.

"Hold this." Blakely pushed her shift to her waist. He spread his hands on her inner thighs. "Do not make a sound."

He angled his head and surged upward, latching on to the saturated folds, licking the swollen flesh, eating the very heart of her—and tasting heaven.

He heard her breath catch, the tiny murmurs she couldn't completely stifle. He felt her thighs quivering, drank the wash of desire that flitted past his lips and realized he'd never experienced anything so pure. So perfect as Francine's passion. *For him.*

Her respiration increased and her hips started thrashing, spreading her essence over his mouth and chin. She was almost there. How he wanted to join her. His erection was straining. Rigid. Needing to feel the heated welcome of her body.

He thrust his tongue higher, almost wishing he didn't want her so fiercely. That she didn't taste so blasted innocent. So much for describing what she looked like, for telling her how the toasted skin of her arms and upper chest tantalized him...confessing how the reflected candlelight shining beneath the curtain glinted off her pale hair, creating a halo about her head.

Making her look like an angel. His angel. Cast out from heaven to save him from his cursed existence.

But he couldn't tell her those things. Not and maintain his sanity.

So he growled into her slick opening. Frustrated. Exhilarated.

Hearing her whimpers grow louder, knowing if he didn't do something soon, she was going to shout the curtain down, he took one final swallow and reached between her legs to plunder her wet slit with his hand. She flinched and trembled above him.

Her thick honey dripped down, coating his fingers. He teased the top of her treasure with his tongue and removed his hand to clutch his erection, wrapping his crevice-warmed fingers around his shaft.

He grunted at the sensation and flicked his tongue over her pearled flesh as swiftly as he could. His thoughts flew faster than his tongue. There was no way he'd trust himself to pull out. Not tonight, when the wanting of her was like a fever in his blood. Maybe later, before he took her home. But for now...

Stroking himself, he spread her thick heat along his cock, feeling his ballocks draw up, his anus clench, his pelvis jerk upward, forging his rod through the tight grip of his fingers while his tongue continued its foray into paradise.

Francine bent forward and shoved one fist against her mouth, muffling her cries. He looked up, past her bunched shift, past her exposed and pouty-tipped breasts, to her face. He saw the look of wonder she couldn't hide—didn't try to.

And he exploded, coming so hard, so fast, semen shot from his cock before he could cover it.

To keep from roaring his frustration—his satisfaction—he sucked one side of her labia into his mouth and bit down with his lips, loving her moan of surprise.

His cock jerked twice more. The proof of his eruption oozed past his hand and over his abdomen and still he loved her with his mouth, each one of her tiny squeals spurring him on.

After one last squeeze along his shaft, he unfurled his hand and brought it to her lips. She sucked two fingers into her mouth, hummed and flailed her juicy flesh over his jaw. He slid his other hand to the crevice of her buttocks. Edging between, he rimmed the tight ring. It opened, then squeezed shut against the pad of his finger.

His cock strained toward her in response.

The only warning he had of Francine's orgastic onslaught was the sudden tensing of her entire body. Then she screamed around his fingers and melted, every muscle going limp as she flooded his mouth with her release.

The roar of the applause below masked her throaty cries, her shouted, "Erasmus!"

And damned if he didn't climax again.

9

HORRID HORRORS OF HORRIBLE HUMIDITY

Rowden House, London, Thursday (June 18), 1812

DEAREST KAT—

I trust this letter will find you exceptionally well. Although, it feels as though I have been waiting an age to hear from you, I vow, I cannot let yet another day expire before taking pen to page and sharing my exciting news.

In truth, I stand (or rather, <u>sit</u>) awed that I managed to delay this long, but in addition to needing time to lapse, so that I no longer felt quite in such a dreamlike state as to question the authenticity of what continues to occur around me, I also needed time to help order my disorderly thoughts. Yet the more I mentally ramble about, the less I believe this has proved the case!

Let us not forget, the only way to ensure my letters get posted timely, is to do so myself, and not rely on one of my aunt's servants. Though Burford can be trusted explicitly, too many of them are in her pocket, and report any little infraction. So now that they—and she—have taken themselves off for a short holiday, I can be free!

Free with my time. With my correspondence. Free to indulge myself by divulging the most intimate of details that I cannot imagine confiding to <u>anyone</u> else. Not even young Temperance, though I profess a gladness of heart to impart that she and I are slowly—out of eyesight and earshot of her mother and sister—becoming close once again.

But enough of that. Oh, dearest, I miss you so! When <u>will</u> your wretched husband bring you back to London? Tell him for me, if you would, that another short visit is all I ask —though a <u>long</u> one would prove a thousand times better.

I cannot believe so many months have gone by with nary a note to mark their passing. But neither can I quite believe what I write you next...

What I ask.

About things of an <u>intimate</u> nature.(I am quite certain I must be the most wicked lady in all of London, for what I'm about to share—and with such giddy abandon too!)

Kat, when we were but fifteen, laughing together, thinking about potential beaus and our upcoming comeouts, could either of us <u>ever</u> have imagined how differently things would have evolved? For us both...

Nay. I shall not go looking backward, but ever onward. (You taught me that.)

Now, find yourself a quiet spot, candles if you need, for I intend this to be a long and salacious, mayhap even gossipy, letter, full of all manner of exciting, confidential tidbits whereupon I shall not finish until asking you <u>all</u> sorts of questions about relations. Relations between men and women!

Faugh! Once again I ramble ahead of myself...

———————◦———————

A SOFT KNOCK upon the already open morning room door, not quite audible over the tumultuous downpour beyond the windows, did not prove sufficient to capture Francine's attention.

Not from the onerous task at hand—untangling yesterday's pathetic pictorial efforts in thread.

Nor from the tempest railing just a few feet from her comfortable perch upon her aunt's favorite settee. Which is precisely *why* Francine had chosen to make herself *comfortable* on it.

The dark sky and thick clouds beyond the seldom-used furniture obscured the sun to such a degree that the multiple candle flames surrounding her (many more than would be lit had her aunt been in residence), while not replacing the precious sunlight, at least brightened the room from its meager state prior.

Overlooking the informal gardens as it did prompted Francine to use the space whenever she could. Her preference for this room—when her aunt was away—certainly had nothing whatsoever to do with Aunt Prudence's stingy use of it, forbidding her daughters and Francine from enjoying the serene setting. No matter that she herself usually slept far too late to ever savor the dawn of a new day or witness the colorful, vibrant plants reaching toward nature's mothering warmth as the sun rose from the east.

But not today. No precious sunlight today, neither

early dawn nor after nuncheon, a quick glance out the rattling window confirmed.

Nuncheon. What a pitiful meal that had been, poor Cook floundering when everything she had prepared, along with every transportable kitchen store, had been nabbed by her aunt and cousins before they took off on their jaunt. And on a public coach, no less. Poor horses, forced to trudge miles on a day like today. They were to be pitied—if not the passengers, who made the choice of traipsing through the mire.

Outside. How *she*'d rather be on the other side of the rain-lashed windows, palms deep in the earth, coaxing her summer seedlings along. Of a certainty, despite the mud, rivulets and thunder, how she'd rather be anywhere other than "occupying herself as a well-bred lady ought": fingers knotted in the woven mess of yesterday's unproductive efforts, attempting to untangle what had become of her threads.

Three days.

She tried not to groan at the thought.

Three days now that she'd not seen Erasmus, likely three more before she would, given how his trip to his country estate was expected to last five or six, "a sennight at most" he'd promised when last they'd parted.

After all their efforts establishing themselves as an affianced couple via frequent public appearances these past weeks, the dear man had likely relished his steward's letter requesting his presence. 'Twas no doubt relieved for the valid reason to avoid Francine's altogether unpleasant aunt altogether. She chuckled at the wordplay, however uninspiring.

"At least that takes my mind off wanting to pillory the steward for stealing away my exciting betrothed," she muttered, frantic fingers making little if any progress against the stubborn tangles.

Exciting. Only one of a handful of words she'd used in the long letter composed to her dearest friend back home. Katherina, the only childhood friend she'd maintained any regular correspondence with since her reluctant relocation to London.

Kat had been married for three years now, still without issue, poor dear, and...well...

Well, now that Francine was finally engaged? Finally *engaging* in her own clandestine activities—stolen kisses, brief touches and heated looks aplenty, if not the significantly more she'd rather. Well, Francine found that she *had* to tell someone. Had multiple topics to question her friend on, both about things she and her betrothed had done together—and several they hadn't but ones she wondered about all the same.

Who better than to confide in except her married bosom friend?

"There!" Finally. The worst knot came free, giving Francine a chance to stretch as she pulled the long thread out, her thoughts reluctantly turning to her aunt.

Despite her begrudgingly obsequious behavior toward Lord Blakely, now that he'd ferreted out her secrets, Aunt Prudence had been quite the stickler when it came to observing the proprieties. Almost as though she'd resigned herself to having her niece marry a nobleman not of her choosing—not a gambling cohort, more like—and now that he'd been "secured", in a manner of speaking, she became determined to behave how a true guardian should.

To the point that Francine had spent far less time—alone—with him than she'd hoped. Or expected. "Leastwise he's not here to see the disaster that has become my hair."

Measly solace, that, with the townhouse unaccountably still—normally a boon but not with the wretched storms keeping her confined inside for the second day in a row. Boredom had set in. The dreaded ennui, worse than any she'd ever known.

Time with Erasmus had bestowed such a generous glimpse of pure independence, and she was fiendishly resentful at having it summarily stripped.

At a light yet persistent knocking and slightly louder throat-clear, she lifted her head toward the open door and found their butler, patiently waiting for her head to come down out of the clouds and acknowledge his presence. With so few beings currently in residence, at least she knew who it was, never mind that she couldn't see him well, not through the smudge on her left spectacle, nor even the clear glass of her right, not after concentrating up close for so long.

"Aye, Mr. Burford? Have you come with fortuitous news, perhaps?"

The always pink-cheeked, rotund man put her in mind of an overweight yet spry, nearly silent cherub. Since encountering each other's unguarded expressions when one of her cousins spouted something erroneous, then again when the other used a jolter-headed version of a word, they'd begun exchanging pointed looks upon said occurrences and had become quite the allies.

Whether smiling over ridiculous utterances, compliments of one of her relatives, or exchanging between themselves a handful of grammatically flawless sentences in passing, she felt a true kinship with the quiet servant. "You have ordered off the rain clouds as I requested, is that it?"

"Aye, my lady. Ordered as directed. I trust they will be trouncing off to the south in moments. Told yon sun to rear its beaming head seconds after."

"Excellent news, my good sir. You are to be commended for such outstanding butlering, Mr. B." Though she couldn't see it—or him—worth a farthing, not after focusing on untangling her dreadful coil of threads this last hour, she knew that he smiled. For it shone in his voice. "I shall order you an increase in salary, shall I, the next time I see my aunt?"

He couldn't muffle his snort of laughter at that absurdity. "Always pleased to please my lady. *Ahem.* Lady Francine." His voice got louder and deeper, somewhat languid—his Official Butlering Voice, they'd jested. "My lady, you have a visitor."

A visitor?

A visitor!

She scrambled to her feet, dislodging her detangling efforts to the floor. No time to retrieve the hash! Not when her hands were frantically trying to tame hair that frizzed and frazzled and flew every which way when it rained for hours on end, and a maid wasn't there to lend talents to taming the vexing disarray.

Her agitated motions to curb the frizzled mess knocked her spectacles off.

While her hands valiantly attempted to salvage some semblance of presentability, the rest of her had frozen in place.

"Who?" It came out a squeak, for no one ever visited *her*, not when her aunt wasn't home arranging callers and lives. Not since Katherina had gotten married and stopped coming to London as well. Not when the knocker had been taken off the front door, signaling the family was not at home to receive afternoon callers.

She blinked, trying fruitlessly to focus in the gloom, only to see Mr. Burford turn his attention beyond the room and nod to some unseen person. "My lord."

Then back to her, making a sharp, make-haste motion with his hand, hidden from the approaching visitor.

"Lord Blakely," Burford announced in his intentionally somber tone, causing Francine's heart to leap, her stomach to drop and her arms to fall to her side—as her unruly hair spoke volumes, defying her every attempt at obedience.

"Erasmus," whispered from her, the casual address she shouldn't speak in front of others escaping on a sigh. Then her hands lifted again, patting, tugging, praying for some semblance of muffled order to magically appear upon her blighted head.

ENJOYING every word of the curious and extended exchange between his betrothed and the servant,

Blakely paused at the doorway until Burford called his name much louder than necessary, as though he wanted Francine unaware of how close he'd been. How much he'd overheard. How much he'd *seen.*

During the hours of hard riding yesterday and the agonizing events of last evening he was determined to blot from his mind... During the estate and family matters he'd seen efficiently to beforehand, permitting his earlier-than-expected return...

During all that time, he'd imagined the delighted pleasure on her face when he surprised her with his early arrival.

Yet never could he have prepared himself for the sight that greeted him now. How the perfect blonde ringlets had transformed into an anything-but-angelic halo of chaos. Rioting about her pretty but flushed face as though in battle. Giving her an untamed look, an extraordinary wildness that touched him in an unforeseen manner.

Nor could he have prepared himself for the way her hushed little moan of his name, *Erasmus*, would sound like the sun singing to his dark soul. How inviting her to use it weeks ago would weaken the barriers he normally kept fortified.

How her very presence constantly drew him forth, inviting him to be as free and easy with her, with himself...

How she alone would claw her way inside and start to wind around his chest—

Nay. Erasmus shook himself. Definitely not in the vicinity of the cold, unfeeling organ that resided therein.

Definitely *not* his chest.

His sword.

Of a sudden, quite unexpectedly given his plans for the day, he yearned for her to be his scabbard, yearned to throw her down, toss up her skirts and sheathe himself in the warm, wet welcome he knew would be waiting.

Despite the fetching tumult tempting his fingers to rumple it further, her rattled gaze arrested the ardent impulses. Subdued the growing need.

Eyes wide and startlingly bright from within the center of the white-gold mane of hair all a rumpus about her face. Eyes conveying surprise—and sheer embarrassment if he read her right.

'Twas a struggle, indeed, to keep the smile from his countenance. But one he mastered, lest she think he was laughing at her. It was a sheer delight, seeing this new side of her, one not completely composed. One he suspected few were fortunate to witness.

He felt quite...*honored* at the realization. No matter how peculiar—that seeing her completely undone should bring him *satisfaction* of all things

Then she blinked, slowly...once...twice...and all was erased. Replaced with—now that he'd glimpsed the truth—a bamboozle of poise.

"My lord. Welcome." She even gave a perfect curtsy, not too deep nor too shallow, just contrived enough that he knew he had ascertained her embarrassment accurately.

"Lady Francine, shall I send for..."

Behind him, the butler's words dwindled, distracting Francine and tugging her gaze from his.

Erasmus shifted so he could observe them both.

"No need," she told the other man calmly. "Lord Blakely has called before. As my betrothed, there exists no harm in us spending a short time alone."

The butler inclined his head. "As you wish, my lady. Refreshments, then? Shall I send those in?"

She hesitated, so Erasmus stepped in, removing his gloves and placing them, along with his already discarded overcoat and hat, upon a small table near the door.

"Burford, thank you, but nay," he told the man. "Refreshments are not needed. Just leave us please, for —" He snared her overly bright gaze, doubtful he successfully banked the hunger gleaming from his. "For ten minutes. No longer."

"Aye, my lord. As you say." Responding to the authority of a peer who knew how to wield it, Burford bowed out the door, silently tugging it closed behind him—all but three inches.

How very unexpected—Lady Francine, the most serene, pulled-together female of his London acquaintance, mortified at being caught not quite at her best?

A sense of ease expanded his chest once they were blessedly alone, for 'twas almost a balm to discover his perfect intended wasn't. Wasn't quite the sublime English miss she presented outwardly to all and sundry, had her own little foibles, in fact. Lord knew he had his.

Made her seem a little more...approachable. Keepable, even.

Don't go there, you knave. Keepable? 'Tis not even a word.

He slammed the lid on the interruption.

Did he chaff her over it? Tease her? Put her at ease?

Or did he do the opposite...

Attempt to teach her a lesson for not being completely truthful with him, never mind that it was her own feelings this time, not some bounder of a tale perpetuating fabricated lists of other men?

A snarl threatened at the thought of other fellows sniffing around her. A twitch of his shoulders and he shook it off.

She hadn't moved, looked like a figurine, or two halves of one:

The perfect half? Her day dress of ecru and apricot; her slippers and the glimpse of peach-colored stocking (only seen as the back of her skirt had caught on the settee behind her, leaving the hem angled, did she but know it, and exposing an enticing amount of ankle and lower leg).

The other half? Above the lace-edged, puffed sleeves and straight-across neckline?

Above the elegant cameo brooch he'd given her as a private betrothal present, it being more to his taste than the gaudy array of diamonds and emeralds he'd handed over publicly to further cement their agreement in her aunt's eyes...

The beautifully carved shell, portraying some Roman goddess—he knew not which—bedecked with little dangling bits and bobbles that she'd fastened around her neck with a ribbon... That she wore, even now, when she had no expectation of seeing him today?

The disheveled portion above that?

Called to him more than enticing ankles ever could. For 'twas the rapid heartbeat pulsing in her neck, the swift intakes of air, the breathless way she held his gaze, left off her frenzied smoothing of hair and dress. And waited.

Ah. This should prove interesting.

You're not truly becoming interested, *are you? Attached?*

All right, then, not interesting, *per se*. Amusing.

Time to amuse himself. That's all this was. *Amusing* himself with a pleasant frolic before the urges commanded his full attention.

Time to test her.

But first, to ascertain whether to anticipate an annoying visit from her aunt. "What, no chaperone today?"

"Not today, for we have limited staff at the moment."

"Hmmm." Limited staff? When it wasn't as though he'd ever noticed a multitude of servants underfoot during his prior visits. Was her uncle having solvency issues? Could the man not afford to pay his people? Erasmus shrugged broad shoulders that seemed to carry more weight with every passing year. Something to have his man of affairs explore... Whether or not the family had more pressing issues than her aunt's gambling travails.

"Only ten minutes?" Fuddled by his arrival she might be, but her disappointment wasn't masked in the least. Her utter frustration.

So, despite the lukewarm reception, she wanted far longer together? Fighting the flare of heat that realization brought, he glanced behind him at the door that had been left ajar.

With a self-satisfied smile, he stepped back and, with one finger, pushed it the rest of the way shut, just short of clicking.

When he turned back to her, he intentionally made his voice brusque. "Retrieve your embroidery from the floor. Spectacles also."

Mayhap she'd not seen this side of him sufficiently, for she hesitated. Mayhap, in her disharmony of the moment, she simply forgot that part of their agreement was her complete obedience. Regardless, he expected compliance. "Now, my dear. Place them on the table there in front— Nay, not your spectacles. Keep those with you for you will no doubt need them later. Your pocket is fine.

"Now come here." As she slowly obeyed, portraying self-assurance in every line—that wasn't her hair—his pride in her grew. She really was a fetching little thing.

Little? She's taller than nearly every woman you've ever been with.

Aye, but trimmer too. Almost ethereal at times, with that controlled comportment that so drew him.

She stopped four feet away.

"Nay. *Here.*" He lowered his gaze to the floor in front of his polished boots and waited until she approached, stood directly before him, still holding his gaze.

Their proximity magnified everything he already sensed about her.

Mortification had been replaced, not with trepidation or even hesitation. But with desire. He caught it in the molten turn to her normally sedate blue eyes, in the way her mouth parted slightly, tongue grazing her bottom lip. Scented it, some unique attraction reaching out from her toward him, luring him closer. Physically, yes. But on other levels as well.

Ones he shouldn't admit, not even to himself—not if he was to fulfill the duties he'd been tasked with.

You can also scent it from betwixt her legs. Why don't you—

Nearly biting his tongue off in an effort to thwart that direction of thinking—to completely realign the current tenor of the day—he had to unclench his teeth to say what he'd come here for in the first place, as silkily as he could manage, "Retrieve your cloak—and your cousins, if you must—for I have come to escort you on a surprise outing."

HER MARAUDING HAIR muffled as well as she could manage, Francine stood before Erasmus, praying the trembling of her knees wasn't evident.

"An outing?" When all she really wanted to do was launch herself in his arms. When all she really wanted to say was, *You look exhausted. Marvelous. Like manna to my starved senses.* Instead...

"'Tis wonderful to see you. Especially so much sooner than expected." That serene voice was hers? Even given how he'd just ordered her about, bent her to his will with nary a peep of protest ushered from her lips? Caused a riotous tumult to storm through her when he firmed his voice, his expression, yet couldn't stifle the caring in his gaze? "I trust your trip proved a success?"

He made some sort of noise in his throat. A decided non-answer. To either question.

Lingering embarrassment shimmered through her, consumed by the yearning his nearness wrought. His eyes glittered down at her, intensifying the latter. "Erasmus?"

"This is quite becoming a habit, my dear. You care so little for your work that you discard it upon the ground?" He glanced behind her, at the table where she'd placed the fallen embroidery, then his gaze shifted back to capture hers. "Or is it my appearance that causes your efforts to leap from your lap?"

Heat flared anew across her cheeks. "I have, ah, trained it do tricks, you see."

One brow above the sable of his eyes arched at that. "As you would a dog?"

"Nay, for a dog is taught to jump *in* one's lap."

The sardonic tilt evened out as a subtle, pleased gleam took hold. "Though it demonstrates a decided lack of restraint upon the part of one who prides himself on that very quality, I vow, I cannot wait a moment longer to hold you. Come here."

His words were gruff; her delight boundless.

He caught her to him in a fierce hug that lifted her feet right off the ground.

After weeks as an engaged couple, one might think their attraction to each other would have waned. That the lift of spirits caused by hearing his deep voice or seeing his stern countenance might dwindle from a veritable vault of elevation to a mere nudge. One would be wrong.

His solid arms held her easily aloft, positioned her

face next to his for a quick nuzzle—his cheek against hers. She inhaled his invigorating presence clear down to her toes.

Giddy of a sudden, for he'd seen the monstrous beast her hair could become and hadn't run screaming in terror. Nor had he taunted her with jests as she'd suffered as a child. But more than that, he seemed so very pleased to see her again. And he was strong. Impressively so, to hold her long self aloft with nary a grunt.

Was there a better man anywhere?

"I cannot believe you're here! You dictatorial wretch, and after telling me you would likely be gone a sennight." She laughed, feet dangling in the air.

Her fingers stroked over one side of his face. Only the tips touched the angled perfection of one side whisker. The rest caressing soft skin. "My oh my, Erasmus, but your skin feels wickedly smooth today."

And warm. Inviting.

After strengthening the force of his hug for a moment, he released her, placing her carefully back on her feet—but kept her far closer than custom might dictate with one hand braced around her nape, his thumb caressing the back of her head. "Gratified, am I, that you noticed. I told Franklin 'twas time for a new blade."

Francine toed one of his shins with her right foot. "For shame. I have no doubt that Franklin himself suggested the new blade."

Completely unrepentant, he stepped back, out of toe-poking's way, and slid his hand from around her neck to clasp them both behind his back. He gave her a slight bow. "As to that, 'tis neither here nor there. I pay him well enough."

Franklin was her betrothed's most efficient valet. The man responsible for keeping Erasmus in such a fine twig. Today he wore midnight-blue pantaloons, rain-spattered—but still impressively shiny—Hessians, an embroidered waistcoat in ivory, and a burgundy tail-coat, with everything topped off by the most majestic neckcloth arrangement she'd yet to see grace his publicly haughty self.

For herself? She'd quickly ascertained the arrogant air was a pretense. A convincing one, to be sure. Though he might bluster about in front of others and make demands in public, in private? In private, when he wasn't trying her patience—and causing little darts of exciting unease to trample her midsection as he'd just done—he *could* be all that was considerate. Charming even, a time or four.

When she wasn't noticing something deeper, *darker*.

As she did now. Now that she'd moved beyond her initial surprise and hair-induced angst, she looked beyond the exhaustion and studied him. Noticed the polished veneer seemed just that—a little more forced, a tad less authentic. Noticed his increasing discomfiture the longer she stared.

He took another step back, shifted his regular russet-brown gaze of the moment (no glow in evidence) toward the rattling window—*brown* being such an insipid word to describe the deep luster of his eyes.

She followed his retreat, to better gauge his

response. "What is it? What has happened? Your trip home—did it not go as planned? Is your family well?"

He looked startled, though he tried to hide it, the depths of his rich, russet eyes more haunted than she'd seen in a long while.

"And pray, do not claim 'tis nothing," she instructed when his tongue dallied—giving his garret time to come up with a clanker, no doubt. "I can see something's occurred. Something that troubles you greatly. How may I be of assistance? Tell me, please."

He brought his arms around, clasped his hands together in front—a white-knuckled grip that gave him away.

"Erasmus?"

Seeing the direction of her gaze, he slid his fingers apart and made a great show of smoothing his already perfect attire. Then he retrieved his tall hat from where he'd placed it upon his arrival, and raised it between them like a metaphorical shield—then started worrying the brim. "'Tis nothing you can help with. Merely a trifle. Disregard it."

At least he didn't lie to her, deny that there was something going on. "Merely a *trifle*, hmm? My..." she challenged, not attempting to subdue her sarcasm, "you rumbled that out as though you mean it."

He gave her a condescending look that clobbered her over the head. "I most assuredly do. Leave my concerns to me." Whatever bothered him now was great indeed for him to draw up haughty and stiff with her, with no one else around to witness the charade.

He squeezed his eyes shut, gave his head a sharp shake, then blinked them open, giving her what—in another man—might be considered a contrite, almost apologetic look. "Please, my dear." His lungs expanded on a full inhale, contracted on his loud exhale. "Today is for you." His posture relaxed—as much as it could, with him nearly strangling the stuffing out of his poor, innocent hat brim. He gave her a tight smile. "I have been looking forward to delighting you with a certain excursion. Do not take that from me."

Not a trifle her aunt's plump posterior.

"Well, my lord, when you put it like that..." She strove to erase any evidence of confrontation from her countenance. "How may I assist you, then?"

"Grant me the pleasure of your company and think of nothing more than enjoying yourself without worrying over trifles, that is all I require. All I desire."

"Consider it done." *And consider my curiosity delayed, not forgotten.*

"Your cloak and cousins?" Back to his customary polish, now that she wasn't hounding him, she noticed, his fingers took to tapping lightly upon his hat instead of mangling it. "Mayhap an umbrella if you have one at hand? I can battle the storms well enough for you, but cannot block them sufficiently if we add another three to our number."

"I believe that can be arranged—the umbrella."

She let him have his way. She might want to share his burdens, feel an absurdly strong desire to ease them completely if she could, but she, more than most, recognized the value in keeping one's own counsel.

She'd respect his need for privacy. For now. Especially since he'd shaken off what worried him to give her a true smile, even if it didn't manage to completely mask the concern from his eyes. "And the others?" he queried. "Cloak and cousins?"

"In my room and in Brighton. Aunt Pru decided I had quite enough caused sufficient uproar with our precipitous announcement catching the collective *ton* off-guard and knocking her matrimonial plans for me askew. When Patience's betrothed suggested a holiday, she jumped, taking herself and my cousins off early yesterday." Indicating, the evening before, when she'd ordered the trunks brought round, 'twas Francine's duty to maintain things here. Alone. "She knows me not at all, if she considers leaving me here a punishment."

'Twas the most relaxed Francine had felt in ages, what with her uncle off on another trip which left Francine inhabiting the townhouse with the few servants who remained. The life of an independent woman could not come soon enough for her.

But that means no more surprise visits or unexpected outings from Lord Blakely.

The price one must pay for happiness...

Shaking off the maddening reminder, she asked, "Where are we off to? How shall I dress?"

"Do you not comprehend the meaning of surprise? You shall find out upon our arrival. Not a moment before. And your current attire"—he gestured from her neck to her feet, but not her head, she couldn't help but notice—"is more than adequate."

"Have I time to work a miracle and dress my hair?" 'Twas an exercise in restraint, to not reach upward and try to disguise the disaster she now inadvertently drew attention toward, but then, not wanting to leave him alone with whatever thoughts troubled him so, she suggested instead, "Or a bonnet, perhaps? That should tidy matters sufficiently." And swiftly.

"And spectacles—keep those with you," he called after her as she raced from the room. "It might be dim in places and I promise that you will want to see all you can."

1 0

THE MUMMY AND THE OTHER MARQUIS

——⊃●⊂——

DEAREST ERASMUS,

Now that we have confirmed, beyond wretched certainty, what happened to your father, God rest his tortured soul, I leave these letters for both you and your brother as I depart upon my own quest.

Please, Erasmus, heed me on this: do not attempt to follow me. Watch over yourself and our home. Watch out for your younger brother. Read these pages with diligence and care, committing all that resides within to memory.

Heed these warnings. Take the snippets of advice and build upon them.

Most of all, my dear boy, live your life.

Do not let the Dire Tenants set forth herein and the responsibilities your father now tasks you with to drain from you every ounce of joy.

Find love and your own redemption wherever, however —and from whomever—you may.

If my journey proves successful, I'll rejoin you both by next June, before either you or your cousin have to fight The Change on your own for the first time.

If it does not...

If I am not successful at what I now seek, at what I must do...

Then, forgive me, for I may be absent an indefinite amount of time. While I am away, I shall send my love hourly.

Your Loving Mama

(who must now ~~#### ### ### ####### ## ### ###### ############~~)

THE LAST LINE of script was scrawled through so many times as to be completely illegible. What had called to his mother sufficiently to take her from them?

To keep her away for long months, before sending yet another letter, this one telling him she'd found what she needed, and wouldn't be returning? Ever...

Hours earlier today, exhausted by the long night, needing a measure of solace once he returned home, Erasmus had eased his flat palm and outstretched fingers over the well-worn missive. The one he'd first seen bundled around the letters that had changed the course of his life once sufficient time—and tragedy—passed to the point that he believed.

Live your life.

His dear mother's counsel.

Live. His life.

Should he? Dare he?

But now...

With this latest revelation. Was it just a coincidence?

Or was it more. An omen?

A direct link? To his club.

A mere two blocks away.

A direct threat to the other women who worked there.

A direct threat to Francine.

⸺⸻◦⸻⸺

THE MOMENT they stepped inside the museum, his nose wrinkled. What was that? Peculiar smell for an exhibit advertised as: Flora of the Globe. Upon hearing of it, he'd known at once how much his unintended intended would appreciate such a thing. How he now had a legitimate reason to rush his business and race back to London.

But *ew*, what was that noxious scent? Nash would no doubt know in an instant, his brother's unparalleled beak putting even Erasmus's impressive one to shame.

Beside him, his lovely companion inhaled clear to her slippers. "Oh my, how lovely!"

"You do not notice anything...amiss?" Rotting?

She fairly beamed at him, then gave the muscles in his forearm, where her hand lightly rested, a quick, finger-clenching hug. "Only the fragrance of blooms not yet studied nor committed to memory. I declare, you most darling of men, your surprise is beyond thoughtful!"

He tried not to snort at that. "'Darling'? Please, my

dear, do not let such a rumor abound. 'Twould quite destroy my hard-earned disreputable reputation."

At his side, she fairly buzzed with the need to explore, but she stilled of a sudden and gazed up at him. "You know your secrets are safe with me, my lord. All of them."

When she stared intently at him just-so... When she left off with her usual lighthearted mien and became serious... When she calmly held his gaze as though peering into his soul, it never failed to raise his awareness of her and heighten his interest.

It should be raising your guard.

Yet still, underlining the perfume of the plants she found so intoxicating, that odd offal made his nose twitch. To clear his brain of the unwelcome odor, he flicked the much-needed bonnet to the side, then pushed it off altogether, letting the ribbons securing it beneath her chin do their job of keeping it from the floor.

"God's teeth and witches' tits, Francy, but you possess enough frizz to stuff a mattress."

"Francy?"

"Aye, an amalgam of fancy and your name." Something he'd thought of in the wee hours of the morning —when he should have been sleeping or pondering solutions to troubling thoughts, not indulging in arous-ing, *fanciful* ones. "Or does it bother you?"

"Though it is only one small S-sound away from Franny, it does not. Not in the least." She tilted that inviting, stubborn chin toward him. "Now, what was that you were saying about my head belonging between the sheets?"

He barked a laugh somewhere between a chuckle and a guffaw. "There is much of you I would like to see between the sheets, but that is neither here nor there today. Although, now that I think on it, is that not one of the few places we have yet to indulge?"

That frank speaking had her scrambling behind her back for the recalcitrant bonnet. Once she had it in her possession, she started patting the mess atop her head and narrowed her eyes at him, directing her gaze upward past her forehead. "You wretch, to remind me."

"Nay, not yet." He halted her frantic bonnet-dressing motions by shackling both her wrists in one hand while he leaned down, halting at the top of her head, to inhale her clean scent.

Ah, heather and sunshine. *Francine.*

"Erasmus. What are you—"

"Partial improvement." So he did it again, burying his nose in her disarrayed ringlets where they dangled just over one ear.

"Stop that, you knave," she giggled, if anything, coming up on her toes and arching her neck for even better access.

"Tickly?"

"Tingling."

"Mmmm."

Then she was off, dragging him hither and yon, exploring the wide variety of flowering plants and other specimens that had been brought in for the exhibit with a wild abandon that helped erase, at least for the first hour, the niggling worry that seemed to be his constant companion these days.

⎯⎯⎯◦⎯⎯⎯

HE'D BEEN RIGHT.

Only years of practice kept the gloat from his expression.

From the moment he'd brought his betrothed into her element, his little independent, scientifically minded miss had been reduced to one-word, chuckle-headed squeals of delight, marveling over the botany exhibits with all the enthusiasm of a child going sledding for the first time. "Brilliant! Prime! Zounds!"

While she'd flitted higgledy piggledy like a boosey butterfly from one specimen to another, exclaiming, reading the placards aloud, he'd drawn upon every ounce—every year—of experience at his disposal, perfecting the art of portraying sincere interest. Pretending.

Because for the first time—the only time—since they'd met, entertaining, wholly engaging Lady Francine, of the fashionable coils and unfashionable spectacles, did not command his full attention.

Not because he was bored.

Not because he tired of her and wanted to end their arrangement early—heaven forfend. In fact, he'd become quite fond of her innocent wonder over things he took for granted or never thought to notice. ("Erasmus, did you see this majestic leaf? Why, 'tis as wide as your forearm is long. Come, let me compare!")

Not because he wanted to be rid of her—perish the thought.

Because he feared for her life.

And not at his eventually clawed hands. Which made the worry triply concerning.

Last night at The Den—

He swallowed hard, forcing down the bile that rose at the images that churned to the surface once he cracked the lid off recent memories, allowed them to command more of his attention than he'd like...

THE PREVIOUS NIGHT

'TWAS LATE—OR early morning, depending upon how one viewed things—when Erasmus let himself into The Den via his covert passage.

The entrance that led straight to his private office by means of the *other* private office he used at times. This particular space disguised further by a small storage room. One complete with a secret door and corridor that let him access—or exit—his club without it being obvious.

Part of the beauty of owning more than one building along this street and leasing the portions adjacent to his club to a mercantile and a pair of apothecaries that shared a common storage section along the back and entertained customers during daytime hours only, which gave him further freedom.

With only the front portions of these businesses open to the public, the remainder reserved for merchandise and administrative concerns, 'twas easy enough to construct a connecting corridor between the buildings, to reserve the space leading to it for his personal use as part of the lease terms put forth by his solicitor.

Gave him the ability to come and go as he pleased, with no one the wiser, save Adam, the only other person with the keys—and permission—to use both.

Even the misters Worsley, Everett and Grimshaw, the proprietors of the neighboring enterprises, did not possess a key to his private area, or the wherewithal to know what all went on next door, in the hours their shops were closed, much less the means to access either.

He made his way through the darkened interior of Worsley's, no candle necessary given the sparse street lamps reflecting through the curtained front window, stepped around a stack of boxed inventory not yet received and blithely made his way to his office in The Den, locking each door behind him as a matter of habit. Ingrained caution and all that.

Travel weary but relieved to be home, he'd stopped off at his townhouse to let his coachman and carriage horses turn in for the night before hailing a rare hackney for himself. At nearly three in the morning, no sense rousing staff and equines to require another team be made ready.

Not when he expected naught but a brief report to ensure Adam fared well during his brief absence. Then 'twas straight to bed.

And the lovely, lively Francine a few hours after that...

A time or two in the last weeks he'd started to wonder whether he ought to be wooing her in truth.

But nay. Though more suited to him than he could imagine any other if he searched the world over,

Francine remained so blasted determined to gain her vaunted independence. Making sure to remind him once or twice a week that she hadn't changed her mind. Would jilt him as planned. That she valued her blighted freedom above all else.

Well, damn it.

What if he wanted her to value *him* above all else?

What if he'd come to care—and far more than was wise?

What if you come to destroy the one person you want a future with?

Aye. That exactly.

Hell. He had half a mind to stop being so free with his favors. *Ha. As if you could stop the sun from rising.*

Mayhap, though...

A little less frisking; a little more flirtation?

Satisfaction roared through him as he contemplated the notion.

Shaking off the distraction, however pleasant, he left his Den office and sauntered out onto the main floor, finding Adam at his command post, exactly where he'd expect to: the pulpit-type podium he'd sequestered from somewhere to act as his informal office. The ornate wooden platform, complete with open shelves, locked drawers and secret compartments, where he stood as gatekeeper and self-appointed Guardian to their exclusive, by-invitation-only club. Where his business partner and closest friend oversaw everything from membership to supply orders to the well-being of their working "ladies".

"Hey, stranger." Adam greeted him when he opened the office door. "Didn't expect you here for several more days." He took Erasmus's outstretched hand in a firm grip, exchanging a good shake before releasing to glance at his unusual timepiece. "Though I think you shortchanged yourself on a night or two's sleep to arrive home so quickly, it's good to see you back safe and sound."

"Even better to be returned." Erasmus gestured to the big room and pointed overhead. "How many are still here? Seems quieter than usual this time of night."

Adam checked his ever-present notebook, made a notation, then snapped it shut, a habit he'd developed when he discovered one of their patrons nosing around his notes. The "gentleman" had been escorted off the premises and invited never to return. "By my count, only eight remaining tonight. The five down here and three others upstairs. And it has been quiet—all night. From what I've gleaned, a couple of huge and competing society to-dos have drawn most of town before everyone heads to the country for the remainder of the summer."

A squeal came from the elevated platform across from their small nook.

"Well, quiet except for Lucy Mae's shrieks."

Adam, who always impressed him with his ability to remain unflappable in a crisis, might've gotten a little red around the ears. "That woman enjoys sex with a lusty abandon I never tire of hearing."

"Aye, that she does." Erasmus confirmed, having been on the receiving end of that *abandon* more than once himself. But not recently. Not since his lascivious interest had fixated on a sun-bronzed beauty whose adorably tilted chin just begged for kisses. "How about the rest of her crew? Are they still amusing clientele or have they retired for the night?"

Lucy Mae's Lusty Ladies. She might not be the oldest, but her loud, cock-sucking mouth and obvious enjoyment had earned her appreciation from the men and respect from the other women Erasmus liked to have on hand. Mostly tough, street-bred wenches who weren't averse to a bit of rough bed sport in exchange for a good time, a full belly, and significantly more renumeration than they would earn on the street or at a common bawdy house.

Regardless, the primary reason his club never lacked for eager, employable evening "ladies", Erasmus knew, was the safe place to reside during non-working hours he provided on the third level—exclusive to the women, the second floor being where they entertained club patrons who didn't want to perform, share, or be seen in the larger common area.

Adam consulted his notes before continuing. "Janie and Lizette are upstairs with Fullerton and Kendall, and young Anne's with Tate."

Ew. *Tate.* Only years of practice kept the revulsion from showing.

One of several challenges with courting unsavories, seeking to befriend and align to better oversee their activities and monitor any savage feline tendencies, was that after they turned five and twenty, and without a roar to be heard or a fluffy mane in sight, it often proved difficult—if nigh on impossible—to rid himself, and his club, of the rabble. Baron Tate was one such vermin.

Adam chin-nodded across from them, pointing to

the few people remaining. "Bunnie is keeping company with Lucy—"

Who happened to choose that very moment to traipse in front of them, dragging the hand of a disheveled lordling, the newly fortunate recipient of her attentions, over to one of the settees set up for the express purpose of illicit entertainment.

"I stand corrected. It seems Lucy Mae has found her own patron to pleasure."

And if Erasmus wasn't mistaken, she was also doing all she could to snare the interest of his friend. "There stands no rule against dallying with her if you have a mind to."

"Ah... No."

Hmm. Brief answer for his normally verbose friend. "Have you prepared that roster of members we discussed? Looked into finding an investigator to delve into anyone I'm not already familiar with?" Ascertain their family origins. With the goal of giving him a more narrow focus of who needed watching.

"Sure have. The tricky piece in all that is finding someone we can trust who's capable of providing what we need and, moreover, doing it *discreetly*." That went without saying. "The agency sent over two, but I wasn't favorably impressed with either."

"That surprises me. The agency comes well recommended."

"I tried to like them, but it wasn't happening. The first was too interested in trying to ogle the women. The second seemed more focused on pelting *me* with questions—and I was interviewing *him*. No. Neither struck me as particularly capable for our needs. Just mediocre. I choose not to settle."

"I agree with you on that. Not with lives at stake." And wasn't Adam proving as particular and pernickety as he himself would have?

"Yeah, if I don't think they'll do a better job than I could, we're not hiring them." Adam stretched his arms overhead from side to side, as though he, too, felt the weight of responsibility—which had never been Erasmus's intent.

When his arms came back down, Erasmus gripped one muscular forearm. "I do not consider this your problem. Trouble yourself no more—"

"You can't say that." Adam slipped his arm free and gestured widely. "I may not have come into this by any explicable means, but here I am and here I'll stay until my own quest is fulfilled. What's more, not only did you give me a home"—Adam had converted rooms into a space of his own in the basement level—"but you've given me purpose. And I'm not dealing with nearly the amount of shit you are."

That brought a grim smile.

"I'm good. Promise. Besides, I've got an appointment with another potential investigator tomorrow and one for early next week if needed."

"Fair enough. And for someone *not* interested in Lucy Mae, your gaze keeps seeking her out rather regularly."

That brought Adam's attention back to him. His mustache rolled as he pursed his lips. "Didn't say I wasn't interested. Just that I wouldn't have sex with her. Not while we both work here and I'm her boss."

"You, my friend, have some odd notions at times."

"Marsh and I do just fine. I prefer my bed partners to have fleas," he said, referring to the feline who shared the basement with Adam and had free roam of the place once they were locked up for the night. "Not esteedees."

Another of those strange words his friend sometimes muttered. Erasmus had learned his lesson about asking, tended to let them pass without comment these days. No need to borrow his friend's difficulties when he had enough of his own.

With only a light grunt, Adam slid over a packet of papers. "Here. These are the first four I've started looking into. Didn't want to wait." He tapped his notebook. "I've added another three to that—do you recall how Tyndale asked if he could invite his two cousins? Well, they showed up while you were gone, and brought a friend. He's an albino chap, seems cordial enough on the surface, but I don't know, there's something about his eyes that seem a bit peculiar." Adam drummed fingers on the podium and winked at Lucy Mae when she slurped off the spent penis of the gentleman she'd fetched mettle on remarkably quickly, her gaze immediately going to Adam as though to make sure he'd noticed.

Which he had.

Neither had he lost his train of thought. "But it might be nothing. The last thing I want to do is take aversion to someone harmless just because of how they appear on the surface."

Adam wasn't one to sense trouble from nothing. "Is

he here now? Mayhap I could meet him, take his measure myself."

"Good idea. I'd like to hear your take. But he left about an hour ago, so you'll—"

A cacophony erupted from the portal that led to the club's exterior, shielded from their inner sanctum by a manned entrance area.

The heavy door separating the two thumped hard against the wall when three men shoved through. His guard and two new hires racing straight toward him. Men he'd employed recently, to keep an eye on the club and its environs. "Lord Blakely! Mr. Nicholsen! Both of ye, make haste."

"Come quick!" the other shouted, pointing back the way they'd come. "There's another! The dogs are raising a rumpus—and the blood—'tis fearsome. Your missing Diana, I be thinking. He got 'er this time..."

⸺⸺◦⸺⸺

"Lord Blakely! *Woo-hoo*, Lord Blakely!" The loud, feminine summons jerked his attention back to the present.

Erasmus glanced over and saw a couple bearing down on him. Actually, the flighty female of the two was waving, trying to snag his attention while her more sedate companion—a powerful man much on par with Erasmus himself, in size, stature and title—if not in curses and lady friends—was doing his best to hold her back without making it obvious.

"Louise."

Just that one word, deliberately uttered by her

companion, arrested her over-eager pursuit of Erasmus's focus.

But 'twas too late, for the spouting redhead, all excitable, jawing excitement, had caught Francine's attention as well.

As Lord Tremayne, a marquis in his own right, slowed the exuberant march of his mistress toward them, 'twas Erasmus who acceded to the inevitable.

"Friends of yours?" Francine inquired, coming up to his side, in that soothing, poised voice of hers which never failed to do distracting things to his innards.

"*He* is. We sparred at Jackson's on a regular basis before I became quite so inundated with estate and family"—oh and pesky curse—"business." One of the few men Erasmus didn't have to hold back with, Tremayne being a fine and adept boxing man in his own right.

Francine much closer, tipped her lips to his ear. "She's not, then?"

Louise, Last Name not Important enough to recall. Courtesan Extraordinaire.

More sense betwixt her legs than her ears. Certainly not something he'd tell his betrothed about.

Pretend betrothed, which you seem to have forgotten over the few days.

Erasmus dismissed the reminder as easily as he had his prior interactions with the auburn-haired beauty.

No denying her splendor, though. Her enthusiasm for life—always nattering on about one thing or another—the few times he'd been around her long enough to listen. Back when The Den was in its inception, before it had the name, location and elite reputation he'd worked to cultivate around the place, before Tremayne had ever made her his paramour, she'd entertained at the private parties Erasmus held.

Hell, even before *he* worried about the silly curse himself, more interested in sowing his own youthful, naïve oats.

"'Lakely," Tremayne greeted him, the sedate confidence in his manner and bearing completely at odds with the over-excitable female at his side. The one who positioned herself between them and then—very inappropriately—proceeded to grope his backside.

Something that might have incited an answering caress a dozen years ago but now left him cold, disgusted even, that she'd treat her protector with so little respect. Until he sensed Tremayne gripping her wrist and twisting her arm behind her back, slowly, with a chiding click of his tongue, just until she looked demurely away. Giving Erasmus the perfect moment to greet his friend.

"Tremayne, good to see you." Erasmus clapped his hand to the other man's shoulder and gave a brief shake. "It's been an age since we crossed paths."

Lord Tremayne gave a brief nod, a slight smile directed toward Francine, then looked back at Erasmus. "Aye, has."

Louise started to spout off—but the sharp shake of Lord Tremayne's head—accompanied no doubt by the pressure on her arm, kept her quiet.

Tremayne again looked at Francine and performed a subtle bow. "Lady Francine Mmm—"

"Montfort, my lord." She gave an airy laugh, accompanied by a gentle smile. "'Tis no wonder you forget. I don't claim to know how anyone keeps all these names straight. Especially when we have only been introduced once and that years ago."

"'Ratulations," sped from his mouth, the deeply rasped sentiment accompanied by a slightly wistful look, did he but know it.

"Congratulations?" Louise trilled, a calculating expression filtering across her features as she looked between them. "You are *married*, Blakely?"

"Engaged," Erasmus all but bragged. Quite unlike him. But if Louise hadn't known, giving her absolutely no doubt about his interest being fixed elsewhere, which would have two beneficial outcomes: one, she'd realize he was *taken*. Off the marriage mart. *Pretend engagement, lest you forget.* Two, the way she liked to socialize and chatter, everyone else in the world of demi-reps would know as well. "Aye. Delightfully so."

"When is the ceremony?" Demanded as though she didn't quite believe it.

"*Louise.*" Tremayne again, attempting to muzzle a dog who insisted on barking.

Francine, eyes wide, stared up at him beneath the brim of her head-saving bonnet. *When?* she mouthed.

Erasmus hugged her to him. Bent his knees slightly to kiss her cheek before straightening to answer, "November. Unless I convince her to have me sooner."

"Autumn." Tremayne encompassed them both with the sincere grin that flashed across his features. "P-perfect season."

"Hopefully, one with less rain." Francine recovered swiftly.

"Oh, has not this entire week been utterly wretched?" Both arms now freed, Louise smoothed the front of her dress, making sure to draw the fabric snugly over her attributes. "It has been a veritable chore, I say, to get this one to take me out." She rolled kohl-rimmed eyes toward the big man at her side.

Then she wagged fingers at both her protector and toward Erasmus, but spoke to Francine. "La, we certainly do not want to bore ourselves further with the weather or boxing, which is where conversation between these two brutes is heading, I wager. Come now..." And Louise tugged Francine a few feet away, in the guise of looking at another specimen.

More likely to glean whatever gossip she could, Erasmus knew, lending one ear to the ladies while the rest of his focus remained on Tremayne.

"I should offer my sympathies on the loss of your father," Erasmus told the other man. A death that had occurred not that long before, giving his well-deserving friend the title his father had worn with all the grace of a worm. "But even to an outsider, he seemed a complete arse."

Tremayne chuckled. "Accurate assessment."

Courtesy made him add, "In truth, though it does pain me to express it, you and your sister—you only have the one sibling now, correct?"

"Aye."

"You are both likely much better off with you at the helm."

The big man sighed. Nodded. Held Erasmus's gaze in complete accord. "Astute of you."

Never was one to blather unnecessary sentences when a word or two would suffice.

He suspected the other man was painfully shy.

Never had visited The Den. Not for an oat-sowing or even to jaw over a glass. Good cove. Solid.

Erasmus's right arm twitched with the need to punch him. "Miss sparring with you, Tremayne."

What he wouldn't give to just let loose right now. Exorcise the fears and frustration hounding him with an exhausting round of exercise. "We're well suited in the ring," he added. "Not something I can say about many others."

Tremayne smiled, and it reached his eyes this time. "Agreed on that score."

Or, some devilish part of him prompted, *instead of swelling your knuckles, risking a sore arm or bruise to your face, you could simply exhaust yourself swiving Francine on the way home.*

The two ladies were stirring the air between them, exclaiming over different aspects of the exhibit. At one point he caught Louise blathering about "the mummified feline in the next hall" and barely avoided cringing when Francine glanced at him, eyes wide and curious.

A glance that told him he'd likely not be enjoying her on the way home as soon as he'd hoped.

What happened to flirtation not frisking?

"'Angerous...business—*that.*" Tremayne eye-pointed toward where the women were jabbering like long-lost bosom chums. "Should we halt it?"

Given how he could still hear every word... "No need. Lady Francine, however sheltered her upbringing, is wiser in the ways of the world than you might think." *Only because you continue to corrupt her.* He didn't try to stifle his self-satisfied smile at that reminder. "I am fine to let them share a moment." For now. "As long as you have no objections?"

Tremayne inclined his head in tacit agreement.

"Oh. Speaking of danger with all seriousness, Tremayne, there is one thing to note. ..."

"Aye?"

"London's become fraught of late, with new menaces lurking everywhere these days. Cut-purses turning to cutting throats not far from my club. Mind your lady folk, do not let them venture out. Alone. Or after dark."

"Never." A single, decisive nod accompanied that, his jaw and the muscles in his neck growing taut. "Sister's in London. Shipping her b-back..." He paused to clear his throat. "To the country p-posthaste."

"I think that is likely wise, especially if she's agreeable."

His jaw relaxed marginally. "Very."

"Your sister need not feel banished indefinitely. I have some men on it, patrolling and whatnot. Hoping—"

"Heavy...burden, 'Llakely." Tremayne shifted, frowned. Brought one hand up to massage the muscles along the side of his neck, so his words came out a bit muffled. "N-*not* yours t-to carry."

"We both know the night watchmen are not exactly up for protecting our fair citizens." London's ill-equipped, under-trained, often elderly and bosky watchmen, armed with nothing more than a baton and their sleepy wits, were no match for the evils prowling the city.

"So..." Erasmus didn't want to antagonize his

friend, but was vastly curious nevertheless. And determined to change the subject. "Cannot help but notice that you are *still* with Louise. Have not moved on nor made any effort to set up your nursery."

After all, as peers, that was their primary responsibility, was it not? At least as far as the rest of the world was concerned—their duty, to make healthy boy babies to secure the line.

"G-good God, no!" Tremayne coughed into his fist after sputtering that out. "No interest in...breeding."

We're agreed, then, Erasmus wanted to share, but didn't, long habits of keeping himself aloof and apart too ingrained. *But not with Francine,* that annoying part of his mind prompted. *With her, you seem to jabber almost as much as a bunch of hens.*

Tremayne gave the women a lingering glance before turning back to Erasmus. "Happy to see... You found someone."

Uncomfortable at the thought of deceiving his friend, knowing he and Francine were a temporary—if convenient—match, he spoke without thinking. "But Louise? Still? Have you not grown tired of her?" Tired of her sometimes crass, sometimes flighty ways?

"We suit."

Hardly.

"In the bedchamber, no doubt," he offered with his practiced air of not caring beyond anything save bed sport. "You are to be commended, then." Commitment, whether to a spouse or one's fancy piece shouldn't be made light of, not in today's society. "For finding and securing her."

"Not averse to change. Only..." Tremayne nodded

once, almost as though convincing himself. "Convenient, she is."

Erasmus chuckled at that. "A man's convenient, should be, do you not agree?" As talk turned to the last session in the House, he heard the women deep in discussion over the exhibit where they'd paused, studying the fly-eating *Dionaea muscipula* on display, the wicked little tipitiwitchet out of North Carolina.

"Did you see this?" Francine asked her companion. "It says here 'twas discovered in America in the late 1760s or thereabouts…"

Even with most his attention on Tremayne, he could so easily pick out her dulcet tones, savor their sweetness—

"Seems America is good for something other than war with France or England, then," Louise enthused, sounding as though she shuffled closer to the specimen. "What a sinfully delightful plant! Do you see *why* the British naturalist Mr. Ellis named it *Venus's Flytrap*?"

"I do indeed." More hushed now, but no less appealing, his betrothed gave a light, almost embarrassed laugh. He eagerly listened and felt no compunction whatsoever at eavesdropping on the ladies' discussion. Especially when Francine continued…

"I used a mirror once—to see down there. Scientific curiosity and all that." Erasmus smiled inside. *Of course* she'd used a mirror to look at herself, his inquisitive little innocent.

He couldn't be more proud.

"La, my dear," Louise exclaimed, "your face is as pink as this fly-catcher. Venus mound, indeed." The auburn head tilted toward the bonneted blonde, as though imparting a confidence. He listened even more intently. "My compliments to you, *Lady* Francine. I am quite gratified to know you have no squeamish airs about you. Blakely and his kind are not the sort for squeamish misses. Not with..."

"With what?"

"The ribald group activities and such..."

"Oh? What group might—"

Time to halt that. "Let's rejoin the ladies, Tremayne, shall we?"

"All means."

"What all have you two been discussing?" Giving them no further time to exchange confidences—or for Louise to corrupt Francine *(why should she need to, when you're doing quite the spectacular job on your own?)*— Erasmus barged right in, Tremayne on his heels. "What's this I hear about a mummy?"

"Interesting, seeing that," his friend volunteered.

Francine turned smiling, if curious—no doubt still thinking about that prior exchange with the blowsy redhead—eyes toward him. "Louise says there is a magnificent exhibit on the other side. Even a cat! Can you imagine?"

How well he could, with all that he had seen in his life. And the exhibit, at least, explained the peculiar smell that had been plaguing him. Whatever embalming methods the Egyptians employed, seemed his cursed conk could still ferret them out.

"Oh, do! 'Tis divine." Evidently giving up on inappropriately stroking other men, Louise turned all her attention to the self-possessed one at her side. "After seeing the magnificent jewels that have been recovered in their tombs? I told Tremayne exactly what I want next!"

His stoic friend gave a slight shake of his head, as if to impart, *Women.* "Storm's likely lessened." He glanced pointedly at his timepiece.

"So...time we leave?" Louise pouted, then brightened. "Ah, since you think the rain has moved on by now"—she practically climbed up his side to loudly whisper in his ear—"can my strong man enjoy himself without a raincoat this time, eh?"

As Tremayne once again restrained her overzealous actions, he shared both *a look* and a small smile with Erasmus. Louise might be lacking in finesse and tact, but she definitely made up for both with a lusty love of lewd lovemaking the other couple would no doubt be indulging in soon.

Frisking? Or flirting?

Still unsure exactly how he planned to go on, he nevertheless tucked Francine into his side, as they watched the other couple saunter off.

"I like your friend. Though I have only interacted with him once or twice—and then even with the most fearsome bruising lining his jaw—I always thought that he has kind eyes."

Was that jealousy threatening to claw its way out? Because she merely said a man he also liked and respected had pleasing eyes?

"Although... Louise now." Francine took one step away from him, to better gaze off at the retreating couple, before lowering her voice to add, "I'm not sure I have her figured out. She did not even give us a chance to finish introductions before tugging me away. Though she seems friendly enough, she doesn't quite seem a proper match for Lord Tremayne, does she?"

A proper match? He didn't try to subdue his grin, but did attempt to make it not quite so derisive. *She's not. At all.* "Why? Who do you think she is?"

"His wife?" Her tone lilted upward at the incredulous look he didn't try to hide.

He gave a bark of laughter. "Hanging on to him as she was?" Then Erasmus demonstrated, extending one arm toward his lady's backside. "Brushing her fingers over my duff after she approached? Nay, my sweet, innocent Francine." Would he shock her? Was he trying to? "She is his mistress."

"In truth?" Her eyes widened, the spectacles she wore only enlarging them further. "I do not believe I have ever met a man's mistress before. Not knowingly."

And if he was any sort of gentleman at all, he would have ensured she hadn't today. But instead of apologizing, of trying to shield his faux affianced, he all but boasted, "You have now."

What was it about this demure yet outspoken, inexperienced yet game lady that only made him want to corrupt her further? To bask in her enjoyment of the bawdy?

Her brows knit in a frown and both hands came to her hips. "And the wretch put her paws on you?"

"Mm-hmm." He watched with interest as she breathed in, then out, lifted her shoulders up, then rolled them back and relaxed her arms out to her sides.

Lightly, she flicked her gloved fingertips across his shoulders and chest, then walked around him, doing the same to his back—and lands lower—as though erasing the uninvited touch, the earlier caress he'd found oddly offensive, given its lack of welcome.

"She did indeed," he said once she again held his gaze.

"Quite without your permission?"

This time. "Quite. Utterly and completely."

What would his little debauched, pretend intended think of that?

"I do not believe I care for her, after all," Francine said primly, not a hint of jealousy in her voice. Only in her eyes, as she now stared daggers toward the no-longer-visible couple. "He can do better, I am convinced of it. Significantly better."

11

CONFESSIONS & WARNINGS, AND PROMISES BE DAMNED

Dearest Erasmus,

Again I must beg of your indulgence. I had thought to return by now, but Fate has decreed otherwise.

In finding the answers I once sought, my journey has taken me in an entirely different direction. One I must follow to its conclusion—alone.

Do not seek me out. Nor let your brother think to. But remain bound to each other knowing that I love you with every breath, every sunrise, every cloud upon the sky...

Now that I know what became of your father, I shall seek my own peace in time.

For now...

For now—

For now, my dear boy, do not neglect to <u>live YOUR life</u>.

. . .

THE WRITING WITHIN THIS LETTER, unlike the last she'd seen delivered into his hand so many moons ago, was shaky and blotched. Smeared in places. But no less dear.

Ending abruptly and causing him to defy the edict set forth and seek her out, but to no avail. Weeks he'd searched on his own, only abandoning his efforts and returning home when the steward's letter reached him, speaking of difficulties with tenants that needed a master at home to tend.

Then for months after that, paying for the search to continue. Yet still without success.

Until finally, one lonely sunrise, as he watched the clouds scud across the orange sky, thinking of his dear mama with every one of his breaths, he finally accepted her wishes and said goodbye...

UPON LEAVING THE MUSEUM, Erasmus told his coachman to circle London until directed otherwise. He wasn't ready to end their little excursion. His huge escape.

For once he returned Francine home, 'twas time for him to return to the unpleasant but necessary business of seeking out a killer. Damn his responsibilities.

Rain still slicked everything, but now more of a drizzle than a deluge.

He handed her into his carriage, that fancy bonnet hiding the Medusa-like, writhing strands of what could no longer be called hair. Not the way it moved every which direction, defying gravity—and now, even the bonnet.

He climbed in and settled himself on the opposite seat. Before the horses even left the curb, he reached across and untied the ribbons at her neck. "Be comfortable," he invited, pointing to the cushion next to her. Then he gestured to his temple. "Unless you need your spectacles here?"

"Not this close to you." They disappeared quickly inside her reticule, which she placed upon the seat. She hesitated but a moment before also removing the elegant contraption she wore, her fingers checking the multitude of pins she'd added—which didn't do a damn thing to tame the frizzled, blond serpents if she but knew it.

No time to entertain her this evening, blast it all. Not after being gone for several days. And while escorting her to a public place with the window curtains hooked back—only because he couldn't take advantage of an open carriage on a day like today—had edged the line of propriety much closer than he'd like, at least it'd been daytime.

He wasn't about to risk an evening closed-carriage excursion with no semblance of chaperone in sight.

Now you want to consider proprieties? Bats, buffle-head. They swarm your belfry like flies do a carcass.

Shut the deuce up!

The gentle touch upon the back of his hand halted the nagging internal voice. He removed his glove and flipped his hand upright, to grasp hers and tug her across the carriage next to him.

"Tell me more of your family?"

"Whatever for?" Could he help it if he sounded irritated by the simple question?

"You never speak of them. I admit to vast curiosity."

"Choke it off." He thought that'd be the end of it.

Hardly.

She gave his fingers a squeeze, then drew hers away to remove both her gloves while giving his side a nudge with her shoulder. "Do you not hear yourself? You can be quite abrupt at times. Severely private."

"Yet you refuse to heed it."

"For I know 'tis an act."

He missed her touch. And because he wasn't above being an arse if it suited him, mouthed off, "Much like our betrothal?"

"Nay. Vastly different."

Her speculative gaze, fixed decidedly upon his person, made him want to fidget. He stared straight across at the unexceptional, empty carriage seat as though nothing could interest him greater than her discarded bonnet. Pointedly refusing to apologize and make the effort to charm his way back into her good graces—as he knew he should.

A few heavy seconds later, she said, remarkably evenly, "I could pout and flounce about, or do the opposite and pretend I care not, but you demanded honesty between us, so you shall have it."

She never stopped surprising him. Wasn't going to whimper and whine? Was only going to employ logic to make her point?

"You know much of my regrettable past, my sorrow. You knew my father, even. You know of my shame, my flighty cousin, the one I am—secretly—becoming friends with again. You know of my wastrel aunt. Even the disaster upon my head should rain dare to fall." He finally looked at her, opened his mouth to halt the discourse, but she shook her head and only spoke louder, both to gain his attention and because raindrops started pounding the carriage. "You know of my lackadaisical uncle."

Ah, her uncle.

Easily, could he cross paths with her uncle, attempt to have a conversation with him. He had no aversion to the man—other than his choice of wife. Would be good to befriend him, perhaps. Ensure he learned of his wife's perfidy. Had they not sat on the same side of the vote the last time Erasmus had troubled himself to attend Parliament? Minute, but something perhaps to build upon.

Build upon? Befriend him? Have your wits gone begging? It is not as though you are joining the family in truth.

"You know of my fortune, my love of dirt, my—"

"Stop." He shifted to cup her cheek, tilt her head and lose his ire in the sky blue of her peaceful eyes. "Your point stands made and it gouges me right here"—he brought his other hand to his chest—"rather effectively."

FRANCINE SENSED he wanted to huff and bluster about, to escape the carriage into the downpour and restrained himself from doing so only by the sheerest of wills, the impressively long and controlled breath he let lightly escape his slightly parted lips. "Francine... What is your second name?"

"Sarah. Was I not the miracle child?" She referred to the Bible story of Abraham's wife and the wonder of motherhood at an elderly age. "The one Papa so desperately needed?"

At the self-mocking tone she employed, he slowly drew his fingers down and off her face, leaving tingles trailing in his wake. She closed her eyes a moment, to better savor the sensations. Then blinked them open to finish, honestly and without the hint of bitterness that had coated her prior sentence.

"Although my choice to be born female proved entirely disastrous to Papa's line, he never—not once— made me feel inferior or rejected. 'Twas loved and cherished from my earliest memories. It is the only reason I have managed to abide Aunt Pru's criticism and restrictions, her harping and confining ways without circling Bedlam. The memories, the feelings of such a warm and lovely childhood."

Though his posture remained stiff, he swayed his upper body toward hers. "When you speak thus"—his tone had softened too—"I swear, Francy, I can *feel* the love. 'Tis quite disconcerting, I admit. Especially given how..."

"How?"

For a moment, he refused to reply, instead turned away, this time to look out the uncovered window, though no scene remained visible, not with the constant trickle of water streams parading downward, blurring the view beyond.

She gave him those solitary moments and was

rewarded when he lifted his arm to draw the curtain partially across it before turning back to her. He took up her hand, lacing their fingers tightly together to bring the back of her hand to his lips.

The silky glide of his tongue upon the sensitive flesh threatened her concentration. So she rotated to climb over his lap, ungainly perhaps in the smallish space, skirts rustling and bunched. But this way, for a moment at least, her hands now bracketing his face with him staring into her eyes and his lips no longer wreaking havoc upon her skin, she could attempt to finish what she'd started.

"Shall I complete the thought?" Her fingers made his head nod while she mimicked his deep tone, "Why, certainly, my dear Francy, will you not avail me of your wisdom?"

His lips quirked. Eyes started to glow.

Still imitating his voice, she said, "I am at sixes and sevens, dearest, to hear your wisdom."

He snorted. "*That*, I would never say that."

She released one side of his face to trace the pad of one finger over his bottom lip. "What? That I am wise?"

"Sixes and sevens."

Because his supple lips nibbling upon her flesh now threatened to snaffle her concentration, she finished in her regular tone. "Might you be disconcerted by *feeling* something given how, for some unfathomable reason, you have distanced yourself from people close to you?"

Because the noise beyond their secluded space howled—his poor coachman, she couldn't help but spare a second to think—she tensed her thighs and changed her hold from his face to brace herself upon his shoulders, speaking directly into his ear. "Though you appear to be surrounded by a great many friends at all times, I begin to think that is another fallacy you portray..."

Beneath some bristly whiskers along his jaw, next to his intentionally thick side whiskers, a muscle pulsed. Hadn't that area been smooth only scant hours before? "Your facial hair grows astonishingly fast."

When had his hands gripped her hips?

She only noticed now as his strong fingers pressed in and slid up to her waist. Angled her until he caught her eyes.

"My early years were not cold nor harsh. Not as doting nor demonstrative as I suspect yours were. From birth, I was reared to assume the title and all its responsibilities, after all," he astounded her by confiding. Not so much by what he said but by the fact that he *shared*.

"But warmer than most I surmise. 'Tis not my mother's blame I claimed self-reliance straight from the womb. Growing up, I was closest to my cousin Phineas. He was only a year and a half older. While my brother, Nash, is several years younger *and* a natural ne'er-do-well, one who eschewed responsibilities while I embraced them." As though the confession had overwhelmed him, he lunged forward to claim her mouth. But once their lips touched and clung, he changed the pressure until it was the merest butterfly wing of a caress, the lingering kiss soft and slow, before relaxing back against the squabs and turning to look once again out the partially shaded window.

Desperately, did she want to ask about Nash and

Phineas. Where were they? Had either of them been one of the men surrounding him the night she'd approached? She squelched her curiosity, though, hesitant to interrupt whatever turbulent thoughts entrapped him so. For like a hare caught in a snare, once again, she sensed the hunting of his soul, the haunting, that she did not understand.

"I know not what, precisely, happened to my mother," he said evenly, without inflection, but without meeting her gaze either, "but I suspect she chose to join my father after his demise was made known to us."

"She took her own life?" Francine's heart ached with the weight of grief he must have suffered—stoically endured—but she knew better than to say more, not while he finally confided the very things she held such curiosity over.

"She took herself *off*," he corrected, his fingers flexing. "Beyond our estate. Ostensibly to learn more of Father's last few weeks. Sent word that finding answers brought her a measure of contentment if not peace, and then..."

His head wrenched round and he rested his forehead against hers, but not before she saw him close his eyes. "Then... Nothing. So yet another family member I failed."

He took on so much! Her arms went to his neck, as she lifted onto her knees the best she could, hugging him to her. "Answers—about your father? Did she divulge her discoveries?"

"Nay, other than to write his last days were likely spent among friends. Some solace, that, I suppose."

"How long ago was this?"

"Nearly two years after his death."

Tempest, along with her fascination of heraldry, took joy in perusing their volume of *Debrett's Peerage*, and studying family histories. After their reunion at the musicale, her cousin wasted no time revealing what she'd discovered of Lord Blakely's. "So you have not seen nor heard from her since your twenty-first year? Your father since your nineteenth?"

"Aye."

"If I am not mistaken, lions are vastly social creatures and—"

His head whipped up and his hands snaked from her waist to clutch her arms, pull them from around his neck and use the pressure to push her away, so he could snare her gaze. His eyes glittering and more intense than she'd witnessed yet. "What did you say?"

"You are not meant to be so alone."

The pressure on her wrists increased. "Before that."

"Umm... Social—" To shouts on the street, the carriage gave a lurch and she shifted above him.

"Nay. *Lions*. What the deuce made you utter that?"

"Your charges. Upon your shield." His family's coat of arms. Specifically *his*.

For Tempest had taught her that a coat of arms belonged not always to the entire family line but to the specific qualifying individual who had it granted by the King of Arms, often with a small change that made a particular design unique to one individual and *his* immediate family. "For unlike your father's shield that pictured two lion charges, you added a third. 'Twas the only change you made. I surmise the great cat has some manner of significance to you, else you—"

He released her wrists only to bring his fingers up against her lips. "You see too much. They represent myself, Nash and Phin, the current generation of Hammonds. Though Phin does not share our surname, we grew up alongside each other." And for all he knew, there were hordes more walking London... Ones not yet identified or known to him.

She reached up to bring his fingers away from her mouth, holding on to his hand with both of hers and giving a slight tug. "You see? *Social.* You are not meant to be so alone."

"I have Adam."

"Ah, the gentleman you so rarely reference. I begin to wonder if he's a phantom, a figment, for your Mr. Adam is remarkably reclusive."

Erasmus managed a laugh at that, despite how it hurt, being so exposed, reliving losses and enduring damn *feelings* normally kept well buried and completely out of sight. The past few minutes had worn him out like a well-wrung rag.

But, oddly, it wasn't sex he craved. The oblivion of a well-debauched orgasm. It was her smile.

He needed to lift the sadness lingering in her gaze. Needed to hug her and hold her against his heart until her bright soul soothed his tortured one.

"Adam—reclusive? Not at all." Just completely devoted to business at the club, and not titled, so therefore not able to mix and mingle among the *ton*, at the elegant activities where someone in Francine's set would have met him.

"Lest you forget, minx, he works for a living, managing things for me." His fingers flexed within her hold, restless. As though even they were uncomfortable that he'd revealed so much, and on so many topics, the last few minutes.

"And now, confession is over." He'd not be having her hound him with more questions, thinking this new verbose manner would be the norm. *"For the summer."*

She jabbed him with an elbow for that. "Very well."

But talk of Adam only reminded him of what else he needed to mention, no matter that it had the potential to ruin the flavor of the afternoon. "I need your solemn vow on something."

"Aye. I will jilt you as planned."

"This is no time for jesting, Francine."

Her smile faltered, faded from her eyes but remained, marginally so, upon her lips. "My solemn vow? You have it."

"You would agree so swiftly? Without learning of what I ask first?"

"That, dear sir..." She lightly stroked his fidgety fingers. "Is what comes from trust."

He gave a grunt. "You shall not venture out. Alone. At night. *Especially,*" he spoke over her when she would have blithely vowed again. "Alone and at night. Swear to me."

She held his gaze in such a way that time paused. Halted heavily between them, the stillness unnerving, perhaps, to someone who didn't care as much as he did for gaining her word. The stillness, now that the clouds, too, seemed exhausted, the tempest outside having paused, rendering the silence between them so very loud that he knew she finally *heard* him. Was debating her response. "Swear to me," he urged, his voice rasping out harsher than he'd like. "Do not venture out onto the streets of London at night. Ever. Else I walk from our bargain now without—"

"Nay," she chastised. "Threats, coercion—whatever you term it—do not become you. Nor do they respect what we have built between us." The gentle caress that had moved to his palm didn't change. "I often venture out—alone—into the garden adjacent to Rowden House. Sometimes at night, much more frequently during the day."

She watched him unflinchingly after delivering that challenging statement.

He forced himself to do the same—silently holding his tongue as she slowly worked through to her ultimate agreement.

For he'd accept nothing less.

"But I do not think that is of which you speak." Here, she pressed the full of her hand upon his, and it was all he could do to allow his flesh to remain passive against hers, to not squeeze her tight to him and never let go. "So you want me to be accompanied at all times or remain bound to home. Have I the right of things? And you want a solemn vow on it?"

"For now, aye. 'Tis not safe for young ladies to be out unescorted."

"I suspect there is much more to be learned upon the topic but also suspect, based on that muscle dancing upon your bristly jaw—time to shave again, my lord—you will refuse to divulge further reasons tonight."

'Twas unnerving, how well she read him.

She drew in a slow breath that made him wait a decidedly long time before it eased out and relaxed her posture. Smiled at him—with her eyes again. "I know you have your reasons even if you will not confide them yet. Very well. I agree."

"Your cousins too. Secure their promises."

"Even Patience? You know talking to her is nothing but a chore." The kinked-up fuzz atop her head waved to him when she rolled her eyes. "If it's not outright stupidity, she projects belligerence a thousand times ten. Even worse now that she has caught Temperance and I sharing giggles and gossip—but only once, mind. For we have been exceedingly careful ever since."

"Did I not tell you this is not a jesting matter? Aye, you must caution Patience as well."

"I shall, you may depend upon it, you mysterious and frustratingly silent man."

"Silent? When I have set myself to entertaining you every moment of this excessively long, interminable afternoon?" His palm got abandoned so he could receive another pointy elbow—this one in his ribs.

And now, he intentionally sought to lighten things, to return the sparkle to her cheeks his sordid past and rash promise-demand had stolen from her. He smoothed the mutinous mass from her forehead. "Francine, tell me, would that inquisitive mind of yours like to know exactly how to mummify a cat?"

She gave him a sidelong glance, as though she found the swift shift in topic pitch-kettling. "Without the proper tools, I doubt it would prove anything but an extended disaster."

"Oh, I do not know...I remain confident you could do it."

"Do you now?" Skepticism became her, the growing flush upon her cheeks, the quick thoughts racing across her expression. "So, I'm to believe you have a collection of everything I would need? Natron, beeswax, loads of linen, sawdust, herbs and oils"—my, she really had paid attention at the exhibit—"and resin? Not to mention a few amulets and possibly charms, if I really wanted to do it right? *And* the space to lay everything out?"

"Most of that is neither here nor there." He discounted her impressive list. "In truth, I think you could accomplish it in a trice without bothering with all that."

"In a trice? Do tell."

"If it was raining, of course."

"Raining?" He'd thoroughly stumped her now, one eyebrow winging upward.

"Of a certainty. All you need is a willing cat."

"Willing? Do you not mean deceased, poor thing?"

"Nay. A lively one would work brilliantly. I am convinced of it. For, you see, all you have need to do is stare at it—and take off your bonnet."

One turn of the carriage wheels.

Another.

Then...

Thwack! "You wretch!" She laughed, pummeled his shoulder with several light slaps of her palm. "After today, my poor mattress-head will never be the same."

"Neither will the cat..."

She chuckled along with him.

Equilibrium, lightness of heart, balance of being restored between them once again.

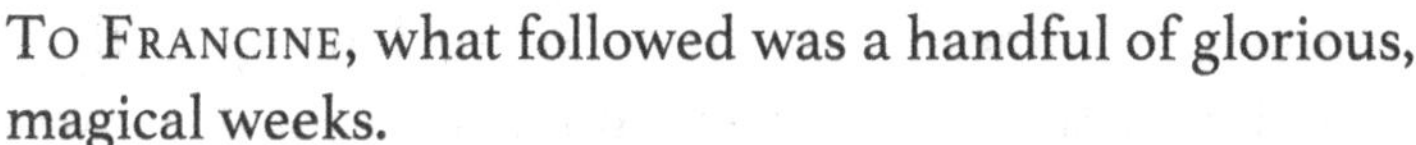

To Francine, what followed was a handful of glorious, magical weeks.

Erasmus was at her side frequently, escorting her to the few remaining balls, routs and fêtes. Finding other entertainments once those dwindled to a halt as, now that sessions in Parliament were coming to a swift close, so many retreated to their country estates. He even fostered a growing relationship with her uncle! The two bonding over some legislation they'd both supported and ensuring her aunt did nothing further to disgrace herself or risk the family name.

It appeared as though the quick jaunt to Brighton had only increased her love of deep play—and her debts, something neither man considered remotely appropriate. Especially given how Francine had confided to Erasmus about sweet, spirited Tempest being won by Lord Wylde across the green. "Thank God he is conscionable," Erasmus had remarked, eyes glittering in that way that never failed to tighten the muscles in her middle. "Not one to take advantage. Had it been another rake of the *ton*... Well, Francy, no need to dwell on mayhaps and might-haves now."

Delighting in each other's company, they engaged in spirited discussions covering a host of far-ranging topics from Wellington's recent victory at Salamanca to debating which one of her female relatives was the most irritating—Patience and Aunt Pru tied, being equally so.

It seemed as though Erasmus made it a point to suggest some type of outing almost daily and she noticed each time they were together that the constant, haunted loneliness in his eyes, so evident upon their first interactions, lessened, until one day, it was vanquished for several wondrous hours completely.

In exchange for his sheltering presence, which usually meant that Aunt Prudence kept her opinions and protestations to herself, Francine made it her utmost priority to please him intellectually *and* sexually. Once or twice he got a little wild—a tad rough—then expressed regret afterward but...well, truth be told, she *loved* it, couldn't imagine the sad state of her life had she never experienced his unbridled form of lovemaking. So she gave herself over to it, reveled in it, savoring every aspect of the wanton she became in his arms, positive she never wanted her birthday to arrive.

Who needed money and freedom when they had perfection?

The end of the Season approached inexorably closer, unremarked upon by either of them, as if by not articulating that the official time to terminate their farce was fast approaching, it was of no consequence.

Erasmus continued to squire her about town, accompanying her to London amusements she'd always wanted to explore but had never been able to escape Aunt Prudence's overbearing thumb long enough to do so. Each evening, when he escorted her home, whether they "indulged" themselves physically or not, he always seduced her lips with his before echoing the reminder to never go out alone.

Francine was all too happy to agree. Aunt Prudence was just plain *dis*agreeable—her French chef had resigned. And Uncle Rowden no longer permitted her any say over the household funds—or her daughters. Taking now the active role in his household he'd previously avoided. "Both gels are engaged, Pru. Francine too. *Leave them be,*" he ordered one night during dinner. And then, after one more mouthful of the kitchen girl's mediocre efforts, "My stomach cannot tolerate much more, so aye, find us a chef. The blunt shall be spared for that."

And if, as time wore on, Francine noticed that Erasmus occasionally seemed even more distracted or abrupt, that the haunted look returned—and with a vengeance—well, all men had their moods—didn't they?—and she was certain he continued to be as satisfied by their unusual alliance as she was.

Or so she convinced herself. Or tried to.

No longer able to imagine her life without him in it.

Then came the dratted notes.

All from Erasmus and all with but one purpose—canceling their plans.

The first was a carefully penned epistle, the bulk of it apologizing—and profusely so—for the night before when he'd whisked her from the townhouse and into the garden, only to make the most violently passionate love to her. To leave her breathless and panting, her lips swollen from his kiss, her shoulder burning from his teeth, her heart rejoicing that she'd found such a thrilling, responsible man.

But an encounter he obviously regretted.

For, along with begging forgiveness, he explained that he had business to attend and must, with great regret, withdraw from that afternoon's activities but that he would see her the following day as scheduled.

The second note, which arrived on said "following day", was a bit shorter, a bit less personable and ended with a brief, *Looking forward to our next excursion*, but making no mention of when that might be.

By the third note, Francine knew what to expect.

By the fourth, Aunt Prudence was overjoyed—it seemed Lord Blakely had finally come to his senses and thrown Franny over...*and* she'd just hired a new chef.

By the time the fifth missive arrived, Francine could read it straight through without crying.

By the sixth, she was thoroughly vexed.

When the seventh note in as many days arrived with a scrawl so illegible she could barely make out the scribbled, *I cannot see you again until deep into next month, E*, Francine knew exactly what she had to do.

Do not venture out. Especially alone and at night. Swear to me.

Promise or no, she'd not languish away worrying over him for naught or pining for him if he'd decided he'd been her champion long enough.

For six full days she'd portrayed admirable restraint, though it had demanded extreme effort. Who knew being silent and still for days on end could wear one down to the bone?

And now that he'd sent round the notes for an entire sennight? She wasn't some hen-hearted female lacking in pluck. Nay, 'twas time she knew for certain whether he'd tired of their arrangement or—and this notion made her cringe—tired of *her*.

And if something else occupied his time, one of those secret wounds she'd long suspected he harbored, then was it not her duty to rescue *him* this time?

What? You'll chance the night and your hampered vision to salvage some savage lord who's merely been dallying with you these last months?

As though witchy Aunt Pru perched upon one shoulder, pointed-toe boots and broom handle digging in, equally pointy black hat swaying in mockery, Francine heard her worst fears. *Against his express orders? Franny, have you no shame?*

The wretched mental cackle accompanying these words dredged up shudders.

Ugh. But, by now, she certainly possessed the wisdom to ignore any advice from *that* quarter.

Francine looked around her bedroom, desperate to concoct another Plan of Genius, one that would, without any further ado, see her safely to his home. But first, she needed to ascertain exactly *where* that was.

⬥

One Week Earlier
The Second Evening with The Sun in Leo

"You're not looking so good, you know." Adam frowned, his words making Erasmus doubt his actions of the last two minutes, letting himself into his private office at The Den via his secret passageway.

On the other side of the locked door, where he'd paused only seconds ago...questioning...reliving...

He'd taken a harsh breath, gathering himself a moment before going through the door and making his presence known.

He hadn't seen Francine in over twenty-three hours; no sexual release since then either.

Not since he'd stolen her away from her aunt and uncle's small dinner party, snuck her outside to the garden wall bordering the mews. Shoved her face up against the wall and taken her hard and fast when the feral need struck between the pineapple ice and the gentleman's port.

Slammed into him like a bolt of lightning, catching him off-guard for the first time in memory. Gave him no warning to fortify himself. Agonizing to the point that it was all he could do to slake his savage lust like the barbarian he was, straighten her gown, and then bruise her lips in a kiss meant to salvage whatever humanity still resided in him—while his flagellating conscience berated him beyond measure.

You reprehensible reprobate—not minding the calendar as though her life depends upon it? When it most certainly does!

Being caught unaware to the point that your teeth become pointy? That you don't notice the impending thickening and sharpening of your nails? And every other sensation heralding The Change?

Pricking imbecile!

Immoral swine! To risk the most precious—

"Enough!" he'd roared, clamping his lips—and teeth—to her shoulder as he rode out the angst, ripping his body from hers at the last possible second to spend in the dirt.

Shaking. Vibrating. Lips and tongue damn-near quivering upon her flesh.

Disgust seething through him at his unrestrained, inexplicable behavior toward her—only compounded a thousand times over when the taste of her blood met his mouth.

He'd bitten her?

His Francy?

Even now, his nose twitched.

Fingernails felt heavy.

Teeth poked.

While his conscience waged a war: Find Francine and fuck till the insensible somehow made sense? Put her further at risk in the process...

Or chain himself up? Battle the curse as he never had, but knew his father had somehow managed?

Or—

The scents of sex wafted from the perimeter of the locked door in front of him.

Or...

You're not looking so good.

BUT NOW, with Adam's critical greeting ringing in his ear, he wished he'd halted—remained on the other side of the corridor, braced the ramparts of his will with anything possible and shut himself off. Sped the other direction, into the night. Where the monsters roamed.

Too late now...

Braving it out, he stalked out onto the main floor, giving Adam no choice but to follow. This early, a decent crowd milled about. Many simply occupying themselves with a stiff drink while they rubbed up a stiff stander, usually with the help of one of his "ladies".

This close, the scents of sexual lubrication and release nearly felled him. Two couples finished up on the stage, and two more stepped forth to take their place. Turning his back on the scene, he shifted toward his office. Contemplating escape. Or the oblivion behind him?

Making the choice—for the moment—Adam came through the office, shutting the door behind him. He leaned heavily on his podium, evaluating Erasmus, from his cringing toes up past the unbuttoned tailcoat and haphazard hash of a neckcloth to the strands of his stinging hair. "Who am I to give you advice when it comes to proper English appearance?" he asked drolly. "But I sincerely doubt you'd let any new member join our ranks looking as you do now."

Refusing to acknowledge what he didn't want to hear, Erasmus foraged clumsily in his pocket before dropping a small package on the podium in front of his friend. Something he'd been meaning to give him for weeks. "Here. Compliments of Franklin and myself."

Fighting against the fine trembling that had taken hold of his limbs, he clenched the muscles in his arms and legs and stood, as still as possible, while waiting for

Adam to unwrap the plain brown paper and reveal the pamphlet, razor and strap within.

Giving a derisive snort, Adam lifted the pamphlet and waved it between them. "Are you joking? *A Treatise on Razors?*"

"No jest. Sixth edition. Read it." Keeping his hand as steady as possible, Erasmus pointed to the fine-edged, heavy blade. "Since you refuse to let a barber tend to your beard, learn to use it. With that furry behemoth covering your lip, you draw too much attention otherwise. Cannot operate with the anonymity we both need at times."

After interviewing half a score of men, professed investigators, and finding them all wanting, Adam had decreed he would look into their unknown patrons on his own.

"Fuck it. You're right." Catching himself brushing the mass of whiskers beneath his nose, Adam made a show of checking his timepiece—interestingly, he wore it on some sort of band strapped around his wrist instead of keeping it tucked in a pocket and secured by a fob. "Another twenty-four hours and you're still squiring about the lovely—unharmed—Lady Francine?"

His jaw grew tight. "That I am."

Adam gazed off toward the far wall of the main, cavernous room. "Not concerned about the time of year?"

More than you could fathom. "Aye. But more concerned about you poking that big nose of yours where it—"

"Hold up, E." Adam's gaze returned to his and he

put his arm out between them, palm up. "Is not part of my job *as your friend* to look out for your interests?"

"Keeping Francine safe interests me greatly," Erasmus said roughly.

Adam only stared. Quirked his lips in such a manner that the giant mustache took on a life of its own. "Safe?" Adam drew the word out in such a way that infused it with skepticism. "From yourself? Or others?"

The sound that came from his throat sounded like that of a rabid dog; something no self-respecting man —feline cursed or not—would ever permit.

The pamphlet and blade disappeared in the leather satchel Adam squired about. He shot Erasmus an overly casual glance as he finished his task. "Why not just have her take care of you?"

Her? *Francine?* "I do not want her near me right—"

"E, sex appeases the urges, right? So have at it. The two of you have been going at it like rabbits based on that dopey grin of yours. Why not—"

This time his throat made a strangled hissing noise, one sufficient to halt Adam's inopportune advice. "One, I am not sure what you mean by 'dopey', but I daresay that insipid word most certainly does not apply to me. Two, *going at it like rabbits*?" Sounded more like a snarl that time. "Do not speak of her in such a manner."

Adam took a step away, hands raised in surrender. "Apologies, my lord. I—"

"Three," Erasmus interrupted without compunction. Adam only ever *my lorded* him when he knew he'd blundered—and badly. "Sex lessens the urges. Does not erase them. I refuse—" He interrupted himself.

"Three *point* five—do not even dare *think* of her and sex in the same sentence. I would hate to break your jaw."

Adam bit his lips against a smile, damn him. He knew Erasmus too well. Knew he might threaten but would never harm his closest ally. "Never again, my lord."

"Back to three. I refuse to sully her with the curse." His friend wavered. Which meant either his sight was weak—an impossibility—or his legs were shaking. Trembling like a virgin's on her wedding night, damn him. Fighting the urge to roar, to deride the weakness quivering through him, he hardened his resolve—and his voice. "We shall be apart for a few days. I will take care of things on my own and she will remain safe. All will be well before she has time to miss me."

"Take care of things *on your own*?" The smile was gone now, replaced with censure. "We both know that doesn't work. You'll need a woman."

True. Palming his staff by himself wouldn't mitigate the urges a shred. Only carnal attention from a female would do that.

Adam cleared his throat, then added, "Already need one, by the looks of things."

Bracing one hand on the podium, Erasmus turned to survey the tables and stage area—currently occupied by several bodies in various states of dress and disarray. Lucie Mae caught his eye and waved before turning back to her energetic tonguing of the bagpipe before her. "Then 'tis a good thing I have plenty of women right here to satisfy my needs, is it not?"

12

TIME TO BRAVE THE NIGHT

RUM

totally out - look for whatever we can get

GIN

Gordons - 4 bottles
Plymouth - 3 bottles

WHISKEY

Jameson – 0
Bushmills – 2 bottles

PORT

Smiths - 4 bottles
Sandeman - 2

Morgan's - 5
Ferreira - 2
Gould's - out
Hunt - out

~~*W*HAT *I* WOULDN'T GIVE *for an ice-cold bottle of Budweiser*~~

BRANDY
   Martell - ½ cask
   Hine's - out
   Ranson - nada
   RMartin - nearly full cask
   Hennesey - 2

ALE

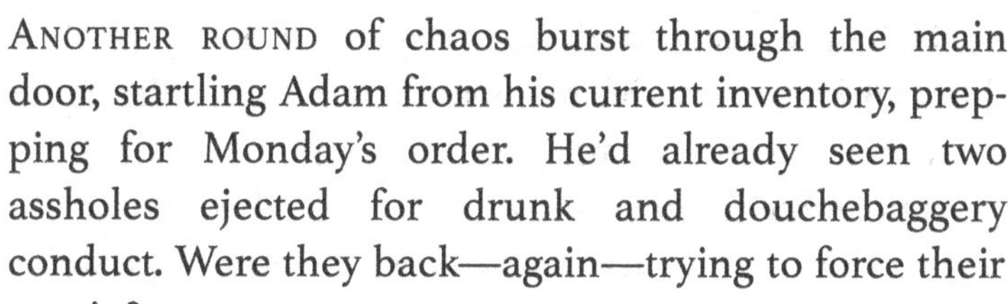

ANOTHER ROUND of chaos burst through the main door, startling Adam from his current inventory, prepping for Monday's order. He'd already seen two assholes ejected for drunk and douchebaggery conduct. Were they back—again—trying to force their way in?

"Lord Blakely!"

"Lord Blakely!"

Both high and low pitches voiced the loud cries.

"Mr. Adam!"

"Mr. Adam! Are *you* here?"

Before he could even begin to respond, the same two tones started yelling his name.

People shouting for him in voices he wouldn't recognize if his life depended upon it. By the way they were hollering, you would think someone's very well might.

Their doorkeeper was having a hell of a time keeping the two from shoving their way into the main room. Abandoning his scribbles, he hustled their direction, taking them in at a glance. Definitely never seen the pair before. A tall boy and his... Sister?

Girl? Doxy-for-the-evening? No, for she was barely out of the schoolroom, brandishing a leather duffle and looking as though she was ready to move in.

No way was he letting these two inside tonight—what was left of it. Or any other. Not even with hell raining down on him, given how incapacitated Erasmus had been these last few nights, leaving Adam jumping through hoops like a trained rabbit, trying to keep all the spinning plates circling his head from crashing down around his ears.

His bulk combined with Baywick's easily pushed the two back into the foyer and he yanked the main door shut behind them.

The entry room was just that—a smallish space, no bigger than twelve feet square, with plain dark walls, no windows, and little furniture save a lone desk and chair in the corner facing toward the single narrow door that led out onto the street. Not much light either, just two lanterns, each on opposite walls, kept intentionally dim. The goal being that if anyone who didn't rightly belong wandered in by accident, their doorkeeper of the night, already attune to the shadows, would usher them right back out.

Baywick, a former military man, took his sentinel duties seriously and had the brawn to back them up. Except, it appeared, when the intruders were wispy enough it looked as though one clout from him wouldn't just send them packing, but might flatten them straight to the floor.

The man wore a floppy hat pulled low, shielding half his face. The lower half had certainly never seen the sharp side of a blade. Lad couldn't be old enough to shave. Had a pudgy middle quite at odds with the slim jaw and long neck. Hmm.

The female at his side, a few inches shorter, eyes wide and cheeks flushed, was eagerly inspecting everything in the room, from Baywick...to *him*.

Both stopped their caterwauling long enough to finally take a breath now that they'd gained attention.

Seeing the tall gentleman readying himself to do battle again, Adam waved the hired man down. "I've got it from here, Baywick."

Knowing better than to keep the Inner Sanctum unguarded—sound from upstairs didn't travel well through the thick walls into this room—he jerked one thumb over his shoulder pointing the way he'd just come. "Keep an eye on things in there for a minute, will you?"

"Aye, sir."

The second the door was secured behind the other man, he turned to the two invaders.

He didn't have time for this shit. Maybe he could intimidate them out?

Glaring at them equally, he led with, "Who the devil are you and why the hell are you trying to barge in?"

As though they really were related, their eyes bugged in unison. It wasn't until seeing the twin expressions on their faces that he realized, man's clothes or not, he was facing *two* females. Likely ladies, judging by the tasteful, no doubt expensive, gown on the shorter, younger one. And he'd more than blundered, speaking as he would have in front of males. Or common folk. *His* folk.

The "man" of the pair stepped right up to him. "Are you Mr. Adam? I need to see Lord Blakely. Immediately. The matter is of the utmost importance."

"Please," the younger one added, transferring the bag to one hand and snaking an arm out to halt the forward progress of her companion. Leading him to realize she was a bit older than he'd thought at first. Definitely more forthright than he'd expected, given her assuredly sheltered upbringing.

In all the time he'd worked with Erasmus, a true young lady—of the innocent, ingénue sort—never set foot in The Den. His friend and boss would have laughed their asses right out the way they came.

Sure, toffs sometimes brought their women with them. Mistresses, street workers who made their living on their backs—or on their knees. Not well-bred, virginal ladies.

Had he even met one before? A virgin? Not in two decades for sure.

Don't you mean two decades and 200 years? part of him snickered.

A part he'd become accomplished at ignoring.

Erasmus might have run what basically amounted to a gentleman's club with hookers, but he did it in style. With class. If that could be applied to doxies and strumpets. Regardless, these two had no business, absolutely *no* business—

"If you could only help my cousin. She needs to find her betrothed and we are lost as to what other avenues might be open to us."

Wrenching his gaze from the wide-eyed lady whose confident nature tugged at him, he swung back to the one in gentlemen's clothing. "*You're* Francine? Blakely's *Francy*?" Yeah, E had let that pet name slip once and Adam hadn't let him hear the end of it since.

But...

Oh God. Of all the rotten timing. Of all the completely insane possibilities. His boss's woman. Here? Now? In the dead of night—with the curse in full fledge? Lord have mercy.

"Aye. The very one." As though to confirm it, she tugged off the floppy cap. Hair of spun gold cascaded down, soft ringlets bouncing into place along her neck and ears. She was lovely—even with the paunchy middle he knew had to be part of her disguise.

And looked much like the younger one, who was also bouncing, just on her feet not with her hair. No springy ringlets in sight, her smooth, fair hair coiled demurely atop her head with a few straight strands pulled down in front of her ears from her temples. Even he knew that wasn't the style, just a small something to set the bouncing beauty apart from the others he'd glimpsed from afar. Had he ever had that much energy?

"I need to see him." The serene, non-bouncing one spoke again. "Right now, if you will, Mr. Adam. Lord Blakely, that is."

"It's just plain Adam, no mister. He's not here. He's—"

"Is he away—to his estate again? Nay." She answered herself almost instantly. "He would have written that—"

"He's written you?"

"Daily. Here." She fished a small purse from a baggy pocket and thrust a packet of letters under his nose. "I know he still cares, else he would not have bothered. And if he no longer wanted to be betrothed, I have no doubt he would come right out and state that as well. Will you help me, please?" Pale eyes *beseeched.* "Take me to him, Mr. Adam..."

Her gaze drifted overhead. "Whether he really *is* here, dallying with others or—" She looked back at him, unshed tears turning her eyes lustrous. "If he has set up a brothel in his bedchamber at home, take me to him regardless."

"I can see why he loves you." Damn. Not what he meant to say. But she was remarkably composed, this woman his friend had claimed, even in her distress.

The other stepped sideways, placing the duffle on the floor and putting an arm around Lady Francine's waist. "Please, Mr. Adam, sir, Lord Blakely made Francine promise to not traipse through London on her own—and yet, she was willing to do so. I had to force her to let me accompany her. She only wants to help him." She lifted the small stack of notes from his loose possession and returned them to her cousin.

But not before running a finger over the ink smeared on what he surmised was the latest one. "You see how his writing has deteriorated? We are not fabricating his distress, I assure you."

Distress? "That's one word for it." Adam had only witnessed the beast once, the night they'd met. A here-today, gone-yesterday mirage that wreaked havoc with his already stunned senses. Causing him to doubt what he'd seen for a full eleven months—until witnessing the extreme change in his new friend's behavior the following year.

He'd not doubted again.

Nor had he been privy to the ultimate torment; only witness to the heightened senses, the ferocious need for fornicating and the ever-revolving parade of young peers his friend sought to mentor. Until exactly one week ago. When he'd seen the beginnings of the worst, he'd feared. Watching his stalwart, take-care-of-every-one-and-everything-in-his-path friend start to break apart...

"You know exactly where he is," she said with assurance completely at odds with how ridiculous she looked in the borrowed clothing. "I can tell by the way you consider my request. Take me to him, please." When he remained silent, still contemplating, she added, "Posthaste, if you would."

As though determined to override his hesitation, the younger one released her cousin and moved into the shadows, pressing her spine flush against the wall.

"I shall stay here till you return. Then you may escort me home. I'll not utter a peep."

"Even a peepless *lady* in these environs is trouble beyond compare," he told her, impressed with how very English he sounded. He'd been practicing. The better to blend and ask questions, he'd learned. Even if, against E's advice, he had held on to his mustache.

Her spine popped upright. "Then take me with you and—"

"No. Hush now. Let me think."

One female, he could protect, his years of illegal fighting gave him advantages over regular Regency street thugs. But *two* ladies? That would put him at a disadvantage, especially as he'd no idea how Erasmus would react. No idea if he would even come to the door. Or if he could. Or if, even now, he was frolicking in bed with his own private harem.

He addressed Lady Francine. "I don't know what sort of reception—"

"It matters not." Her hands, clutched over her heart, should have looked melodramatic. Instead, they came across as sincere. Her entire demeanor impassioned, worried...yet impressive in a crisis. Even a blind man could see she was exactly the type of woman his friend needed. Capable. Bold. Yet alluringly demure as well. What a combination. "What does matter is that he needs me."

Damn.

"And I am not a real lady," the other one piped up.

"You're peeping," he told her.

She snickered. "Well, I am not. My father was a

country vicar. Even though my stepfather is titled, I remain only a simple, unadorned miss."

"Miss pain in my ass," he muttered, startled when the younger one laughed outright.

Even as the older one gave a sad smile. "You will take me to him, then?"

Instead of answering, he pointed to them each. "Stay here. Both of you."

He wrenched the inner door open and stepped through, scanning who was left of the crowd. To shield the innocents behind him from the debauchery within, he closed the door all but a few inches, letting his bulk block the opening.

"Tyndale!" he barked without thinking. Shit. He moderated his tone to one of deference instead of demand. "Lord Tyndale, may I kindly have a word?"

Playing the subservient always stuck in his craw. But at least the man was fully clothed, which was more than he could say for most of them.

A few months back, when Tate's crowd roughed up Bunnie, Tyndale had stepped in. At the moment, that was the best reference he could find. That and *clothes*.

"Lord Tyndale?" A feminine voice piped—peeped —from beneath his outstretched arm. "*He* is here?"

Damn it! "Did I not tell you to stay put?"

"You did but—"

"But nothing!" Seeing Tyndale approach, a look of inquiry on his swarthy features, Adam turned to shove the annoying little "not-a-lady" lady back into the anteroom.

"Nay! You cannot." She shoved back, surprising him with her strength.

"Don't tell me 'Nay' in my own damn club!" Okay, yeah, mostly E's club, but partly his too. As of two years ago, they were officially partners. Had acted like it for several before that.

His brute strength easily overpowered hers, gripping her upper arms and simply lifting and rotating—

He stopped dead. "Oh shit."

Tyndale bumped into his back, lanky where Adam was beefy, the other man easily saw over his shoulder. And whistled his appreciation.

"I told you!" His little miss hissed, jostling them both back into the main area and following this time, pulling the door shut behind her.

"Heavens! *Men.* She is changing into a *dress.* You cannot expect her to greet him fashioned as a man!"

Great.

Jim. Fucking. Dandy.

Adam could feel E's right hook connecting with his jaw even now.

For both he and Tyndale had just gotten an eyeful of the Marquis of Blakely's future wife.

In a magnificent state of complete and utter disarray.

With nary a stitch upon her person.

⸺◦⸺

Earlier That Evening

FRANCINE PLOPPED herself down in the hack they'd hailed and scooted over to make room for her cousin, tugging on the crotch area of the men's trousers that she wasn't used to wearing. "My, these saw into you when you sit."

"I daresay, 'tis your hips. They're wider than Tom's"—Temperance mentioned her stepfather's coachman—"and it was not as though I had time to search further than the laundry. His were only set aside because of the rip in one leg."

"I'm not complaining, 'tis just..." She tugged again, trying to resituate her backside so the front wasn't cleaving into that delicate area. "Decidedly uncomfortable."

"Here." Temperance clambered up next to her and settled a packed valise upon Francine's lap. "You may have need of this. I folded one of your dresses, stays and a clean shift for later. So you can greet him attired properly. We cannot have a marquis seeing you masquerading as a man."

"Excellent idea."

"What a Grand Adventure!" her cousin enthused, head swinging every which way, to look out beyond the hack they'd waved down several streets from Rowden House. "I have always craved having several, you know."

"What? Adventures?" No, Francine hadn't known, not because she didn't care, but because Temperance hadn't confided in her for years. This getting to know another person, when you had to snatch brief conversations, here and there, was taking longer than Francine had hoped.

And now wasn't the time for her to indulge her excitable cousin, who'd thoughtfully—forcefully— joined Francine on her quest after a hurried, hushed argument Temperance only won because Francine had not the fortitude to fight both her cousin and her own escalating worry.

Thank goodness, too. In her haste to act, once she finally made the decision to, she'd stupidly left her spectacles in her room.

Traversing London on her own would have proved a nightmare.

As it was, Temperance was just coming home from an evening out with friends and encountered Francine tiptoeing down the stairs, hoping to find Burford, to ask if he knew where she might locate some men's clothing.

"Dearest," Temperance had exclaimed once she finally pressured the story from the nervous and anxiety-riddled Francine, "you cannot enlist his aid. Not with his advanced age. Should Mother learn of it, why, I have no doubt she would delight in dismissing him without a character or a farthing to his name."

While Francine doubted her aunt still wielded that amount of power, not now that Uncle Rowden had finally taken an interest in curtailing her nefarious activities, she agreed risking Burford's livelihood wasn't ideal.

"Return to your room. I shall bring what you need posthaste." As though she planned secret exploits routinely, Temperance took over, soon delivering clothing Francine shrugged into as fast as she could and then meeting her cousin by the servants' entrance as agreed.

"Thank heavens Patience is still out with Mother and Lord Hansen," Temperance whispered on a giggle as they'd let themselves out of the still and silent home behind them. "Else she would have either demanded to accompany us or put a halt to everything and completely ruined our fun."

Fun wasn't what Francine would call it. Not even close.

The hack was decent, an open carriage intended for four, with the top pulled down, leaving them both exposed to the night and her with the ability to make out the driver's back just a short distance in front of them.

Heart fluttering madly because now it was time she took on the masculine role they'd agreed, Francine turned her attention to the driver.

Significantly louder than the hushed whispers she had exchanged with her cousin up to this point and using her *imitating a haughty lord* voice, she informed him, "We are off to The Den, fine sir."

"The Den now, eh?" Their driver sounded dubious. "Are ye certain 'bout that?"

"Most assuredly. Be quick about it," she ordered, hoping that she sounded sufficiently authoritative—something she certainly didn't feel.

"Pity that Wylde is from town," Temperance leaned over to murmur. "For I have no doubt we could enlist his assistance elsewise."

Francine wasn't so sure. Nor sure how many others she wanted privy to her desperate behavior. Scandalous was one thing, but *desperation*? Not something one liked to advertise.

Knowing her feminine hands would easily give her away, she kept them stuffed in pockets or hidden beneath the jacket's edge, her bare fingers worrying themselves sick. "Gloves? Did you think to bring those?"

"Drat. Nay, I did not, nor fresh stockings either. Ack. I fear I'm not as accomplished an accomplice as I might have hoped."

The drive proved an unnerving blur, Temperance keeping up an animated discourse that Francine was starting to think was intentional, something to set her mind at ease—something that wasn't working nearly as well as she wished it would.

When the hack horses slowed, then came to a halt beside a curb, she took what stock she could of their surroundings. No lanterns burned on this street, the store fronts decidedly dark, empty and intimidating. If it weren't for the lamps on their hack, she'd see nothing at all.

As it was, they'd paused directly in front of a nondescript narrow door set off by several feet of empty wall on either side, situated between an apothe-cary and a mercantile, both of those fairly easy to discern, due to the glass windows fronting the dark shops and the large signs marking their existence. (Aided, no doubt, by Temperance whispering in her ear what *she* saw, bless her thoughtful heart.)

"This is it, then?" Francine asked, both forgetting to use her low voice and that she should have brazened it out, pretended as though she knew exactly where she was going. *Ugh.*

Hoping to cover the blunder, she started to rush from the hack.

Temperance held her back with a firm grip upon her arm. "Nay. Wait. You are attired as a man, lest you forget. Move... *Clunkier* than you would as yourself. Mayhap swagger a bit."

She heard their driver chuckle. No wonder. She did not see herself as the *swaggering* sort.

He turned his head to the side and spoke over his shoulder. "Are you bof certain 'ere is where you ought to be?" He seemed of a fatherly disposition. Perhaps indulging them the entire way? she started to wonder. Had he purposely made it take longer than it needed to, hoping they'd cry craven? "I'm thinkin' I best wheel you right back where I found you."

"Nay, please," Francine said without any attempt to disguise how she sounded. "My betrothed is in there."

I think. I hope. *I fear.*

"All the more reason why chasin' 'im down ain't the smartest move, ye 'ear me?"

"We shall be fine," Temperance spoke to him. "I will pay you extra to wait here until we are safely inside."

He shifted round, placed one arm across the back of his seat so he could look at them, an evaluating stare that made Francine start to sweat in her borrowed disguise.

"You want I should wait beyond that?" He grumbled on a bit about lost fares but seemed kindly enough.

Francine was tempted to take him up on his offer.

"Nay," Temperance said. "That will not be necessary. Just ensure we are both safely inside, then you may drive off."

"Are you certain?" Francine hissed under her breath to her cousin, starting to question this whole outing now that they were here. Now that she was likely to find him hale and hearty—and in the arms of another. Oh, why had she taken on this wretched business? Why had *he* not simply been truthful with her in his notes?

His notes. She reached deep into the unfamiliar jacket's pocket and gripped them. *This was why.*

He'd not been himself this past week. He needed her. She just knew it.

"Absolutely, I am certain," Temperance said with staunch conviction. "You do not want to give him an easy way to reject you, do you? To send you on your way. Not until you have had a chance to secure his presence and the answers you need, correct?"

"Aye."

And then proceeding to prove her worth far and away that above simple companion, Temperance counseled, "Now, do not go in there screaming for him like a *girl*. Remember, you are a man at the moment. Behave as one."

A man. Right. Shouldn't be overly difficult to recall, not with the groom's hat Temperance had brought her, cramped tight over her skull and holding all her thick hair up. Or the way she'd bunched up her shift, above the too-tight trousers, stuffing the lower portion inside the loose-fitting shirt that belonged to someone other than the owner of the borrowed trousers. All the extra fabric around her middle concealed the curve of her breasts every bit as much as the heavy jacket they'd pinched off a peg down below. The boots, at least, were hers, her oldest pair usually reserved for stormy days, and fortunately with a low heel.

"*Man*. Aye." She reminded them both out loud,

taking a huge breath and praying for courage. "I am ready. Let us alight while the street is still empty."

"I shall do it." Temperance followed close behind Francine as they disembarked. "You be quiet."

"Quiet? Whatever for?" Did that not completely contradict their very purpose in being here?

"I shall ask for Lord Blakely. You remain silent."

Francine stumbled to a stop, gripping the bag with both hands. "Nay. *You* shall stand there silently. I will not see you ruined too. You are not disguised. Anyone could recognize you."

"Posh." Temperance pried Francine's grip from the handles and took the bag. "I care not about that. You know I entertain myriad interests beyond making a match and making babies. You are the one engaged to a marquis, the one we cannot allow to be recognized."

Rather than argue, Francine marched forth and tried the door handle.

Locked. By the blazes. One more obstacle.

With a closed fist, she assaulted the door.

Whether she sounded like a *girl* or not, she'd give someone on the other side two seconds to answer before she started screaming in truth.

ADAM.

They'd found him.

Francine wouldn't admit out loud, but certainly would to herself, how very much more at ease—if one could count their teeth rattling and body quivering *at ease*—she'd been since locating this friend of her betrothed's, the man who insisted she dispense with the *Mr.*

Above a tall, very muscular body, dark blond, longish hair was brushed back from a strong, mayhap handsome face. Hard to tell with half of it obscured by the thick mustache she'd noticed he ran his fingertips over when he was debating something—such as whether or not to help her.

But he'd agreed.

And she could breathe once again. Now that she no longer had to navigate the dark streets of London on her own, for that's how it'd felt. Temperance's company might have been an unexpected boon, but having her along, while giving Francine a much-needed distraction, had also caused her to worry more.

Was she now putting her cousin at risk, letting her also be out at night?

Uncaring at being caught changing, she'd quickly drawn her fresh shift and dress over her head—who had time for stays on such an errand?—and finished making herself as presentable as she could given the lack of light and mirror. Given the lack of steady hands.

"I cannot drive a pair worth shit," Adam told her minutes later when she balked at mounting the giant stallion he called a mere pony. An ironic appellation, to be sure.

She stood there, uncertain, in the mews a block from the club. Shifting her feet, feeling the press and glide of her inner thighs once again against each other and not coarse fabric, her previously abused tissues thanking heaven.

The horse might be devastatingly large, but the

men's trousers were gone. Her Venus mound sighed in blessed relief every bit as much as it blossomed in anticipation of seeing her man.

Adam huffed when she made no move toward the horse. "Lady Francine, this is it. Your only choice. I'm not risking *either* of us by walking."

After he'd taken such extreme caution, just gaining the short distance to the stables, she had no doubt of his conviction. He might be able to see perfectly well, but he obviously had no desire to chance this portion of London on foot. Certainly not the worst area she'd been in, nor the most fashionable, but somewhere betwixt the two, she suspected, certain there were other gambling hells and likely brothels nearby.

After leading his horse away from the sleeping groom, Adam had saddled it himself and now expected her to simply, "Climb on."

Bringing the beast right up to her, barely a foot away.

"With you?" That was not how ladies rode a horse, not that she'd had much practice in years, Uncle Rowden keeping horses for the carriages but not for much else.

"Of course with me. I'll ride behind you."

This deep into the night, with no spectacles and lanterns sparse and few between, so much of the journey had been a black blur. The horse now?

Just a giant black beast, bigger than many she was used to seeing, not nearly as refined or tame looking either.

It seemed as though, the more she hesitated, the more the horse aimed a baleful, disapproving eye her direction, as though he knew it was *her* fault he'd been roused and forced back into duty when he thought his workday was over. She *would* be in a position to see that!

"It's the fastest way," he said impatiently when she still didn't move. "Thought you were in a rush."

"Never before have I ridden astride."

"Oh, for the love of God." In three seconds, he had her plunked on the beast, legs hanging down on either side of the large animal, Francine scrambling to stuff some of her shift between her thighs—lest her *intimate* regions meet the saddle. Astride was one thing; plastering herself indecently *there* quite another. As to indecent, her skirts rode up to reveal a significant amount of lower leg and thigh.

Sparing her exposed skin not a single glance, he hefted himself up behind her and grunted as he unwound the reins. "Huh. For all your height, you're a dainty little thing, aren't you?" He turned them toward the exit and clicked to his horse. "Smell a hell of a lot better than this place too."

That was all he said, galloping through London in such a way that were less at stake, the ride would have been exhilarating. As it was, every minute only tumbled the nerves tighter in her belly.

Once they reached the area where larger, more elegant townhouses resided, he slowed the animal to a sedate pace, making sure to take to the shadows any time a carriage or hack lumbered past, preserving what little modesty she no longer claimed, but the gesture appreciated nonetheless.

During one such moment, as they waited, hiding,

tense and still, for people to disembark and their carriage to be taken round back, she asked, "How did you and Lord Blakely meet?"

"You wouldn't believe me if I told you." She was about to argue the matter when he added, "Not now, you wouldn't. Maybe after tonight though..."

Cryptic. Curious. Not important enough to follow up on, not when all her turbulent thoughts brawled through her brain like unruly street bruisers, clashing for dominance.

"I can't believe you aren't scared," he murmured, the words breezing past her ear and jostling her hair. "At least...*wary* of arriving at his doorstep, unannounced."

"Are you daft? I'm terrified."

He grunted a low chuckle. "Impressive. Must be that stoic English upbringing."

More like the habit of hiding what I feel and think. "I have become adept at shielding my true nature."

He stiffened behind her and she rushed to explain, "But not with your friend. Never with Erasmus. With him... I am amazingly free. Utterly myself, I assure you."

As though sensing his master's easing, the animal beneath them ruffled his lips in a long, snorted whinny.

The people and conveyances finally cleared and Adam ordered his beast to move out once again. It wasn't but a handful of blocks later that she began to recognize several streets. Oh, if only she'd known. Lord Blakely's home wasn't overly far from Rowden House.

Before turning down what she assumed was the

last street, Adam pulled up at the end, halted the horse and sat there silently for a few seconds.

The cool evening breeze that kissed through her hair, the lone carriage that rolled by, bringing more late-night revelers back home, the single laugh she heard someone utter from a distance...

It all seemed so very normal.

When inside her entire world was breaking apart. A fine trembling had taken hold of her limbs.

"Why have we stopped?" Over the furious pounding of her heart, she asked the question, afraid of the answer. "You have not reconsidered, have you?"

Quietly, the words whispering past her ear, he said, "There's more than a fair chance your Lord Blakely will have my head for this, Francine. I'd hate to lose my job —or my best friend—over bringing you here."

Please don't change your mind.

"But I've seen him act differently the last couple months and all for the better. I know he needs you too. I'm just not sure..."

Not sure about what?

It took greater strength of fortitude to remain silent, let him work through things on his own, than it had to ride astride for the first time, the unused position starting to strain her thighs.

"Truth is...I'm not sure you're ready for what awaits you inside."

"I am." *I have to be.*

"Just..." He swore. "Prepare yourself. I don't know how bad it's gotten, but he won't be himself, that I can guarantee."

Her legs and every other muscle tensed. "What do you mean *how bad*? What exactly is *it*?"

"That's for him to tell you. Not me." He hefted out a big sigh. "Damn. I cannot believe I'm letting you go in there alone. Maybe I should..." As though sensing his master's indecision, the big horse shifted his weight, rocking them both with a creak of saddle and leather.

"Shall I take the decision from you? I shall speak with him *alone*. Face whatever"—whomever—"he keeps from me on my own. I need to do this."

He clicked to his horse and tightened the strong legs behind her, nudging the animal forward with his heels. "All right. I'll wait, though—out of sight. For five minutes, no more, in case you change your mind. Then I really must get back to the club."

"I will not change my mind."

"I'm still waiting."

"Make it three minutes." She tried to compromise. "I do not want to take you from your duties. I don't claim to know what all they are, but Erasmus speaks very highly of you."

"Not after tonight, he won't."

13

ANGST, ANXIETY, AND DEMMED ANIMALS

SEVERAL DAYS AGO,
IN A RARE MOMENT OF ANGUISHED CLARITY

DO THIS FOR ME—FOR yourself—for every Hammond that has come before either of us and I pray may come after: save yourself, and your family. Take whatever measures you need to in order to remain whole. I pray your love for me, and yourself, outweighs your hatred of what you become, of what I ask of you.

Be at peace, my Erasmus, my precious heir, be at peace.

ERASMUS'S ACHING fingers strained to close around the old pages from his father, to crush and crumble. Squeeze the life out of them and throw everything into the fire. Then jump in after. The weight of its requests heavy indeed. Nearly beyond bearing.

Had he not done all that his father asked? All that he could to identify any stray, cursed family members? To save Nash, if not Phin?

To keep his own seed from perpetuating?

And where had it landed him?

Beset with guilt.

Bombarded by questions. Where the hell was his brother? What had happened to Phineas? Was The Den and his work there doing enough to keep others safe?

Had he fallen blooming in love with the most sexually eager "innocent" a man could hope to frolic with?

"God help me." The letter gripped tight in his trembling fist, his head thumped down on his bent arms. He didn't need the distraction. Not now, not with lives at stake. So many lives.

But the thought of sending her away? Of never seeing her again? Not waking up, with the notion of basking in her smiles, her wit propelling him out of bed... Instead, the idea of waking with the dark, interminable dread of knowing he wouldn't see her in a few hours, might never see her again?

He couldn't fathom it.

But if he failed the men closest to him—failed to protect his club, his cubs—and the ones they might be a threat to, how could he ever hope to help others? To help himself?

How could he justify keeping Francine, when every facet of their agreement, their every conversation, kept reminding him how he was supposed to give her back? Return her freedom. Grant her that ultimate independence she so craved.

Even if he'd be giving away his bloodied, ensnared, godforsaken heart in the process.

The one she'd rescued.

The one he couldn't live without. The one she held in her dainty, dirt-dusted, lovely hands.

CASTING one last glance beyond her shoulder, where she knew Adam waited, watching over her, Francine marched up the steps to the townhouse he'd indicated Lord Blakely owned.

Nothing to hold on to save her resolve and the valise she'd brought with her, now carrying the discarded men's clothes—and Erasmus's precious letters.

Where was a doorknocker when one needed it? Needed to desperately lift the heavy metal and bring it crashing down as hard as she could, hear its metallic clangs echo satisfyingly in the air?

"Nothing for it." She kicked the door sharply with the side of one boot, swinging her leg as hard as she dared. "There now."

That thumped pleasingly loud.

No one responded to her summons, so she banged on the door again, this time with her bare knuckles.

The night was cool and she set the valise down to pull the big jacket tighter around her middle. Muted thumps echoed beyond the paned windows, confirming Adam's assertion that someone was home.

And what was that? She pressed her ear to the window beside the door. There it was again—something long and animalistic...sounding suspiciously like a roar, of all things. *What* was going on in there?

She straightened and pounded against the thick door with both hands. Hit the solid wood with such force, it jarred her teeth. Kicked it again for good measure. *Who needed a doorknocker when they had determination?*

"Erasmus! Let me in," she called from her position on the stoop, heedless of who might overhear. The jacket's long sleeve got in the way and muffled the next round of pounding.

Her breath coming in gasps, she tried the handle.

Locked. No surprise there.

Where were his servants? Why did no one respond? Abandoning decorum, she lifted part of her long skirt and wound it around one hand to bang harder, thrashing the impenetrable wood with all her might.

She worried he might be dallying with another woman.

She worried he might be sick, or worse.

She worried about *him*.

"Erasmus Hammond! Open this—"

The door swung open abruptly. "What th' hell do you want?"

"Erasmus?" Francine stared at the...*person* before her. It was him. But it wasn't.

Sun-bleached streaks lightened his coal-black hair and it had grown! Several inches at least—in a week? His already-muscular chest had expanded, was hunched forward and bowed inward from some invisible weight he carried on his back. Golden whiskers covered his cheeks and jaw, extending down his neck and replacing the dark shadow she'd come to expect by the end of their evenings.

She stared in shock. Erasmus had thought her false betrothal proposition was ludicrous? *This* was insane! Grown men did not turn into hairy beasts in the span of a few days, not in the nineteenth century!

Not in any century!

But *he* had...

Nay! It couldn't be. 'Twas a parlor trick, a cruel jest.

The pressure behind her eye sockets heralded the arrival of unwelcome tears. Her ungloved fingers dashed them away. She didn't have time for silly female emotion.

Shaking off her confusion, she swept up her bag and poked him in the chest with it, propelling him away from the door. She stormed over the threshold, turning in dismay when a low rumble erupted from his throat.

My. Even disreputable and...well...somewhat hairy, he was a sight to behold. Never before had she faced such raw power, so much brute strength, especially in the form of the person she'd come to care about more than any other.

Feral energy radiated from him. Effectively intimidating, if her racing heart were any judge. But she couldn't deny the flash of excitement that flared in some latent part of her either, the extreme wildness beyond exciting. What did that say about her?

Debauched, indeed.

He'd often been a little untamed in their lovemaking, but nothing like this. Never a total barbarian...his eyes now cullish, hooded, no longer bright and clear.

All tolerant amusement gone; all indulgent consideration wiped free from his face.

Her resolve firmed. This wasn't like him and she wasn't leaving without answers. "Are you drunk? In an opium haze?" She leaned in, hoping to catch a hint of his breath—not that she knew what opium might smell like.

She bustled several feet from the doorway and spun to face him, clutching her shaking fingers tight around the handle of the valise, praying for courage. "I refuse to leave, so you have no choice but to tell me. Erasmus, *what* has happened?"

He rammed the door shut so hard it bounced back off its hinges. He kicked it closed, fumbled with the lock. Then whipped around and advanced. "So, *malaya*, you finally saw your way to showing your face? About demmed time!"

The angry words were snarled with such hatred that she stepped back, a frisson of true fear latching on to her heart.

Where was the gentle, caring man who had escorted her everywhere these past weeks? The man who arranged for packets of seeds from his estate's garden to be sent to her? The man who once arrived, one magical time, with a tipitiwitchet! The difficult-to-come-by plant that he said needed her soft touch to tame it and that she was to think of *his stalk* claiming *her* "luscious pink interior" every time she glanced upon the wicked specimen? Who'd been her staunchest defender and biggest supporter since the night they'd met?

Where was the man who had captured her heart, for surely this beast wasn't him.

She stood tall, determined not to let him intimidate her. "I refuse to be bully-hectored by you, no matter—"

A tormented wail came from overhead, followed by such a commotion that the ceiling-mounted chandelier swayed. She gripped his arm. "What is going on up there? Did you decide I wasn't enough to satisfy your 'extensive appetites'?" She bit her lip, refusing to be cowed when he turned hate-filled eyes on her. "I thought we had an agreement. One you obviously—"

"Forget your bloody agreement." He shrugged away from her hold and ripped her valise out of her hands, hurling it to the floor with a threatening growl.

She retreated, bumped against a table, that spark of fear igniting...

Be strong. He'll not hurt you.

She was starting to question...

"Are you here to save your lover?" he spat the words. "Can you manage such a sacrifice, I wonder?"

"Sacrifice? Erasmus, what—"

Another crash sounded from upstairs the very second she noticed his nose. It was smooth and blemish-free. No scar marred its even surface but two slightly larger nicks slashed across his lips, the faint lines almost obscured by the heavy whiskers furring his face.

Faster than plucking a weed, awareness swept through her. "Where is Erasmus? I demand you take me to him!"

Realizing this barbarian wasn't her beloved returned all her confidence and then some. She grabbed the impostor's linen shirt, barely noticing how frayed it was at the seams. Tears gathered and fell from her eyes as she suspicioned this detestable man must have harmed her beloved.

She fisted her hands in the ragged material, also catching the chain he wore beneath. Further proof! Erasmus never wore jewelry. No chains, ever. Only his beautiful signet ring handed down to him from his father.

Pummeling the shammer's chest, she screamed, "What have you done with Erasmus? Where is he?"

"Franceeeeeeeene!"

The bellow came from upstairs.

Her attention diverted from the one before her, it took but a moment to realize he'd shoved the heavy jacket from her shoulders. It landed in a heap with a *whoosh-thunk*. The stranger stood appraising her, a wary, disgruntled expression settling over his menacing features. "Scrawny. Shit. You aren't near strong enough. Too fucking innocent, just like he claimed. *God damn it!*"

Giving her no time to make sense of his words, the man before her swayed, gesturing with disgust, an odd puffing noise coming from his open mouth. He motioned for her to leave and she caught sight of his hands, the nails elongated, pointed, curving into *claws*.

"Erasmus!" she shouted, stumbling from the monster before her. "*Erasmus!*"

Another roar. She jumped. It seemed as if the plaster directly above them was about to come falling down.

She returned to the stranger, digging her fingers

into his shirt and hammering him with her fists. "Take me to him!"

Fire burned in her heart, the breath heaving from her lungs. She struck his burly chest over and over as hard as she could, the action ripping the top of the worn shirt until it exposed his upper chest. His skin was covered in thick, tawny hair, so unlike Erasmus's smooth, shapely muscles. The difference goaded her on and she struck him with more force, not caring that tremors were shuddering through him, increasing the glaze that filled his eyes.

"Please!" Francine cried. She pulled at the hair covering his pectorals, trying to get his attention, trying to *hurt* him. "Please. You have to tell me! What have you done to him?"

"Quiet!" He clutched her arms, and for a fraction of a second, his face gentled. Refinement overlaid savagery. A modicum of peace settled across his fierce visage, then it was displaced when another convulsion ran through him, almost dislodging their combined grips. "Listen well, *mwanamke*," he gritted out. "I am Nash, his brother. The Change is upon us. He refused to call for you and..." Low growls vibrated from within his throat. "He refused to fuck any of the women I brought here, damn him. He remains in agony, *suffering*, because of you. And 'tis making *me* suffer as well, damn you both!"

Nash threw her from him and Francine crashed into the small table.

"Leave now. If you value your life...leave!"

As she watched, he shuddered again, his hair and

nails extending. He hunched over, his arms hanging perilously close to the floor.

"Franceene..."

The cry was softer now, more anguished. She looked toward the staircase, torn, not understanding.

The man-beast before her roared and she saw fangs.

God have mercy.

"If you value your life, *leave* or I cannot promise what..." Nash stumbled toward the staircase, landing on all fours. He loped partway up the steps, turning to look at her over his shoulder. Stringy hair hid most of his face. Her lack of spectacles blurred the rest. "Or, Lady Francsheene..." His words were slurred, garbled. "...falloww me...schraight intoo *hell*."

Ascending faster than she would have believed possible, he disappeared up the stairs.

What had just disappeared? The younger brother to her beloved? Or a monster?

Gasping, Francine looked around her, one hand going to the tender spot on her hip where she'd collided with the table. The house appeared typical, if sparsely furnished, but for the inconsistent thumps from overhead.

Secrets. She'd known Erasmus had them.

Had that not been part of his allure?

The haunted look in his eyes she'd sworn to ease? Perhaps erase?

And now...

Now—

The wounded cries came again. Fainter but no less intense. Such an unfamiliar, foreign noise but one that captured her, rooted her feet to the spot as surely as the kindness and passion that Erasmus had wrapped her in these past months had planted seeds within her, ones that had quickly become entrenched, intertwining throughout her body and heart, blossoming into something much more than she'd ever expected.

Another moaned wail, drawing her gaze toward the stairs. Yet trepidation sent it scurrying toward the locked door. The one she could open, could escape through... Return to Rowden House with no one the wiser.

Nay. For that way lay heartache. Shame. *Loneliness.*

If they were to be her lot in life, so be it, but she'd not choose them. Not when it was time to save her man.

Secrets be damned.

Though her mind railed at her to leave, her heart stood firm. She wasn't going anywhere without answers —or without Erasmus.

Her gaze jerked overhead.

She tasted blood and realized she'd bitten her lip. Scared, nervous—oddly exhilarated—she closed her eyes and prayed for strength, because, God help her, whatever the sacrifice, she was going to save the man she'd come to love.

⸻⬥⸻

MIRED within The Change unlike anything he'd ever experienced, Nash struggled more with every second. How much longer could he hold the fiendish elements off? Keep them from overpowering what humanity he still claimed?

Part of him sensed what an utter bastard he was being. But the beast controlled him now—or nearly so. He had no patience left, no soft nor refined feelings.

No feelings at all. Other than the need to fuck, clawing at him so assiduously, 'twas a wonder he still stood.

Oh wait, he wasn't. Standing that is. Racing up the stairs faster than lightning, seeing the carved balusters pass at eye level in a hazy, reddened blur.

How was it he seemed to be suffering more than Blake? As though loving the blighted bitch somehow gave his brother more strength than Nash could dredge from the depths of his soul.

It had been like this for days—unceasing, the relentless pressure to succumb, to let the monster take hold. And it only grew once he reached London a few nights ago, hoping to find answers for why this year was different than any other.

Previously, whether he and Blake were together battling The Change jointly or whether they did so apart, only referencing it briefly the next time he was in town, 'twas always a—fairly—simple matter of securing a wench. Slaking the Beast Lust and functioning, more or less, as a normal, lusty wastrel the rest of the time.

Or not.

"Regular" sexual urges increased during The Change, but didn't overwhelm—or reign supreme—as long as that female-brought-about orgasm occurred daily.

But this year, no matter how many willing wenches

Nash found, or paid, the urges only gained strength. And knowing better than to take on the responsibility of a horse—or any responsibilities, for that matter—he'd hired a gig and driver and made haste to London, hoping for answers.

Only to find Blake a broken shell of himself, hiding out in his bedchamber, struggling, pleading for Nash to only leave and let him fight in peace.

Pah. The way his brother looked, he wouldn't last the month.

So despite the stupid lout refusing any help, Nash did what he could, in the moments of sanity he could secure, at least seeing them both fed and the more breakable possessions cleared out.

He'd suspected 'twas a woman to blame. Had only taken Blake's fevered rambles to confirm it.

He also suspected the only way for either of them to truly find a measure of peace this year, was for them both to succumb to the beast—not an option—or for Blake to finally bed a bitch.

And now the very one his blighted brother yearned for had delivered her treasure straight to their doorstep?

If Nash could just push back the agonizing pain long enough to remain sensible, keep the beast caged long enough to keep from scaring her and her tasty little slit off...

He hurt. Hurt with such a relentless ache, he wasn't sure whether he could endure it from one minute to the next. Hated how rough and uncouth he'd become. How his mind and thoughts had reduced the alluring female form he normally appreciated in all its soft, gentle glory to naught but a resented means to stop the agony.

He wasn't a monster. He wasn't!

And he proved it eleven months out of the year, when he did... Well, not much of anything in truth. But certainly nothing harsh. Nothing unkind. Certainly nothing *intentionally* and overly rude.

Eleven-twelfths of the year, he simply looked out for himself. What was the harm in that?

He knew better than to depend upon his brother to smooth his way—Blake already did so much more for him than Nash deserved, providing money, a home even. What sort of irresponsible knave would he be to expect his remaining family to put to rights his beleaguered existence when he wallowed in the uncertainty of it?

Why trouble Blake further when it was Nash who couldn't figure out what he wanted from life?

He wasn't duty-conscious enough to buy into the military. Certainly wasn't clerically minded. An educator? A scholar? *Absurd.* Intellectively inclined, he was not.

He'd laugh if his demmed fangs weren't poking into his bottom lip.

Or perhaps, secretly he did know, down deep, *exactly* what he wanted. But also knew he claimed not the worth to wish for it so...

What second son, cursed with an inherent dislike of responsibility—oh, and the pesky trial of becoming *Felis leo* each summer—who secretly yearned for a refined "lady" to call his very own had *any* chance of ever gaining his dreams?

None.

Nullus.

Hakuna hata.

None, but such remedy as, to save my aching head from such ludicrous dreams, would be to cleave my heart in twain.

His ridiculous dreams...

Craving a soft, sweet-smelling female to hug him and hold him when the urges became too great? Pah. He knew better. Knew better than to dream or expect.

Knew better than to think beyond the difficult night ahead. And the sole goal of surviving the tortuous hours any way he could.

***

IN THE END, Adam waited seven minutes. Nearly dismounted at how disreputable his friend appeared when he tore open the door, but also saw how the man looked at Francine as though she would be his redemption. So he slowly settled back into the saddle.

Still unnerved. Still worried.

Definitely straining his ears for the blood-curdling scream of a victim or the roar of a predator going in for the kill—his entire body shuddering at the thought. And when he didn't discern either, he slowly guided Magnum around the way they'd come, kept his pace as sedate as he could to not draw attention in this part of London, and as soon as he felt comfortable, lit a fire under his trusty steed and raced back to the club.

The Den and the second English "lady" he needed to see secured for the night.

God help them all.

"Where is she?"

His eyes already accustomed to the dark, Adam heaved the door practically off its hinges in his rush to get back, scanning the foyer.

But she wasn't there. No one who mattered was, certainly not one particular not-a-lady *lady*.

"Where the devil is she?" he bellowed, not receiving a single response to his first—more calmly voiced —question.

Tyndale finally looked up from his lounging position behind the desk, where he was scratching out something with the pencil and paper Baywick usually kept neatly stacked, now sprawled over the desk— almost as though someone had brushed across it, all the pages haphazardly splayed. Had the bounder decided to use it for naughty or nefarious purposes?

"What did you do with her?" Full of worry and quickly filling with rage, Adam advanced. "Where is she? Why is the desk all—"

Tyndale gave a relaxed laugh and pushed to standing in a meandering, uncaring way that made Adam want to shake him till he cracked one of the buffoon's teeth. "You know, I think I may have a word with Blakely about your attitude toward your betters."

Grinding *his* teeth so hard they squeaked, he gritted out from between compressed lips as cordially as he could manage, "Pray, my lord, forgive me. I am quite on edge, you see. Where, please tell me"—before I break your damn neck—"*where* has Lady..."

Fuck it all. He *still* didn't know her name?

Rounding the desk in a leisurely move that just

made Adam's fist yearn to slam hard into the man's neck—yeah, fighting dirty wasn't above him, not the way he felt right now—the other man raised his arms overhead and clasped them together, then stretched from side to side as though he had not a care in the world.

Adam stood there seething, giving off so much heated anger he was surprised the low ceiling overhead didn't start to melt.

Only after a big yawn, another interminable six seconds of stretching that was stretching Adam's vanishing patience to the breaking point, did the asshole of a London lord finally snap to and act as though he had a clue what Adam was talking about. "Oh, you mean that wild little piece?"

At least, that's what he heard. *Wild little piece*, having no idea that, in fact, the other man had said Wylde's little piece.

Just as the muscles in his upper body instinctively tensed, readying to throw that punch after all, Tyndale finished, with a dismissive flick of his fingers toward the door Adam had just come through. "Scurried out of here when—"

"You let her *leave*?"

In a flash, Tyndale slammed into the wall, Adam's shaking fists at his throat, knotted in the voluminous neckcloth and drawing it perceptively tighter every second. "You motherfucker! Do you not know what's been happening around here? There's a killer on the loose, for God's sake. Baywick!" Adam finished in a roar.

Tyndale's eyes got wider than a flying saucer. Didn't

know if it was how he'd just been addressed, the tightened neckcloth possibly starving air from his imbecilic brain, or what he'd just been told.

Maybe a bit of all three.

Adam didn't care.

"Baywick!" he hollered again, shoving the lord to the side with a vicious thrust of both arms and turning to wrench the inner door open just as the doorkeeper did the same.

"The other one—" He held his hand out, chest high, indicating her height as opposed to the tall one. "She's gone? Left?" he asked the man.

Baywick scanned the inner sanctum. "No, sir. She was here not three minutes ago."

Three minutes. Three fucking minutes!

Red-faced and jaw clenched, Tyndale was already climbing from the floor. Sparing not a thought to his ridiculous rank, Adam speared him with a finger in his face. "We're getting out there and finding her! And if we don't—if something's happened? You'll be next."

Without stopping to think or arm himself further, he was gone, racing out the small door, running to the right after gesturing Tyndale back the way Adam had just come from, thinking she must have gone the other way or he would have already seen her.

Could this night get any worse?

14

THE SAUCE BOX TO THE RESCUE

———◦———

AND THAT'S ANOTHER THING—SOME *unknown language I speak with ease, without even realizing I'm doing it. So very deuced perplexing at times—how foreign sounds flow from my mouth when the beast is upon me. Beyond uncomfortable, I tell you, speaking in a tongue one has no recollection nor recognition of. Only discovered what the strange syllables meant upon viewing an exhibit focused upon The Peoples of Africa months ago.*

Imagine my astonishment, if you will, when I started translating a series of engravings before ever noticing the English versions beneath. Even stranger, I was unaware of my audible translation until the curator called it to my attention—and that only because he overheard me saying something different, and more accurate we were to learn later, than what was written.

What other unknown abilities might this curse bless— or blight—us with, I cannot help but wonder...

———————◦———————

Swallowing her unease, Francine darted up the staircase after Nash. At the top of the landing, her steps faltered. Which way?

"Erasmus!" she called with all her might, half afraid a round of servants would come running and chase her out. Although, wouldn't they have already done so?

But no... No one came.

So she called out again. Waited...

And received a tortured, soft "Francy" in response.

Allowing the muted cries of her name to guide her, she charged down the hallway past several closed doors until she reached the one fairly brimming with untamed energy.

Apprehension spiked through her as she gripped the knob. It wouldn't turn. She leveraged her weight to—

The door handle ripped from her grasp.

Nash stood—nay, he *hunched*, bent to the side, blocking her entrance. But more human than the *thing* that had escaped up the stairs. "Says *no*, wants you gone."

"Nay! Let. Me. In!" He tried to pull the door shut but she wedged her body against his and shoved with all her might. "You fiendish brute!"

The scent of tallow thickened the air. An abundance of candles burned in the background and she stood on her toes, craning to see over his shoulder to assess the chaos she faced.

Royal blue, floor-length curtains hung in tatters, shredded from the bottom up. Furniture was toppled, drawers and their contents thrown haphazardly about the chamber. Her nose pricked. Beneath the burning candles, the room smelled of sweat and damp...*fur?*

"Where is he?" She scanned the vast area, seeking—

There. As removed from the door as possible.

Shoved against the far wall, a huge bed, the glazed chintz hangings every bit as destroyed as the curtains. A man, tied—bound in the middle.

"Erasmus!" Seeing him renewed her resolve and she ducked beneath Nash's outstretched arm, barging past him to race to the bed where Erasmus struggled against restraints.

Primitive, completely naked, he appeared a stranger, every bit as uncultivated and disreputable as his brother. "Oh, my..."

No wonder she'd mistaken him downstairs. The feral savagery emanating off them both erased any hint of refined veneer. The change in his appearance defied the sennight they had been apart.

"Fraaaanciiiine." Heart wrenching, it was, the way the sound tore from his throat, the anguish upon his features. "Here? *Now?*" He blinked fast, as though disbelieving what he saw. "Night...?" gasped from his throat.

As though to confirm 'twas dark beyond the curtains, he twisted his head to the side, toward the shuttered window. Then back to her, all color leaching from his face beneath the whiskery stubble. A tormented cry raised the hair along her nape, along with *"Night!"*, snarled as though the very concept should be condemned. Hate and self-loathing evident in his harrowed gaze.

Gingerly, she cupped one bristly cheek, staring into eyes the color of molten lava. The deep red scared her as nothing else. They'd only ever glowed golden before. "Oh, my sweet. I am here."

He moaned at her touch. His muscles jerked against his bonds as he seethed the word again: "Night..." as though uttering the vilest of curses.

Nash staggered over to aim one shaking, barbarian-looking hand at his brother. He all but spat, "See what you have done to him? How knowing you rendered him savage?"

"*Me?*" He'd come up directly behind her and now sniffed along her ear. She turned and swatted him away. "Stop that, you fiend."

"Absolutely, *you*," Nash grunted, body heat coming off his hulking form in waves. "Too *fragile*, he said." Mocking Erasmus with his delivery. "Cannot help us, he claimed. Said you were too *delicate*. Nay! I fear 'tis he who is too pigeoned by the pink."

Ignoring his crude taunts, heart thumping madly, she turned back to face the agony. "Oh, dear man, how can I ease your suffering?"

Eyes closed, Erasmus bucked against the ropes tethering him to the bed and she saw what she'd missed before.

There was more than simple twine wound about his limbs.

Leather straps and manacles secured his arms. Chains, his ankles.

Chains?

Francine whipped around and slapped Nash hard across his wild face. He barely budged. "You animal."

Making no move to retaliate, he only hovered there, watching her, glowing, amber eyes narrowing.

"What have you done to him, you blighted savage?" She slapped him again before swinging back to Erasmus who watched her, nostrils flaring. She clambered atop the mattress, ignoring the low rumbles emanating from both men as she scrambled to unfasten the ropes and leather straps securing her beloved.

He looked no better than Nash—his black hair and beard turned to gold, fine fur lightly covering his chest and legs. Bulging, corded muscles twice their normal size filled out his entire frame, and his eyes, now that she was closer...

Despite the unholy color, they conveyed the same emotions as the night they'd first talked. As the times she'd glimpsed his soul prior to that:

Lonely. Haunted. *Hunted.*

Until he slammed them shut, turned from her.

"Stop!" He strained against the bindings, against her—still attempting to push her away. "Leave me. Go!"

Every word he uttered shattered another piece of her heart. She fought him, practically sitting on top of him as she battled the locks and rope and his resistance. "Quit working against me!"

When he refused, kept trying to shove her bodily off him, she hollered, "Lord Blakely." The strident call at least snapped his head back to her, his eyes open again. "Already, have you rescued me more than once. Let me do this for you."

With an anguished howl, he stilled, breathing hard and heavy.

Despite her frantic efforts, her fingers met unmovable resistance.

"Where is the key?" She stumbled off the bed and spun toward Nash. "The key!" Her fist bounced off his hard shoulder, and when he didn't answer but only looked at his brother, she slapped his cheek, bringing his fiery attention right back to her. "*He* is not in his right mind. *I* am. The key? Where is it?"

An odd glint came into his gaze. Mayhap respect? More likely murderous intent, his eyes glowing so, like her beloved's yet differently too. "No. He told me—"

"Never mind that, you swine. I do not care to hear what he told you. *Where* is the blasted key?"

A hiss came from his throat as he whipped the chain over his head, tripped over to a trunk and rummaged inside. Tense moments later he thunked a large, sturdy key into her waiting palm.

"Your own brother," she shrilled, wanting to stab him with the damn key, uncaring if she appeared the deranged one. Instead, she ran to the foot of the bed and stabbed it in the lock around one ankle. "How *could* you—"

"Not me," Nash spat and gestured past her shoulder to the man-beast now staring at them both. Jaw locked as tight as the chains. Eyes as cold as the metal she now lifted from one leg. "Him. *Choice.* Mattered not that I offered, brought them here."

Applying the key to the other leg shackle, she paused. Refused to glance at the lightly furred stranger trembling violently beneath her touch and captured Nash's gaze. "Brought *them*. Other women?"

"Aye, but he refused—"

Erasmus growled.

"Brought them *here*?" she demanded, still staring at Nash, part of her recalling something he'd said downstairs. When she was too distraught to listen. "For sex?"

The glint in his eyes was answer enough.

A heave of her right wrist and the second lock clicked open. Too impatient to remove the shackle, she left it open, chain dangling—for him to kick off.

Nash grunted. "Still, he refused—"

"Erasmus!" Rounding on her man and the bed, she thumped his naked thigh. "Why did you not call on me?"

As though ashamed, he squeezed his eyes closed. "Cannot. Not see me thus."

"Of all the..." Three steps along the bed and she plied the key in the wrist restraint closest to her. "Asinine...impossible... *Argh*." This one proved stubborn. "Chained yourself to the bed?" In that moment, she didn't know what she hated more—the stubborn lock or the stubborn man it held. "Stupid, deuced... *Lock*." Finally, the key turned and she wrestled the manacle off. It clanged to the floor, the chain still secured to the bed frame. A grim reminder that whatever had gone on the past week was far, far beyond anything previously known in her sheltered circle.

She caressed the reddened flesh of his wrist. He curled his hand into a fist and bent inward, muscles drawn taut, concealing his expression. Hiding from her.

"Erasmus, what is—"

"No, Francine. Nay! *Moyo wangu*," he murmured, the words agonized but making no sense. "Go. Not want...see me thus..." He refused to look at her, even when she touched his cheek. "Francy... *God's sake, go!*"

"Never," she swore, climbing back over him to work furiously on the last lock. "Hold still." Once she did finally free him, would he abandon her all over again? Take off into the night?

This lock opened faster. But this arm also had the leather straps. While she battled the buckles, her heart raged, beating so fast she felt lightheaded.

Blazes! His heat rose up through the thin layers of her skirt and shift, met her skin and scorched her. Inside and out.

"Almost..." Poor, blighted man! What in heaven's name was he going through? "There!"

Unleashed, Erasmus lunged upward and his arms encircled her waist and back, crushing her torso against his. He swallowed her in his embrace, something she'd half feared might never occur again when he'd started avoiding her by means of those confounded notes.

The scents she'd smelled upon entering the room only strengthened within his hold, the singe of burnt candles, the strange odor of animal pelt, but stronger than both, more welcome than either, was the blessed, yearned-for comforting and invigorating spicy musk of her man. Her nails dug into the skin of his back, validating his solid presence. So precious, so real. "Erasmus..."

He hugged her so hard she thought her lungs

would burst, his breath exploding from him in a sound of wounded relief.

Lips at his ear, she rained kisses over his neck and shoulders, luxuriating in his taste, his presence, so dearly familiar yet overridden with a feral sensuality. "I will not let *you* go," she swore. "Never. So stop pushing me away."

He grunted, vised his arms and trembled against her. The primal need radiating stronger until it seared her too.

"*What* has happened to you?" She leaned back to cup his cheek and run her thumb over the surprisingly soft whiskers. "Your hair...your face... What is it?"

Even more than his shocking appearance, he exuded a ferocity unlike anything she'd ever encountered. The force of the primitive energy suffused the space around them, painting the air with heady longing.

The next second, he sent her flying to the other side of the mattress.

With a roar that shook the rafters, he bounded to all fours, that one chain still dangling from his ankle. She shrieked when he flipped her over, facedown, and came down on top of her. His weight so very welcome.

"*Hapana*," grunted from him. The heft of his body vanished off her and she wanted to cry. Protest.

But he gave her not the chance.

His grip at her hips wrenched them upward, brought her to her knees. Head still down, her fingers twisted about the sheet, heart pounding madly.

He wrestled with her skirts. Cool air assaulted her skin.

No preliminaries.

He plowed into her, his shaft finding the path slick and ready.

Ahhhh...mmmmm. Francine closed her eyes. So very relieved. So thankful.

He was back. In her. Wanting her. *Loving* her.

The thrusting was unlike any other. Fast. Hard. Relentless.

Over way too quick.

His rough hands stroked up the side of her back, over the deuced dress she wished anywhere else. Clutched her shoulders—kept her head down. Pinched. Caressed. And when she thought he was nearly finished—

When his thrusts became ever more harried and forceful, he fell atop her. Plastered his mouth to the curve of one shoulder as he'd done the week prior. And his teeth made impressions. Bit down...*just so.*

This time, unlike the others that came before, he did not wrench his body from hers. Didn't abandon her and leave her slightly bereft at the last second. This time, when his teeth pressed down and his pumping ramped up, the hard hold on her shoulders firming, *this time,* he ground his shaft in further, released her shoulders to slide his arms around her middle and hug her to him.

As though he'd never let her go.

Her heart and hinterlands rejoiced at the truth of it, at the realization. At the reality of his touch: rough, present and *returned to her.* Even as sweat slicked her face and the sheets... Even as the fast lunges became a series of staccato bursts, nearly cleaving her in two but still, so very welcome...

Even as he spent his seed inside her, crying, insensibly, "*Ningewezaje!*" Francine felt at peace for the first time in days.

And still so needy. For him. For her own completion.

OH GOD, *thank you.*

Erasmus could breathe again.

Could feel the precious body quivering beneath his.

Could smell everything about her and actually recognize individual scents now, not just the jumble they'd been since he first gained a whiff of her arrival downstairs.

Heather.

Sunshine.

The lilac soap she used.

The growing damp from outside, confirming the rain he scented moving in.

Leather.

Horse.

Adam?

Later. His bamboozled brain could make sense of it all later—or not. For now, every fiber of his body *hurt.* He felt exposed.

Raw.

Unlike anything he'd experienced before.

She laid him bare, this—

Nay, not her. What loving her does to you, man. Makes you weak.

Nay. The opposite!

Although...right now...as the last few moments came back to him in a rush, the vision of what he'd just done, how he'd just *used* her...

As his thoughts returned with a clarity that had been lacking for days, self-loathing came storming in as well.

You say she makes you strong? You just treated her like a whore. No better than an unrigged drab. Not as the dress-wearing lady she is.

To the devil with him!

He finally, *finally* succeeds in gaining her presence in his home—in his bed, by damn—and he attacks her as a reprobate would a slattern?

But oh, her glorious arrival!

Raging at him. At Nash.

Those cultured, serene tones that had seduced him from the beginning projecting every man's inner fantasy: Passion. Anger. Impatience.

The *need* for her man.

Him.

In the seconds after orgasm, all that and more ran through his beleaguered mind...

So exhausted.

So thunderingly exhausted.

Wait.

Why was she here? *How* had she come to be—

Nay. Too tired.

Time enough to deal with that. Tomorrow. No energy to think now.

He just needed to lie here, holding her, hugging

her. Needed to sleep with her in his arms, next to his heart. Needed—

Wait.

The fine hairs covering his entire body prickled. Teeth twinged...started to throb.

When his body should be returning to some semblance of normalcy, when the beast should be abated, for a few hours at least, if not the following twenty-four, it was hovering? Looming?

Pressing in again?

The blame beast was back? So soon?

How?

Because he'd denied himself for so long?

Across the room, he sensed Nash more than heard him. As though in answer.

Or because they were together? Ever before, during The Change, when they'd fornicated jointly and freely to ease the urge, neither had denied themselves. Neither had struggled against the beast, only indulged it. Frolicked away with willing wenches because neither of them had any reason not to.

Until this year.

Had thinking only of himself put them all in danger?

He'd not realized Nash struggled as well, until he'd appeared, looking no better than Erasmus, even though he'd been indulging. He'd battled his brother as well as himself ever since.

And now, even as he felt the beast strengthening again, he sensed his brother's inner monster taking over as well. God help them.

After slaking his lewd need on the precious one

beneath him, he now ached to *do it again*? Nash needing just as much?

His arms convulsed around her as he swallowed hard. Not his Francy.

What have I done? "*Ningewezaje!*"

WITH A STRANGLED CRY that pierced Francine's heart, Erasmus leapt off and thrust her away.

"Stop shutting me out." Still on edge, in no way lethargic, she rolled up to her knees. Responding to the anguish imprinted upon his savage features, the way he started shaking his head, she lunged forward to hug him again.

He held her back with one strong hand splayed in the center of her chest, more nonsense coming from his lips.

She ignored it and slammed her hand against his bare upper arm, digging her fingers in.

He shuddered beneath her touch. "Damn you! Still need to fuck you so badly," he said, shocking her with his language. "Cannot control..." Legs crumpled beneath him, head bowed, he pounded the bed with his fist. Behind her, she heard an unfamiliar *pfffting* sound and turned to look at his brother.

Who was gone.

Shimmering... As though his very form was being replaced by a giant feline, one with strangely glittering eyes and a full ruff. A...lion?

Impossible! She wrenched her head to the side.

Heard a snarl. A yell.

Gathered courage and turned back, only to see

Nash again. But golden, *glowing*, unreal... Glittering in the air, the atoms of his body vibrating betwixt that of man—

And an animal!

Oh, Nash was still present, the tortured, wild shell of a man, his tattered shirt, torn trousers indecent coverings at best.

But overlying his human, physical form, was a ghostly, glowing one.

A giant wild cat... It *was* a lion!

One who was stalking toward the bed.

To her astonishment, the feline howled and convulsed, leaving a human form—Nash?—contorting back into his former shape. That of a man...but not.

Fear catapulted through her chest and she dove forward, gripping Erasmus around the neck. His shaking had increased. "What is that? What just happened to your brother? I don't understand! What do you need? Tell me and it is yours." When he remained agonizingly silent, she shook him and screamed, "Tell me!"

With brute force, he pried at her arms, attempting to loosen her hold. She clasped her fingers together and secured them behind his neck. "I told you—I'm not leaving without answers." *Or you.* "I won't leave you, Erasmus. No matter what." The promise shrilled loudly in her ears. She didn't try to soften it. "Not in a hundred years. A million sunsets!"

At her vow, his ruthless motions to dislodge her calmed. "Francine...listen." His words panted from him as though he'd raced across all of London. "We are doomed...coexist as lions. We—"

"Impossible."

But you just saw it.

Saw Nash turn into—

"*Inawezekana.* Our control... 'Tis weakened until the sun...passes out of Leo. Thought I could..."

He ground his jaws together and closed his eyes. His body convulsed again, the tremors clamoring through him so strong they almost freed her grip.

She tightened her fingers, resolved. Fantastical secrets or impossible lies, she wasn't letting go.

That strange *pffftting* emerged from his throat too and she saw that two of his teeth had shaped to points and were extending beyond the boundaries of his lips. "Erasmus. Talk to—"

"Need sex. Need your body...any *body* would do, but yours is the only one I— God forgive me... couldn't be with anyone else. Else I'd not be so far gone."

In a tender motion defying all that had gone on since she arrived, he ducked his head and nudged the top of it against her chin. The shudder that attacked him running through them both. When he lifted his head to again look at her, his heated gaze glowed as never before. "Need you to..."

He stopped midsentence and slammed his mouth over hers, plunging his tongue inside. Francine started, not expecting the sudden invasion nor the voracious roughness of his tongue as it licked and caressed the cavern of her mouth. Not expecting the way his teeth would feel nor how he would sense the small cut where she'd bitten herself earlier...sense it and begin sucking the flesh around it, drawing her blood, her very life force, from the tiny crevice and taking it into *his* mouth...devouring her.

"Francine," Erasmus ground out against her lips, then released her abruptly. "Get th' hell out of here *now*, 'fore we both take you like animals. Fighting it but —" A rumbled roar blasted from his mouth and he shook his head, making his tawny hair fly. The ends whipped her face. "Go, damn you!"

Nash snarled. She jumped. She'd all but forgotten him.

Startled by the threatening rumble, Francine's eyes darted toward him. He'd come up to the head of the bed, looking more human again—or at least he did until she saw him placing one *clawed* hand on the bed.

His weight caused the mattress to dip as he slowly climbed up next to them. His clothes nothing but shreds now, Nash sniffed the air, a predatory gleam in his eyes.

"Stay," Nash pleaded, his earlier anger transformed to pain.

Twin shudders racked both men.

She leaned forward and kissed Erasmus's mouth slowly, feeling the tiny pricks from his teeth when their lips met. "What do you need?" she whispered, thinking she already knew and knowing she'd give him anything, offer him anything, even...

"*You.* Forgive me, *mpenzi wangu*, we both need you."

"Take me, then. If it will ease your pain."

"*Both* of us?" Nash asked, leaning over to sniff along her neck.

Francine shook with reaction and stared into her

lover's eyes. The loneliness was tempered now, eased by a softer, gentler emotion. "Erasmus?"

He nodded slightly, turning away, closing himself off.

Nay. She wouldn't let him hide from this, *from them.* She coiled her fingers in the long hair streaming past his face, tugging hard until he looked at her. Gazed at her as though he didn't know whether she was his salvation—or his damnation.

His hands came up to grip her arms. "Cannot believe the first time...have you...in *my* bed, 'tis to share you..."

Desire battled with propriety. Why wasn't she protesting? Shouting that this wasn't natural, that it couldn't be happening? That she didn't want it.

Because you do.

Despite everything, possibly because of it, she trembled with a need so strong she questioned reality. But the sounds of the men's breathing, of her racing heart resonating in her ears, the echo of the passionate little cries that escaped her parted lips on each exhalation...every vibration thrumming through her convinced her that this *was* happening. It was real.

Nash licked her ear and sensation raced down her neck. His body hovered behind hers, his heavy staff nudging her back, seeking solace.

Erasmus's erection pressed tight against her stomach.

She shivered. With fear, yes, but also with the unwavering realization that what they asked of her, *needed* from her, she wanted as well. To ease their pain, to show Erasmus how very much she loved him. To experience it all—unbridled lust. Love.

She loosened herself from his grasp, nudged Nash back, and in a flurry, gathered the skirt of her dress to lift it up and over her head, dropping it uncaringly behind her. Wearing naught but her thin shift, she braced herself against Erasmus's chest. "Take me, then. I offer myself to you. I—"

His lips assaulted hers, brutally, all-consuming. Purely divine. She didn't expect how much she'd love the primal atmosphere that surrounded them, the raw desire and hot need surging through her, quickening her blood, calling forth a rush of moisture that flooded her channel.

As if sensing her increased arousal, both men made that puffing noise, airy grunts that came from their throats.

Erasmus abandoned her mouth, his eyes wild. "Francine, *mpenzi*," he pleaded. "Please...*tafadhali ondoka*."

"I do not understand. What are you saying?" *And in what language?* It wasn't Latin, nor French. Not even German nor Italian. "What do you want?"

Erasmus blinked, confusion evident in his eyes. The short whiskers covering his face had thickened, further hiding his beloved features. "*Ondoka!* Go! Before it is too—"

"Nay!" Nash tore off his ragged shirt and ripped away the remnants of his barely there trousers. He exposed his savage strummer and Francine felt compelled to caress it, to gentle the beast that raged within him as well as her cherished Erasmus.

Her hand gravitated toward Nash but Erasmus clasped it and stilled her movements. "*Ondoka!*"

"She stays," Nash grunted, suffering through another racking vibration. He gripped her waist, holding her in place. "We take her now...else control is gone..."

"Leave!" Erasmus commanded again, attempting to shove her from the bed, even as he stared into her eyes, his face haggard with unquenched passion. His eyes hunted... Yet hopeful.

Nash held tight, hissing in her ear.

Both men seemed to have forgotten that she lay melded between them. "Please, Erasmus, you cannot do this. Do not make me leave. I love you!"

He released her at once, horror etched on his face.

"Nay. You cannot..." His voice shattered. Hope extinguished.

"I most certainly can!" Francine beat at his chest, forcing him back down. A move he allowed, causing her to realize he'd finally acceded. She didn't cease until he reclined beneath her, allowed her to straddle his abdomen. She aligned her hungry body over his erection and rode him through her shift. "Let me help you. Both of you... I want to help..."

Nash's hands moved to her shoulders, anchoring her between them. His nails burrowed beneath the material of her shift and he ripped the material to her waist, exposing her naked back.

Erasmus slid his hand under the remaining fabric. He found her slit—wet, swollen...*ready* for his possession. He nudged his knuckles along the crevice, pressing deep, then retreating. One nail edged through her curls in a jerky, winding path, the sharpness bordering on pain and heightening her response. She twitched, then grasped him with her feminine muscles when he twisted his knuckles between her folds again, glorying in his touch, his willingness to finally take from her what he so desperately needed. He pulled free of her body and passed the back of his fingers under her nose, painting her lips with the creamy secretions. Her own scent had never been so strong.

Nash pressed his fur-lined chest to her back. The surprising sensation had her arching up, away from him, into him...confused. He leaned forward, blanketing her with his torso and brought his face to her shoulder, watching. His breath was hot on her cheek. "*Kaka, mgao*?"

Erasmus's eyes burned but he removed his fingers from her lips and brought his hand to his brother's face.

Nash proceeded to lick Erasmus's fingers, groaning. Her inner muscles clenched, empty, excited. Her hands tangled in the rough mat of hair covering her beloved's chest and she sought his mouth.

"Wait." He shuddered again, dipping his other hand past her folds. Once more, he gathered her honey, then brought it to *his* lips, licking them clean. "Francine, love..."

Nash clenched his fingers in her hair, stinging her scalp, bracing her. He situated his erection along the indentation curving her lower back.

Erasmus lay beneath her, his shuddering body turned to stone. Raw need glistened in his eyes. She was lifted fully on top of him, stretched upon his length. The tip of his cock poised at her entrance, all three of them breathing in unison.

Pliant, she willingly succumbed to their joint guidance.

"Aye. Like so..." Nash rasped, directing her entire body downward with his weight, seating his brother in her so deeply that she screamed. Tried to angle herself against him even more. Deeper. As far as she could take him, she would—and then some.

Erasmus united his mouth with hers. Their tongues intertwined, as she sought out every succulent taste she could discover. The passionate kiss sent her head spinning.

Nash raised off her, tore her shift, not only from her hips but clean in two, exposing her nude backside to the room and his attentions. Her lower body jerked reflexively, thrusting the rim of her sheath onto Erasmus's lightly furred abdomen.

Sensation streaked through her. Centered above her cleft, the riotous sparks ricocheted down to her toes.

She kissed Erasmus harder in response. He growled into her mouth and his rough tongue lapped at her lips, ate at her face, the furious undulations of his hips increasing.

A sudden sting landed upon her backside, causing Francine to flinch.

"That's for the slaps earlier," Nash whispered in her ear.

He swatted her significantly harder on the other side. "That's for me."

Her inner workings constricted against the shaft she rode, a light sigh escaping past the kiss.

"These now?" Nash all but groaned. "*These* are for you."

Several more sharp slaps stung her newly awakened flesh, his palm against the virgin skin raining sensation over her buttocks and thighs, then his mouth was there too, upon her arse, teeth prominent as he kissed her bottom. He hissed, slapped her again, then returned, licking...*biting*.

The unfamiliar stimulation caused her derrière to burn. The fire raging in her blazed higher. She squirmed around Erasmus's cock, stretched wider and plumbed deeper than ever before—yet still, she ground against his pelvis, seeking *more*. Concentrating on her mouth, he refused her unspoken plea, instead ravaging her lips, her jaw...her neck. Her lower body thrashed between the men. They roared her name in unison, synchronized in some otherworldly way.

She felt loved, needed.

Unheeded, tears of raw emotion slipped from her eyes and landed in the light, whiskery fur surrounding Erasmus's face. When the drops pooled and sank to his skin, he groaned wildly, thrusting her arse higher in the air as his hips lifted off the bed.

His hands framed her face, roughly wiped her tears away, his kisses never stopping.

Behind her, Nash left off focusing on her bottom and instead mounted her back, once again aligning his hard flesh along her spine. His hands cupped her flaming cheeks, massaging the tender skin as he began his own ride, sliding his erection against her skin in long, gliding lunges.

In seconds, his shaft began driving raggedly—small frantic jerks across her back in time to the stinging swats he landed again upon her thighs. Seconds later, he lurched against her and groaned, and she felt the hot spill of his semen on her skin.

She clamped around Erasmus's driving erection and squeezed, fluttered her muscles, but she still *ached* down there.

Still needed, in a way that mocked restraint or self-control, her body now a slave to desire.

An unfamiliar command rumbled from Erasmus's throat as he paused in kissing her. Nash lifted off her back and moved to the side, looking decidedly more human. "Here," he said, almost kindly, "let me."

He slid one hand between them—a normal-looking appendage, some part of her noted. He secured his other around her nape.

"Lean back now," Nash murmured, tightening his fingers behind her neck and supporting her, guiding her slightly back so he could lower his splayed palm down her stomach to her mound.

His fingers spread her open. Tapping and circling the flesh above where his brother thrust. She clenched harder around the hot shaft pleasuring her so. At the next swipe of Nash's touch, her body blossomed, moistened even more, slicking everything. Inciting whimpers, heart palpitations, breathless pants beyond measure...

At a grunt from Erasmus, Nash leaned in, angled

his head to lick and suck the overly sensitive area. Kissing her deeply as she rode his brother.

Her head spun faster and she mashed her lips together to stifle a squeal.

Her intimate muscles contracted just as Nash brought his tongue into play. She cried out. *How much more can I take?* she wondered, at the same time thinking *Please, never let this end.*

Shifting his knees behind her, raising her up toward him, Erasmus gripped one shoulder, used the sides of his fingers to ply at one breast as he caught her gaze with his ever-glowing eyes.

Nash's tongue flew over the knot of nerves he'd discovered, making the tension tighten.

Plucking at one nipple with his rough fingertips, Erasmus flexed his upper legs, then brought his other hand to grip her jaw. He pushed one long finger past her lips, giving the command to, "Suck."

That did it. At the unplanned taste of him inside her mouth, so firm, so *needed*, so blessedly *missed*, her building orgasm thundered free. Every muscle constricted, then sighed. Bloomed as breathing became optional. Lightning exploded from her core, encompassed every part of her loins and flowed outward, leaving her cells singing, shattered, humming with the aftermath. Numb.

Completely numb.

It was so beautiful. Her chest hurt. She cried harder.

When did I start crying?

Erasmus lunged inside her, thrusting high, heaving her body upward. She hung suspended above him, impaled upon his massive shaft, held in place by his strong arms and strong legs. Nash licked all around, seeking out the liquid of her desire and the fresh wash of her release.

"Francine." Erasmus stared into her eyes. "My love!" His tortured face was blurred.

"Nay. I..." She tried to hold on, to tell him of her love but her forehead creased, clouds covered her mind, buried thought. She couldn't catch her breath. 'Twas so exciting, being here, with them. Yet she was so exhausted, after days of worry. The last two sleepless nights. So enthralled...

Spots danced in front of her face. Circled around her head. Stars blasted behind her eyes.

Breathe.

An anguished howl came from Erasmus as she felt him unleash his seed inside her body for the second time.

"Not now." She battled the onslaught claiming her but it proved too strong. "Nay! Leave off!" *Nooo...*

An avalanche of nothing rolled over her mind. Pressed hard against her forehead.

And swept her under.

THE BESPECTACLED BEAUTY TAMES THE BEAST

ONCE AGAIN, to my heirs, my wonderful boys, Erasmus and Nash. Never doubt my love. Never that.

I hope these pages, these glimpses into life as I now know it may explain, in some manner at least, why your sire never was the overly affectionate sort.

A few blessedly quiet, typical months have passed since the last Change. Thought I'd scribble out some less dramatic, less agony-filled thoughts.

For you see, most of the year I am simply a man. A husband, a father. Most of the year I function like a normal, red-blooded British male. I love my wife, my boys and a good, smuggled-in French brandy.

I also love <u>not</u> gnawing on raw beef bones, fighting a part of myself I sometimes sense growing stronger every year and always loathe. I keep telling myself that, somehow, by educating you two, we might halt this deadly curse before it touches yet another generation.

But how can I contemplate ordering you boys to never marry? To never father children? How can I expect you to give up something that has brought me so much personal joy?

Enough of that now. This was supposed to be a light-hearted entry.

Erasmus, you're 14 and off at Eton. Nash, we had your 9th birthday celebration just last week. I gave you a volume of selected works by Shakespeare, most notably A MIDSUMMER NIGHT'S DREAM, my particular favorite, hoping to entice your interest in literature (which proves nonexistent at the moment). But alas, it remains the archery set chosen by your mother that you gravitate toward.

"Let the boys be boys," she told me when you ran off, pell-mell, to put it through its paces. "Plenty of time for them to falter under the weight of life and responsibility later."

She is right. Still limps from what I did to her, damn my hide, but right all the same. So I think I shall set this aside and find you, Nash. See whether I can challenge your aim. Let us all be boys, for once, eh?

NASH WANTED TO HOWL.

He hated his demmed brother. Bastard had made them both suffer all week because he wouldn't simply take a crack to soothe the beast.

He hated his demmed grandfather, whose selfish and thoughtless actions brought the curse careening down upon their heads in the first place.

But most of all, right this second, he bloody hated Francine.

His blasted brother's little *Francy*.

Nash knew he'd acted the total arse, goading both his brother and his woman. *Too pigeoned by the pink.* Had he really said that? To a *lady*? He should be pilloried. Piked. Banished to the pigsty to forge within. For was that not where pigheaded pricks belonged?

In the mud.

He'd listened to them coo and kiss deep in the night, after she roused from the stupor they'd put her in. Had wanted more than anything to roll over and slake his frustration out on the smooth curves of her body. But already, recriminations gonged about his garret like a tide of Vikings laying siege to his brain.

Aye, you arse, *'Twas your pleasure, and now your own remorse*, he bent Shakespeare, as he was wont to do, to fit his particular situation.

How could he? How the devil could the urges have taken hold with such ferocity that he'd been reduced to covering his brother's woman?

Good God. Blake would likely never want to look him in the despicable eyes again.

The sharing? That was of no matter. They'd shared before, more times than he wanted to count. It was the *commitment* part of it that skewered him like a poor, severed head perched upon a pike.

For the mighty Marquis of Blakely had fallen irretrievably *in love*, and that Nash could never forgive.

Not when the two of them kept spewing whispered words of adoration on their side of the huge bed, as though he didn't exist. Heard her whispered question, "Why so many candles, Erasmus, for I know you do not need them?" And then his brother's rough, husky-voiced reply, "Trying to banish the night. Without you in my life, all was night." The nausea-inducing exchange at least explaining why Blake had been so insistent Nash kept them burning.

Sickening, the way they practically purred for each other.

Especially when they'd exchanged an entire one-word conversation that nearly made him cast up his accounts, bantering about such overly sentimental drivel as *endearing, my heart* (granted, that was two), *stalwart, masterful, salvation*....

Putrid, that's what it was.

He'd known this was coming. Had gone searching for it, in fact, when his brother refused to explain fully *why*, chancing across more than one startling set of papers on Blake's desk his first night back, searching for clues as to the identity of the woman to blame for their wretched condition.

Only he'd found something far beyond a mere infatuation. Notes, showing the parish church where Blake had paid the minister to start reading the banns...

Nearly three weeks ago, which meant the fool already planned to marry this woman before the beast took hold.

How could he?

Not just *how could he fall in love*, but how the devil could Blake expect to marry someone he hadn't yet confided their Deep Dark Secret to?

That bothered Nash twice as much as the rest of it.

Never being in love—never planning to—he'd no idea how anyone could contemplate that sort of hurly-burly commitment without being honest with the other. Why multiply an already cursed situation through silence?

Not only because his brother's action of "endureth all things" by "not forsaking thee" (on occasion the Bible snuck in when Shakespeare didn't come readily to mind) *and taking others* had magnified the urges to the point of insanity for them both, but because his older, perfectly responsible, perfectly proper, demmed stinking *perfect* brother had found the one thing Nash knew he never would—

A woman to love.

One willing to do *anything* for him. Even prick *his* sorry arse.

When the low drone of their voices started again, he roused himself enough to roll off the bed, landing more agilely on his feet than he'd expected. Leading him to realize, now that Blake had finally sated the beast, it no longer hunted Nash as well.

For the first time in days, he was able to stand upright with ease, look down his nude body and see skin and the standard light covering of body hair. He held one hand out, gratified it was stable. Steady. The nails blunt tipped and regular.

He knew from experience much of the night would fade from his memory the first time he slept deeply—possibly even sooner. The Beast Lust had never ridden him so hard. Before, he'd always pricked away the urges, enjoying himself in the process. But this time? He was drained like an empty pond. Completely worn down to the point of utter exhaustion.

Was concerned if he didn't escape now, but waited, the urges would strengthen and he might cover her again. Mount her and this time not have the wherewithal to remain *outside* the alluring body presented so willingly to him.

And while he might profess to hate his brother—and the woman who'd made Blake both stronger than Nash ever thought to witness, but weaker as well—he respected and revered the man far too much to risk coming between him and his love.

No wonder Nash always did everything he could to avoid commitments, avoid so much as *looking* at women when he took them. Why bother? One was just as good as another. And he wasn't about to get duped into *caring* for one. Not with this curse business always looming every summer.

So he'd take himself off to the chamber his brother always kept readied for him, despite it only being used a handful of nights each year. Clothing, money. His perfect brother would have arranged for both, well before the season warranted it.

From there?

To the entrance hall, to upright the table and anything else he'd smashed. Tidy what he could.

And then? Was anyone's guess.

Mayhap back upstairs to sleep the day away...find another faceless, willing London wench tomorrow night.

Mayhap...Scotland. Or perhaps...Cornwall and a dockside doxy.

At the doorway, he couldn't resist a last glance,

would have denied with his dying breath the envy inherent in it, upon seeing the intertwined couple.

For no matter how many times he told himself he hated Francine, God help him, he wanted someone exactly like her...

Someone who would look at *him* the way she gazed at his brother. Someone who would risk *everything* to see him unharmed and cared for...

Withdraw yourself, and leave them here alone, his blighted brain once more misquoted. But wisely.

And so he did.

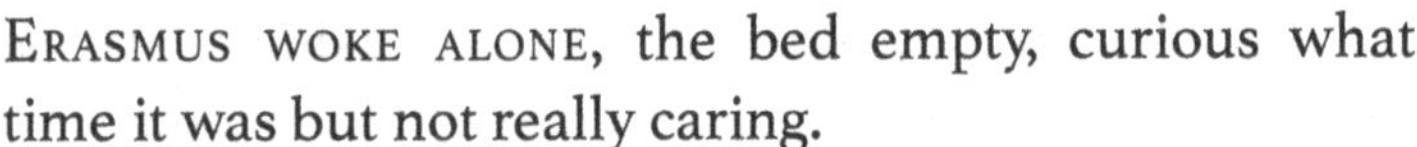

ERASMUS WOKE ALONE, the bed empty, curious what time it was but not really caring.

Francine was gone. Nothing else mattered.

Stale sweat and sex permeated the air, doubling his regret. Why had he not spoken to her sooner? Attempted to explain the...inexplicable?

You know why.

He did.

Fear. The very real possibility that she'd have nothing to do with him once she knew the truth.

Too late for regrets now. All he could do was look to the future.

He walked to the window, naked and fully upright, his hair, face and form returned to their customary appearance. After so many days denying himself physically, his cells had altered to the point that he'd feared harming Francine—or anyone else who dared enter his domain. Hence, his demand that Nash restrain him.

Nash, who had suffered almost equally, the ease he'd found in various women since his unexpected return lasting only a brief time, their proximity causing The Change to affect them both differently than they'd experienced before—when Erasmus *wasn't* denying himself. But at least his brother had managed to find some moments of clarity.

For Erasmus, the past few days—even most of last night—were a haze. A haze of pain, longing and regret. And hatred. Couldn't forget that, now could he? Hatred turned inward for being such a clodpate as to think he could dally with innocence and allow it to remain unscathed.

Drawing open the ruined drapes, he unlatched the shutters, inviting fresh air into the chamber.

Though it was raining, a persistent sheeting turning everything grey and dreary that had started sometime during the night, all he saw, felt, *breathed* was sunlight.

Sunlight.

Sunshine.

Francine.

Steeling himself against the pain of her loss, he idly wondered how his other male relatives might be handling The Change. Especially Phineas, poor bastard, the cousin once closest to him and also the person who had suffered more than any other because of their affliction. Alive or dead, sane or crazed, the not knowing...

God, he was a wreck. He leaned against the shutters, inhaling the humid air, imagining he could smell her again. Fresh. Unspoilt.

Before they'd gotten their wretched claws in her. He *and* his brother.

Nash had vanished again, during the night, likely taking the first ship to France or the first stagecoach to Scotland. Leaving the country like he always did—another sudden arrival and abrupt exodus—leaving Erasmus to make do with nothing more than the half-arsed correspondence he'd send once or twice a year and always from a different location.

The blackguard, availing himself of the purest part of Erasmus's heart—Francine—and then abandoning him to deal with the aftermath alone.

Always alone.

Eyes squeezed tightly shut against emotions he didn't want to face, he bellowed, "Franklin!"

His valet could attempt the unenviable task of making him presentable. Then he'd present himself, hat in hand, at Rowden House, seek an audience—

Not today, you won't.

"By the devil." How could he have forgotten? His valet, along with the entire staff was on paid holiday for the month. A tradition started by his father, one that made the various Hammond residences much-desired places for employment.

He'd thought the loneliness might be over, that the companionship and, yes, love, he'd so unexpectedly found with his Francy might carry him through this year, give him the strength to control the beast within. To resist altering into a maniac.

He'd been wrong.

He might have been able to resist the lure of other

women, which had been less difficult than he'd anticipated, but as the sun crept into Leo, his traitorous cells had grown more demanding every day, until now, not even near the zenith of the zodiacal sign and he'd been near destroyed, broken. Without the respite garnered from her welcoming body, he shuddered to imagine what—

The sound of someone furiously assaulting the front door broke through his thoughts.

Probably the constable, come to cart him off to Newgate. Or Francine's uncle, come to cart him off to the dueling field.

The man, once he'd returned to town, had been agreeably tolerant of the amount of time Erasmus spent with his niece. And—after Erasmus dropped a hint or two, leaving Francine's aunt little choice but to confess her nefarious plans concerning Francine's inheritance, along with her own gambling foibles— he'd been completely supportive of their "betrothal".

That last dinner—before The Change snuck up on him and he whisked her off to have his wild and wicked way with her—he'd even thought he and Rowden might become something of friends... So much for that now.

If it *was* her uncle come to put a ball of lead through him, 'twas nothing less than he deserved. Exposing Francine to himself—and his brother—as he had, using her precious body for their own gain...he was a prigging animal. Who deserved to be shot. Drawn and quartered too.

Dipped in hot oil, rolled in grouse feathers—

The persistent clanging reverberated throughout

the house. Threatened to burst his overly sensitive eardrums.

Damn him. He should have confided in her long before now.

You think of that—now?

One of the few clear moments he had of last night were her last words to him, crying for him to leave her alone, to stop touching...

Nay! Leave!

Had anything as heart wrenching ever crossed his ears before?

Which is where the bulk of the self-castigation came from. How his selfish actions had brought her to that place.

More pounding attacked his chest and head.

Leave off castigating yourself and answer the damn door!

Wrapped in a dressing gown, still moving slug-gishly from the effects of The Change and the hours of bliss-induced relief he'd give anything to recall with more clarity, he made his way down the stairs to the entrance hall where the noise only increased, the blasted thumps clamoring in his brain.

"'Tis not even locked!" He wrenched the door open before the person on the other side broke the blasted thing down. Snarling, "What in Hades—"

Only to be brought up short when a dripping umbrella poked him in the chest.

Francine barreled her way in, looking more pure than a heathen even had a right to behold. The umbrella hit the floor and her reticule collided with the side table just as vehemently as her accusing gaze collided with his, her vibrant eyes magnified by the eyeglass lenses.

An avenging angel come to life, but his angel no more? If that's what she thought, he'd correct her soon enough.

Let her say her piece. Let her ire carry her through, however she needed. He'd give her the remaining three weeks, while he got through somehow, and then, by damn, no matter what she said to him in the next few minutes, he was going after her. And he was going to claim her. Forever.

"I am here to conclude our bargain, my lord." She faced him, removing her spectacles and carefully placing them on the small table with her reticule. "But first, I rather think I deserve an explanation. A thorough one."

"Aye, you do. Apologies, as well. But you may not believe what—"

"*Erasmus.*" Exasperation coated her tone. "I saw your brother practically turn into a slathering lion and you were not far behind." Calm, cool, her voice held no accusation, simply truth, as her fingers went to the bow beneath her neck, untying the bonnet she wore. "I daresay I can safely guarantee I shall believe most anything you have to tell me. Now start flapping your jaws."

As she drew out the long ribbon, he noticed scratches her gloves couldn't hide—the ones that streaked down her arms. Sheer surprise made him recoil.

"Oh-no-you-don't!" Francine fisted one lapel of his dressing gown, halting his retreat. "Do not dare turn from me as you tried to last night. How can you think that I—"

"By the blazes. I hurt you. Look!" He raised her hand and pointed to the thin cuts crossing her sun-browned forearm above the glove. And the paler skin on her upper arm when he runched her sleeve. "Here too?"

She gestured to her arms. "These happened when you were trying to push me away and I was holding on for dear life. Did it occur to you that keeping me with you might have been safer than sending those dratted notes?"

Knowing he looked guilty—because he felt guilty—he didn't complain that she'd pinched skin when grabbing him. Too damn relieved to see her. Have her in his home again.

"When will you get it through that thick, some-times furry skull of yours—I cannot claim to know why, but I *like* it when you become wild and on edge—and a little rough. I know that makes me..."

"Wicked." Did she know that the more she spoke, claiming to like his wild ways, the more perfect she seemed? Nothing could please him more.

"Depraved," she countered on a frown.

"Debauched." He grinned when he said it. An unholy grin that spread his lips wide and showed off—dare he hope?—normal-shaped teeth. "I must say, I do like how very debauched you have become, Francy."

Everything would be all right between them. For, after that confession, he'd move heaven and hell to make it so.

"Stop tempting me to wipe that wickedly alluring

grin right off your face," she huffed, her frilly untied bonnet still perched upon her unhappy hair, gloved hands propped at her waist, slippered toes tapping, face full of righteous indignation.

"You are smashing in high dudgeon, did you know that?"

"I am unwilling to simply banter—no matter how tempted—when still more exists to resolve between us." She grew deplorably serious. "You should have told me before now. Not kept me utterly in the dark. After all we have shared!" That did it. Wiped the mirth clean off his expression. "You would have saved us both some angst."

"I concur. Can only claim my wits went begging." He groaned, slamming one hand on the side table, causing something to flutter to the floor. Distracted, he looked down, muttering, "Surprised you can bring yourself to look at me this morning."

"'Tis accomplished quite easily, I assure you. Magnificent specimen and all that."

But he was no longer listening, bending to pick up the fallen, folded paper.

She jerked it out of his hand and tossed it back on the table, skewering him with no small amount of ire. "Have at it. Enlighten me. Thoroughly."

And best make it good. She's as pissed as she has a right to be.

"I... We..." Since when did he ever fumble about? Staring into pale blue expectant inquisitiveness, he swallowed and tried again. "My family— The males that is..."

How could he just blurt it out? He battled the

multitude of lies that rose to his lips and finally surrendered to the truth—most of it, for now. Beneath her imploring regard, he could do no less. "Our grandfather was on African safari, hunting elephants, lions, zebras—anything he considered exotic enough for his trophy room. He was still a relatively young man and boasted more pride than sense."

Unable to bear the distance, he stepped forward and hauled her to him, burying his face in the warm curve of her neck, knocking her bonnet off and not giving a damn. Her frizzed, not-about-to-be-tamed, pinned-up hair muffled his next words. "After the greedy bastard had already killed more animals than he could even transport home, he came upon a herd of lions and..."

"And what? I need to know," she whispered, hugging him fiercely. *Not saying nay now, is she?* "And you, I believe, need to tell me."

He lifted her off the ground so that her feet dangled, holding her as tightly as he dared. "He had already brought down two and was reloading for a third kill when another lion came from behind and attacked. Grandfather nearly bled to death right there on the savannah."

"Oh, Erasmus..." Her fingernails scraped along his scalp, pushing him away or pulling him closer, he didn't dare contemplate.

"'Twas no more than he deserved, extinguishing those beautiful animals for nothing more than sport, hoping to impress his friends back in England." And how could he be condemning his grandfather's actions? Since when did *he* feel empathy for the blasted animal whose form tried to overtake his own every year?

Her nails dug deeper. "Then what? Did your grandfather recover?"

"A tribal healer was summoned from a nearby village. He told Grandfather that the disembodied familiars were angered over his greed and disregard for life. The man said he had called on *Felis leo* spirit medicine, but it would only be available if a reciprocal exchange was offered. The healer gave him two options —either agree or surrender to fate and most likely die."

"He agreed," she whispered when he paused, squirming in his embrace. "Tell me the rest."

He lowered her feet to the floor but held fast, inhaling the subtle scent of lilacs, sunshine and earthy, fragrant woman, absorbing the refinement she exuded, his soul soothed for the first time since he'd come to and found her gone. "On the verge of his last breath, Grandfather consented, unaware of what he had done, as the man had spoken in another tongue. Grandfather only knew what the single remaining packman had shared—the others having scattered—which was a fraction of the truth."

"How did you discover the rest?" she asked, still gripping his hair, now making him face her.

"From letters and journals. My father's and grandfather's. Only studied a fraction; some is in code." He tilted his head, nuzzled his cheek along hers, wishing —for her sake—that his stubbled face had seen the sharp side of a blade in the last week.

"Mother gave them to me after his death. Actually,

arranged to have them delivered into my safekeeping *after* she left."

Those had been dark days, not long after his father's bloodied body was returned to the family amidst scandal and speculation. The rumor circling round being that the prior marquis took the embarrassing, foolhardy, dicked-in-the-nob way off the shores of England and shot himself in the head; the truth *suspected* by him and his mother even more ruinous to the family name than that spot of tragedy.

"I glanced carelessly over things, shared the absurd claims with Nash and Phineas." Somehow, he no longer held her nor her him, instead he now paced across the entrance hall, as though to outrun the naïve memories. "We thought 'twas rich amusement, the whole lot of it nothing more than a jolly tale." What else could they have thought?

'Twas nonsensical blather claiming that he and his brother and cousin had *Roho ya Simba* coursing through their veins, the Spirit of the Lion. And him having to track that tiny spot of knowledge down by consulting with a scholar interested in African tribes and their various languages.

"We were convinced 'twas merely something our parents had contrived—a jest on wild boys to keep the oat-sowing to a minimum. 'Tis all. Thought Mother shared when she did only to keep my focus off where she had gone.

"We never believed it. None of it. Not even her letter confiding the mangling of her leg was not a carriage accident at all but the result of our father turning on her the first time he faced The Change." Now that he'd started blathering the family secrets, seemed he couldn't stop.

"It was not until later, when our cousin Phin had his devastating wedding night and disappeared in a flurry..." He came upon another wall and paused, slapped his palms to the decorative paper he hadn't changed since inheriting the London home so many years before. Stood there, breathing hard, staring at the floor between his bare feet. "Not until we saw the bridal room he left behind, the mangling of blood and golden fur, did Nash and I finally believe. Then I battled the curse the very next year. Nearly succumbing, until I had no choice but to take my father's impassioned warnings to heart and do everything I could to stop it. As I have been doing every year since.

"And you know the rest." Or enough of it.

"The curse? Have you knowledge of *how*?"

He nodded abruptly. There were still journal entries, additional ramblings he'd yet to share. There'd be time enough in their future. She hadn't run screaming yet; he'd no intention of ever letting her go. Even if he couldn't face her quite yet. "In parts. Not everything."

"Why did you not struggle when we first met?" She placed a tentative hand on his shoulder. He couldn't control the flinch that ran through him. "Why now?"

He swore. Since when did he find his bare toes so enthralling? *Since they look like toes and not like paws?* "That part has been the biggest hubble-bubble, figuring out how it all works. Time and observation have filled in some blanks."

His shoulders started to feel the strain and he

pushed off the wall, straightened to his full height and slowly spun to her, finishing with a light shrug. "Too bad there's not a fortune-teller in our midst. Best we can determine, when the sun is in the constellation Leo...traveling through that zodiacal portion of the sky...

"For those few weeks every year, the lion spirit is stronger, overpowering, as if the essence of what makes us human has slowly seeped away. It extends beyond belief, I know."

She waved his words away, a measure of realization dawning in her expression. "*This* is why your eyes glow at times, is it not? I always thought it was mine not seeing clearly."

"Francy, you see more clearly than any person I have ever met."

At that very moment, her calculating mind appeared fast at work. "Although...*lion*. That does make sense, I suppose. The charges on your coat of arms. The three lions—you, Nash and Phineas." Then she blinked and turned her focused gaze back to him. "What became of him—your cousin?"

"I know not. No word has been heard from him since that day." Hadn't seen hide nor tail of his elder-by-a-year cousin since the man's wedding night.

God Almighty, *Phineas*. Was he even alive?

Or, heaven forfend, had The Change taken more than his soul? Landed him a trophy on some disgustingly vile and clueless lord's hunting-lodge wall?

Nausea plowed through him at the notion. He squeezed his eyes shut to blot out the image.

• • •

FOR THE MOST PART, Francine had listened in stillness, breathing deeply, lips clamped tightly together to keep from peltering him with questions. The grief over his missing cousin as obvious as what she'd seen last night. Certainly more plausible.

She was still absorbing all that he shared, trying to grasp the enormity of what haunted not only him, but his family as well.

"Answer something for me, if you can?" She whispered the request, unsure of its reception.

Until he opened his eyes and braced himself, facing her straight on. "Certainly. You have every right to ask anything you wish."

"Now that I have seen the toll it demands, can you explain why you persist in fighting it so hard?"

"How can you even consider that?" Shock stiffened his posture further. "'Tis an unholy, unnatural curse. Lions are predators. Carnivorous ones. Should I endanger all those around me by not doing all—"

"Shhh. Shh." His voice had grown in proportion to the agitation she so easily sensed. Lightly, she placed four fingers on his chest and tapped, two of them on the dressing gown, two slipping over warm skin. "So you fear losing control? Harming"—she could not bring herself to say *eat*, not in the most literal of senses—"those you love?"

"Exactly."

"Have you considered you might not?"

"Eh?"

"That you, perhaps..." *Tap, tap.* "Remain in possession of your wits, just not of your form?"

He swore, captured her fingers and pressed her

palm firmly over his heart. "Would you have me risk it? For I will not."

"There is no need. As long as you let me, I shall tame your beast."

"Ah, Francy," he chuckled, the first sign of true mirth she'd seen since arriving. "Despite last night, your demands I leave you alone, you are still my little innocent, are you not? Tame my beast, indeed."

"What do you mean *demanding you leave*? I never! I did all I could to pour myself into your arms, fighting back *your* constant rejections."

"Mayhap I misinterpreted?" Looking thoughtful at the possibility, he took her wrist and began divesting her of the long glove she still wore.

"You most certainly did. Yet still... Everything you just shared. Last night. Curses! Lions..." Her mind a complete rimble-ramble over all he'd told her...

No matter that she'd witnessed the truth of his preposterous claims, knew firsthand the veracity of them, everything he spoke of was just so...utterly and completely...

"Impossible." Succinctly, she summed up the last twelve hours and his Banbury tale—the one no rational person would ever believe. But she'd seen...

"Fact." He stoically insisted, pinching the glove in between her fingers and pulling it loose to toss it over his shoulder.

"Improbable."

"Fact."

"Insane."

"Aye." He agreed with a tight smile, releasing that hand with a kiss upon her palm and snaring the other.

"Cursed?"

"Forever." His brow drew taut upon uttering that, as though pronouncing his own death sentence.

She infused her response with every ounce of raw feeling she now possessed, thanks to knowing him. "Cherished."

"Ensnared."

"Loved."

"*Married.*"

"Married?" He'd said it with such assurance, she had to issue protest. Best she start training him now, she thought with a self-deserving bit of pique, how she planned to go on. Could not simply let him go around assuming things without asking. So she drew back, leaving him holding nothing but the second glove and started shaking her head. "But that is *not* what we—"

"Damn it, Francine!" He advanced. "Do not gainsay me on this. I will give you any freedoms you want, but agree to marry me in truth or, upon my word, I shall not allow you to leave."

"Ever?"

"Never."

"Hmm." Making him wait—had he not forced her to do the same, and for an entire week?—she weighed the freedoms he promised with the threat of absolute confinement he hazarded. Wanted to call him on his rapper, point out the blatant contradiction.

But not now. He'd had a difficult night.

A difficult week. Mayhap a difficult life.

And she could ease that for him. Could keep him laughing. Keep the haunting secrets that hunted him so persistently at bay—

"Um..." She made a prolonged show of consideration, layered heavily with skepticism. Because she'd yet to share her own secret. Still confessed to more than a tiny seed of anxiousness over how he might respond. "This—the whole *Felis leo* thing." She swept her hand between them encompassing the entrance hall and the stairs leading up to the bedchamber overhead. "*This* is your deep secret, correct? You do not have others I need to know about? Anything worse—uh, belay that—more *unusual* for me to learn of?"

The Den.

The Curse.

Family Responsibilities.

He thought a moment. Chose not to worry her sweet head with his other suspicions...

Possible connection to horrific murders. Tracking the monster committing said murders.

Time enough for that. *After* the wedding. The one she'd yet to agree to.

"Nay. That all seems more than sufficient to me."

"Who else knows?"

"About the curse?"

She nodded.

"Members of our family, Adam. Most of our relatives reside in the northern shires. I cannot but feel it necessary to make a life in London, to—"

"Your cubs!" she exclaimed, more astute than he would've wished. "You living here is about those fellows you befriend, is it not?"

"Aye," he sighed. In for a penny, in for a crown. "My

grandfather and a couple of uncles were more indiscriminate than wise. Given the infidelities rampant in society, especially after the first two sons are sired, I decided to keep an eye on various coves carousing in and around London. In case any of them show tendencies toward being afflicted."

'Twas also best not to mention the "debauched orgies" she once questioned him about—how every year he planned those toward the middle and end of summer, recruiting jaded women who liked hard liquor and hard loving, hoping to be in close proximity should any of the young bucks display animalistic leanings, knowing the only way to halt them would be immediate sex. In the years he'd looked out for the cubs, none had shown signs of The Change that he was aware of.

"Where is Nash? Upstairs still?"

"He has disappeared again. Like someone else I know."

"I had an errand to run, one that could not wait. I expected to return before either of you awoke. But, smart lady that I am, I came back."

"For which I am most appreciative." He couldn't stop himself from hugging her. Didn't try. "When I woke this morning and you were gone, and I could not remember much of last night—"

"You cannot remember?" She sounded quite affronted at the notion. "You do not recall my time in your bed?"

"Very little. The blighted curse, stealing those all-important hours from me."

"So you do not recall professing your enduring

love? Nor swinging up onto the canopy, swaying from the hangings, imitating a gorilla?"

"I would *never*—"

"Tell me you love me or behave like an arse? I mean ape."

"How you make me laugh, and how I love you. When I awakened alone, I feared you might hate me, that you had left for good. Though I was coming after you..." He hugged her tighter. "Well. Quite relieved you saved me that trouble."

For that, he received an elbow in his side. "*Trouble?*"

He wisely returned to the prior subject. "I never know when I might see or hear from my brother. He battles The Change by running from it, pretending nothing of it exists until he is faced with it every year. He arrived a few days ago, claiming that my internal struggle had heightened his, begging me to..."

"Be with a woman?" she asked, and he gave an abrupt nod, relieved when all she did was give him an indulgent smile.

"Impressive restraint." A gentle nod of thanks, before she was moving on. "As to Nash, when do you expect he will return?"

"I know not. I never know. Here." He handed her the note that had fallen to the floor. "Evidently, he paused long enough to leave this. It is addressed to you."

Standing within the circle of Erasmus's arms, her back snug against his chest, she read the missive out loud.

Dear Francine,

*My Brother is a Lucky ~~Bastard~~ Cove to have found
You. You're his Salvation. Not certain My own
exists.*

*My most Sincere Apologies for how I Behaved. Did
not mean to Attack you. Know that your Selfless
Sacrifice gave me a few hours of Peace. My Humble
Gratitude for that.*

Be Well. Nash

*P.S. I'll kneel down and ask of thee forgiveness, shall
I? I do beseech thee, grant me this...*

"That is very poetical, and a bit odd...the
postscript."

"'Tis most likely Shakespeare. He butchers it regularly to suit his purposes when his own words should
suffice."

Her eyes raced over the last line, but she chose not
to read it out loud, instead to bask in the suspected
meaning behind the cryptic words.

*P.S. 2 ~ Banns, Blake? And before you've even
professed your Sins and Secrets? For Shame, dear
brother.*

"Beautifully written," she said, folding the note
until only her name remained visible. "But unnecessary. Nothing exists to forgive."

"I doubt that. Through the murkiness, I seem to
recall the jackanapes calling you a bi—"

When he bit off the word, she asked, "A what?"

"Ahem. Something I should have pummeled him for."

"I think you misremember."

"Mayhap he spoke in the African tongue? God knows neither of us were in our right minds. 'Tis the only excuse I have for how crudely we behaved."

She smiled to herself. "Mayhap he only called me brilliantly debauched."

"If you are, you only have me to thank."

"Do not deride yourself." She leaned back, pressing her entire backside all along his muscular front. "I adore knowing that you tend to lose control around me. Your unbridled actions make me feel alive. Until we met, I kept parts of myself stifled, not allowing myself to feel—or love—because I knew the emotion would not be returned."

His chin rested over her head. "It is now. You know that, do you not?" She felt the kiss he gave her next. "A thousand times over."

"I do. But as to Nash..." She ran her fingers across the harshly scrawled line of her name and looked over her shoulder at Erasmus. "His pain is apparent."

He hugged her again, strengthening the security she always felt in his embrace. "Only until he finds someone like you."

She exchanged the note for her reticule, loosening the drawstrings. "I have another proposition for you."

He relaxed his arms and turned her to face him. "As long as you are not asking me to vacate the country, I accept."

"Without even knowing what it is?" She laughed, relieved, nearly giddy. "You are very brave."

"As are you." The heat in his eyes made it clear he was referring to last night.

The sharp bite of renewed desire ran through her as she pulled out the bank note she'd obtained that morning, after making arrangements with her solicitor for it to be ready and waiting. "Today is my birthday, you know. Your payment, my lord. Now our original bargain is complete and... What?"

Erasmus was already shaking his head. "I refuse to accept your money. That was never part of anything."

"You paid my aunt's debt to Peterson. I owe—"

"Not a shilling of it, Francine."

"What about my body? My heart? Does that proposition interest you?"

"Now that is most definitely worth discussing." The bank note forgotten, he picked her up, curving one arm beneath her knees and securing the other at her back. "Are we talking the same terms as last time? You fulfill my desires. I fulfill yours?" He began ascending the stairs in a steady, measured pace.

"Of course, for as long as you want."

"Forever?" He hefted her closer. "Because that is the only duration I will accept."

"Forever..."

"Why are you hesitating? Now that you know *what* I am and I have you in my arms, I shall not be letting you go. Your independence? Are you concerned I might stifle you?"

"Never. I experience a greater sense of freedom

with you than I ever thought to. 'Tis only..." She spread her fingers along his neck and stared over his shoulder.

"Tell me, woman. What makes you hesitate? Have you not laid all my secrets bare?" When she remained silent, he added, "Most of them, of a certainty," prompting a reluctant smile.

One that faded when she murmured, "What about my eyes?"

Erasmus reached the landing and paused. "What about them?"

"You know I need spectacles."

"No wonder. With all the stitchery you persist on doing with such a frown. Have you any idea how many times I arrived at Rowden House, when the weather was unfavorable, to find you hunched over a task you obviously find unpalatable?"

His arms strengthened beneath her bent knees and gave a little shake, inviting her to look at him. "When you ply a needle, you frown as though you have just caught sight of your hatless head on a rainy day."

He imitated, pinching his forehead and pursing his lips till she laughed. "What a piercing scowl, indeed."

"Then why do you do it? Persist in an activity that gives you no joy?"

"I have done it to hold tight to her memory—Mama's."

"Francy. You know better. Her memory is here." His arms lifted her until he could place a tender kiss between her breasts. Then shifted his stance, returning her to his chest where he could kiss her temple. "And here. Not to make light of your concerns, but they certainly do not pose a reason sufficient to keep you from me."

He hugged her tight and began walking again.

"My eyesight. It is waning. Which is why procuring my inheritance and freedom was so vastly important, you see."

"I begin to." His strides slowed.

"I needed the funds to accommodate myself and a companion, perhaps a small staff, in a cottage. Mayhap by the sea, so I could hear the ocean. Somewhere *flat*. With rich soil—"

"For a garden."

"Exactly. I needed time to ensure that the space was arranged properly, the soil prepared, with everything dug and marked so I could identify what is planted and where. Plenty of seeds..."

"You do realize, do you not, that particular dream is not one that only works in isolation."

She arched an eyebrow at him. "Oh, do tell. You have a cottage by the sea to tempt me with?"

"What you envisioned and just described? Mayhap not the ocean out your back door, but the rest of it? Certainly." And while she started to breathe easier— for had he not confidently dealt with her concerns?— he added, "Is this why, in near darkness, apprehension takes hold?"

As it did right then at his perception, the arm not wrapped around his neck fidgeting with the empty space near the bridge of her nose—where her spectacles usually resided. "Long-held anxiousness, I confess. Worry over being trapped by a husband without your unique view of things, one who might have... Kept me intentionally locked away."

"Oh, sweetheart. My brave, intriguing baggage."

"It sounds ridiculously silly now. Especially given the exemplary example of my parents' most unusual match. But tales of Aunt Prudence's first marriage and seeing what it did to her?" Restless now, she swung both her feet. "There you have it."

"Francine." He waited until she looked at him again, then continued. "I can see well enough for the both of us and bring the light to where ever you are."

"My dark lord with the glowing eyes." Her restless hand went to one side whisker. She blinked up at him, tracing the edge and imprinting his beautiful, tired face in her mind.

He reached a chamber she hadn't noticed the night before, wrenched the door open, walked through, then slammed it shut with his foot. He approached the large, handsome bed—forest-green hangings and draperies intact—dominating the room and dropped her onto the middle.

Following her down, he brushed her hair back from her forehead. "Do not let those concerns cross your mind ever again. Listen to yourself. Do you really think that I, of all people, would find fault with your eyesight? As if I do not have any demons lurking in my dungeon."

"You have a dungeon? Hmmm."

"Francine," he said with a frown. "Do not interrupt me when my goal is convincing you how wonderful you are." He kissed each eyelid. "In fact, I think these are exceptionally lovely."

"Thank y— Stop kissing my eyes!" She squirmed, shaking her head. "I cannot help but worry. Aunt Prudence always said—"

"Your aunt belongs in a dung heap," he surprised a smile out of her by saying. "If the idea of anyone learning your secrets bothers you, I shall insist on being unfashionably droll and always keep my wife by my side."

"Wife." She clutched his shoulders, her eyes and cheeks still tingling from his kisses. "That does sound rather decent."

"Decent? *That* is all you can muster? You should know by now I am not nearly buffle-headed enough to let you get away. Ever." He began peeling down the neckline of her gown, baring her shoulder.

"I should hope not." Her skin sizzled at the look on his face. "You will not ask me to leave again? Even when the beast returns?"

"I vow, I shall never ask you to leave again." The soft glow started up, heating his gaze from within. "No notion of what I was thinking, really, to not tell you everything before."

"Perhaps all that hair on your face last night got tangled in your brain." When he tugged harder, she arched her back so that, together, they could slip her arms from the sleeves, leaving her dress loose about her waist, her shift the only covering. "Did you really have the banns read? I thought both parties had to meet with the minister first."

"How did you—? Nash. Caught." Caught, mayhap, but not repentant. Not when he gloated, "It does help, having a soul doctor not opposed to extra coins in the plate. How could such a pious body of divinity not want to assist granting my heart's fondest desire?"

As she started to dismiss his flim-flam, he turned serious. "For what began as a farce, thanks to a stubborn chit with frizzled hair and a fine mind, truly has proved my salvation."

Her eyes tracked over his countenance. So strong. So dear. His longish hair hung down, giving him a bit of a boyish air she'd not seen before.

His fingers continued their downward trek, pulling her shift indecently low. "Ah, I do believe... Aye, I have located the lovely...boundary..."

Curious what he referred to, she tilted her head, only to see his fingers tracing the narrow path where her skin took on two distinct shades. "Now that I finally have the time, wherewithal and mental capacity, I shall apply myself to divesting you of every article of clothing, so I may satisfy a particular longing... That of appreciating, of mapping, that fine line between your sun-kissed skin—and the porcelain portions normally hidden from view. The portions I want reserved only for *my* lips and gaze henceforth."

Her throat made a sweet-sounding little moan. "Agreed."

"I admit to pondering any number of things of late —when my mind was not crazed with The Change. 'Tis time I put forth a new proposition to you. One I expect you to accept with all due haste." His gaze abandoned where his fingers explored the pale skin he'd exposed to give her a heady look from beneath his brow. "Do you remember *my* original terms? You were to obey me in all things."

"What a royal clanker!" Though 'twas hard to protest, given the way he was staring at her with such an indulgent expression of caring, of love. "Your memory is faulty, Erasmus. I do believe I agreed to service your physical needs or absent myself—"

"Have we not established that there will be no more absenting? I forbid it." Though they made her giggle, the words were heartfelt and he left off gazing at her to scoop her in his arms and roll over, balancing her on top of his chest. "I, in turn, shall spend the next several decades convincing you of my sincerity."

She cupped his face, skimming one thumb down his dear nose, then she leaned forward to place a kiss right on the scar. "I might just have to spend the next several decades taming this monstrous beast I recently found lurking in my garden."

"Monstrous?" He slid his hands down her back and filled his palms with her glorious arse, using the hold to slide her...exactly...where he...*needed*. "Would you be referring to this, my lady?"

"Nay, I was not." She laughed, giving a delightful wiggle until she cradled his rapidly firming erection. "But if it will make you feel better..."

"Only one thing will make me feel better: having you by my side. Always."

Sky-blue eyes, full of serenity and love gazed down. "What about on top of you?"

With a growl, Erasmus William Charles Hammond, Lord Blakely, the former avoider of innocents and current purveyor of pleasure, proceeded to show his lady that it didn't matter how well she could see or exactly where she was positioned—beside, on top of, *around*—he would love her forever, any way he could have her.

Author's Note

THANK you for reading *Ensnared by Innocence*. I hope you loved meeting my shapeshifters and their world. If you enjoyed the story, it would be terrific if you could please leave a review at your favorite retailer, telling others. Reviews really help authors!

The novel-length version you just read is *three* times as long as the short novella originally released a number of years ago. I am so, so happy Erasmus and his Francy finally got their full-fledged love story.

Those who've read *Seductive Silence* may have recognized Lord Tremayne at the museum—several years before he meets the love of his life (most definitely *not* his current mistress!).

As you can tell, I'm expanding my Regency world, including different aspects of the paranormal—and time travel—along with fabulous mere mortals, who aren't always aware of what else is going on in their fair city.

Stay tuned, Nash's story is next! Keep reading for details...

ANYONE with a keen interest in lions may have recognized the *Felis leo* classification used throughout the story and wondered *What is Larissa thinking? Everyone knows lions are under the genus Panthera.* True, which is why, in the early version of this story the men struggled with their *Panthera leo* essence.

As I was rewriting this, doing additional research on

word choice—always attempting to portray the Regency era using words that were common in the early 1800s instead of our more modern equivalents (except in Adam's case!)—I discovered that it wasn't until 1816 when the "Panthera" word was first proposed. Meaning that my 1812 Regency gents, and their ancestors, would have been familiar with *Felis leo* instead, a term in use since the late 1750s.

Now it's Nash's turn!

Cursed into the form of a lion without nightly sex, Lord Nash Hammond wants only two things—his liquor strong and smooth, and his wenches wild and willing. What he doesn't need is a virgin!

Turn the page for a look at the blurb and most of the first chapter.

PREVIEW: DECEIVED BY DESIRE

BOOK 2 - ROARING ROGUES REGENCY
SHIFTERS

In *Deceived by Desire*...

*Meet a Shakespeare-quoting shapeshifter who wants
nothing to do with love...*

Nash senses the man across from him in the cramped
stagecoach is trouble, a danger to the veiled woman
accompanying her lofty "protector". Nash knows *he's*
no hero, yet she keeps asking for his help. And how is it
the vexing female knows so much about *his* secrets?
Ones that could rip her apart if she only knew it...

*And the spunky "lady" from the streets who masquerades as
another man's mistress...*

Blessed with the second-sight—or cursed, depending
upon which relative she believes—Laney sees her two

possible futures: bleak and a soon-deceased victim (ack!) or frolicking with her fellow stagecoach passenger: a golden-eyed, tawny-haired gentleman—who's anything but.

The miserable rip who's already stepped on her dress, who keeps *staring...*

Nash is surly and rude and resistant to her every effort to speak with him. When they stop for the night and she overhears him order a "strumpet" to bed, Laney takes the doxy's place, convinced she can pretend well enough. After all, she's *pretended* to be a mistress for years. She'll satisfy his needs, but refuse his money—demand he listen and help her instead. Then she'll be safe.

Until, along with her body, Nash starts to claim her heart as well.

Reader Advisory: While Deceived by Desire is laugh-out-loud funny in places, it contains a short vision of violence and brief references to past abuse. Beyond that, expect a fun and steamy good time because...

Changing into a lion is all fun and growls—until it isn't.

— ⋅◦⋅ —

Standalone ~ HEA ~ 80,000-word Novel ~ Book 2 - Roaring Rogues Regency Shifters

DECEIVED BY DESIRE - PART OF CHAPTER 1

The Wretched Hat and the Wretched Man

Nash roused from his latest bout of self-pity long enough to crack open his eyes and watch the new passengers climb aboard the already cramped, soggy stagecoach and settle in directly across from the corner he'd occupied for the past several hours.

He shifted and pressed his foot solidly against the floor of the coach.

Demmed inconvenient it was, having to share the dank spot he'd staked out as his own with the outwardly perfect pair. He kept his head lowered in the guise of dozing and refused to admit, even to himself, that he'd cared enough to peek.

People. Who needed 'em?

Certainly not Nash Hammond. The stagecoach, on the other hand? Now *that* he needed, though if the blasted sky would just cooperate, not for much longer. He had enough money that he could buy his own horse —a damn fine one if he wanted. Hell, an entire stable full if he so desired and actually had a stable. But then he'd have to care for it. *Them.* No demmed matter!

It was easier to put up with public transport.

Gave him something to think about other than his own contemptible problems.

"Pardon me, sir, but your foot's snagged on my dress." The cultured voice cascaded over him like a heaven-sent waterfall, at odds with the jarring way she tried to wrench her long, surprisingly dry skirts from beneath his boot.

Nash refused to budge, kept his boot clamped down and continued to feign sleep as he'd been doing ever since the horses had splashed to a stop, the stagecoach rolling to a sodden halt behind them when the driver paused for a fresh team and additional passengers.

Experience had taught Nash that folks usually left a sleeping man alone, thinking he was drunk most likely, and would refrain from asking him to scoot over. That was the pertinent motivation—if he was going to be trapped inside, then he'd make blame certain he had all the space he could muster. He always left a couple of extra inches between his body and the side of the coach, celebrating privately whenever he managed to secure more than the typical sixteen inches allotted to paying dolts like himself.

He'd begun his flight out of London as an outside passenger on the Royal Mail Coach—because it moved faster than lightning—but the incessant rains drove him inside and onto a public conveyance. He never could abide being exposed to the elements when it was pouring.

"Mister! My dress," the female hissed, trying in vain to arrange herself across from him. "It's caught under your boot!"

She pulled harder and he glanced at her through slitted lids, but the frilly contraption perched precariously atop her head completely hid her face.

Did she know that he'd stepped on her trailing hem on purpose?

Could she tell he was fighting back a smirk at her pathetically puny efforts to free her skirts? Did she have any idea of his pathetically useless existence?

Just as Nash tensed the muscles in his thigh to lift his foot, a ripping sound exploded from the floor and she plopped backward on the opposite bench, her skirts flying up to expose surprisingly inviting petticoats.

"Wretched man!" he heard her mutter under her breath.

Acting no better than an unlicked cub, he was amusing himself at her expense. He should apologize.

But he didn't move.

Or say a word.

He was too busy rumbling a fake snore or two and inspecting the luscious treat whose lacy hem remnants lay trapped beneath his sole, and the fop who'd just climbed in after her, lurching more than a bit in the process. The fop who she appeared to be wedded to, if the dandy's sour look toward Nash was anything to go by.

Figured.

Refined thing like that. Her in her fancy hat and frilly white traveling dress—white! As if she shouldn't be covered from head to toe with a thick layer of mud and grime. How she managed to look so pristine and proper on a day like today, with her apricot-colored kid slippers, closed ruffle-edge parasol that matched her dress to perfection and immaculately gloved fingers was beyond him.

Her generous bosom looked anything but refined

though, ready to spill from the not-quite-decent neckline with just the slightest encouragement.

Nash strangled on the sudden growl of desire that threatened to erupt, turning it instead into a garbled snore.

Damn cock. Rearing up as if it needed a warm cunny, as though he hadn't attacked his brother's woman just hours before. Damn him! His penis deserved to be ground beneath *her* heel.

"All set, m'dear?" the red-haired dandy asked on a hiccup, squishing close to the woman and placing his arm across her shoulders in a proprietary move while he cast Nash a glower as if he could read minds.

Nash heard the slight hitch in her breathing, caught a hint of fear, just before she answered. "Indeed, Mr. Tate. Thank you for asking."

Her cultured tones had turned puny. From vibrant waterfall to watered-down dribble.

Nash hunched lower, slightly lifting his lids to gaze at her from beneath the overlong fall of hair that blocked half his face. Some sort of netting hung from the brim of the ungodly confection perched atop her head, fully hiding her features. He could just make out the curve of her cheek, but that was it.

Probably had the face of a sow. God surely had to give such a one a curse to balance the bounty of figure He'd blessed her with.

The dandy patted his pocket, drawing Nash's attention. The man pulled out a snuffbox and made a great show of meticulously placing a pinch just inside his lower lip, which he ruined with another hiccup, then did everything in reverse, returning the snuff to his pocket. His actions were ludicrous, done with one hand as the other was still firmly ensconced atop the sow's shoulder.

Nash hadn't seen more flounces even at court. How the dandy could even talk with so much starched linen and lace at his throat was beyond him. The clunch likely spent more time at Weston's than he did his own dinner table.

And shuddering fear, and green-eyed jealousy! his conscience taunted, compliments of Mister William Shakespeare.

Jealous? Jealous of the overdressed man and his feminine fortune? *Never. Never!* As if hearing the mental shouts, the man echoed...

"Never fear, m'dear," Dandy drawled, "only two days confined in this infernal conveyance—three at the most if this Scotch mist keeps up—and we shall arrive at our destination."

She left off gazing at the torn hem fraying in her fingers and glanced through that damn netting at Dandy. "Will you please bring yourself to tell me where we are going?" she inquired so softly if Nash's hearing hadn't been exceptional he would have missed it. At the dulcet sound, he realized he could never think of her as a sow again. Pig-faced or not, she had the voice of a princess. "I am quite sure it will not ruin your surprise if you—"

"No! And leave off asking!" The dandy swatted her shoulder sharply. "You will enjoy it," he added cajolingly. "I can assure you."

At the threatening undercurrent in the man's voice, Nash lifted his head and uncrossed his arms. He intentionally remained slouched, giving the appearance of only casual interest. "You would not be taking the lady somewhere she prefers not to go, now would you?"

The woman flinched. Nash smelled her fear. It had grown stronger.

"Of course he is not!" She trilled a practiced laugh. "Mr. Tate is forever treating me to new experiences and surprises."

"Mind your own bloody business!" the dandy bit out loudly.

"Here! Here!" an older man in the opposite corner grumped. "Females present and all that. Mind *your* mouth!"

"Forgive me," the redhead said urbanely, but Nash saw how his knuckles whitened on her shoulder. To the others, he was all polish and shine. Slime.

Nash wanted to lose his breakfast on the man's gleaming Hessians. Instead, he tried to see past the netting, clueless where his sudden bout of chivalry had sprung from. "Ma'am?"

He sensed her nervous smile, could almost taste how close to tears she was. "I am wonderful. My life is...wonderful."

"See?" Dandy boasted, as if there had never been any doubt.

She was lying.

Nash cursed himself for caring. For even asking.

He didn't want the responsibility of sheltering a damn horse. What made him think he was up for the challenge of saving a bountiful-breasted, soft-voiced princess?

Sow, he told himself. A veiled sow. Oink.

Oink, oink! so cries a pig prepared to the spit. He intentionally butchered Shakespeare's original line, but couldn't stop from wondering...

Did lions eat pigs?

HEAVENS. The look on the stranger's face made Laney feel all twittery inside. On edge. Just like being with Reginald did, but in a not-quite horrible way. Almost a good way, for even though her stomach felt lodged in her throat and her skin buzzed at the fiery glint in his eyes, she couldn't look away.

Mayhap 'twas simply riding backward? Squished between the side of the carriage and the man who *owned* her—body, *not* soul—until her indenture expired. If she didn't expire first, that recent—*dire*—vision overriding her every waking thought and action the last few days. Until this gruff stranger demanded her attention and refused to let go.

Her stomach pitched again. Knowing the four horses and driver were just a meager distance away, barreling forward at a breakneck pace, didn't help. Certainly, they were traveling too fast for the inclement weather. But then, Reginald had insisted they both change clothes after the morning's coaching debacle and she'd just seen him tip their new driver substantially to "Push on, man. Horses are strong, make 'em earn their hay."

Thanks to Reginald and his ill-timed impatience, she was now stuck enduring not only the stranger's avid inspection, but the coach jiggling her body so ferociously it was stewing up the meager toast she'd eaten to break her fast. She'd known better than to indulge in her love of sweet breads, not when such an arduous, unknown journey awaited her.

No, Laney immediately reconsidered, the heat from the stranger's expression warming her straight down to her previously wet toes, it wasn't the public coach ride responsible for the feelings fluttering in her belly. It was *him*. The surly looking man whose knees were only scant inches from her own.

One would think the scowl on his face would do damage to his countenance, but on the contrary, his churlish expression combined with the daring lack of care he showed in his dress only piqued her interest further. His jacket wasn't properly buttoned and his neckcloth was tied so haphazardly she could see the hollow beneath his throat where his collar bones didn't quite touch. Absolutely scandalous!

Now if *he* owned her instead...

Laney groaned at her fanciful imaginings. Only one person owned her at the moment—for the next ten months, twenty-two days and some-odd hours—and that was Reginald Tate, the handsome...bastard next to her.

To distract herself, both from Reginald's smothering arm across her shoulders and the stranger's piercing gaze, Laney chanced a look at Reginald, confirming his attention was elsewhere, and left off tearing the torn hem to shreds to bring her reticule to her lap. She heard the comforting rustle of paper. Mary Delilah's letter. She'd read it again this evening, after they stopped for the night, see whether she could make heads or tails of her friend's uncharacteristically wild rambling.

Reginald patted her shoulder then removed his arm. Finally! She took a shaky breath but still felt smothered by his presence. Calling him *Reginald* in her mind was just one of a handful of defiant measures she'd undertaken lately to assert her independence, whether he knew it or not.

Why couldn't the knave have remained outside and ridden on top of the coach? The loud blast of thunder overhead mocked the question even as she thought it.

"I'll just enjoy another little nip, m'dear. I daresay it'll help the time pass." He scooted closer, branding her entire side, then pulled his ever-present flask from inside his coat pocket and tipped it back, pouring the contents down his gullet as if it were a race he had to win. At this rate, he'd be out before the next stop.

Would the stranger disembark there or remain on the coach? If that was his destination, would Reginald notice if she disembarked with him and never got back on?

Oh, the fanciful ideas running through her mind. The tingly quivers running through her abdomen…

Laney somehow found herself unraveling her torn hem again and trying not to notice the increased flutters in her stomach at the thought of intentionally putting herself under the stranger's power. She should know better. She'd already put herself willingly under one man's control and that certainly hadn't improved her lot in life, now had it?

Reginald Tate…

The man she once thought the answer to her

prayers. The man she now concentrated heaven-bound prayers on nightly, requesting Divine escape.

She'd been barely sixteen when the dashing Reginald Tate had begun frequenting Mrs. Michaels Millinery and Fine Accoutrements where Laney had been indentured shortly after she turned thirteen. After three solid years making hats and waiting on "ladies" who looked down their fashionably pale noses more often than not—and pricking her fingers with milliners needles, hat pins and bracing wire just as regularly—the flattering attention the handsome Mr. Tate showered on Laney practically made her swoon.

Two scant months after they met, he'd offered to buy her papers from Mrs. Michaels. Laney secretly suspected he wanted her for his "Lady of the Night" and other than being woefully uneducated in the art of nighttime activities, she was otherwise agreeable. Since losing her grandmum and mother within a few months of each other and being passed from one relative to another until winding up on the doorstep of an aunt who was already burdened with her own gaggle of children and certainly didn't want Laney, indenturing her at the first opportunity, Laney was nothing if not practical.

The allure of being pampered like a "lady"—even one bought and paid for—far surpassed the daily drudgery as the life of an unappreciated servant. At the time, her indenture to Mrs. Michaels was for another interminable four years, which to the young Laney was a veritable lifetime. The position offered by Reginald seemed a godsend.

Instead, the rotten Mr. Tate had only wanted her to

pretend to be his amour while he'd dallied with those she'd often heard called "lower elements". Certain *men* —she could hardly think the thought without blushing, even now, half a year after Reginald had parted ways with his *male* paramour and renounced his *despicable, detestable acts*—Reginald's words, not hers—only to turn his immoral attention to her. Immoral because he didn't want her physically, but he kept trying to take her anyway.

Although in the last few moments, since being stuffed like kippers on a plate with the other passengers, Laney's mind swam with all manner of possibilities. What if she'd declined Reginald's offer and remained with Mrs. Michaels? Would she have, perhaps, crossed paths with the gentleman sitting across from her?

And should he even be termed "gentleman"?

Most assuredly not. Not with the way he went without a hat when everyone knew the importance of fine head wear. "Choose your hat first," Mrs. Michaels had always told her customers, "the rest of your ensemble will then magically follow."

And *not* with the way he brazenly persisted in staring at her so intently, his eyes glowing like orange embers, causing Laney to feel as if her veil hardly shielded her at all.

"Stop staring." The words were out of her mouth before she knew it.

Reginald had gone slack. He leaned heavily against her, indicating his slumber, and Laney supposed she'd unknowingly relaxed her guard as well. Relaxed too much, given her awareness of the man across from her and her hastily spoken command.

Judging by the increased heat in his gaze, he hadn't stopped contemplating her either.

Did no one else notice his unusual eyes? The way they fairly shimmered with heat?

"Remove your hat."

The lace slipped from her fingers. "I beg your pardon?"

He leaned forward and caught the scrap before it drifted to the ground. Their knees collided. "Take off your hat. You appear to be the best view around, and I want to see the rest of it."

"Shhh!" she sputtered, never more grateful for the shielding gold netting than she was at this very moment. She tried to angle her legs from his, but between Reginald's sleeping body weighing against her side and the stranger's knees pressed intimately against hers, she couldn't move. "Please. You mustn't say such things."

He gave Reginald's sleeping form a disdainful glance and leaned even closer. "Why do you fear him?"

How did he know? "*What?*"

"You heard me." He made a show of returning the torn hem to her gloved hands, giving hers a gentle squeeze before releasing them. She felt the touch clear to her toes, which were locked between his heavily booted feet.

"I asked why you fear him." His rumbling voice had gone all low and smoky.

"I'm quite sure you must be mistaken," Laney whispered, glancing at the other passengers. Everyone seemed intent upon passing the uncomfortable time as privately as possible, gazing out the windows or snoozing.

How was it no one took notice of anyone else? Least of all the intimate encounter between her and a stranger? Or how Reginald's head lolled about his neck with every jostling revolution of the coach's wheels? Laney couldn't miss how Reginald's jaw hung unattractively unhinged, his sour breath breezing over her shoulder. She had the sudden urge to upend the contents of his flask inside his mouth. Maybe he'd drown.

"You do not deny it." The firm statement, voiced with perfect elocution, drew her attention back to the ill-dressed man before her. The most unrigged gentleman she'd ever seen.

Gentleman? Gads! She had to quit thinking of him as such. No matter that his speech was as fine as she strived to make her own, he was nothing more than a shabbaroon. But one who so boldly demanded, "Remove your hat. I will not ask again and I want to see your face."

His tone made her think he'd be uncouth enough to rip it from her head if she refused to do as he bade. "You cannot! *I* cannot. Oh, do please sit back."

She couldn't think with his knees touching hers, with his finger idly nudging her leg. Was this desire, then? This awful achy, nervous, *wonderful* feeling? The need to brush his hair back, to really see his face? The need to be *his*?

For the thousandth time, Laney bemoaned her

misspent youth and cursed her impatience. She hated Reginald and Mrs. Michaels all over again.

"How long have you been wed?"

His words startled her. "Wed? I assure you we most certainly are not!"

"Related?"

"Heavens no."

And just like that, he was gone. No more teasing fingers. No more obscene nuzzling of her kneecaps. No more glowing eyes.

"Ah," he murmured once he'd straightened and returned fully to his own seat. His expression once again inscrutable, the playful, albeit intent, interest he'd shown seconds before wiped free.

"And what, pray tell, does that mean?" She couldn't keep quiet. "*Ah?* You say that as if you pass judgment upon me. Are not negative judgments reserved for those of clerical persuasions?"

If anything, he looked darker, more brooding. She heard him fairly growl from his shadowy corner. "You claim not to be bound to him, yet you choose to remain," he stated with obvious disdain. "Keep the blasted hat on, then. I no longer care what you look like."

Unaccountably, she cared that he no longer cared. Stupid, stupid. She should be jumping from the stagecoach and running as far away from Reginald as she could instead of bantering with a moody stranger.

"You don't understand," Laney hissed, incensed with herself. Why in the world should it matter whether he understood or not?

· · ·

NASH TURNED AWAY from the shrouded feminine mystery, dismissing her and pulling the thin volume of Shakespeare from his pocket. One could only feign sleep for so long. "I no longer have the inclination to understand. Keep your protestations and your fear to yourself, madam. What you choose to do with your life is of no interest to me."

It was a blatant lie, but Nash hoped if he said it enough, it would become the truth.

He had no business caring for anything, much less any*body*, at the moment.

Damn her and infernal voice for tempting him to think otherwise.

For unlike his older brother who preferred hardened women—at least until Lady Francine came along—Nash himself had always lusted after innocence and purity. *Virgins.* From the moment he became cursed and realized his body was no longer his own, he day dreamed about once-upon-a-times and happily-ever-afters, envying ordinary men with ordinary wives living ordinary lives.

He dreamed of one day having a pure wife. An innocent. As long as she composed herself as he imagined a lady would—caring for her family (which, to his way of thinking, meant her man—*him*) and caring for her home (the one he'd never had, not since his mother abandoned them shortly after his father did the same)—she didn't have to be a *lady* in truth or even very beautiful. A simple refined peasant or even a clean servant—he wasn't overly particular—would suit him fine. A woman who had saved herself just for him. *That* was what he truly desired.

But those were imaginings—the two to three minutes of fantasy he allowed himself in the moments before full wakefulness intruded and reality crashed down around him. He couldn't take a virgin. He couldn't have a wife.

Or children, or a family of his own. He wouldn't have peace.

Not as long as he was a monster.

Who'd practically raped his brother's woman.

Feeling the irate attention the veiled, behatted female still directed at him, Nash moved the curtain that was drawn against the rain and peered out of the coach, making a great show of gauging the location of the sun. Asinine, as it was blocked by storm clouds. "By my reckoning," he said as if to himself but intending that she should hear, "and barring a broken wheel or axle, or washed-out roadway, we should arrive at our overnight stop in six and a half hours." He sighed wholeheartedly and sank back into his corner, letting the curtain drop. "Plenty of time to find myself a pretty wench for the evening, one who avoids wearing ugly hats. Or anything at all..."

"Wretched, wretched man!"

Good. He'd gotten to her. So why did he feel lower than the bottom of muddy pig's feet?

And why couldn't he rid himself of the unwanted concern mired in his chest?

Learn more:
https://www.larissalyons.com/series/roaring-rogues-regency-shifters/

ABOUT LARISSA

HUMOR. HEARTFELT EMOTION. & HUNKS.

A lifelong Texan, Larissa writes sexy contemporaries and steamy regencies, blending heartfelt emotion with doses of laugh-out-loud humor. Her heroes are strong men with a weakness for the right woman.

Avoiding housework one word at a time (thanks in part to her super-helpful herd of cats >^..^<), Larissa adores brownies, James Bond, and her husband. She's been a clown, a tax analyst, and a pig castrator (!) but nothing satisfies quite like seeing the entertaining voices in her head come to life on the page.

Writing around some health challenges and computer limitations, it's a while between releases, but stick with her...she's working on the next one.

and wit, and Thea realizes she's about to break the cardinal rule of mistressing—that of falling for her new protector. *Egad.*

Daring Declarations, Part 3

An evening at the opera could prove Lord Tremayne's undoing when he and his lovely new paramour cross paths with his sister and brother-in-law. Introducing one's socially unacceptable strumpet to his stunned family is *never* done. But Daniel does it anyway. And it might just be the best decision he's ever made, for Thea's quickly become much more than a mistress— and it's time he told her so.

Lady Scandal

Sparks—and stockings—fly when an interview for a husband turns into a game of forfeits—played with articles of clothing—a scandalous lady and one handsome rogue learn how very right for each other they are.

Lady Scandal **awarded the Golden Nib!** "I can't praise this book enough. Regency fans, if you like gorgeous wit in with your devilishly superb, well written, sexy reading matter, Lady Scandal should be on your 'Must Read' list." *Natalie, Miz Love & Crew Love's Books*

Top Pick from ARe Café: "[Lady Scandal] is the most flirtatious, sensual, and delectable treat." *Lady Rhyleigh, ARe Café* ~ Selected as a **Recommended Read!**

Miss Isabella Thaws a Frosty Lord

Blind from a young age, a Regency heroine risks her overbearing father's displeasure by attending a house party, never dreaming she'll meet a formidable lord who will discover all her secrets and still want her for his own.

Top Pick! "This entertaining read conjured up the atmosphere and exquisitely formal dance of manners so beloved in Jane Austen's books...I am enchanted by the grace and artful wordplay that accompanies this tale." *ELF, Night Owl Reviews*

"I love the way that the book reads as if it were written in Regency times. I'm a fan of Carla Kelly Regency romances and I was in the mood for another story of that caliber. I definitely got that with *Miss Isabella Thaws a Frosty Lord*." *EKDuncan*

www.ingramcontent.com/pod-product-compliance
Lightning Source LLC
Chambersburg PA
CBHW011206190726
48288CB00013B/3342